Sherlock Holmes: After the East Wind Blows

Part II: Aftermath
(1919-1920)

Sherlock Holmes:
After the
East Wind Blows

Part II: Aftermath
(1919-1920)

Edited by
David Marcum

Belanger Books
2021

Sherlock Holmes: After the East Wind Blows
© 2021 by Belanger Books, LLC

Illustrations for "His Last Bow"
by Frederic Dorr Steele, Alfred Gilbert, and R.W. Wallace
IN THE PUBLIC DOMAIN

For information contact:
Belanger Books, LLC
61 Theresa Ct.
Manchester, NH 03103

David Marcum can be reached at:
thepapersofsherlockholmes@gmail.com

derrick@belangerbooks.com
www.belangerbooks.com

Cover and Back design by Brian Belanger
www.belangerbooks.com and *www.redbubble.com/people/zhahadun*

CONTENTS

Forewords

Adventures

Aftermath

(Continued on the next page . . . .)

COPYRIGHT INFORMATION

The following contributors appear
in the companion volumes:
Part I: The East Wind Blows (1914-1918)
Part III: When the Storm Has Cleared (1921-1928)

Editor's Foreword:
Holmes Retired? Not So!
by David Marcum

So Moses stretched out his staff over Egypt, and the Lord made an east wind blow across the land all that day and all that night.

– Exodus 10:13

"There's an east wind coming, Watson."
"I think not, Holmes. It is very warm."
"Good old Watson! You are the one fixed point in a changing age. There's an east wind coming all the same, such a wind as never blew on England yet. It will be cold and bitter, Watson, and a good many of us may wither before its blast. But it's God's own wind none the less, and a cleaner, better, stronger land will lie in the sunshine when the storm has cleared. Start her up, Watson, for it's time that we were on our way. I have a check for five hundred pounds which should be cashed early, for the drawer is quite capable of stopping it if he can."

– Sherlock Holmes and Dr. Watson
"His Last Bow"

"There's an east wind coming," said Sherlock Holmes to Dr. John H. Watson on the second of August, 1914 – *"the most terrible August in the history of the world"* – as they looked out over the moonlit sea off the Essex coast, (then called the German Ocean, and soon to be renamed the North Sea). This conversation is chronologically the last Canonical appearance of Holmes and Watson, at the conclusion of "His Last Bow". Britain would declare war against Germany just a couple of days later. The events of this particular story cover only a few minutes, giving hints at Holmes's activities as "Altamont" in the previous two years leading up to that night, and implications of what Watson might be doing in the days

soon to follow, but it can't be considered in vacuum. Holmes and Watson's war service started over a decade before the events of that adventurous August night . . . .

In the fall of 1903, Sherlock Holmes retired. Since the mid-1870's (except for a three-year stint when he'd faked his own death to go undercover, alternately tracking and fleeing from the agents of his enemy Professor Moriarty, and carrying out tasks for his brother Mycroft,) he'd been working as a Consulting Detective – the first to do so – in London, initially living in No. 24 Montague Street alongside the British Museum, and then, after 1881, at 221 Baker Street. In 1903, Sherlock Holmes was forty-nine years old – rather young to retire, especially for someone with his energy and unique gifts.

The Sherlockian Chronologicists among us can determine that Holmes retired in 1903 because that was when Watson was finally allowed to publishe "The Empty House", relating just how Holmes had managed to survive his encounter with Professor Moriarty at the Reichenbach Falls on May 4th, 1891 – "*Reichenbach Day*" – over a decade earlier. Not long after that, a grieving Watson, with the assistance of his literary agent, had begun publishing narratives of Holmes's adventures in a newly created magazine, *The Strand*. Although two of Watson's tales had previously appeared in print, *A Study in Scarlet* in late1887 and *The Sign of the Four* in early 1890, they hadn't generated the excitement that *The Strand* stories did. Between June 1891 and December 1894, there were two-dozen of Holmes's cases recounted in the magazine, before the public – those who didn't already know of Holmes's death back when it happened in May '91 – was shocked to learn that he had supposedly died over two years earlier.

The three years when Holmes was missing are called *The Great Hiatus*, stretching from his encounter with Moriarty on 4 May, 1891 to 5 April, 1894, when he suddenly reappeared in London, with the time now right to clean up a last bit of business with the Professor's right-hand man, a killer named Moran. One can imagine Holmes's reaction upon seeing those copies of *The Strand* with his cases written up as only Watson could – but not as scientific treatises that he would have preferred. It's almost certain that this is when Holmes forbid Watson to write any more of them.

For it was in the opening paragraph of "The Empty House", published in *The Strand* in October 1903 (and September 1903 in

Collier's) that Watson wrote an explanation why it took him so long to relate that Holmes was still alive, and *how* he was still alive:

> *Let me say to that public, which has shown some interest in those glimpses which I have occasionally given them of the thoughts and actions of a very remarkable man, that they are not to blame me if I have not shared my knowledge with them, for I should have considered it my first duty to do so, had I not been barred by a positive prohibition from his own lips, which was only withdrawn upon the third of last month.*

Holmes had "*barred*" Waston from sharing his knowledge with readers with a "*positive prohibition*", but it hadn't been entirely enforced. Holmes had allowed Watson (along with the first Literary Agent) to publish *The Hound of the Baskervilles* in *The Strand* from August 1901 to April 1902, but that was an adventure set in the late 1880's, *before* Holmes's supposed death, and it would have done nothing to inform those many people who hadn't had personal interactions with Holmes since his return from The Great Hiatus know that he was actually still alive. No, it was only with the publication of "The Empty House" in late 1903 that the world in general knew that Holmes still lived – and that some unexplained event had finally prompted him to remove his "*positive prohibition*" granting the publication of this knowledge – and also most certainly that of his retirement.

But why would it be important that this retirement be revealed? Knowing what we do of Sherlock Holmes, it was intentional, and it was certainly a distraction – something flashy happening in one hand while the other hand, unnoticed, performed the actual trick. In fact, Holmes wasn't retiring at all. True, he left London and settled into a "*villa . . . situated upon the southern slope of the downs, commanding a great view of the Channel*", but he didn't become a recluse, washing his hands of his former life, as some might picture. Rather, his life and work transitioned into something else entirely. He was too young to retire, and there was too much that needed to be done. He had other business to carry out, and it was important that people think he was no longer a relevant factor.

For decades, those who could see the signs – people like the Holmes brothers, Sherlock and Mycroft – perceived that war was coming, a terrible and entangling monster that would eventually drag in the whole world, country after country after country. Germany, for centuries a series of small bickering kingdom-states, had unified in 1871, and its leaders had a hunger for respect that became more and more reckless.

Italy had unified in the same way a few decades earlier. For decades, various smaller wars across Europe served to shift borders and loyalties, while ratcheting up inescapable tension. Germany and Italy, and other Continental players such as France and Belgium, the always-turbulent Balkans, and Russia to the East, were all rubbing up against each other in a small space. Each was growing more and more nationalistic, and to feed their ambitions they needed raw materials – lots of them, to be plundered by way of a race for colonies around the world, regardless of the cost to the native inhabitants of these lands. Obtaining and keeping these colonies meant a lot of stepping on one another's toes – and ever-growing strain. Of course England, with its mastery of the sea, was thickly involved in all of this as much as their Continental neighbors.

The leaders of a great number of these countries ended up having interrelated ruling classes, with many connected by close blood ties to Queen Victoria, the multi-generational British monarch. In spite of their ambitions and jealousies, these countries began to rope themselves together – both openly and in secret – with ever-tightening treaties and counter-treaties and secret agreements. It was an increasingly dangerous and flammable situation, and someone was bound to light a match. Sherlock and Mycroft Holmes knew this, and John Watson as well, and they worked together to prevent it – or at least to delay it as long as possible.

Almost one-fourth of the Canonical narratives regarding Holmes and Watson's activities occur after the start of the Twentieth Century . . .

1900
- June 8-10   "The Six Napoleons"
- Oct 4-5   "The Problem of Thor
                    Bridge

1901
- May 16-18   "The Priory School"

1902
- May 6-7   "Shoscombe Old Place"
- June 26-27   "The Three Garridebs"

4

- July   "The Disappearance   of
                 Lady Frances Carfax
                 (Various Dates)
- Sept 3-13   "The Illustrious Client"
- Sept 24-25   "The Red Circle"

1903

- Jan 7; 12   "The Blanched Soldier"
- May 26-27   "The Three Gables"
- Early Aug   "The Mazarin Stone"
- Sept 6; 9;   "The Creeping Man"
      15-16

1907

- July 23; 30-31 "The Lion's Mane"

1914

- Aug 2   "His Last Bow"

. . . but only two ("The Lion's Mane" and "His Last Bow") occur post-retirement. The former, narrated by Holmes himself, gives us guarded details of where he lived, and the impression that he didn't do much more than keep bees, walk along the cliffs, occasionally converse with his neighbors, sometimes swim in the ocean at the base of the nearby high chalk cliffs, and devote himself to his studies. *"At this period of my life,"* Holmes wrote, *"the good Watson had passed almost beyond my ken. An occasional week-end visit was the most that I ever saw of him."*

This carefully constructed vision of Holmes as hermit is corroborated by Watson's "Preface" to the book *His Last Bow*:

> *The friends of Mr. Sherlock Holmes will be glad to learn that he is still alive and well, though somewhat crippled by occasional attacks of rheumatism. He has, for many years, lived in a small farm upon the Downs five miles from Eastbourne, where his time is divided between philosophy and agriculture. During this period of rest he has refused the most princely offers to take up various cases, having determined that his retirement was a permanent one. The approach of the German war caused him, however, to lay his remarkable*

5

combination of intellectual and practical activity at the disposal of the Government, with historical results which are recounted in His Last Bow. *Several previous experiences which have lain long in my portfolio have been added to* His Last Bow *so as to complete the volume.*

John H. Watson, M.D.

This to also gives one the impression that Holmes didn't do much at all during those years between late 1903, when he "retired", and 1912, when he agreed to take on the role of Altamont, a two-year task leading up to the events of 2nd August, 1914, as he worked his way into the existing German spy network that was trying to gain advantages for their side, damage the British, and influence events leading up to the beginning of the inevitable war.

But Holmes was not a man to simply retire at age forty-nine. Clearly he had more to do with his life, and there were certainly many more adventures than the two published post-retirement Canonical tales that have been left to us. The Canon is the fundamental structure upon which to study the lives of Sherlock Holmes and Doctor Watson, but the overall sixty stories from which it's comprised are truly just the tiniest fraction of what Holmes and Watson did, and fortunately, a number of other later Literary Agents have followed in the steps of the first one, bringing literally thousands of additional adventures to light that reveal what else happened.

I've referred in the past to this vast interconnected network of further narratives as *The Great Holmes Tapestry*, with the sixty Canonical adventures serving as the main ropes, while all of the other tales serve to fill in the background threads. Since discovering Holmes in the mid-1970's, I've been collecting and reading and chronologicizing as many of these other adventures as I could, and by this point I believe that I own and have read almost every traditional pastiche in existence, except for some truly obscure pieces that I may never find – no life is long enough, nor are resources plentiful enough, to get all of them.

By way of acquiring and studying so many post-Canonical adventures, I've been able step back and see the Big Picture, with stories running from 1840, concerning Holmes's father and how he saved the life of Queen Victoria, all the way through to the morning of 6th January, 1957, when Holmes passed away while sitting on the cliff-tops above his Sussex home. Being able to study the overall gestalt of the *entire* lives of Holmes and Watson – and not just the pitifully few sixty Canonical stories – is truly a blessing.

By way of the chronology that I've constructed based on the Canon and these additional adventures, it can be seen that there are literally hundreds of cases that occur in the years between Holmes's supposed 1903 retirement and the beginning of the war in August 1914. Likewise, there are many adventures set during the war itself, and also quite a few during the 1920's which follow.

There are a few who chronicle these years that incorrectly give an impression that Holmes and Watson lost touch with one another during that time – that Holmes did indeed became the reclusive apiarist hermit character that he wished people to believe, completely withdrawn from his former life, wandering among the beehives and slowly curling in on himself, suffering with increasing rheumatism, or even dementia, and then an early death. Watson isn't given a much better fate by some of these later chroniclers. These visions of Our Heroes could not be further from the truth.

The purpose of this collection, *After the East Wind*, is to provide additional accounts of Holmes and Watson's wartime adventures, and also what happened during the post-war peace – what actually occurred, and not the idea that they simply drifted away into obscurity. The contents of these books don't pretend to offer a definitive and complete *A*-to-*Z* account of what happened during those years – for how could they, when there are so many other stories which also add threads to this particular part of The Great Holmes Tapestry?

There are some other notable adventures that took place during the war that should be located if possible: *Hellbirds* (1976, later re-titled *Sherlock Holmes and the Hellbirds*) by Nick Utechin (who generously provided a Foreword for this anthology) and the late Austin Mitchelson. I was particularly pleased when I first discovered this volume years ago, as it includes a most memorable encounter between Holmes and Watson, in disguise behind enemy lines and in the German trenches, and a shabby fellow there named Schicklgruber, whom Watson unfortunately allowed to live.

Besides countless short stories, other longer wartime adventures include *Sherlock Holmes and the Lusitania* (by Lorraine Daly, 1998), *Son of Holmes* and *Rasputin's Revenge* (1986 and 1987 respectively, by John Lescroart, serving as valuable links between Holmes and Nero Wolfe), *The Case of the Reluctant Agent* (2001,

7

Tracy Cooper-Posey), and *Sherlock Holmes on the Western Front* (2000, Val Andrews).

One war story that deserves particular mention is "The Case of the Last Battle" by L.B. Greenwood (1997, included in *The Mammoth Book of New Sherlock Holmes Stories*). It's a wonderful tale of the very end of the war, and how Holmes and Watson brought that about.

After the war, London tried to get back to normal, although it took a while. Fortunately, Scotland Yard had learned the lessons that Holmes had so valiantly tried to teach them, and other consulting detectives had stepped forward to fill the void, including Solar Pons, Hercule Poirot, Lord Peter Wimsey, and Albert Campion – all of whom have some small connections to this anthology.

Poirot, living at 14 Farraway Street, had a number of interesting cases before he too retired, traveling for a while and then settling back in London in Whitehaven Mansions while continuing to consult on a much more limited basis. Lord Peter, at 110A Piccadilly, and Albert Campion (at nearby Number 17A Bottle Street, Piccadilly), were more dilettantish about their investigations, but they were nevertheless quite effective. Certainly the best and most consistent of them during that time was Solar Pons of 7B Praed Street. If the reader hasn't yet met Mr. Pons, please do so at the earliest opportunity.

As I edited this set of stories, I was also concurrently working on the most recent set of the MX Holmes anthologies, *The MX Book of New Sherlock Holmes Stories*, Parts XXV, XXVI, and XXVII, and also *The Meeting of the Minds: The Cases of Sherlock Holmes and Solar Pons*. There were stories in the former's Part XXVII, and many in the latter set, which very much overlapped those contained in this anthology, and I highly recommend also seeking out those other books for additional narratives that help to fill in and around the Canonical ropes in The Great Holmes Tapestry.

There are many other amazing post-war and post-Canonical tales besides those contained in these volumes, but I must point out that after looking through my Chronology, a great deal of what's shown through the 1920's turns out to be *Prologues*, *Forewords*, *Postscripts*, and *Addendums* related to earlier adventures. Watson spent much of these post-war years writing up his notes before adding the manuscripts to his Tin Dispatch Box, or sending them to those who might be interested, such as individuals who had been involved in the original investigations. Thus, it's through Watson's monumental efforts during this decade, leading up to his death on

24th July, 1929, that we now have so many of these additional tales to augment the original sixty Canonical accounts.

For too many people, there is a belief that Holmes and Watson simply ended on 2 August, 1914. This is absolutely not true. There are so many other adventures that followed "His Last Bow", and the stories in this new collection will fill in some of those gaps, and also hopefully encourage Mr. Holmes's admirers to seek out the others. After 1914, Holmes didn't vanish, for *After 1914, he's still ours!* – the traditional Canonical hero that is just as important today as he was then.

* * * * *

"Of course, I could only stammer out my thanks."
– The unhappy John Hector McFarlane
"The Norwood Builder"

As always when one of these Holmes anthologies is finished, I want to first thank with all my heart my incredibly wonderful wife of nearly thirty-three years, Rebecca, and our amazing son and my friend, Dan. I love you both, and you are everything to me!

Also, I simply cannot find words to express the gratitude I have to all of the contributors who have used their time to create this project. I'm so glad to have gotten to know all of you. It's an undeniable fact that Sherlock Holmes authors are the *best* people!

Additionally, I'd also like to especially thank:

- Nick Utechin – Nick and I began exchanging emails in early 2014, when our mutual friend Roger Johnson forwarded a fan letter from me to Nick. We quickly determined that we are both Rathbones – each of our mothers was originally a Rathbone. Nick has traced a fairly close connection directly to Basil Rathbone, while I've yet to firmly establish the path from "Cousin Basil", as my sister and I always called him, to the American Rathbones.

  In 2015, I was in England for my Holmes Pilgrimage No. 2 and staying for a few days at the home of Roger Johnson and his wife Jean Upton. I mentioned that the next day I was going to Oxford, and Jean called Nick on the telephone and asked if he'd be my tour guide. He met me at the station the following morning and graciously set aside a

9

huge part of his day. He is a resident of Oxford and alum of one of the colleges, and as such, he was able to take me into many colleges, buildings, dining halls, libraries, chapels, and gardens where I would have otherwise never been able to visit. (If I had gone by myself, I would have likely traveled a few of the main streets, thinking that I'd "seen" Oxford, and then caught the next train back to London.)

Additionally, Nick took me that day to several J.R.R. Tolkien spots, including The Eagle and Child Pub – where a shelf above Tolkien and C.S. Lewis's regular table wonderfully had a copy of *The Hound of the Baskervilles*, and also out to one of Tolkien's houses. (This side-trip satisfied my curiosity, and also was for my wife's sake – for she is a Tolkien fan at the nearly same level that I admire Holmes. In fact, she made her own Pilgrimage to England and Oxford, focusing on a Tolkien agenda, several years before I met her.)

It was while Nick and I were eating lunch that day that he expressed an interest in contributing to a future edition of *The MX Book of New Sherlock Holmes Stories*, and he ended up sending me several very fine stories over the next year or so, including one based on an Oxford statue (and the backstory related to it) that he and I had seen during his tour.

Since then we've stayed in touch, and I was fortunate to see him again in person most recently when he was at the amazing *From Gillette to Brett* conference in Bloomington, Indiana in 2018. I hope to run into him again in the future, either in the United States or in England, and I'm very thankful that he contributed the Foreword to this volume – which is especially fitting, since his 1976 pastiche *Hellbirds* was set in this period, and I'd enjoyed it long before I ever knew that I'd get to meet him.

- Derrick and Brian Belanger – I first "met" Derrick when he graciously reviewed one of my early books. Then he interviewed me several times, and when I had the idea for the first MX Holmes anthology in 2015, he quickly joined the party and contributed a fine pastiche. From there he's written a number of others, and then he formed Belanger Books with his brother, Brian. It's turned into a Sherlockian powerhouse, and I'm very grateful to have this and other opportunities to contribute to The Great Holmes Tapestry by editing and writing stories for their different anthologies. Derrick continues to write, but he also stays quite busy as a noted teacher, as well as running Belanger Books with Brian.

Over the last few years, my amazement at Brian Belanger's talent has only grown. I initially became acquainted with him when he took over the duties of creating the covers for MX Books following the untimely death of their previous graphic artist. I found Brian to be great to collaborate with, very easy-going and stress-free in his approach and willingness to work with authors, and wonderfully creative. His skills became most apparent to me when he created the cover for my 2017 book, *The Papers of Solar Pons*, which was one of the most striking covers that I've ever seen. Later, when the Belangers and I began reissuing the original Pons books in new editions, and then new Pons anthologies, Brian's similarly themed covers continued to astound me. He truly deserves an award for these. In the meantime, he has become busier and busier, continuing to provide covers for MX Books, and now for Belanger Books as well, along with editing and occasionally writing. (*Brian: I'm still waiting for you to write a pastiche for something that I edit!!!*) (*Note the three explanation points at the end of that statement – for I am not kidding.*)

I finally met both Brian and Derrick in early 2020 at the annual Sherlock Holmes Birthday Celebration in New York City, and they're just as great in person as they were by way of email. Keep up the good work, both of you, and thanks very much for all that you do!

Finally, last but certainly *not* least, **Sir Arthur Conan Doyle**: Author, doctor, adventurer, and the Founder of the Sherlockian Feast. Present in spirit, and honored by all of us here.

As always, this collection, like those before it, has been a labor of love by both the participants and myself. As I've explained before, once again everyone did their sincerest best to produce an anthology that truly represents why Holmes and Watson have been so popular for so long. These are just more tiny threads woven into the ongoing Great Holmes Tapestry, continuing to grow and grow, for there can *never* be enough stories about the man whom Watson described as "*the best and wisest . . . whom I have ever known.*"

David Marcum
May 4th, 2021
The 130th Anniversary of
Reichenbach Day
(When Sherlockians celebrate
"The Detective Who Lived")

Questions, comments, and story submissions
may be addressed to David Marcum at
thepapersofsherlockholmes@gmail.com

Foreword
by Nicholas Utechin

The period from August 1914 onwards in the Sherlockian Canon is especially fascinating. But there is nothing in the Sherlockian Canon covering that period. Therein, of course, lies the fascination.

The Valley of Fear and no fewer than thirteen of the short stories were published after the vital events of "His Last Bow" took place (including, naturally, "His Last Bow" itself); but all were actually dated (specifically or by scholars) previous to those events. "Shoscombe Old Place" was the very last tale to be published in *The Strand Magazine*, in April 1927, but its Canonical dating was actually – oh dear, here we go (damn those chronologists): 1882, 1883, 1894, 1897, or 1902! Sherlock Holmes was, we take it, only sixty in 1914 and Dr. Watson not much older. There was surely more to come in their lives.

In my own contributions to "The Grand Game", I have ventured only twice in this direction. In 1997, I much enjoyed discovering that from 25 April to 20 June 1913, the position in the British Government of Solicitor-General for Ireland was held by a certain J. Moriarty – which provided for added depths in researching Holmes's activities in the lead-up to the case of LAST. [1] As is the way in such matters, I chose to ignore the fact that the minister involved was John Francis Moriarty and – this *is* interesting – was one of the two Moriarty brothers who attended Stoneyhurst College at the same time as Arthur Conan Doyle: Wheels within wheels where worlds collide, indeed!

Twenty years later, I had an opportunity [2] to range far more straightforwardly over one specific area of work carried out by Holmes and Watson in the years following the First World War: How they collated the various notes of old cases (see above) for publication – and why. Somehow, I was led to what in the end seemed an inevitable conclusion: That Sherlock Holmes died in 1927, an outcome that had certainly not been on the cards when I first accepted the remit to write the paper.

That fine scholar, D. Martin Dakin, decided that Dr. Watson had passed away before then [3]. Having decided that "The Blanched Soldier" and "The Lion's Mane" were not only not written by Holmes, but perhaps even fictitious, he goes on: "*Why did not*

Watson instantly denounce these amazing forgeries? That he did not do so points, I fear, to the inescapable conclusion that the good doctor was by then deceased. Since the last undoubted publication by him was the introduction to His Last Bow *at the end of 1917, and the series in question started in October 1921, we may safely assume that his death took place between those two dates . . . ."*

Most scholars have tended to go no further than T. S. Blakeney – and usually along much the same lines [4]: "*No student of Sherlock Holmes can doubt that the years 1914-18 found him hard at work in the nation's interests – doubtless the perspicacity of the genial but anonymous head of the Secret Service secured the willing assistance of one who stood head and shoulders above the common order of men.*" June Thomson – in the biography [5] she wrote which is often overlooked by those who only know her for her pastiches – is similarly inclined: " . . . *[G]iven his specialized knowledge of espionage and the activities of the Irish Republican movement, it is possible that (Holmes) remained in London, acting as a Government adviser, or travelled to and from Sussex to attend ministerial meetings.*"

In terms of pastiche, no one has realistically taken matters further down the Sherlockian time-line than Mitch Cullin, whose 2005 novel *A Slight Trick of the Mind* placed Holmes in the year 1947 [6].

On a personal note, however, I find it recorded that it was in the year 1976 that I co-authored the second of two pastiches which appeared in the United States courtesy of a soon-to-be-defunct publisher [7]. It was probably not as a direct result of our post-*Seven-Per-Cent Solution* outpourings that it went bust, but they will not have helped. The events covered in *Hellbirds* opened in Baker Street on 18 December, 1914 and proceeded via The Tower of London, Dover, and the Western Front, to come to a resounding close in the Royal Albert Hall. Forty-five years after I wrote them, I see the final words read: "*Outside, the first snow of 1915 began to fall.*" En route – on page 144 of the book, to be precise – my co-author and I committed one of the most ludicrous examples of "Look how clever we (think we) are" in Sherlockian pastiche history. I fear it was my idea.

But memories of inadequate pastiches should not be allowed in this volume. David Marcum, in his quest to squeeze the very last droplet of new story material from the quivering wrecks of writers old and new, has succeeded once again. The breadth of invention and intriguing plot-lines is impressive: Among them, we have more

Irish skulduggery, a pleasing re-appearance of former Irregular Wiggins as a middle-aged civil service mandarin, and a tale with strong *Titanic* links.

The East Wind blew strongly indeed, but so does the quality of present-day pasticheurs.

Nicholas Utechin
Oxford, U.K., 2021

NOTES

1. "Holmes's War Service: The True Story", contribution to *An East Wind – The East Coast Expedition of The Sherlock Holmes Society of London, 4-6 July 1997*. Sherlock Holmes Society of London,1997
2. "Aftermath – Holmes and Watson after 11 November", contribution to *Trenches – The War Service of Sherlock Holmes*, The B.S.I. MS series (LAST). The Baker Street Irregulars 2017
3. *A Sherlock Holmes Commentary*, David & Charles 1972 – This book is a completely essential contribution to the scholarship.
4. *Sherlock Holmes: Fact or Fiction?* John Murray 1932 – As is this, for historical reasons.
5. *Holmes and Watson*, Constable 1995
6. The novel was of course turned into the film *Mr. Holmes* (2015), starring Ian McKellen.
7. *Hellbirds*, with Austin Mitchelson. Belmont Tower Books 1976. (The first, also published that year, was *The Earthquake Machine*.)

Sherlock Holmes: After the East Wind Blows

Part II: Aftermath
(1919-1920)

The Old Sweet Song
by Margie Deck

Chapter I – The Enthusiastic Admirers

"I'm afraid breakfast is a bit sparse this morning, Watson," Sherlock Holmes said, motioning to the coffee and toast on the table. "The housekeeper set this out and abandoned us until tomorrow night for a family duty of some sort. Although with rationing what it is, breakfast would perhaps be the same even if she were here fussing about as usual."

I took what had become my usual place at the table when visiting. "After my time in the wards, I can assure you this breakfast is more than sufficient. Munificent even. These weeks here in Sussex are doing wonders for my health and morale. I thank you again for the unexpected invitation. I'm recovering because of it, and perhaps because some remnant of the resilience of my youth exists even at this late date."

Holmes didn't acknowledge my thanks, but I hardly expected him to do so. In many ways he was still the man Stamford had introduced me to all those years ago. He moved the morning *Times* across the table.

"The Paris Peace Conference opens today with the Prime Minister center stage and concern about the further spread of the flu from the November celebrations are the topics of the day. Thankfully, I'm not interested in the criminal world any longer, for I see nothing that could possibly challenge me. Your mail is on the sideboard."

He pushed back from the table and repositioned himself into his reading chair near the fire with the book he'd started last evening. I knew he wouldn't stir again for two hours.

A glance at the paper proved Holmes's summary accurate. I stared hard at the *18 January, 1919* at the top of the newspaper for a moment. Three weeks had passed since my arrival at Holmes's door the day after Christmas, weary to the bone, weak from illness, and more devastated than I had been in the weeks following Maiwand some forty years ago. My wife's duties had kept her from immediately returning home. Twelve weeks treating soldiers stricken with the so-called "Spanish Flu", and the resulting septicemia in so many, combined with six weeks of my own bout, left me well aware of the joint catastrophe of war and flu. No, no newspaper then. I was determined not to lose my optimistic mood, my first such in several long months. I poured a cup of coffee and retrieved my one piece of mail.

"I don't recognize the name on this envelope, but a St. Dunstan's Lodge return address can only mean The Blinded Soldiers' and Sailors' Hostel," I said, more to myself than to Holmes.

"Certainly, the hostel," said Holmes from his book. "A former patient then. A patient who has been in residence there for a few months. Note the lack of errors in the typing. He has been at the typewriting class for a while. The *D.J.* – more than likely a David James. What would be more prosaic? And Shaw. Did you not tell me once that Hayter's soldier godson was a Shaw from the Surrey branch?"

I smiled at the back of Holmes's head. Yes, still the man from our Victorian adventures. I opened the letter. The contents proved Holmes correct on all counts as to the identity and circumstances of my correspondent, although I didn't specifically recall treating him.

I read the letter several times, unsure if I should share the contents with Holmes. "Well, Watson," Holmes said, with his nose still in the book. "What does he want from us?"

"How did you know he wanted something that included you?"

"You don't remember treating him and he hasn't written to you before, or you would have recognized his name immediately on the envelope. You aren't friends. Why then would he go to the trouble to find you here?"

"Yes. There is a small conundrum at the hostel he thought might interest you. He tells me that he reads and rereads all our published adventures. One of his fellow lodgers noted his interest in my books, and suggested that he seek your counsel concerning some watches being taken and then returned repeatedly."

Holmes closed the book and dropped it to the table with some unnecessary force. "Watson," he said as he turned to face me, "I didn't know you made your coming here common knowledge. You know how I value my seclusion, and I am no longer in practice."

"I told no one I was coming here, Holmes, beyond those necessary for my income to be available to me," I said with a hint of sharpness in my tone. "This Shaw reports it was a brother of the fellow lodger who advised him of my whereabouts – although how he knew of them, I have no clue."

To my great surprise, a smile crept across Holmes's face. "I see. Who are these brothers so keenly interested in us?"

"The letter doesn't say." I tried to pass the letter to him, but he waved it away.

"If our past behaviour is so admired, then perhaps we should behave as we did then. Custom dictates you should read it to me." Holmes turned back around in his chair, stretched his long thin legs towards the fire, and closed his eyes. I settled myself down and read the letter aloud. It ran in this way:

My Dear Dr. Watson,

> *I trust you will forgive my intruding upon your visit with Mr. Sherlock Holmes. On the basis of how kind you were to me when you helped me at the Fifth London General Hospital, and of all the stories my godfather, Colonel Hayter, told me about you, I believe you will not find this intrusion untenable. I must add I feel like you are a friend of mine, as I have read your words many times in your books about Mr. Holmes's cases.*

> *You may not remember when you treated my eye injuries in May of this last year. I know many hundreds of injured soldiers passed through the Fifth's doors. I recovered enough to be discharged and have been in residence here at Sir Arthur Pearson's hostel since July. I have busied myself learning typewriting as the baronet and the aftercare leader, Captain Fraser, believe the world is never so dark when one has a Braille watch and a typewriter.*

> *My sister, wishing for me to feel at home, kindly brought over a box of my favorite books and a few new ones. I couldn't fault her for this, although I can no longer read the books myself. Luckily one of the fellows here in my rooms has a brother that visits often, and he has been kind enough to read your books to us. He is quite impressed with my connection to you, even though it is second-hand through the old Colonel.*

> *Now as to the reason for this letter: We need help solving a mystery and, as my reading friend Ned said, who better to ask to solve a mystery than Sherlock Holmes and Dr. Watson? I had no inkling of where to*

21

send a letter but, somehow, he turned up with your address, care of Mr. Holmes.

When a soldier arrives here for training, he is gifted with a Braille watch. There were hundreds of these pocket watches brought in from Switzerland last year due to the generosity of the National Association of Goldsmiths. One morning, four weeks ago, we discovered three of the watches were missing from our rooms. After a search, the watches were found in the most unlikely of places: Behind Gog and Magog in the surround of our old namesake clock. A few days later, this same inexplicable exercise was repeated, but with ten watches from the storage cupboard. Watches from different parts of the grounds have disappeared and are returned in the clock on varying days since.

As it happens, we were rereading your story about the Six Napoleons when these strange occurrences began, and we, as in myself and the brothers, think perhaps someone is looking for a specific watch but is unable to find it. We cannot think why a certain watch would matter when they are all the same, as far as we can tell, but it would seem to explain why the watches are taken but then returned.

I hope you and Mr. Holmes will come to the lodge and help us. We realize the matter is a perfectly trivial one, but after so much desolation, we are quite excited by our little mystery and the possibility of a visit from you both.

"Signed '*Sincerely yours, etc., etc., from Corporal D.J. Shaw*'. So, Holmes, what do you make of it? Could you possibly want to trek to Regent's Park?"

"Yes, I will go. Do you feel well enough to make the journey?"

"Of course. I wouldn't miss the opportunity to go on a case, no matter how minor, with you again. After all, it has been more than four years since my adventure with that fellow Altamont."

"Minor? Hmm . . . We shall see. Ring St. Dunstan's to advise we will arrive by the mid-morning train out of Eastbourne. Then I'll call round to Stackhurst's. One of the coaches can give us a lift to the station."

The morning *Railway Time* proved accurate for once, and after finally securing a cab, an old Darracq which had seen better days, we arrived at the front gates of the fifteen-acre spread of house, gardens, outbuildings, and magnificent clock that make up the St. Dunstan's Lodge grounds. A beautiful, tall young woman, brunette with a creamy complexion and a sharply pointed nose greeted us warmly as we stopped to admire the life-size wooden figures inside the clock striking the bell on the quarter-hour.

"It is a monstrous beauty, is it not?" the young woman said. "It dates from 1671. We are fortunate the clock came here when the ancient Church of St. Dunstan in the West was remodeled. We are watched over by these magnificent renditions of the Guildhall giants of myth, Gog and Magog. Oh, where are my manners? "

She extended her hand to me, and then to Holmes.

"I am Irene Mace, long-time V.A.D. assistant to Sir Arthur, and recent fiancé of Captain Fraser. You are undoubtedly Sherlock Holmes and Dr. Watson. It caused some excitement when you telephoned this morning. We do have celebrities here from time to time – Shackleton, the renowned Antarctic explorer was here last year – but to have the great consulting detective and his chronicler here is a special honour. If you will come with me, I will take you to Corporal Shaw. I'm afraid Sir Arthur and Captain Fraser are both away today. They will be so disappointed to have missed you."

She flashed a lovely smile and beckoned for us to follow as she made her way past the huge clock towards a side building. I docilely followed the lady, but Holmes lagged, obviously studying the clock and its surrounding area. He suddenly took three long strides and fell into place at our side.

"Please tell me, Miss Mace," he said, "are there any restrictions here as to how your residents come and go, or perhaps, as to their visitors?"

She stopped, gave Holmes a puzzled look, and then answered the question in a careful, measured tone.

"No, Mr. Holmes, not at all. This is a home for the men until they have completed their chosen training. While obviously we are a healing and teaching institution, we try to make this hostel as comfortable as possible. All of our residents are soldiers. We believe we can depend on them to be respectful of our staff and grounds."

Holmes nodded. "Yet the watches of these soldiers are taken from them. What do you make of it?"

"As for this watch business, I make nothing of it." she said without hesitation. "Sir Arthur and Captain Fraser are convinced it is a lark – one of the men having some fun with the others, and I agree. We don't see anything sinister in it, as the watches are always

23

returned in the clock. After all these men have been through, a harmless practical joke is a welcome small diversion. We were surprised to learn this morning that Corporal Shaw had written to you about it. Perhaps he simply wanted to meet the two of you?" She smiled once more and again motioned for us to follow.

Miss Mace directed us past the carpentry, switchboard, and shorthand training areas and into the ground floor sitting room of the sleeping quarters. The nicely furnished room, arranged with a deliberate sparseness, featured several large sofas, broad windows, several desks with typewriters and supplies, and slightly roughed flooring without rugs. Low bookcases ran under the windows, filled with books, not all in Braille, but all clearly labeled with large Braille tags.

"Forgive my impertinence, Miss Mace, " I said, "but why so many books the blind cannot read?"

"The gentlemen chose their favorite books by reading the titles in Braille, and our volunteer readers, or sometimes friends and family, read to them. As a medical man, a soldier, an author, and a reader yourself, surely you can see the value? Also, some of our more enterprising typing students practice their skills by typing what is being read to them. It is a marvelous training exercise. Now, gentlemen, I will tell Corporal Shaw you are here, and I hope to see you again before you leave. Please make yourselves comfortable."

I remained standing until she had closed the door, and then dropped wearily onto the nearest sofa, a sad acknowledgement of my reduced health. Holmes wandered around the room, lightly touching various surfaces, and glancing at the bookshelves. To me, who still recognized his every mood and habit, he seemed particularly interested in a shelf on the lower right side of the window, but I couldn't see why that shelf, or the books on it, would be of any more interest than the others.

The silence of the room vanished with the entrance of three young men. A tall, affable-looking red-head could only be Corporal Shaw, as the other two, one blind, and one not, bore a strong resemblance to one another. The taller and older looking of the brothers gently guided the other over to where I now stood in front of the long sofa.

"Dr. Watson! We are so glad you are here." He offered his hand to me. "I am Ned Hewick, and this is my younger brother, Alec. And here is your old friend Hayter's godson, David Shaw," he said as the red-head joined us. I greeted each of them, shaking each hand in turn.

"Ned – actually Edward – and Alec Hewick. Sons of Baron Edward Hewick, once Paymaster-General of the previous administration," Sherlock Holmes said from across the room. All three men turned to the sound of his voice.

"Surely it is Mr. Holmes. How do you know us?" Ned asked. "We haven't met before."

"As you may know from your reading, it is my business to know things, " he replied, waving a hand over at the bookshelf he had previously examined.

The older Hewick appeared oddly confused for a moment, and then crossed the room to offer his hand to Holmes. "We are glad you came today," he said. "Maybe you can make some sense of our mysterious watches."

The two soldiers followed him to greet Holmes. He wasn't effusive, but he kindly received their praise for his previous cases. The red-headed Corporal went to the bookshelf, quickly scanned some titles with his fingers, and returned with the volumes distributed as *The Adventures of Sherlock Holmes* and *His Last Bow*.

"Dr. Watson, we read them all, but these are our favorites."

"Yes, I know," Holmes said.

"But how?" Shaw exclaimed. "How could you know?"

"The corners of your favorites are more bent and worn smoother than the corners of the other ones in the collection."

Shaw laughed and nudged Alec. "I should have predicted that. To be honest, I find them more quickly, Braille tags aside, because I know the feel of the book covers and those corners."

Alec picked up *His Last Bow* and turned it over a few times. "I can always find this one without the tag because it has a particular smell. I think from time to time someone smokes a pipe while reading it."

I took the book from him and brought it close to my face. The smell was certainly familiar, but I couldn't name it. "I suppose it isn't surprising that it smells of pipe smoke," I said. "Nearly every soldier I treated smoked as often as possible. Smoking is ubiquitous." I handed the book back to the younger brother.

"Not a pipe," said Holmes. "Cigarettes – more than likely Smith's Glasgow Mixture."

"Ah, yes, all the types of tobacco monograph," Ned said. "What was that? 'Boscombe Valley'?"

He took *The Adventures* from the Corporal, thumbed the book to the proper page and read aloud from it: "'*I have, as you know, devoted some attention to this, and written a little monograph on the*

25

ashes of one-hundred-and-forty different varieties of pipe, cigar, and cigarette tobacco.'"

Holmes took the book from him, looked over the page, and then thumbed the volume before handing it back. "That was a long time ago," he said. "Tobacco and smoking practices have changed. I see you do not smoke in this sitting room."

"Sadly, we do not," Alec said. "It is far too easy for one of us to possibly cause a fire. Soon we will be more comfortable with our limitations and can choose to smoke indoors or not once we return home. With everything provided for us here, not smoking inside isn't too much to ask." Shaw and Ned nodded in agreement.

Corporal Shaw then flashed a smile at me. "I do have a question before we talk about these wandering watches. Tell us, Dr. Watson, are the stories true? I'm always prepared to swear to the veracity of your stories. Please tell me my faith is well-placed?"

I shot a glance at Holmes. He shrugged his shoulders and said nothing. I thought for a moment.

"The tales are as true as I can make them while still protecting the people who need to be protected," I said. "There is fundamental truth in all of them, and there is a common thread of fiction in all of them as well."

The three seemed surprised by my answer and were quiet for a moment.

Ned Hewick broke the silence. "I suppose protection and timing must always be considered. Perhaps that is why you didn't publish the events of 2nd August, 1914 until two years ago? You can imagine how interesting we find the story, considering our own war service. Alec, pass that one to me. This is our favorite quote from 'His Last Bow'."

He opened the book, thumbed quickly to the desired page, and read aloud:

> "'*I shall get level with you, Altamont,*' *he said, speaking with slow deliberation,* '*if it takes me all my life I shall get level with you!*'"
>
> "*The old sweet song,*" *said Holmes.* "*How often have I heard it in days gone by. It was a favourite ditty of the late lamented Professor Moriarty.*"

The three laughed. "Yes, the old sweet song!" Alec said. "But we know he didn't get level with *you*, Mr. Holmes, because here you are. We have often wondered why 'His Last Bow' wasn't written in

Dr. Watson's voice as most of the other adventures are. Is there a special reason for that, Dr. Watson?"

I have many reasons, but I wasn't going to discuss them. I decided to ignore the question. "Now, gentlemen, perhaps we best talk about these watches that go missing and then are later found in the clock. This day is going to get away from us. Possibly we should walk back to the clock, and you can tell us exactly what has transpired."

"I will walk as far as the clock with you," the older brother said. "Then I'm afraid I must tend to some business for my father. I know he'll be thrilled that Alec and I have met the two of you. Won't you both join us for dinner so that I might introduce you? He's in London for the day. We're meeting at Simpson's at 8:30. Despite the rationing, Simpson's will feed us well on salmon, sole, and turbot."

The younger Hewick looked surprised. "I didn't know you were leaving, and I didn't know Father was in town. What can the old man possibly have for you to do? Either way, at least by dinner time we might have an answer to our conundrum. Yes, please, Dr. Watson and Mr. Holmes, join us for dinner – and you too, Shaw. A meal away from here will do us both some good."

I started to voice a polite refusal, but to my surprise Holmes interrupted.

"It will be a pleasure to dine with you. Watson and I plan to stay over tonight in London. However, you can appreciate that at the moment we are weary from our journey, no longer being the young men in the adventures you are so fond of. Watson and I will go to our hotel and return here in time for tea. With my housekeeper away, breakfast was light, and we will be quite ready for tea. At that time, the three of you can tell us all the facts of your little mystery and we'll see if we can bring the case to a successful conclusion."

He turned to Ned Hewick. "I assume you can complete your father's business and be back at that time?"

"Certainly," he said as he returned the two books to their shelf.

"Shall we go then?" Holmes said as he made his way to the door. Accustomed to following orders, the three men gathered themselves together and followed Holmes out, apparently not realizing that less than an hour had passed since our arrival.

I stood there for a moment thinking about what had transpired. I knew that Holmes and I weren't spending the night in London, as I was sure we weren't having dinner with Baron Edward Hewick, and possibly we weren't having tea here either. Holmes had reason to create an illusion of a London stay, but I didn't understand why, any more than I understood why we were leaving so soon after our arrival. Once again, my friend had seen or deduced something remarkable that had completely passed me by. I hurried to catch up with them, closing the door firmly behind me.

Chapter II – Tracing the Paymaster

"Tell me," I said as soon as we were out of the gates and out of earshot, "where are we actually going?"

"Do you not know? I thought you might have worked it out already. You have made progress over the years. A younger you would have asked to which hotel we were going." He laughed in his hearty, noiseless fashion. "We are going home, Watson, because we are going to have a visitor. We have to hurry, because I want to be there before he arrives."

I turned the events of the morning over in my mind once more. "Ned Hewick is coming, isn't he? I don't understand why, but all my instincts tell me this is what you expect."

"Ned is a nice persona, but I believe this afternoon we will have Edward, first son and heir to Baron Edward Hewick, of Sutton Court in the County of Somerset. Now, let us see if we can hire a car. We don't have time to wait for the next train. "

"How are you going to do that?" I asked. "With the shortages, it's difficult enough to get a cab here in the city."

"Whitehall. The Holmes brothers may have officially retired years ago, but we served our government in a myriad of ways, some official and some not, over many years, including the last few difficult ones. My name should be enough to obtain the use of a car and driver for a few hours."

Holmes wasn't wrong. In short order we were in route to Sussex in the luxury of a Vauxhall 25-horsepower, driven by a Lieutenant who seemed surprised at his assignment. I wanted to discuss the morning's events and to know what to expect once we were back in Sussex, but Holmes wouldn't talk. He shook his head, pointed to the driver in the front seat, and put his finger to his lips. I knew there was no point in arguing with him. I decided to simply enjoy the ride. After all the raw January rain of the first weeks of the new year, today's air was clear and brisk, and I felt more alive than I had in ages.

At Holmes's request, the driver allowed us to keep one of the lap blankets from the car and dropped us a good half-mile from the villa.

"Watson, I couldn't risk having the car take us all the way, should he already be there. I don't think Hewick has had enough time to get ahead of us, but we cannot be certain. We lost some little time arranging the car, but he would have needed a little time to disengage with his brother and the corporal and to place a watch in the clock for us to find at tea-time. I made sure there wasn't a watch in the clock when we arrived."

"Then he is the one taking and returning the watches?"

"Of course he is. Now, as ridiculous as it may seem in our current state, we need to be as unidentifiable as possible as we walk this last part. I don't believe that he could have made it here before us, but we must consider he might pass us here on the road. He will be in a hurry. If we look even mildly different, he may pass us by without a thought. We need the element of surprise."

Holmes pulled his hat low on his brow, turned his collar up, and wrapped the blanket around his shoulders. He stooped over a bit and started the walk with a noticeable limp. I nodded my understanding, adjusted my own clothing, and walked around to hold Holmes's right elbow, appearing to be assisting him with his walk. Holmes smiled. "Excellent, Watson."

I am sure we were an odd sight, but our luck held. We made the walk without disturbance and found Holmes's rooms as we had left them. Holmes took us in through the back entrance, double bolting it behind us.

"We won't make things too easy for him, Watson. He must come through the front hall, which puts us in a much better position to surprise him. We cannot risk any fire or light that might betray our presence. The villa must look deserted. I'm sure you noticed I pointed out the absence of the housekeeper during our conversation today. He must have been thrilled about that unexpected bonus – one less thing to worry with." As he spoke, he unlocked the Spanish colonial sideboard, withdrew two revolvers, handed one to me, and slipped the other into his pocket.

"I don't think we will need to protect ourselves to this extreme, but it is best to be prepared. He will come alone, and although we are older, we are two. I don't have what he wants, so it's possible he will simply deflate when he sees his plan has been for naught."

"I did notice your unusual comment about the housekeeper. I also noticed you going on about resting and eating and socializing. You may have changed some over the years, but not to that extreme. Will you please explain to me what is happening here?"

"Patience! We need to take up our positions. I expect him now. I know he planned for his supposed errands to run long and force him to miss tea – I did make that easy for him, did I not? He knows he will have to be finished here by 5:30 to have any hope of making a last-minute appearance at 8:30 for dinner. He could telephone in some indisposition to miss dinner as well, but it might look too suspicious."

We settled in to wait on either side of the front entrance as the clock chimed three. I was grateful to sit down. "But why is he doing this?"

"Because of two sentences you placed in 'His Last Bow', my dear Watson."

I couldn't believe what he'd said. "Me? I'm the cause of this . . . ? Whatever it is? I don't know what to call it. How is that possible?"

"Watson, keep your voice down. It isn't entire – " He stopped in mid-sentence, and suddenly stood with his ear against the door jamb. He motioned for me to stand and put his finger to his lips. I heard the purr of the motor in the drive.

In a moment or two we heard the back door rattle, but it held fast. In another minute the front doorknob shook, and the door creaked as our visitor pressed hard against it. Holmes reached over and flipped the latch. With the next hard turn, the door flew open, and the elder Hewick brother fell through the doorway and onto his knees.

"Hello," Holmes said as he placed the revolver to the back of the intruder's head. "In all your reading, you should have studied a more elegant way to deal with a locked door. I believe I have said it before: Read it up – really you should. There is nothing new under the sun."

Edward Hewick looked wildly at the two of us in disbelief. He turned so sharply from side to side that he fell off his knees and landed in a full sit on the hallway floor. Holmes smiled. "Perhaps you should have given two old hounds like Watson and myself a little more credit." Holmes nudged him with the revolver. "I suggest you stay still."

"Well, Mr. Holmes. Here we are, the old sweet song. Looks like I'm not getting level with you any more than our German friend did."

Holmes smiled again. "Now, Watson, if you would be so kind, please turn on the lamps. And then, if you will, find the coil of rope resting on the floor by the back entrance. I believe our guest would be more comfortable tied."

30

We tied him into the chair I had used that morning as I read the letter that began this inexplicable course of events only eight hours earlier. Holmes and I sat silently across from him, watching him struggle with his ties and his emotions until he gave up on them both and sat dejectedly with his head down.

I poured a glass of whisky-and-soda for the two of us and lit a cigarette for myself. Although I seldom smoked anymore, I felt I had earned it. "I believe I am due some sort of explanation," I said. "But first, I'm going to telephone the hostel and ask the lovely Miss Mace to extend our apologies for missing tea, as I'm suddenly feeling ill. Even in these dark days, we are still gentlemen."

"Quite so, Watson," Holmes said as he lit a cigarette of his own. "The younger brother and the corporal are unaware of the situation and will be awaiting our arrival with their youthful enthusiasm. In a way, I'm sorry to disappoint them. In my quiet life here, I had somewhat forgotten the impact of your work upon your readers." He looked thoughtful for a moment and then returned his attention to his captive.

"I'm sorry, Edward, but we don't have your favorite tobacco, Muratti Ariston cigarettes. The specific smell of your brand is evident on your clothing, and in Corporal Shaw's books. Don't look too surprised. I did tease you a bit by misnaming the odor as Smith's Glasgow Mixture."

Edward responded with a defiant lift of his chin. "I suppose I should have known I couldn't get past you, Mr. Holmes. You do understand I had to try. My younger brother is going to need help for the rest of his life, my father is a broken man and, with the war's end, I cannot risk too much attention suddenly being cast upon events that have been, so far, swept aside in the chaos. I need to retrieve the proof. If only you ever left this place of your own accord, things would have been so much simpler. I have kept watch over your door as I could."

Holmes nodded. "Yes, but even so, it would have done you no good. The tracing isn't here. I don't know what happened to it. As Watson so faithfully reported in the text, I put the papers in the valise of the fellow he delightfully dubbed 'Von Bork'. The story indicated a plan to turn him over to Scotland Yard, but that is another one of Watson's common threads of fiction. The fellow and the valise were turned over to Whitehall. I never saw him or any of the papers again. I haven't asked what happened to him or the valise. I agreed to find the fellow and stop him. My job ended there."

Hewick looked incredulous. "But the stories say you keep all your papers!"

"Don't be ridiculous. You are chasing shadows. I followed the career path of your father through the end of 1914, and when I saw he wasn't offered a ministerial post when the 1915 coalition government formed, I knew at least one person had put the connections together. No public scandal ensued, and your father was apparently allowed to retire quietly to Somerset. Why are you so concerned now, four years later?"

"Because it is right there in the text. Shall I quote it for you?

> *"'Hullo! Hullo!'" he added, as he looked hard at the corner of a tracing before putting it in the box. "'This should put another bird in the cage. I had no idea that the paymaster was such a rascal, though I have long had an eye upon him."'*

"I have read it a million times since September. *The paymaster*. Do you know how many people have read those words, first in *The Strand* and now in that blasted collection?" He cast an accusatory glance in my direction.

I had listened to this extraordinary exchange without comment as the pieces of the puzzle fell into place for me. I thought for a minute more and then addressed the accusatory glance. "You are working from incomplete information and faulty assumptions – positions Holmes's stories should warn you against if you take them as seriously as you say you do," I said. "I will not discuss the circumstances behind the creation of 'His Last Bow', but I can tell you I know nothing of your father, and there was certainly no intent to draw attention to him in anyway."

"But yet there it is!" Hewick shrieked.

"Stop it and be quiet!" Holmes said in a harsh authoritarian tone. "Think this through. Four years have passed. If your father were to face any retribution for his minor, although still treasonous, information sharing, it would have happened in 1914 when Von Bork, as we will continue to call him, was taken into custody. You need to understand the history is much more complicated than presented in Watson's little patriotic tale designed to stir up support for the war effort. Your father was a minor, disposable player in a grand game, and he was disposed of with more kindness that he probably deserved. You have given him much more importance in your mind than he ever had in fact."

Holmes picked up the revolver he had laid on the table and extended his hand to me. I passed the revolver I had to him. He reopened the cabinet, replaced the guns into storage, and relocked the cabinet.

He turned back to the limp figure in the chair. "The odds are astronomically against anyone not found in the deepest bowels of Whitehall ever making a connection between this story and your father. How many times have you read the story with your brother and Shaw? Has either one even once mentioned the fact the word *'paymaster'* appears in the story and your father was once Paymaster-General? Alec is his son – has Alec ever said anything?" Hewick shook his head.

"Go home. As far as we are concerned, you were never here. It will all be forgotten, just as your father has been." Holmes untied him and pointed to the front door. "I think you can find your way out."

Chapter III – A Last Quiet Talk

I watched him leave and then poured myself another whisky. Although the mystery was minimal and the villain hardly a challenge, I found myself exhausted. Holmes thankfully started the fire as the evening cold was beginning to creep into the room.

"Holmes, tell me: When did you first suspect something wasn't quite right?"

"From the beginning. How did this brother of the blind lodger suddenly have your address? I only agreed to go because I knew there had to be something more to it. I wasn't sure what the something was until I added the Hewick brothers together with their so-called favorite tales. Do you remember I thumbed *The Adventures* after he read from 'Boscombe'?"

"Yes, I noticed you reviewed the page, and gave the book a once-over."

"The most used-looking page in the book was the denouement in that John Clay business, 'The Red-Headed League'. It smelled of the tobacco, which means it was being read over and over outside by the same person. It smelled like Edward Hewick. Why was he reading it over and over?"

"Because the entire point of Clay's plan was to get Jabez Wilson out of his own space."

"Exactly. As he said, he has been watching the house for some time as he was able. I suspect it wasn't often, or I would have been aware of it. But, still, once the connection to you was found through this Shaw fellow, he saw an opportunity to possibly draw me away from here with you if a compelling event could be manufactured."

Holmes lit another cigarette and stretched his legs out to the now glowing fire. "We begin with what Shaw said in his letter – the watch business started about four weeks ago when they were rereading 'The Six Napoleons'. No coincidence there. The Napoleon story gave Hewick the idea to use the watches as a mystery, especially as he could rile up the other two with theories about a supposed thief searching for a certain watch. Remember how they followed him and listened to him? He obviously could manipulate them into an excited state. Note the watch mystery failed to excite any interest from the leadership of the hostel. Your lovely Miss Mace certainly put me to thinking with her statement 'Perhaps he just wanted to meet you.'"

I listened carefully, reimagining the conversations in the sitting room. "I follow you completely. The two younger soldiers were led by this elder Hewick, physically because of their blindness, and mentally because of his age and magnetism. I believe his worry about his father must have become almost a mania with him. What he said about protection and the timing of the publication of 'His Last Bow' certainly takes on more meaning in hindsight."

Holmes took a long draw on his cigarette and stared into the fire for a moment. "In some ways, the case is sad. This son is traumatized not only by his war experience, but also by his brother's war disability, and his father's shame. Remember how strong the smell was in the other volume? He must have spent many minutes holding that book to his face, smoking and thinking, thinking, thinking. Perhaps we have helped him by giving him more of the truth than he had in his own mind."

"I know what I have in my mind, Holmes. I wish we were having dinner at Simpson's at 8:30, with or without Baron Hewick. I'm starved."

"I'm not convinced the father was in London at all. His unexpected appearance in town on the same day we made an unexpected appearance at the hostel is too much coincidence. I have a suspicion the three soldiers and the two of us would have made up the dinner party."

"I wonder what kind of story Ned will weave for his brother about all this business. I suppose we may never know. I do know it would have been good to eat at Simpson's. Perhaps the housekeeper left us some dinner?" I said hopefully as I dropped the remainder of my cigarette into the fire. "As this case is over, I will start a new one. I will investigate the larder now."

"I still never get your limits, Watson. Lead the way," Holmes said with a wave of his hand as he followed me into the kitchen.

The Seventh Shot
by Paul Hiscock

"Who can that be?" I muttered irritably to myself, as my breakfast was interrupted by an insistent knocking at the door.

I looked at the clock on the mantelpiece, only to discover that it was already ten o'clock – hardly an unreasonable time for someone to call. However, in the months since the Armistice, with few calls on my time and the country at peace, I had taken to rising late and starting the day in a leisurely fashion.

The man standing on my doorstep was blonde, clean-shaven, and wore a dark sack-cut suit with the narrow lapels that young men seemed to favour.

"Doctor Watson?"

"Yes? How can I help you?"

"I've been sent to fetch you."

He gestured behind to where a car was parked, its door open wide in anticipation.

"Fetch me? Fetch me to where? I have no appointments today, and I have certainly never met you before."

"Indeed, we have never met, Doctor, but Mr. Holmes told me that you would be available to attend upon him immediately."

My mood brightened immediately at the mention of my old friend. "Why did you not say so immediately? We are bound for Sussex then?"

"No, he is in London," replied the young man, seemingly surprised at the question.

I wondered what manner of case could have drawn Holmes out of retirement once more, and hurried to fetch my overcoat so that I could join him without delay.

It was only when the car pulled up outside a familiar building in Pall Mall that I realised I had made an erroneous assumption.

"You will need to be silent inside," he said as he opened the door for me.

"Of course." I was already quite familiar with the rules of the Diogenes Club.

He led me into the Stranger's Room, closing the door behind us.

"I have brought Doctor Watson as instructed, Mr. Holmes," he said.

Mycroft Holmes stood with his back to us. When he moved, I saw that his large body had concealed a table covered in documents, from which he picked up a thick file.

"Very good, Hargreaves," he said. "These must reach Paris without delay. All the usual precautions."

"Of course, sir," replied Hargreaves. He took the proffered file and left without another word.

"Doctor, it is good to see you again," said Mycroft once the door was closed and he was sure that no sound could escape into the club beyond. "I see that you have been busy writing up more of my brother's cases for the enjoyment of the masses."

I looked down at my hands and spotted ink stains that I hadn't realised were there.

"Very good, Doctor. Your deductive skills have certainly improved since we first met."

"It was hardly a taxing conclusion to draw," said a voice from behind me. "You might as well have told him that he had egg for breakfast, or that he had attended a reunion of his old regiment last week."

I turned around and was delighted to see Sherlock Holmes standing there, positioned so that he would have been concealed by the door as I entered. I hurried over and shook him by the hand.

"Now that those pleasantries are concluded," said Mycroft, "please can you attend to the business at hand? I have been advising on the negotiations taking place in Paris."

"My brother is too modest," said Holmes. "He is the primary architect of our government's strategy for the peace accord."

"Why are you not there?" I asked. "Surely you can do very little from here?"

"On the contrary, Good Doctor, it is here that I can achieve the most." He waved his arm over the table full of papers. "Here I can collate the reports of every one of my agents across Europe, and draw all the necessary conclusions without once having to set foot in France or suffer days locked in a room full of politicians."

"But you haven't called us here to assist you in that regard," said Holmes.

"No, this is delicate work that requires a subtle touch. However, yesterday someone almost undid all my painstaking labours with an attempt to remove one of the major players in the negotiations."

He picked up a newspaper and offered it to us. Holmes declined, no doubt already aware of its contents. I took it and saw that it was that day's edition of *Le Petit Parisien*. On the front page was a picture of a man with a thick white moustache under the headline, "*Attentat Contre M. Clemenceau*".

"Someone tried to kill the French Prime Minister?"

"Indeed, and they almost succeeded," said Mycroft. "He was shot, although luckily the perpetrator was a poor marksman and failed in his attempt."

"A dramatic incident, to be sure," said Holmes, "but hardly one that necessitates my involvement. If you read on, Watson, you will see that the would-be assassin, one Émile Cottin, was arrested on the spot."

"Where there is one anarchist," said Mycroft, "there are usually more. Our own Prime Minister is worried that he might be next, and is demanding assurances that this was an isolated incident. The French police aren't inclined to spend time investigating when they already have the culprit and, in any case, I wouldn't trust such an important matter to them. I need you to root out the man's accomplices so that I can concentrate on putting the pieces of Europe back together without further interruption."

"I fear there will be little in this case to occupy my mind," said Holmes, "but since I have come this far, I will follow the matter through. You will join me, won't you, Watson? I doubt it will take long – a day or two at most."

Mycroft barely gave me time to nod before thrusting a pair of tickets into my hand. "You are booked on the boat train via Folkestone this afternoon. Clemenceau's Chief-of-Staff, Mandel, is expecting you. I trust that you will send a report post-haste."

Then, he opened the door and ushered us out into the corridor and the silence of the club before either of us could utter another word.

The newly resumed service to Paris made for a smooth and speedy journey. It afforded me a chance to catch up with Holmes and we passed the time engaged in the pleasantly inconsequential small talk and companionable silence that is only possible between close friends. Upon our arrival, a car was waiting for us and we were taken straight to the hospital where the French Prime Minister was being treated.

There was a wiry solider leaning against the wall in the corridor near the Prime Minister's room when we arrived. My initial impression was that he didn't seem very alert for a man on guard duty, but he dropped his cigarette and moved to intercept us quickly enough as we approached.

"These are important detectives from England," said our driver, who was escorting us to the room, and waved the soldier away.

The soldier went and knocked on the door to one of the rooms. I assumed he was asking permission for us to enter, and was surprised when our driver opened a different door and ushered us inside.

There were three men waiting in the room to receive us, and I immediately recognised Clemenceau from meeting him the year before. He was sitting up in his bed and seemed quite cheerful in spite of his injuries. The man to his right didn't look so happy. Georges Mandel had oily black hair, parted in the centre. A stubby cigarette hung from the side of his mouth, which seemed to be fixed in a permanent scowl. The third man was M. Clemenceau's doctor. I didn't know Antonin Gosset personally, but I had heard of him and knew him to be a skilled surgeon.

"Mr. Holmes. Doctor Watson," said M. Clemenceau. "It is a pleasure to once again meet England's famous detective and his chronicler. However, I fear your Prime Minister has sent you here under false pretences. There is no mystery to be solved. I was shot and we arrested the man responsible. It is done."

"How are you, sir?" I asked. "Were you badly injured?"

"Hardly anything worth mentioning. The man was an incompetent. We have just won the most terrible war in history, yet here is a Frenchman who misses his target six out of seven times at point-blank range. He must be punished for the careless use of a dangerous weapon and for poor marksmanship. I suggest that he be locked up with intensive training in a shooting gallery. Do you not agree, Mandel?"

"Of course, sir," said Mandel, but I saw his eyes roll as he replied and had the sense that this was already an old joke that had been repeated many times.

"You shouldn't make light of your injury," said Gosset. "You know that we are unable to remove the bullet. Doctor, if you would care to look, I have the X-ray here."

He held it up to the light and pointed out the white spot of a bullet lodged near M. Clemenceau's heart. I passed it to Holmes, who glanced at it before handing it back to Gosset.

"Doctors," said M. Clemenceau. "They think they know everything. Is that not true Mr. Holmes? I should know – I used to be one of them."

He laughed at his own joke, and I felt a pang of sympathy for my French colleague. It is often said that doctors make the worst patients, and I could tell that the maxim held true in this case.

"I'm glad to see you in such good humour," said Holmes. "If you will allow me to ask but a few questions, maybe I can persuade Mr. George to share your outlook."

"If you can get that man to agree with me, then you really are the miracle worker Doctor Watson portrays in his stories. He is thoroughly intractable and impossible to negotiate with."

"I am more interested in your relationship with your attacker," said Holmes. "Had you ever met him before?"

"I don't believe so."

"And do you know why he attacked you?"

"I believe he claims to be an anarchist, or Bolshevik, or some other brand of malcontent. It is all the same to me. We have restored order to our country and they want to tear it down again."

"They? Then you do believe he had accomplices?"

"I know there are others who share his views, but if you want to know who his friends are, you will have to ask him yourself."

"I will do that," said Holmes.

"Good," said Gosset. "While you are gone, my patient can get some much-needed rest."

I could see that he was correct. The exertion of speaking with us and maintaining the façade of good health was obviously taking its toll on Clemenceau.

Mandel stamped out his cigarette on the floor. "If you come with me, I will speak to the *Sûreté* and arrange access to the prisoner," he said and led us out of the room.

However, we didn't get very far. As we stepped into the corridor, we were almost knocked over by two men in French military uniforms, emerging from the neighbouring room. One was the soldier we had met before. The other man was older and, judging from the insignia on his uniform, he was a high-ranking officer.

"Is he ready to see me now?" barked the older man. "We were meant to have met yesterday. There are matters of state we must address."

"He is tired," said Mandel, "and even if he weren't, he has left specific orders that he doesn't wish to be disturbed by you, Marshal Foch."

40

So this was the man who had led the combined forces of the Allies in their push to end the war.

"Maybe he isn't well enough to resume his duties," said the guard, who hovered behind Foch's left shoulder. "If that is the case, he should hand over his responsibilities to someone more capable – especially the negotiations."

"There is no one more able to conclude the treaty negotiations." Mandel tried to sound confident, but I could see that he was worried about how long it would take M. Clemenceau to recover.

"Negotiation?" asked Foch. "More like capitulation. If Germany is allowed to keep the Rhineland, France will never be safe! We mustn't concede, whatever it takes."

I tried to remember the news reports I had read about the negotiations. I was sure that this was M. Clemenceau's view too, against opposition from my own country and the Americans.

I said as much to Foch and he snapped at me. "Clemenceau is weak. He will back down and we will be left defenceless."

"If that anarchist hadn't been such a poor shot," said the guard, "he could have solved all our problems."

I was about to berate him for making such a callous comment, but Foch reprimanded him before I could.

"We mustn't allow subversives to interfere with these negotiations. The border with Germany is a military matter, and we must be the ones to resolve it. Come, there is work to be done, and nothing to be gained from talking with these English."

"Sir, should I not stay here?" asked the guard.

"I need my aide with me, Captain Bresson. Besides, Clemenceau has no need of a soldier to watch his room. He already has his own guard dog." Foch pointed at Mandel and laughed, then set off down the corridor, his aide trailing reluctantly behind him.

When we arrived at the *Sûreté*, Holmes asked to be taken straight to the suspect. However, upon entering the cell, my first thought was that they had taken us to the wrong man, as this was obviously the victim of a violent crime. Émile Cottin had been badly beaten. There were bruises all over his face, both eyes were swollen, and there was a large cut below the one on the right. The rest of his body was in no better condition, as he groaned with pain every time that he moved.

"What happened to him?" I asked the *Sûreté* agent, Labaigt, who had joined us to observe Holmes's interview.

41

"It wasn't me," he replied, sensing my implied accusation, "although I won't say he didn't deserve it. A mob gathered as soon as we arrested him. I was lucky not to be badly hurt myself, and Ravery received a nasty blow to the head. The people of Paris are patriots. They have no time for anarchist traitors."

"Has someone attended to his injuries, at least?"

"The doctor examined him. He will live long enough to meet Madame Guillotine."

"Very well," said Holmes. "If you are well enough to stand trial, M. Cottin, you should be well enough to answer my questions."

"First, may I have a Gitane?" Cottin asked.

Holmes looked to Labaigt, "Can you oblige him?"

Labaigt reluctantly reached into his pocket and took out a light blue packet.

"I have these," he said.

Cottin hesitated a moment before accepting a cigarette from the pack. Once it had been lit, filling the room with the pungent smell of dark French tobacco, Holmes began his interrogation.

"M. Cottin, I don't imagine that you deny attempting to murder the Prime Minister."

"Of course I don't. Clemenceau is the enemy of mankind, because he is war – because he is the obstacle to the renovation of society."

"He has been like this ever since we brought him in," said Labaigt. "He just keeps repeating propaganda from his anarchist pamphlets."

"He had these pamphlets with him when he was arrested?" I asked, thinking that they might be traced back to some group.

"No, but his type always has pamphlets. Horrid grubby things full of phrases like that."

"You discussed your plan with your anarchist friends?" asked Holmes.

"We discuss how the world will be improved when we overthrow the old order. When the next revolution comes, they will be ready to lead us into the future."

"So they helped you," said Labaigt. "Who else was involved in the attack? Give me names."

"We don't talk about the steps we intend to take," said Cottin. "Even one accomplice would place the mission in jeopardy. Right now there are anarchists all over the world, preparing to take action. I don't know their plans, and so you can never force me to betray them."

"If your fellow anarchists wouldn't help you, where did you get the weapon?" asked Holmes. "You cannot have brought it home with you, as it's obvious you didn't serve in the war. The calluses on your hands tell me that you spent the past years holding a carpenter's tools, not a pistol."

"You are correct. I engaged in an honest trade rather than fighting Clemenceau's war, but I met a soldier in a bar who told me all about it. He understood that society needs to be changed, and offered to sell me his weapon so that I could act."

I thought it more likely that a down-on-his-luck soldier had sold his pistol to buy more drinks, hoping to block out the horrors he had seen. Men like that were an all too common sight in the cities when a war ended.

"You'd never shot a gun before?" I said. "That explains why most of the shots missed."

"As soon as I had the gun, I started practising at home," said Cottin, indignantly. "I traced a mannequin on the wall that looked like Clemenceau and I aimed at the head and the heart. I broke a window the first time, but I improved greatly before I ran out of bullets. I had meant to take one out of the gun and save it for Clemenceau, but I forgot."

"Then where did you acquire the ammunition you used to shoot Clemenceau?" Holmes asked.

"I asked all around, but bullets aren't easy to come by. They've banned selling them to honest citizens as part of their efforts to repress us. I was about to give up when I ran into the soldier who sold me the gun again. He wanted to know why I hadn't acted yet. When I told him what had happened, he offered to sell me a box of bullets."

"He just happened to have this box with him?" I asked.

"Of course not. We met again the next day."

"What did this man look look like?" asked Holmes.

"Just a normal soldier. You see them everywhere these days."

Holmes sighed in exasperation. "Was he short or tall, fat or thin? What colour was his hair, his eyes? Give me details."

"He was blonde and a little taller than me, but he walked with a stoop. I remember that his overcoat was old and too big for him, as he was quite thin. I imagine it was given as charity, as the only money he had was what I paid him."

"What happened to the ammunition box?" Holmes asked Labaigt. "Did he have it with him when you arrested him?"

"No, just the pistol and an empty magazine."

"Have your men search his home then. I imagine you will find it there. I would start by looking under his bed."

From the surprised look on Cottin's face, I could tell that Holmes was correct as usual.

While Labaigt carried out the search of Cottin's home, Holmes had an officer take us to the Boulevard Delessert, where the assassination attempt had taken place. Upon our arrival, he took out a newspaper. Unlike the copy of *Le Petit Parisien* that I had seen earlier, *The Excelsior* had filled its front page with photographs, including a picture of the corner where we were standing. It was annotated with little pictures showing the movements of M. Clemenceau's car and the shooter.

I watched as Holmes walked back and forth along the road, studying every detail of the scene. Eventually he called me over and pointed at a tree.

"Look at this, Watson. You can see where one of the bullets struck after it passed through the car's windscreen."

I examined the tree and saw that there was indeed a mark, like a wide scratch, where the bark had been torn from the tree.

"Note the height and the angle," said Holmes. "It is a wonder that M. Cottin hit anything at all. He should have practiced more before making his attempt."

"If he was working with a group, you would have thought they would have chosen someone who was a better shot to make this attempt."

"It is certainly suggestive, but I'm less interested in the shots that missed. That seventh, almost fatal, shot is the one that matters. Now look over here."

Holmes led me across the road to a small passage between two buildings and pointed to the ground, which was covered with ground-out cigarette butts.

"Do you think this is where Cottin waited for the Prime Minister's car to pass by?"

"No, Cottin's brand of cigarette is Gitanes. They are favoured by the Bohemian set. These are Gauloises, like the one Labaigt gave him before I questioned him. Also, note these marks on the wall." He pointed to a series of short black lines. "The person who stood here must have been at least three inches taller than Cottin to have comfortably struck their matches at that height."

"You think someone else was standing here at the time of the shooting."

44

"He was here at least two hours before the shooting. Some of the butts are wet, and it hasn't rained since the early hours of yesterday morning."

"He was clearly here a long time, judging from how many cigarettes he smoked. Do you think Cottin lied and had an accomplice after all?" There was no answer.

After Holmes had gleaned all he could from the road, we made our way back to the *Sûreté*. However, rather than asking to see the prisoner, Holmes had the officers take us to a garage at the back of the building. Inside there was a black car. It was clearly the vehicle Clemenceau in which had been travelling when Cottin attacked, as the back was pock-marked with bullet holes and the windscreen above the driver's seat had been smashed.

Holmes walked around the automobile, examining it from every angle. Then, once he'd finished examining the exterior, he climbed into the back seat and knelt down on the floor.

"There's a torch over there," he said to me. "Please point it at the back of the car."

I did as he directed, moving it to different positions, in accordance with his instructions, until he was quite satisfied.

"It is all a matter of angles. These holes are all relatively straight. The bullets were fired from directly behind the vehicle. Some passed straight through like the one that broke the windscreen and grazed that tree, but I dug this one out of the back of the driver's seat." He passed me the flattened remains of a bullet.

"Now, compare those holes to this one. When I shine the torch straight, the light does not pass through. But when I turn it you can see how the bullet struck obliquely. It was fired from a different position, and would have exited through the side of the vehicle, had it not hit the Prime Minister."

I took the torch and examined the holes myself, in accordance with his instructions.

"It is a pity they couldn't remove the bullet from him," said Holmes. "I would have liked to have examined it."

"Surely there is little need for it." I held up the twisted piece of metal he had passed me. "We have this bullet, which I am sure it will match the ammunition box you have asked the police to find, and that will just confirm that Cottin was the shooter. It doesn't tell us anything new."

"Watson, the bullets tell us everything. Remember what we saw on the X-ray image."

45

"The bullet is lodged between Clemenceau's ribs. I can see why Gosset didn't want to operate. It would be an extremely risky procedure."

"But did you not observe the bullet itself? It was obviously much larger than the one you're holding. A rifle round, probably a Lebel 8mm, although I would need a clearer image to be certain – definitely not the example of the 5mm pistol ammunition that you're holding."

"But Cottin cannot have had a second weapon with him. The police would have found it."

Holmes nodded as I thought through the implications of his revelation.

"That means there must have been a second shooter there yesterday morning – the man who was waiting in the passage."

"Yes, Watson, and he is still out there, free to make another attempt."

We were about to enter the cell to question Cottin again when Labaigt returned.

"Here it is, Mr. Holmes," he said and handed Holmes a small cardboard box. "It was under his bed, just like you said.

Holmes turned it over in his hands, then with a shout of, "A-ha!" he threw it to me. Then he opened the door to the cell.

"How did you know where Clemenceau was going to be?" Holmes asked Cottin as we stepped inside.

"It is near his home. He often drove down that road."

"But you were confident he was going to be there that morning."

Cottin suddenly went quiet.

"Come on, man! Someone clearly told you he would be there," I said. "Which one of your anarchist friends was it?"

"I told you," he replied, "none of my comrades knew what I was planning."

"But the soldier who supplied you with the gun and the ammunition knew your plan," said Holmes.

For a moment I thought Cottin would try to deny it.

"Yes. When he gave me the bullets, he told me the Prime Minister would be travelling along that road to a meeting the next morning. He convinced me that it was my best chance, and that I needed to act immediately before Clemenceau endangered the French people any further."

"Who was this soldier?" Labaigt shouted. "Give us his name!"

46

"I cannot betray him because I don't know! Simply another soldier cast on to the scrap heap after the war, desperate for a few francs and eager to serve his country one last time."

"You are wrong," said Holmes. "The money didn't matter to him. Look at that box in your hands, Watson. See the stamp on it – it marks it as having come from the armoury at the Ministry of War – part of their efforts to restrict access to ammunition now the war is over. A down-and-out veteran wouldn't have been able to procure such an item. Only a serving officer could have taken it."

"But if he had access to weapons and knew the Prime Minister's schedule, why didn't he just do the job himself?" I asked. "A trained solider could have done a better job than this poor wretch."

"M. Cottin was just a scapegoat. A convenient malcontent to throw to the police."

"I shot Clemenceau!" shouted Cottin.

"You didn't," replied Holmes. "I imagine that was the original plan, but the real assassin obviously realised that you didn't have the skills to complete the job. He made sure you were where he wanted you, and then waited to take his shot under the cover of your noisy attempt."

Cottin slumped in his chair, throughly dejected.

"I doubt we will need to speak again, M. Cottin," said Holmes. "However, if you manage to escape the guillotine, I would advise you to confine your attempts to change the world to words in the future. You don't have the skill necessary to achieve your ends with a gun."

"What do we do now?" I asked Holmes, once we had left the cell. "Should we start asking about this soldier in the bars? Maybe somebody recognised him."

"It's unlikely," said Holmes. "To most people, he will have been just one solider among many, and he clearly attempted to conceal his true appearance with his oversized coat and affected stoop. However, he made a mistake when he gave Cottin that box of bullets and laid a trail back to the Ministry of War."

"The Ministry is beyond my jurisdiction," said Labaigt. "If your suspect does work there, this will become a military matter."

However, despite his protestations, he clearly wanted the credit for arresting Cottin's co-conspirator and so elected to come with us.

Upon our arrival, his fears appeared to have been realised, as the guards didn't want to grant us access. Holmes let Labaigt negotiate with them for a few minutes, before he stepped in.

47

"We are here on official business for the British Government," he said and handed the soldier barring our entry a piece of paper. "You will find our credentials here, signed by our Prime Minister. If you don't step aside immediately, you will be responsible for creating a diplomatic incident."

The guard examined them closely, before calling over a more senior officer who also studied them. Then, finally, we were allowed to pass.

"When did you receive diplomatic papers?" I asked.

"Mycroft provided them before we departed. I hadn't intended to use them. I don't like the implication that I work for him. However, it seemed expedient in the circumstances. Of course the signature is a fake. A fine facsimile, but I know my brother's hand, and it is probably backed by greater authority than the genuine article."

Our diplomatic credentials clearly caused quite a stir, as we were taken straight to Marshal Foch's office. The Marshal stared at us in surprise as we were shown inside.

"I remember you from the hospital," he said. "You told Captain Bresson you were detectives, but now I discover that you are English diplomats. Were you sent by Lloyd George to force concessions from our Prime Minister while he is weak and infirm? Well, you might have fooled him into listening, but you will find that I am a more formidable opponent!"

"Your political differences with M. Clemenceau are none of my concern," said Holmes. "I'm only here to prevent an assassination."

"You should read a newspaper," said Marshal Foch. "I can have one brought in for you, or you could just ask the agent of the *Sûreté* standing next to you. The assassination attempt failed and the culprit is now in custody. There is nothing for you to do here."

"The first attempt failed," said Holmes, "but the man who almost killed M. Clemenceau is still at large."

"What concern is that of mine? Do you suspect that I will be the next target? I can assure you that I am quite safe here, surrounded by my loyal men."

"Your loyal men are the problem. We believe one of them shot M. Clemenceau yesterday, and it is likely that he will try again."

"Nonsense! We don't tolerate anarchists here."

"I don't believe this man is an anarchist. I suspect he is a nationalist, and that is no less dangerous. It is no secret that you want M. Clemenceau removed from the negotiations."

48

"Of course I do! The man is risking the future security of France. If he leaves the Rhineland in German hands, they will be back in France before long."

"This isn't the negotiating room," said Holmes. "Save your arguments for those who are interested in playing the great games of state. My only concern here is to unmask an assassin."

"Mr. Holmes," said Labaight, "you don't mean to accuse the Marshal of attempting to assassinate the Prime Minister?"

"No," said Holmes quickly. "I'm sure Marshal Foch would never be found drinking in bars with anarchists or waiting on a street corner to shoot his political rivals. However, I'm certain there are plenty of his men here who share his views."

"This is outrageous!" bellowed Marshal Foch. "I should have you all arrested for suggesting such treason. I would never condone – let alone order – such an action."

"'Will no one rid me of this turbulent priest?'" said Holmes.

Marshal Foch looked confused.

"It is something an old King of England once said," I explained. "His knights misinterpreted it as an order, and killed the Archbishop of Canterbury."

"Ridiculous nonsense," replied Marshal Foch. "Is that all you have – speculation and old stories? Where is your evidence?"

Holmes took out the box of bullets and threw it on to the Marshal's desk.

"This is the ammunition that M. Cottin used," Holmes said. "It came from your armoury."

"Plenty of people could have taken that. It doesn't prove anything."

"In the hospital, you said M. Clemenceau was meant to be meeting you yesterday."

"That is correct. He was coming here when he was shot."

"Who else knew about that meeting?"

"It was arranged late the previous evening," replied Marshal Foch. "The only person I spoke to about it was Clemenceau's secretary."

"Nobody here?"

"No. Well, apart from my aide, Captain Bresson." A hint of uncertainty crept into the Marshal's voice. "I always keep him apprised of my schedule."

Very calmly, Holmes said, "Please can you have Captain Bresson brought to us, Marshal."

"I cannot believe Bresson has done anything wrong. However, if he has acted improperly and shared classified information, he will face a court martial. You may leave and I will question him when he returns."

"When he returns?" asked Holmes. "Do you mean to say he isn't here?"

"He returned to the hospital to watch Clemenceau just before you arrived."

"Why would your aide be guarding the Prime Minister?" I asked.

"He isn't guarding him. He is keeping me informed in case foreign agents, like you, try to influence him."

"Haven't you listened to us?" shouted Holmes. "You have placed your Prime Minister in dreadful danger. We must get to the hospital at once!"

For the first time, I saw the terrible realisation in Marshal Foch's eyes that we might be correct. "I will have someone call ahead to make sure Clemenceau is kept secure until we arrive."

We started to leave, but Marshal Foch stopped Labaigt at the door. "Even if Mr. Holmes is correct, this is now a military matter," he said. "Go back to the *Sûreté* and deal with your anarchist. You are no longer needed here."

Labaight tried to argue, but Holmes cut him off. "We don't have time for your petty squabbles," he said. "The credit for Bresson's arrest will count for nothing if you delay us and M. Clemenceau dies."

A car pulled up outside the Ministry, just as we were leaving, and Georges Mandel stepped out.

"Where are you going?" he said to the Marshal. "I thought we were meant to be meeting."

"I arranged no such meeting. I don't have time to deal with you now."

"But I received a telephone call from your aide, insisting that I come here at once."

"It seems Captain Bresson is removing any potential obstacles," said Holmes. "We must all leave immediately."

We raced to the hospital in Marshal Foch's staff car. As we travelled, Holmes explained the danger to a horrified Georges Mandel.

As soon as the car stopped, Holmes jumped out and rushed into the hospital. He raced up the stairs to M. Clemenceau's room, and I marvelled at his speed as I tried to keep up. Age had aggravated my old wounds, but Holmes seemed as spry as when we first met.

I reached the top of the stairs just in time to see him enter the Prime Minister's room. Then I watched in horror as Captain Bresson appeared at the other end of the corridor, holding a pistol.

In my younger days, I might have tried to tackle him, but I was getting older and he was a man in the prime of life. I was certain that he would overcome me with ease, or just shoot me as I approached. "Holmes!" I shouted. "He is coming!"

Captain Bresson looked at me and scowled. Then he hurriedly went inside the Prime Minister's room.

As I ran down the corridor, I heard running footsteps behind me. By the time I reached the room, Marshal Foch had caught up with me. Further away, Mandel had just reached the top of the stairs and was now bent double, puffing from the exertion.

The Marshal opened the door and we both entered. Captain Bresson had his gun pointed towards M. Clemenceau and Holmes, who was standing next to the bed.

"Captain, stand down!" bellowed the Marshal.

Bresson stared back at him in shock. "You should not be here, sir!"

"You are the one who shouldn't be here!" replied the Marshal. "I am appalled by you, soldier – working with anarchists against our country."

"I would never support them, sir."

"But you helped Cottin," Holmes said.

"I needed Cottin to be there to take the blame. The world will be better off when he is executed anyway."

"So the army was behind this assassination attempt," I replied, "not anarchists."

"Not the army," he said, and for the first time he sounded fearful. "None of my brothers-in-arms knew anything about it. I acted alone."

"Why did you do it?" asked Holmes.

"So that Marshal Foch could take over the peace negotiations and save France," replied Bresson.

"I didn't order this," said the Marshal. "We are soldiers, not murderers!"

Bresson's shoulders slumped and he let his gun arm drop slightly. "I am sorry, sir."

I took a step forward, intending to take the gun from him now he had given up, but Marshal Foch hadn't finished.

51

"Your court martial would be a stain on the reputation of the whole army."

"I understand, sir. I served the Republic in life, and now in death."

By the time I realised what those words meant, Bresson had already raised the pistol to his temple. His shot echoed around the tiny room and his blood sprayed across the white hospital walls.

"Why did you tell him that?" I asked. "He was ready to surrender and face justice."

I was surprised when it was M. Clemenceau who answered.

"It is better this way," he said. "France doesn't need a scandal."

"But he ordered a man to kill himself," I said.

"You heard me," said Marshal Foch. "I didn't give any orders."

"No," I replied sadly, "you never needed to."

The Adventure of the
Suicidal Sister
by Craig Stephen Copland

On Easter Sunday of 1919, Lady Lillian Assherton attempted to take her own life, a second time.

Her first attempt was in the fall of 1917 when Her Ladyship, recently widowed, received news that both of her sons, officers in the Loyal North Lancashire Regiment, had died at Passchendaele.

On that occasion, she had put a noose around her neck, tied the rope to a chandelier, and tried to hang herself. The chandelier became detached from the ceiling and crashed down upon her, rendering her unconscious and inflicting numerous cuts and injuries.

Her household staff rushed her to Barts, and she slowly and painfully recovered. Along the way, she decided that the Good Lord had intervened and that it wasn't yet her time to depart from this veil of tears. Her mills in Lancashire were critical to the war effort and, after the death of her husband, she had been left to manage them, a task she undertook with locomotive energy. She would just have to carry on.

For over a quarter-of-a-century, I had been her personal physician. She first came to my office in her late teens when she completed her schooling. Although not of aristocratic lineage, she came out during the season and, by dint of her beauty and charm, was immediately the recipient of several marriage proposals. She chose the handsome and wealthy Enoch Assherton, Lord Cliffside, of the ancient family seat of Prestwick. They divided their time between the estate and the surging metropolis of London.

I had assisted in the birth of her two sons, Edward and Roland, and had attended to their few medical needs as they progressed through Eton. By the time they moved on to Oxford, I had retired from my medical practice, but, like so many Barts Old Boys, I had been called back to service once the war broke out. Our young doctors had been sent off to the front to attend to the needs of our soldiers, much as I had done nearly forty years earlier in the Second Afghan War.

I stayed on at Barts after the Armistice. Britain was short of everything, including doctors. Scores who had served in the war had died or were grievously injured. Others were so severely diminished by shell-shock that they could no longer function as physicians. New recruits from our medical schools had dried up, and it would be several years before our ranks could be replenished.

Upon learning that Her Ladyship had been admitted to hospital, I informed the administration that, as her former physician, I would accept responsibility for her care. I hurried up to the room in which she had been placed, only to find her unconscious from heavy sedation. The note on her chart was brief and read:

> *Patient ingested mixture of strychnine and gin. Stomach rejected and wretched. Butler and maid forced additional vomiting. Full physical recovery expected. Placed on suicide watch.*

I asked the duty-nurses to have me alerted when she became conscious and coherent. They did so, and seven o'clock on the morning of 22 April, I entered her room and approached her bed.

"Good morning, Your Ladyship," I said. "Such a pleasant surprise to find an old friend on a sunny morning."

She turned and looked at me. In her youth, she had been a vision of feminine loveliness. As a mature woman, she was described in the society pages as "elegant and stately". On that morning, she was wan and weary. Her eyes were bloodshot, and her hair, previously always coiffed and raven-black, was now disheveled and streaked with grey.

"Well, if it isn't my dear old doctor," she said. Then, giving me a look up and down, added, "My old, *old*, doctor. I suppose if I have to submit to anyone here, it is best an old fogey who has poked and prodded every corner of my body already. How are you, Doctor?"

"Well, I'm just fine, thank you, considering the ravages of age. More important is how are you, your Ladyship?"

"Oh, don't call me that. All that was part of life before the war. Now, that whole world has vanished. It's all gone. My husband, my two boys . . . everything. I'm rich, but what good is that? I've lost everything that I held dear. These days, I may as well be just plain old Lilly . . . So, here we are, old Lilly and even older John. If you want to be useful, you can inject me with cyanide."

"That, my dear, is not going to happen. You pulled through after you lost Lord Cliffside and Eddie and Rolly. You can keep going. We all have to. The war is over. No more trying to do yourself in. That just won't do. Your country still needs you."

"No, John, my country does *not* need me. My country does not want me. My country is intent on hanging me."

For a moment, I was speechless.

"What do you mean, hang you?

"I've been accused of having committed treason during the war. There is a boatload of evidence against me. My barrister looked at everything and told me I had no choice but to throw myself on the mercy of the court. Plead madness brought on by the death of my sons. Then maybe I could escape the gallows and spend the rest of my life in prison. That's what my country wants to do with me, John. So, if you want to be useful, help them out. Go and fetch the cyanide."

"But . . . but that's impossible! You could no more commit treason than fly! You're innocent. I'm certain you are. What in the world happened?"

"Of course, I'm innocent. I have been diabolically set up. But what does it matter now? I can afford a dozen lawyers. But the evidence against me is insurmountable. If you will just give me an injection of cyanide, I promise I won't vomit all over the bedsheets. That's what you can do for me."

I took her hand in both of mine.

"I have a better idea."

"Not likely, but what is it?"

"I know someone."

As soon as I had a break in my shift, I went to the administration office and begged the use of their telephone.

I called Sherlock Holmes.

After his sojourn in America and his success in smashing the Von Bork ring of spies, Holmes had been conscripted – Mycroft had something to do with it – to serve the British government as needed for the duration of the war. I ran into him from time to time and, in response to my asking what he was up to, he answered vaguely that he was doing a spot of work for Section Five of the Directorate of Military Intelligence, or for another unnamed section, or for Scotland Yard, or for the Directorate of Intelligence, or for any combination of them. It was all hush-hush, and he gave no details.

The Armistice was signed at eleven o'clock on the eleventh of November, 1918, and by ten minutes after eleven, Holmes had departed Whitehall, made his way to Victoria, and from there to his property near Eastbourne where his long-neglected bee hives had been sitting – feral – for four years.

I had rarely seen nor talked to him since the end of the war, as he had made it clear to me that he was intent on spending the remainder of his days caring for his bees and not caring whatsoever about the sordid activities of the criminal classes of London.

It was my good fortune that when I called him, he happened to be in his cottage and answered the telephone. At first, he was full of pleasant chit-chat and friendly inquiries about my health, my wife, and the prospect of my long-delayed retirement. That attitude changed when I came right out and asked for his help with a case of Lady Lilly Assherton.

"My dear, Watson," he sighed. "I was a detective for many years. I no longer am. I am now a beekeeper. Surely, there is someone else that you can ask for help to solve a crime."

"It isn't merely a crime, Holmes. It is an accusation of espionage and treason, and you remain the nation's most capable agent in dealing with such matters."

"That may very well be and, if there is anything I learned in four years of sullying myself in the world of spies, counter-spies, and diplomats, it is that they all tell lies. Can you be certain that this patient of yours is telling you the truth? In the overwhelming number of cases where the evidence all points to one and only one conclusion, that conclusion is correct."

"Holmes," I responded, "as you have said, a man may lie to his wife, to his children, to his lawyer, to the police, to his neighbor, to his employer, and even to *his mother*, but he cannot lie to his bank book, and he has nothing at all to gain by lying to his doctor. The same goes for a woman."

I then proceeded to browbeat him over our years of friendship, reminding him of all the times when I had come to his assistance, always ready to abandon my patients and surgery.

I imagined that I could hear him sigh all the way from Sussex.

"Very well, Watson. Fair is fair, I suppose. I will take the afternoon train up to London. Meet me for supper at Simpson's and bring all the data you can lay your hands on by that time. Six o'clock. Until then."

He hung up.

"Here is everything that I've learned," I said as we sat in Simpson's and waited as the trolley arrived with the enormous section of roast beef. "I had time to make a few calls. I do know a few of the chaps in the intelligence service. Bob Pollack was a patient of mine years ago, and he was quite forthcoming."

"Excellent! He must trust you, seeing as matters of treason and espionage are invariably confidential. I hope you didn't expose the fellow to reprimand, termination, or worse."

"Well, now, that was the odd thing about it. He told me that even though the matter should be kept secret, it seems that everyone who is anyone in any of those agencies for whom you used to do work knows all about it."

"Indeed? Yes, that is odd. Very well, then, what did he tell you?"

"As you know, Lady Assherton owns all those mills up in Lancashire. She ended up having to run them after her husband, Enoch, died unexpectedly back in 1913. All of the cotton they use comes from either the American South or Egypt. Once the Germans began sinking supply ships in the Atlantic, the cargo from America dried up. Some of the mills across England were facing closure and putting thousands of men out of work. The government stepped in and re-organized the supply that was still coming from Egypt, regardless of which firm had ordered it, and divvied it up amongst all of the mills, so all could keep running."

"Yes, Watson. I am fully aware of that. What happened?"

"Almost all of Lady Assherton's supply came from Egypt, so she was high and dry, so to speak. Many of her shipments were commandeered either by the War Office or the Home Office and sent to other mills. That cut into her profits, but the dear lady has more money than God and didn't object. It was her bit for the war effort."

"Your beef is getting cold, Watson. Get on with it."

"After the Italians finally made up their minds whose side they were on, a number of her shipments were diverted to Genoa for use in Italian mills so their soldiers could have new shirts and underwear."

"Entirely sensible. Italian soldiers may fight, but not if they are poorly dressed."

"I suppose so. Well, some of her shipments landed in Genoa but were then diverted by persons unknown up to Switzerland. From there, they were secretly sent up to Germany. Her cotton was keeping *the enemy* in shirts and underwear. She was accused of violating embargoes and giving succor to the Boche. That is considered treason and subject to hanging if convicted. That is what she was accused of, and they appear to have copies of all of the documents proving it."

"But they haven't yet arrested her, have they?"

"No. Not as far as I know."

For the next ten minutes, Holmes slowly devoured his supper in silence. If I tried to say anything, he held up his hand and bade me keep silent. He finally swallowed his last mouthful of Yorkshire pudding and laid down his utensils.

"A fascinating case, Watson."

"How so?"

"I was in Switzerland several times during the war. It was an incestuous hive of spies and counter-spies, diplomats, importers and exporters, Germans, French, English, Turks, and far too many Italians. Shipments of arms, chemicals, steel, aluminum, wool, cotton, every conceivable foodstuff, and more were traded, diverted, trans-shipped, and forwarded. Much of what took place violated the laws of both the Central and the Allied Powers. The Swiss, being Swiss, arrogantly ignored such minor concerns and made all the arrangements. And they were devious enough to never put everything in writing. All deals were done on a handshake, and funds transferred through Swiss banks. And if you didn't honor your financial or commodity obligations, they simply stopped doing business with you."

"But there are written records of her shipments," I said.

"Highly likely that they were forged. And that means that someone has done an extensive amount of work to frame her."

"But why?"

"Precisely. Why concoct the scheme, and why pin it on this particular wealthy widow?"

"But she could hang for it."

"Highly unlikely. I can name a score of firms and agents who violated the embargoes and sanctions who were found out and, as long as they were still needed by British industry during the war and now, were punished by anything from a slap on the wrist to a stiff fine."

"Well, somebody," I said, "told her that she was a traitor and faced the gallows."

"Yes. And that is where we must start."

"Shall we begin tomorrow morning? You could meet me at Barts first thing."

"No. Time is of the essence. We shall start this evening. You do have her address, do you not? We'll start with her staff. They always know something."

By eight o'clock in the evening in late April, London has descended into chilly twilight. On a Tuesday evening, two days after

58

Easter, Chequer Street, just north of the Barbican, was deserted and damp. Lady Assherton's town home – as much of it as we could see in the dim, flickering light from the recently-installed electric streetlamps – was a substantial terrace house that was a long way from the ostentation of Mayfair and Belgravia.

A knock on the door brought a tall, slender young man who was understandably surprised to find two no-longer-young men calling at such an hour in the evening.

He must have been Lady Assherton's butler, but was dressed casually with no jacket and his fine linen shirt open at the neck. He had a cane in his left hand and was somewhat leaning on it. However, even in this condition, and with his military bearing, he had British Army written all over him, from his neatly trimmed mustache down to his gleaming shoes.

"Good evening, gentlemen," he said. "I'm sorry, but Lady Assherton is not home this evening and may be away for a few days. If you will give me your names and telephone numbers, I will let her know that you called on her, and I'm sure she will call you back when she returns."

I stepped forward.

"I am Dr. John Watson, Lady Assherton's physician. I have been attending to her throughout the day, and I need to speak to you and the other members of the house staff to determine precisely what happened to her and how best to help her recover. Perhaps we could chat with you for a few moments in the parlor?"

I took another step forward as I spoke, and the butler moved back, noticeably hobbling and using his cane for support.

"Oh, of course. Dr. Watson," he said, with a note of unfeigned sincerity. "We were so relieved when we heard that you were looking after her. Please come in."

I wiped my wet shoes on the entry-way mat. Holmes followed me in and did likewise. The butler stared at him.

"Are you . . . Sherlock Holmes?" he said.

"I am."

"Then permit me, gentlemen, to deduce that your visit concerns much more than Her Ladyship's health."

"It does," said Holmes as he walked into the parlor, tossed his overcoat on one of the chairs, and sat down. I did the same.

The butler seated himself across from us, deftly lowering his body into the chair while balancing himself on one of the chair's arms and his cane. Once in place, he sat bolt upright, his right leg bent, and his long, left leg sticking straight out into the room.

Holmes gave an obvious look to the leg and then at the butler.

"Ypres?" asked Holmes.

"The Somme."

"We are," I said, "grateful for your sacrifice. I took one nearly forty years ago in Afghanistan, but I got off lightly compared to you. How are you managing?"

He smiled back at me. "Better than many of my unit, Doctor. I'm alive. Not yet facing decrepitude. With the scaffolding around my leg, I can still walk. My lungs are clean, and my cerebrum, cerebellum and even my hippocampus all still work – or at least I like to think they do, but I leave that for others to judge."

"Ah," I said, "that's the British spirit. Stiff upper lip all the way. Well done, soldier. What happened?"

"I blocked a shot on our goal. But the other team was shooting with grapeshot. Most unsporting of them."

I laughed. There is an immediate camaraderie between men who have served under fire, and particularly with those who have come close to death and made it through. I might have carried on the friendly chat with a fellow veteran, but Holmes wasn't interested.

"What is your name, please, sir?" he asked.

"George Nichol, Mr. Holmes. A few years back, it was Captain George Nichol, but now I am just George-the-Butler."

"It is obvious that you aren't from a family who were in service. How came you by this position?"

"Before the war, I was an electrical engineer, an inspector of lines and poles and transformers and such. You can't do that with a bum leg. After I was shot up, Eddy and Rolly Assherton, Lady Assherton's sons, told me to call on their mum, and they sent her a note asking her to give me a position."

"They were your friends?"

"My brothers-in-arms. I was invalided-out early on, and it looked like they were going to come through *arte et marte* without a scratch. It took me a year to get back on my feet, and Her Ladyship hired me on the spot when I showed up at her door. *Ad libitum* and not full-time, mind you. No need for that. With my small pension, I didn't require much more, and, honestly, I am grateful that she had proper work for me. I started just a week before the telegram came to her about her boys. It was a hard time."

"You were here then," said Holmes, "the first time she attempted suicide."

"I was. She was horribly despondent, and a week after the telegram, she tried to hang herself, but the chandelier came down on

60

top of her when she stepped off of the table. Claire heard the crash, rushed in, and shouted for me."

"Claire?"

"Her previous maid. She was here throughout the war, but the young man she waited for and prayed for every night survived and was demobbed in December of last year. After a short contretemps, they sorted things out and were married straight away and moved to Liverpool."

"Who replaced her?"

"Miss Hope. Hope Leighton. She was a nurse on the front during the war, and Lady Assherton hired her immediately after Claire gave her notice."

"And how was she selected?"

"I'm not entirely certain, Mr. Holmes. But she's up in her room now. Shall I have her come down?"

"In a minute, if you don't mind. Another question or two for you, please."

"Fire at will," said the captain.

"What do you know about the accusations that led to Lady Assherton's second attempt to take her life?"

Mr. Nichol looked quite uncomfortable and seemed to be composing his answer before offering it.

"The day after the men came to visit – "

"What men, please? From where?"

"I honestly cannot say, sir. I had never seen them before. Never. Two men who looked like the type you see all over the pavement down by Whitehall, if you know the type I mean."

"I do. Go on."

"They met with her in private, behind the door of the library, and then they left. Her Ladyship called Hope and me in after and told us that she had been accused of treason related to some of her cotton shipments, but that it was preposterous – imbecilic, was the word she used – and that we should ignore any such nonsense."

"She confided in you, her staff?"

"We had become the closest thing to family she has. After all we had gone through during the war, there wasn't much reason to keep up the rules that segregate the classes."

"And was that all?"

"No. A week later, the day before Easter, the men came back again and talked with her, and this time she was terribly upset."

"What did they talk about?" asked Holmes.

Mr. Nichol didn't answer. For nearly a minute, he fixed his gaze on the shoe of his outstretched leg and shook his head, but only by a degree or two.

"Mr. Holmes, I know that you are here as a friend, and your purpose is only to help her, but it was a deeply personal matter, and I'm still a member of her staff and bound by a pledge of confidence. I regret that I cannot answer your question, and I request your understanding on that matter."

"Mr. Nichol, her life remains at risk. If whatever took place isn't sorted out, she may very well attempt to kill herself again. Surely, you know that."

"I do, Mr. Holmes, I do. But I took an oath. I made a promise. I did the same when I enlisted in the army. I do not violate my oaths, sir. But, if it is of any help to you, Hope visited Lady Assherton this afternoon and reported that while very weak, she was conscious and coherent. May I suggest, sir, that you pay the lady a visit yourself tomorrow morning and ask her what happened. If she wants it to be known, she'll tell you. But I will not."

The two men stared at each other for an uncomfortable half-a-minute. Sherlock Holmes didn't react patiently when his investigations were obstructed and had, during the war, I suspected, carried out countless intense interrogations on behalf of His Majesty. Across from him, however, was an army captain who had been through Hell and back and wasn't about to be cowed by an aging detective. The captain won the duel. Holmes relaxed into a smile.

"An excellent suggestion, Captain. I will do that. Now, would you mind calling Miss Hope and ask if we could have a word with her?"

We waited for several minutes after Mr. Nichol departed, affording me an opportunity to look around the room. It was tastefully decorated with paintings of Lancashire, photographs of husband and sons, and a plaque bearing the popular poem *If,* all illuminated by the latest, flickering electric lamps.

Miss Hope Leighton entered the parlor and, without saying anything, marched across the room and sat in the chair vacated by the butler.

I don't wish to be unkind in my description of her, but the immediate words that came to my mind on meeting her were "Sergeant-Major". She was a solidly built woman whose complexion was etched by what must have been endless days and nights of demanding work. Before either Holmes or I could say anything, she gave us a hard look.

"Well, what is it you two old blokes want to know?"

"Madam," said Holmes, "if you count yourself a friend of Lady Assherton, then I assure you we are on the same side."

"Of course you are. If I thought you weren't, I wouldn't be bothered coming down to talk to you. What do you want?"

"You weren't employed in service before the war," said Holmes. "How came you by the position you now have?"

"I came to chat with Lady Assherton, and she hired me."

"Would you mind being just a little more explicit?" said Holmes.

"Fine. I was a nurse in the ward that Eddy and Rolly were brought to after they got shot up. I dressed their wounds and did all those things a nurse has to do until they died. They asked me to pay a visit to their mum, and I promised I would."

"Just a visit? Was that all?" said Holmes.

"No. They both knew that they weren't long for this world, and they asked me to help them write a note in their New Testaments – just '*Thank you, Mum. Love you.*' that was all – and take them to their mum when the war was over. I got about thirty such requests like that from young lads before I pulled the sheets up over them. Kept me busy for a month or more after I got back to England in December. Lady Assherton was one of my last calls. Her other maid, Claire, had just given notice, and when I told her about being with her boys at the end, she gave me a hug and offered me employment."

"You must have had other opportunities for a better-paying position as a nurse," said Holmes.

"All over the country. But after ten years in a hospital before the war and four years in Queen Alexandra's Royal Nursing Corps, I was ready for a change. You may not understand that, Mr. Holmes, but I'll wager you do, don't you, Dr. Watson?"

"Completely," I said. "If I had been offered a position as a butler in Knightsbridge after my time in battle, I might very well have taken it."

"Well, I was offered, and I took it on the spot. A fine home, three meals and tea, a comfortable bed, clean sheets, my own bath, regular hours, and a good wage. I said 'Yes' there and then."

"And I understand," said Holmes, "that you were on duty when she attempted to poison herself. Would you be so kind as to tell me what happened?"

"Be so kind? Sure, if that's what you want to call it. Yes, it was Easter. Me and George and Lilly – that's what she told us to call her – only had each other as family, so I had ordered in a fine Easter

63

breakfast and had it all set out. George and I tried to be cheerful, but she hardly said a word. After we finished, she said she had to pay a visit to the garden shed out back to get something that she wanted to work on. That was odd as it was still chilly, and the shed would still be there after the day warmed. I was a bit concerned, but it was a bright, sunny day, and I thought the time outside might lift her spirits. It wasn't long after she returned that when I heard her shout in pain, and I rushed into here, the parlor. I saw a bottle of gin on the side table, and what I guessed was some sort of pesticide beside it, and a glass on the floor. I knew right off what had happened, and I screamed for George, and he came hopping, and I told him to hold her arms back, and I forced her jaw open and pushed my fingers down her throat until she vomited, and I kept it up until there was nothing left. And then I forced a glass or two of water down her throat and made her vomit some more. Then she passed out and, by the grace of God, we found a taxi on Easter Sunday and took her to Barts. And you know the rest, Doctor."

"Allow me to commend you for your prompt and selfless action," said Holmes. "It mustn't have been a pleasant experience."

Miss Hope shrugged. "It wasn't the first time someone had hurled their breakfast in my face and all over my uniform. It wasn't even the fifty-first. I'm a nurse. You don't think about it. You do what you have to do. Isn't that right, Doctor?"

"It is," I said. "It goes with the calling."

"Yes, of course," said Holmes. "And did you also know what it was that led to Lady Assherton's desire to end her life?"

"You already asked George that same question. Right? My answer is the same. Go and ask her yourself. I'll be back to see her at the hospital first thing tomorrow morning. If you're there, I'll do what I can to encourage her to talk to you, but that's the best I can do."

"That is more than I can ask for. We shall see you tomorrow."

"Your thoughts, Watson?" Holmes asked me once we were in a motored taxi and on our way back to the Savoy, where he had booked a room.

"I admit that I have a soft spot in my heart for nurses who have served on the battlefront. She is just like so many of those with whom I worked years ago. No nonsense. And absolute integrity."

"And the captain?" he asked.

"He's a fine man. I trust him. He was visibly upset by what had happened – more so than the nurse. Mind you, I suspect he knows more than he's letting on. And, well, he came right out and said so, didn't he?"

"He did indeed. Perhaps we shall learn more tomorrow morning. Do you expect that Lady Lilly will open up to us?"

"I expect that between Miss Hope and me, we should be able to instill enough trust and encouragement to let her disclose whatever it is."

"I hope you will," said Holmes. "Otherwise, this case could take much longer to solve."

At seven o'clock in the morning in late April, London is gloomy and damp. Motorized taxicabs offer somewhat more protection from the elements than the horse-drawn hansoms we used for years. Even though no improvements have taken place since the start of the war, the warm air from the engine takes the edge off the cold, the mixture with fumes notwithstanding.

I hailed a taxi, picked Holmes up at the Savoy, and then the two of us continued on the short distance to Barts. When we entered her room, Lady Assherton was sitting up and, whilst still pale, was looking much better than the morning before. Miss Leighton was already there and must have brushed her hair and put it up.

"Good morning, Lilly," I chirped. "I've brought you a belated Easter present."

"Oh, good morning, John. It isn't necessary to be quite so cheerful. What did you bring me?"

"Not *what*, Lilly. *Who*. Allow me to introduce my old friend, Mr. Sherlock Holmes. Between us, we are going to get things sorted and let you get back to as normal a life as one can have these days."

She gave Holmes the once over and rolled her eyes. "Good morning, Mr. Sherlock Holmes. I didn't know that you were still alive. Didn't you die in Switzerland thirty years ago?"

"I came back from the dead," said Holmes forcing a smile. "And I plan to be alive for a few more years yet – the same as you will."

"That will be the day. Can you give me a good reason?"

"For England, my dear lady, for England. And before you can make a cynical reply to that, allow me to inform you what is patently obvious to me. You are unquestionably innocent and have been set up and framed by some traitorous people operating within the British Intelligence agencies. We don't yet know their motives, but they are intent on dismantling all the efforts of the past year and those still taking place that are bringing the world back to peace. I'm intent on discovering who is behind these nefarious actions. To do so, Dr. Watson and I shall need the utmost cooperation – not only from you, but also from your loyal household staff."

He then turned to Miss Leighton. "May I count on your help, Miss Leighton, in exposing those who have done such harm to Lady Assherton?"

The fearsome nurse looked defiantly back at Holmes. "I'll help you all right. If you can find the blackguards behind all this, I will bloody well cut off their – "

"Thank you, Miss Leighton. Seeing them hanged will be sufficient. And now you, my Lady. May I appeal to your patriotism and your love of country, which I know you have I abundance. You have already sacrificed your two sons. Asking you to assist in bringing vile spies to justice is a paltry additional request. I would hope that you are still sufficiently loyal and committed to England to take on one more assignment."

In a trice, the glaze of hopeless despair vanished from her eyes. She was glaring at Holmes and, to my great relief, was jolly good and angry with him.

"How dare you question my loyalty to King and Country! If you are as good as you appear to think you are and can bring those rotters to justice, then you can be sure that I will be right behind you, kicking your arse to get the job done!

"And John," she added, turning to me. "Get me out of this horrible place and back to my home. Hope, order in a few decent meals. The food here isn't fit for horses."

"Not quite so fast, my Lady," said Holmes. "There is one condition that I must set before we begin."

"Then set it."

"You know perfectly well that the reason you gave Dr. Watson for the accusations against you – the pirating of a few of your cotton shipments – was utter nonsense and could have been easily dismissed. What else did they accuse you of?"

Her body sagged. She gave a pleading look to her nurse.

"Do I have to tell them, Hope?" she asked.

"You have to, Lilly."

For a minute, her face went blank. She shrugged and looked at Holmes.

"Very well, then. If I have to, I have to. You see, Mr. Holmes, throughout the war, I carried on a constant exchange of letters with the enemy."

Both Holmes and I were struck dumb.

"You *what*?" sputtered Holmes.

"Does the name Elsbeth Schragmüller mean anything to you, Mr. Holmes?"

"*The* Elsbeth Schragmüller? The one they called *Fräulein Doktor*? The woman who was the mastermind behind German Intelligence and trained all their spies?"

"The very one," she said.

"In the name of all that is holy, madam, why would you do something so . . . so – "

"So *treasonous,* Mr. Holmes? Because Elsbeth is my sister."

There was an awkward pause in the conversation before Holmes said, "Go on."

"My mother married a German. It wasn't uncommon fifty years ago. Several of the Queen's children did the same thing. I spent my childhood in Schlüsselburg, but my mother sent me to England for my schooling. While I was a student, my mother died, and my father married again. My little sister arrived a year later. We quite adored each other, and I made several visits a year to spend time with her and my father, right up to the start of the war."

"But surely, you knew who she was – what she had become."

"Of course, I was so very proud of her, the first woman ever in Germany to receive her Doctorate in Political Science. She was brilliant. But up until August of 1914, neither of us believed that the world would come to war. Did you? Did anybody? Once all hell broke loose, we agreed that we would only write about personal matters and never say a word about what was going on in the world. We had our letters forwarded through Switzerland and wrote to each other every week. Once the war ended, we were free to carry on as we had before it started. I never expected for a moment that it would come back to haunt me."

"Your letters must have been intercepted and read. Was there anything in them that could be construed as treasonous?" said Holmes.

"Not a thing, but I was accused of sending her coded information, and not merely some facts about how much cotton cloth I was producing, but some message that led directly to the arrest, conviction, and execution of Edith Cavell."

I gasped. In violation of the Geneva Convention, demanding that medical personnel be protected in times of war, Miss Edith Cavell had been arrested by the Germans and charged with treason. As a nurse, she had treated German, English, Austrian, and Dutch soldiers alike with no regard as to which of the belligerents they

67

belonged. However, in 1915, she had also aided in the escape of several hundred English and Dutch troops who were caught behind enemy lines in Belgium. The Germans considered this action a crime and, in spite of worldwide protest, had executed her in front of a firing squad.

She became an immediate, sainted martyr, and throughout the English-speaking world, monuments had been erected in her honor and streets, parks, wings of hospitals, government buildings, and schools had been named or re-named in her memory. Somewhere in Western Canada, a massive, snow-covered mountain was given the name of Mount Edith Cavell.

Lady Assherton had seen the look on my face and hastened to say, "Had I done any such thing, I would deserve to be hanged. But I did not. It was entirely a confection."

"These men," said Holmes, "who informed you of these accusations – did they say which branch of the government they worked for."

"Scotland Yard."

"Did they give you their names?"

"No."

"Can you describe them?"

She exhaled an exasperation. "They were typically English-looking blokes with average height and chubby faces. Grey coats, grey hats, grey suits. They didn't stay long, and they did not leave their cards."

"Thank you, madam, for being so forthcoming. I will find these men," said Holmes, "and discover what has been happening to you."

"How are you going to do that, Mr. Holmes?" she asked.

"I need to review all of the letters you received from your sister during the past five years," said Holmes.

"Fine. Hope can give them to you. She knows where they are. You can read to your heart's content about flowers and birds and nieces and nephews and recipes. How do you imagine that is going to do you any good?"

"I know someone."

The man sitting beside Holmes that evening in a café on Temple Square appeared to be around seventy-five years old. He was a small fellow with white hair and a well-lined countenance, but the rat-like face and sallow hue of his complexion were unmistakable.

"Why, hello, Lestrade," I said as I approached their table. "It's been a year or two. Good to see you."

68

"Feels more like ten years, Doctor. And good to see you as well."

Inspector Lestrade hadn't always been on the best terms with Holmes and me in years gone by. But now, with those days far behind us, I found myself happy to see him, much in the same way as I did an aging rugby player who had tackled me mercilessly when I played for Blackheath.

We chatted briefly, chuckling over some of our more outrageous shared adventures in the previous century. I found myself wondering if Sherlock Holmes and the inspector would ever discuss all that really happened to Charles Augustus Milverton, but now wasn't the time to ask.

Holmes quickly got around to filling Lestrade in on the tragedy that had befallen Lady Assherton and asked if he knew anything about it. Lestrade shook his head.

"I still chat from time to time with some of the fellows I hired or worked with," he said. "But many of them are now also retired. There is an entire new batch of them there now. Some of them came over from the army. Officers. Clever chaps. But no respect at all for doing things by the book. Willing to bend all sorts of rules. I suppose that's what helped them get through the war and win their battles, but it is simply not the way to do responsible police work."

"Are you saying," asked Holmes, "that you wouldn't be surprised if Lady Assherton was set up? Framed by someone within the Yard or the Directorates?"

"It's certainly possible. We would never risk imperiling the life of an innocent person for any reason. But these chaps are somewhat cavalier about that. I suppose that when you have sent men to their death in battle, hoping that by doing so you will come out on top and defeat the enemy, the well-being of one widow is not much to worry about. But it isn't what we would have done. Wouldn't think of it."

"The world has indeed changed," said Holmes.

"And you, Mr. Holmes?" said Lestrade. "You used to break every rule in the book. I tore my hair out many times over your tactics. But the life of an innocent person was sacrosanct."

"It was. It still is."

"Right," said Lestrade. "Now, are you absolutely certain that this woman is innocent?"

Holmes looked toward me for an answer.

"I have known her," I said, "for thirty years. She was utterly loyal to the Empire. Never a doubt."

69

"And you?" said Holmes to Lestrade. "Are you absolutely certain that there couldn't be traitors lurking in the Yard or any of the Directorates?"

Lestrade laughed.

"I'm absolutely certain there are. And I gather that the reason you're buying my supper in my favorite old haunt is your desire to have me go in and smoke them out."

"Precisely."

"I'll see what I can find and let you know. I still have a few friends amongst the old boys. But one condition."

"Yes?" said Holmes.

Lestrade turned to me. "Now see here, Dr. Watson. If we succeed, and you write up this case, no more calling me a little sallow, rat-faced fellow."

"I wouldn't think of it."

He rolled his eyes at me, stood up, and departed, leaving Holmes and me to chat.

"It is useful," said Holmes, "to have some old colleagues. Twenty years ago, I knew almost every one of the inspectors who came here for lunch. Now they are strangers. Lestrade was right. It is a brave new world."

I had glanced over the patrons of the place while we ate. Many of the chaps had a distinct military bearing – former officers, no doubt. What was surprising was how many were disfigured from the war. Some were missing arms, some only hands. Two were wheeled in on bath chairs, several hustled about using canes. At least a third of them bore scars on their faces that had been inflicted by cuts or burns. Four wore patches over one eye but appeared to carry on well enough – happy, I assumed, not to be blind. I kept my eye out for two men with chubby, bland faces, but no such pair appeared.

At two o'clock, lunch having ended, we returned to Lady Assherton's home and met with Miss Leighton. She handed over a packing case of letters, dated weekly beginning in the spring of 1918.

"There are another four cases," she said. "They have been writing to each other for over twenty years."

"This will suffice for now," said Holmes as I carried the case out to the taxi.

Upon returning to his hotel, he bade me come up to his suite and took a bundle of letters from the case.

"These are the most recent," he said. "Let us see if they reveal anything beyond sisterly chit-chat."

He opened the latest to arrive, dated Berlin only a week ago, and handed it over to me while he organized the rest of them according to their dates.

"Your thoughts, old friend. Anything suspicious? Seditious?"

I read it over. It ran:

> *Sister dear: Every day I think about you. Daily, I worry for your well-being. Are you getting on better this week? Not that I doubt your fortitude. Ever and always, you are the strong one.*
>
> *Right now, I am looking out at my garden. Gardens always bring succor to the soul. Gloriosa are starting to bloom in their beds. Narcissuses are waiving their bright yellow heads. Irises have sprung to life along the verges. Rather a lovely time, do you not agree? Better by far than the dreary winter.*
>
> *Shall you return this year to visit me? Rainer, your nephew, keeps asking about you. Every night, he pesters me about his Aunt Lilly. Very soon, he will be sent off to school. God will watch over him, I pray. Nothing untoward will touch his young life. I ask you to pray for him too. Will you, dear sister?*
>
> *Later today, I will walk in the park. You would love to see our cherry trees. Right and left, the blossoms are falling. On top of your head, some of them land. Then there are the chestnut trees. All of them are covered with their lovely cones of flowers. Very attractive, also, are the lilacs. And let us never forget the roses.*
>
> *Last fall, I planted an entire new bed. 8 of them did not survive the winter. 25, however, are growing splendidly.*
>
> *I can only say that I am enjoying my new position in Berlin. Rigorous work helps one to put the war behind. Fortunately, my studies paid off. Though the past four years were terrible. Now we are all hoping for peace and harmony. Ending war forever is the prayer of us all. God grant that our prayers may be answered. Always, we can hope for a better future. Together, all nations can live in peace.*

71

Egon sends his warm regards. Ever and always.
My love and prayers.

I handed it back to him.

"Nothing here," I said. "Meaningless chit-chat between two women. Though, I must say, for a woman who earned her doctorate, even if from a German university, her sentences are surprisingly awkward."

He gave me an odd look, took the letter from me, and took a seat beside the window. He read it and gazed at it for several minutes. Then he paused, lit his pipe, and scrutinized it for another ten minutes.

"A-ha!" he shouted and leapt to his feet. "Here it is, Watson. As I suspected." He was grinning with glee, and he mouthed words while reading the letter one more time. Then his expression changed. His mouth opened, and his eyes went wide with fear.

"Dear God," he gasped. "This is a disaster."

He packed the letter back in the case and lugged it toward the door of the room.

"Holmes! What is it? Where are you going?"

"The Diogenes Club. Enjoy room service if you wish. Put it on my tab. I will call you later."

I thought of hurrying to join him, but it was apparent he didn't wish my company.

I waited up that evening for his call, but none came. At midnight I crawled into bed beside my wife, who, by that time, was sound asleep.

The phone rang at two o'clock in the morning.

"Sherlock," mumbled my wife, "is the only one who would think of calling at this time."

I stumbled out of bed and down the stairs to the unceasing telephone.

"Holmes?"

"Yes," he answered. "I will come by your house in a car at eight. Kindly be ready."

"I'm on duty at the Barts tomorrow morning."

"So tell them you're sick. If they need a medical opinion, give them one. Eight o'clock. Regards to your dear wife."

He hung up.

He was looking highly alert for such an early hour. It was same look I remembered from years ago when he had become a bloodhound about to pounce on its prey. The eyes, now hooded and creased, were once again blazing, eyebrows contracted, and his jaw set.

"Did you sleep at all?" I asked him.

"No, but neither did Mycroft, for which he will be a long time in forgiving me. However, the Savoy has excellent individual baths and strong coffee. Another round and a bite of breakfast will be waiting for us at Lestrade's café."

"Whose motorcar is this?" I asked. It was exceptionally comfortable, quiet, and powerful.

"It is owned," he said, "collectively by the members of the Diogenes Club. I had to promise to have it back by tea time."

Traffic was light at that early hour, and we sped our way through Kensington, along the Strand, and down to the Embankment. As we rode, he had his valise open on his knees and was reading more of Lady Asserton's letters. He muttered a series of oaths under his breath and kept shaking his head. I tried to ask him what he found so disturbing, but he held up his hand and bade me be quiet.

In the same café on Temple Place, Inspector Lestrade was holding a table for us and had already procured a full carafe of coffee.

"Good morning, Inspector," said Holmes. "What have you learned?"

"And good morning to you too, Mr. Holmes. Sit down and enjoy your coffee. Was it really necessary to get me up at this hour of the morning?"

"Time is pressing. Please. What did you learn?"

"Right" said Lestrade. "Well, I called in a few favors from over a decade ago, but they were still good. You wanted to know who the two men were who called on Lady Assherton and caused her attempt on her own life. Right?"

"Yes. Precisely."

"Well, their names are John Peterson and Peter Johnson, and no, I am not making them up. You remember how you so unkindly referred to some of my men as unimaginative imbeciles? Well, this time, you might have been right."

"But who are they? You know what I mean."

"Well, that's the problem, Holmes. They are a couple of new boys who were recruited after being demobbed. Low-level entry

73

position on the Force. But I waited for them yesterday until they were off duty and followed them around to the pub and came and sat down beside them."

"Yes, go on," said Holmes.

"They had no idea who I was, so I said, 'Good day there, lads. I'm Retired Chief Inspector Lestrade. I have an old friend named Sherlock Holmes, who wants to have a word with you about Lady Assherton.' Well, they pretty much choked on their ale. Must say, it was the most fun I've had in months."

"I'm sure it was very amusing."

"They started in straight away, sputtering that they had nothing to do with the case. They were only following orders. They were told they were to make three visits to Lady Assherton, with escalating accusations, and they were free to chat about it with other fellows from the Yard. They felt horrible when they heard about her suicide attempt. No one, it seems, expected her to do that. They weren't aware of her previous attempt during the war, and she had the reputation of being something of a battle-ax. Must say, the two blokes seemed honestly distraught over it. Not much good at hiding their emotions. They won't last long as police officers if they don't learn how to do that. Frankly, Mr. Holmes, I don't know what the Yard is coming to."

"You said *three* visits," said Lestrade.

"Right. I did say that. Well, after the dear lady tried to kill herself following the second visit, the third was called off."

"What was it going to be about?"

"They couldn't tell me," said Lestrade.

"But why? What purpose did it serve?"

"They said that they were told that up at the top of Scotland Yard and the Intelligence Directorate, there had been evidence that somewhere in the Directorates there might be a German agent who was sending secret information back to Berlin. The idea – bloody stupid if you ask me – was to let everyone know that they had found the culprit, and it wasn't anyone on the inside. It was Lady Assherton who was in secret communication with her sister in Berlin, and her sister is some sort of master spy, if you can believe that."

"Odd though it may be," said Holmes, "I can. Now, would these fellows be willing to meet with me?"

"Not on your life," said Lestrade.

"Why not?"

"Because they have read those stories that the doctor here wrote about you, and they don't want their hero to think of them as complete fools."

"I wouldn't treat them as *complete* fools, only partial."

"That's bad enough. A meeting is out," said Lestrade.

"Very well, then. Who gave them their instructions? Did you ask them that?"

"Well, yes, Mr. Holmes, of course I did. They said that the assignment was given to them by Bramwell Duponte, the Secretary to Sir Basil Thomson. They find this Duponte fellow an arrogant prig, but he zealously guards the gate of access to Thomson."

"Basil Thomson?" asked Holmes. "Didn't he run prisons? What's he doing at Scotland Yard?"

"Somebody in the government thought that if he had been in charge of prisons all over England for twenty years, he might be good on the other side and able to catch felons *before* they were sent to prison. Maybe there is some logic to that, but if there is, I don't see it. Whatever Scotland Yard is becoming these days – "

"Yes, Inspector, you were saying."

"Right. Well, Basil Thomson is now not only the head of the CID, he is also in charge over the Intelligence Directorate."

"What about Sections Five and the non-existent Section Six?" asked Holmes.

"No," said the inspector, "they are still run by chaps who know what they are doing. They might cut your throat as soon as look at you, but at least they are competent."

"Can you arrange for me to meet with this Thomson fellow?"

Lestrade gave Holmes a sideways look.

"Mr. Holmes, I'm getting the impression that there is something more going on than a failed attempt to abuse a wealthy widow, isn't there?"

"There is, indeed. Can you arrange such a meeting?"

"I cannot help you on that on, Mr. Holmes. Sorry. However, if I remember, I believe you might know someone who can."

"I do. And I'm most grateful for your help, my old friend. I promise to give a full report the next time we meet at this table."

Lestrade bade us a good day, wished us success, and departed.

Holmes turned to me. "Come, Watson. The game – "

"Fine. You don't have to tell me."

I gulped down a final mouthful of coffee and followed him out to the pavement.

"Back to the Diogenes Club?" I said.

"No. I don't dare. He will still be asleep in his rooms across the street, and utterly dead to the world. No, we have yet another visit to pay to Lady Assherton's."

"But she is still in hospital."

"Precisely."

"What are you two old dogs doing back here?" said Miss Hope when she opened the door. "The Lady is still in hospital. Come back after she returns."

"I need another word with you and Mr. Nichol, if I may, madam," said Holmes. "I promise that it's only in the best interests of her Ladyship. May we come in, and would you mind, please, calling Mr. Nichol?"

"All right. But make things snappy. We're trying to have the place spotless to welcome her home. I have a charwoman here as well as the two of us, and I'm not about to tell her to stop her cleaning just because Sherlock bleedin' Holmes needs to have a word."

Holmes thanked her graciously and we sat down in the parlor. Holmes looked somewhere between serene and smug. I knew that look.

When George Nichol and Hope Leighton were seated and facing us, Holmes smiled at both of them in turn.

"Miss Hope, I do wish to thank you for your complete cooperation and assistance. The batch of letters you gave us may not have been at all instructive, but they revealed a gentle, domestic side of Lady Assherton in a way that touched my heart and made me all the more determined to help her."

"You're welcome. Is that the only reason you came here? If it is, then be on your way. We have a house to get ready."

"I will not keep you long. However, I would be remiss if I didn't offer Mr. Nichol here some basic lessons in the art of espionage. You are not a very good spy, sir."

The captain's spine stiffened.

"I beg your pardon. Now, look here, Mr. Holmes – "

"Oh, come, come. No need to get huffy about it. You just need to learn that if you're going to paste on a mustache, try not to use such a cheap one. Anyone who has ever worked in the theatre can spot it a mile away."

The captain involuntarily raised his hand to his upper lip and quickly put it back down in his lap.

Holmes continued, "And do try not to wear shoes and shirts of such fine quality. Yours cost more than two weeks' wages of a part-time butler. And if you are going to pretend to be an electrical engineer, make sure that the lamps in your house flicker only in unison with the street lamps and with the other houses on the block and not independent of them, indicating that the short is inside the home not outside, and therefore could have been fixed by any butler who claims to have been an electrician."

As if on cue, the lamps flickered yet again.

"And learn," said Holmes, "to hobble using at least three different gaits, and not the same way here in the house as in the pub on Temple Square, where you turned around and stumbled out upon seeing me at a table with Inspector Lestrade. There is no doubt that you are a Liverpudlian. That is obvious by your accent, but your vocabulary was tainted by your years in Oxford or Cambridge. And never add 'honestly' to any answer you give. Men who do that are invariably dishonest. And finally, if you are going to impersonate a soldier who was friends with the sons of the lady of the house, do try not to choose one who is dead and buried in a war cemetery in France. George Nichol died at the Somme. You did not. You did act to save the lady's life, and your distress with what happened to her was sincere. We do appear to be on the same side. But now then, who are you, and to whom are you reporting?"

You could have cut the silence in the room with a knife. Finally, Miss Hope burst out with a colorful oath and, looking at the butler, added, "Yes. Who the hell are you, George?"

The butler had sat still and stone-faced throughout Holmes's diatribe. Now, without altering his posture or facial expression, he looked Holmes straight in the eye.

"Allow me to preface my answer by saying that I told them it was an absurd idea. Putting such a fine woman through what they did was unconscionable. But they insisted. So, yes, Mr. Holmes, I was a captain in the LHL, but in the communications unit. My leg was injured at the Somme in a motorcycle accident. Upon my recovery, I was recruited by the Intelligence boys. They knew all about Lilly's sister in Belgium and her role in training and overseeing German spies."

"That much I already assumed," said Holmes. "Keep going."

"My task was to get a job as her butler, using a feigned friendship with her sons as an entrée. I was to intercept all the letters coming from Germany, open and re-seal them, having made copies. Then take the copies to the Intelligence Directorate. Letters being sent by Lilly were taken not to the post office but to the same office, after which they were sent on to Switzerland. They knew that Lilly was as loyal as they come, but they were looking for anything in the letters from Fräulein Doktor that might be gleaned and give any insight into the enemy's operations. They found nothing."

"Why then the false accusations?"

"There was a reliable report from MI6 that an attack was planned on the meetings in Versailles, killing the leaders of the Allied powers and sending the world back into war. Some fool came up with the cruel scheme that by publicly identifying Lilly as the traitor, the true villain would drop his guard and allow himself to be caught. It failed."

"Who was the fool?"

"That, Mr. Holmes, I honestly . . . that, I do not know. I was given my instructions directly from Sir Basil's office. The plan was approved at the top. I do know that the threats to the meetings in Versailles are being taken quite seriously."

"You told me last time we met that you take your oaths and promises seriously. I'm certain that when you were a boy, you took an oath in Sunday School not to tell lies. I am also sure that the Almighty hasn't released you from that oath. Now then, who are you?"

"I am Captain Robert Sylvester John Faulknor."

"Then allow me to bid you good day, Captain Faulknor."

We rose and departed the parlor. As the front door was closing behind us, I could hear Miss Hope Leighton saying, "And allow *me* to bid you *goodbye*, Captain Faulknor. If you are not out of this house in fifteen minutes, so help me, I will bloody well cut off – "

I closed the door behind me, not wanting to visualize the threat being made to the already handicapped fellow.

"Our next appointment," said Holmes as we walked from Chequer Street out to Whitecross in search of a taxi, "is with Sir Basil Thomson. This plot against Versailles demands my attention."

"We are able to see him so soon?"

"Mycroft made the appointment for me. Somewhere in the vast chasms of his mind, he has stored every detail, sordid and otherwise, of the lives and careers of the entire civil service. He never threatens blackmail. He doesn't have to. His requests are invariably granted."

"Splendid. Are we going there now?"

"No. The appointment isn't until four o'clock. Between now and then, you may as well return to Barts."

"I can't."

"Why not?"

"Because you already had me call in saying that I was too ill to work. I hacked and sputtered into the phone rather convincingly."

"Then tell them you recovered. You're a physician. Heal thyself."

"It doesn't work that way, Holmes. We don't let infectious people wander around hospitals. The place is already overflowing with germs. But I have an alternative solution."

"Yes?"

"I shall wait in your room at the Savoy. I hear the room service is excellent. You can pick me up at the front door at half-past three, and don't be surprised if there are a few more charges on your tab."

It was only a short walk from the Savoy along the Victoria Embankment to New Scotland Yard, and, it being a pleasant April afternoon, Holmes insisted that we travel by Shank's Pony. He preferred to rehearse his forthcoming encounters *en plein aire*.

The Home Office had recently centralized some of its functions within the newly-formed Directorate of Intelligence, housed in the Scotland Yard buildings.

The sweet-young-thing behind the reception desk of Scotland Yard beamed at the two of us when we announced ourselves.

"Oh, my goodness," she said, "are you really *the* Sherlock Holmes and Doctor Watson? My mother read all those stories about you when she was a student. I didn't know that you were both still alive. Please, follow me. Sir Basil's office is on the top floor."

We passed through a corridor of the offices of the Assistant Commissioners of Scotland Yard until we come to a suite labeled *Directorate of Intelligence*. The military directorates were responsible for catching and spies both at home and abroad, but didn't have the power to effect arrests. For that, they relied on Scotland Yard and the service of Sir Basil and his men.

The receptionist led us into an elegant office that had no one in it.

"This is Mr. Duponte's office, Sir Basil's secretary. He will be along shortly and take you to see Sir Basil."

We sat in the comfortable leather chairs and waited . . . and waited. At twenty-past-four, Holmes stood up and began an inspection of the paintings and photographs on the walls. On one wall was a row of photos of quite handsome men, all elegantly dressed.

"These," said Holmes, "are a rogues' gallery of the master criminals and spies Sir Basil has given himself credit for catching."

"Who is the woman?" I asked.

There were three separate photographs of an exceptionally attractive, more-than-somewhat voluptuous woman dressed in varying exotic – indeed erotic – attire.

"She," said Holmes, "it the famous, or perhaps infamous, depending on your sentiments, Mata Hari. Sir Basil interrogated her for several days, then handed his notes over to the French, who subsequently executed her for spying."

"Was she guilty?"

"She was undoubtedly guilty of many sins, both known and unknown, although spying may not have been one of them."

He moved on to another wall and inspected a row of oil paintings, all set outdoors. One was a scene of a village in India, several were of farm animals, and one that I recognized was of the Matterhorn in Switzerland. Each was in the smudged style that the French called *Impressionisme* and not at all to my taste. Holmes seemed quite intrigued.

At four-forty, he sat back down and retreated into his familiar contemplative posture with his eyes closed and his fingers tented under his chin.

It was four-fifty when the back door of the office opened, and a well-dressed man of average height and thickness entered. He was carrying a small stack of books under his arm.

"Oh, good afternoon," he said while shuffling through a stack of files on his desk and not looking up at us. "Holmes and Watson, right?"

"We are," said Holmes, "and who might you be?"

That got his attention, and he looked up, positively offended.

"I am Bramwell Duponte, the Secretary to the Director. And yes, I understand that Sir Basil has an appointment to meet with you. However, he sends his regrets. He is frightfully busy as he is leaving London tomorrow for France. He will be giving a brief to the Big Four, as the press is calling them, at Versailles. I have rescheduled your appointment for a fortnight from now, but he did ask if you would be so kind as to sign his copies of *The Adventures of Sherlock Holmes*. There are eight books in the series, are there not? He has enjoyed them since his boyhood and was, I assure you, disappointed at not being able to meet with you this afternoon, but is very much looking forward to doing so when time permits."

He placed the books on the coffee table and put a pen and inkwell down beside them.

"He may be frightfully busy," said Holmes, "but we need to speak to him about a matter that is frightfully important."

"Oh, yes, yes. I heard you were dabbling in that business of Lady Assherton. Please tell the old girl that she has been completely exonerated, and all suspicions have been lifted. Sir Basil asked me to organize sending her a small gift – a nice piece of Wedgewood or something like that – as our way of apologizing for any inconvenience we might have caused her."

"I'm sure she will be thrilled," said Holmes. "However, our business with him concerns the threats to the meetings at Versailles."

"Oh, you heard about that business as well, did you? Not to worry. An extra guard has been set up to protect everyone in the Hall. No anarchist or crazed German or Turk will get close to them. No need for Sherlock Holmes to worry his old detective brain about it. Now, please excuse me. I have other pressing matters to attend to. Please let yourselves out, and don't forget to sign the books. Good day, gentlemen."

He turned on his heel and departed through the same door as he had entered.

Sherlock Holmes wasn't happy.

"It is time to call in the cavalry," he said.

"Mycroft? Again?"

"Regrettably, yes."

"Shall we head over to Pall Mall?" I asked.

"Not yet. This is the time of day when he has his sherry, then his supper, and then his port. He won't even have me let into the Stranger's Room before eight o'clock."

"And until then?"

"Forgive me, old friend, but I must prepare myself for the encounters we are going to face. Can you meet me at the Savoy at half-seven?"

We departed the Scotland Yard building, and Holmes called for his own taxi.

I made my way to Simpson's and dined alone.

At the appointed time, he appeared in Savoy Court. He had altered his attire and was now sporting his tails, walking stick, and top hat. I made a passing comment on his appearance.

"When the stakes are high," he said, "one must employ every weapon at one's disposal. Come, we are meeting Mycroft at ten-minutes-to-eight. That is the earliest I could get him to agree to."

The porter of the Diogenes Club disappeared into the bowels of the building and reappeared five minutes later, followed by the slow-moving mass of Mycroft Holmes. I hadn't seen him in person for quite a while. He looked every one of his seventy-two years. Were I to describe him, I might compare him to an aging, lumbering Grizzly bear – incapable of moving quickly, but still capable of knocking one's head off with one swipe if one came too close.

"Sherlock," he growled, "I will have you know that I never venture outside before the Queen's birthday. You'd better be sure that this travail is worth it."

"Preventing another war-to-end-all-wars is at stake."

"Right. Get in the car. And wake me up when we get there."

It was only a few blocks from Pall Mall to the home of Sir Basil Thomson in Mayfair, but Mycroft Holmes immediately laid his heavily-jowled head on the back of the seat, closed his eyes, and began to snore.

Ten minutes later, we stopped in front of an elegant home a block away from Grosvenor Square.

"Give me your hand," Mycroft ordered his brother as he extracted himself from the vehicle. He moved slowly up the steps to the front door, taking one step at a time. With surprising forcefulness, he banged on the door with his stick and, for good measure, rang the bell several times.

A butler opened the door and looked aghast at the three of us.

"Gentlemen, please. No one is available to see you – "

Mycroft Holmes pushed his way into the foyer. He looked up the staircase and shouted.

"*Basil!*" Get down here, *now!*"

"Sir!" said the butler. "Stop that. You cannot barge into Sir Basil's house like that. Sir, I must ask you to leave this – "

"*Basil!* You hear me? Come here this minute. I don't have all evening."

"Sir!"

At the top of the staircase, a tall man in an elegant dressing gown appeared. He appeared to be in his mid-fifties, with thinning hair and a lampshade mustache.

"What in the world – ?" he asked. "Mycroft Holmes? . . . Is that you?"

"Of course, it's me, and I'm not coming up, so get down here."

"Mycroft, what are you doing here?"

"You know perfectly well I wouldn't be here if it weren't of disastrous importance to the Empire."

"Can it not wait until I get back from Paris? I will return in ten days."

"After which the Prime Minister of England, and of France, and of Italy, and the President of the United States may very well be dead. Not to mention you, too, Basil."

That brought him down the stairs.

"Whatever it is, Mycroft, get on with it. I'm in the midst of packing, and I have a train at sunrise."

"You can sleep on the train, Basil," said Mycroft. "For the next hour, you are going to sit and read and listen. Now, have your man bring me some port and sit down in the parlor."

He strode into the parlor, but Sir Basil Thomson didn't move.

"*Basil!* Are you deaf?"

"Now look here, Mycroft, old chap. I will have you know that — "

"What I know is that you will not have a job anywhere if you don't move. Dead men don't last long in their employment. Now get in here."

Sir Basil Thomson, the head of the Directorate of Intelligence and the Assistant Commissioner 'C' of Scotland Yard, followed Mycroft Holmes into the parlor and sat down. Sherlock Holmes and I meekly came in after him.

"Sherlock," said Mycroft, "give me those letters. The latest one on top."

Holmes hurried to open his valise and hand a bundle of letters to his oversize older brother.

"Read this, Basil," said Mycroft.

Sir Basil took the letter and glanced at it.

"I saw this a week ago. It is meaningless. Nothing but womanly chatter. You are wasting my time."

"No Basil," said Mycroft, "I am not. I am saving your life. Take this pencil and mark down the first letter of each sentence."

He diligently recorded each letter in sequence. It ran:

S-E-D-A-N-E-R-G-G-N-I-R-B-S-R-E-V-G-N-I-W-L-Y-R-O-T-A-V-A-L-8-25-I-R-F-T-N-E-G-A-T-E-E-M.

Sir Basil looked up at us.

"This is meaningless. Utter gibberish."

"No, Basil, it isn't," said Mycroft. "Read them again. This time start at the end and proceed to the beginning."

"*M-e-e-t . . . meet . . . .agent . . . fri, 25* – Friday? *Twenty-fifth? Eight . . . lavatory . . . Lwing . . .* left wing? *. . . vers . . .* What is that?"

"Try Versailles, perhaps."

"Perhaps. . . bring. . . Good heavens! Grenades? Someone is being told to bring grenades to Versailles this Friday! Who was this sent to?"

"We shall get to that," said Mycroft. "First, read through all of these letters received over the past two months. You might find them interesting."

Over the next half hour, Sir Basil Thomson read backwards through the series of letters. As he did so, his mouth hung open in disbelief, and he repeatedly shook his head. By the time he had finished his task, the color had drained from his face.

"These letters contain the complete plot to destroy the meetings now taking place in France. Leaders of over thirty countries could be assassinated, including Lloyd George, Wilson, Clemenceau, and Orlando."

"Don't forget yourself, Basil. You will be giving your briefing on Friday morning," said Mycroft. "And will be blown to smithereens along with the rest of them."

"But why? Why would anybody want to do this? Who are these people? Are they crazed anarchists who have gone mad?"

"Good heavens, Basil. Are your agents over there utterly useless? Do you not know what is going on in Versailles?"

"What do you mean? The chaps over there are busy writing a treaty to ensure peace, an ending to all wars."

"No, Basil. They are ensuring a Carthaginian peace. As we speak, there is a group from our side who are drafting the chapters on reparations that Germany is going to be forced to pay. And they will be forced to admit that they and they alone are guilty for causing the war."

"And so they should," said Sir Basil.

"And if you were the average Boche, who had been told that you agreed to the Armistice on the basis of that American's Fourteen Points, would you be happy?"

"Oh, yes, that fellow. Almighty God Himself only needed ten. He is a bit much."

"And so are the terms they are going to force on the Germans. The economic consequences will be devastating for decades to come."

"And rightly so. We won. They lost. And they should jolly well accept defeat like good losers. Now then, who is behind these letters and this nasty plot? They were all sent to Lady Assherton. Is she a traitor, after all? We thought it was someone within the Directorates. This makes no sense whatsoever."

At this point, Sherlock Holmes took over posing the questions.

"Is Her Ladyship going to be in Versailles on Friday?" he asked.

"Of course not."

"Is Captain Faulknor? Also known as the dead Captain Nichol."

"No. And how did you know about him?"

"Then who else has seen this letter?"

"Only myself and my secretary," said Sir basil.

"And are you planning to explode yourself on Friday morning."

"Don't be ridiculous."

"Then, having eliminated all other possibilities, who remains?"

"Only Bramwell Duponte. But that is unthinkable! He has been my loyal secretary for over a decade. I trust the man completely."

"Does he have family in Germany?" asked Holmes.

"In the German part of Switzerland, yes. But he hasn't been in touch with them for years . . . not since his grandfather emigrated from Zurich. He has no connection whatsoever with anyone in Switzerland, or in Germany. He is an Englishman through and through."

"Are you certain?" asked Holmes.

Sir Basil gave Holmes a hard look.

"By your question, Mr. Holmes, I perceive that you are not. Explain yourself."

"The paintings on his wall were done by Martha Burkhardt and Friedrich Eckenfelder. They are both contemporary Swiss-German artists. The Duponte family owns one of the largest shipping companies in the world. I'm quite certain that it was he who forged the false shipping documents. I suspect that you know that as well, Sir Basil."

"Yes, I do. It was part of the blind we set up to point the finger at Lady Assherton. But that doesn't mean he was part of the entire plot."

"Would you agree that the communicating of secret information didn't occur in one direction only? Is it highly likely, inevitable even, that secrets were revealed and sent in return to Fräulein Doktor?"

"Well, yes, I suppose that would make sense."

"Who had the opportunity to send such replies," asked Holmes, "other than yourself, sir?"

"Only my secretary. But see here, Mr. Holmes, Bramwell has had my complete confidence for a decade or more."

"And quite possibly was entirely trustworthy before August of 1914. After that date, I would remind you that blood is thicker than water."

"Mr. Holmes, you . . . you . . . ."

Sir Basil was visibly deflated and looked as if his chest had descended into his stomach.

"He has already departed for France," he muttered. "I will call ahead and have him detained as soon as he steps off the boat in Calais."

"Basil!" said Mycroft. "Use your head for more than a hat rack."

"Mycroft, that was not called for!"

"My dear Basil. You move with immediate speed to pounce and capture an escaped prisoner. You move with deliberate slowness when snatching a spy. Has no one ever told you that you tail a spy and wait until he has led you to his contacts, and *then* descend on both of them? What you need to do is have your men waiting for him at the lavatory, watch until he transfers the grenades, and then and only then make your move."

"Oh, yes. I suppose that makes more sense. I will have him brought back to England for interrogation."

"Considering," said Mycroft, "the gravity of the offense, the application of electricity to certain bodily appendages might be called for."

"Mycroft! We are a civilized country. We do not torture prisoners, not even if they are traitors."

"I agree. Then leave him with the French. They have no such qualms."

On Friday morning, 25 April of 1919, four men from that section of Military Intelligence that no one will acknowledge exists, assisted by a half-dozen gendarmes, waited in the vicinity of the lavatory in the southern arm of the *Palais de Versailles*. At precisely eight o'clock, a credentialed member of the British delegation entered the lavatory, carrying a valise. At five minutes after eight, a member of the maintenance staff of the *Palais,* who had been assigned to the care of the Hall of Mirrors, also entered.

At seven minutes after eight, the second man emerged, carrying the valise.

He did not get far.

Neither did Mr. Bramwell Duponte.

I have no idea what happened to either them after that, and I knew enough not to ask.

Had the plot been successful, leaders of thirty-one countries might have been assassinated. It would have been thirty-two, but the entire Italian delegation had walked out of the meetings on 24 April, disgruntled with their allocation of increased territory. They returned on 5 May.

On 29 April, Lady Lillian Assherton was released from hospital and returned to her home. There was no butler there to greet her, and she was, once again, despondent, after learning her sister's treachery and betrayal.

On 1 May, an elegantly packed parcel was delivered to a house on Chequer Street by a government driver. In it was a fine Wedgewood bowl along with a note from His Majesty thanking Her Ladyship for her stalwart patriotism.

She sent a note with her thanks to me and Holmes. We read it together over a glass of brandy in the bar of the Savoy.

"Watson," he said. "Fine work. We have won a final battle. We won the war. However, my dear old friend, I fear the center cannot hold. We may have lost the peace."

On 2 May, Sherlock Holmes returned to the Sussex Downs and his bees.

NOTES

From January to June of 1919, representatives of the Allied Powers met in Versailles engaged in The Paris Peace Conference. The final outcome was the *Treaty of Versailles.* Should you wish to know more about those fascinating days, you may wish to read *Paris 1919* by Margaret MacMillan.

During late April and early May, a sub-committee of the Allied Powers drafted Articles 231 and 232 of the Treaty. These assigned the entire guilt for The Great War to Germany and laid out the requirement for extensive financial reparations. A young economist assisting the British delegation warned that the terms were too punitive and that they threatened the entire future economies of Europe, including Britain. In December of 1919, he published his conclusions as *The Economic Consequences of the Peace.* His name was John Maynard Keynes.

Some historians have argued that these punishments were among the factors that led to the rise of fascism in Germany and eventually to Nazism, the Holocaust, and World War II.

Cotton shipments to England from the U.S. were disrupted during the war and supplies were restricted to those coming from Egypt. The government took over supply management and divided the imports amongst several mills in order to keep as many people as possible employed. Several of the great mills of the time were in Lancashire.

The Loyal North Lancashire Regiment served with distinction during many of the battles of World War I. They were present in the Battle of Passchendaele in November 1917, during which roughly half-a-million men died in a battle that accomplished next to nothing.

Elsbeth Schragmüller is a historical figure and served as described in the story as one of the master spies of Germany and as the trainer, the spies Germany sent into England, France, and the other Allied Powers. There are several fictionalized accounts of her exploits, including several movies. She did not have a sister in England. I made that up.

The reference to Edith Cavell is historically accurate. There is a mountain in Western Canada named in her honor. In August of 1965, I had the good fortune, as a teenager, to visit that mountain exactly fifty years to the day after her arrest. The description of it as "a massive, snow-covered mountain" was written by none other than Arthur Conan Doyle in his account of his visit to Jasper, Alberta in June, 1914.

Sir Basil Thomson is also a historical figure who had served with some distinction as the director of several of England's largest prisons. During the war, he was appointed as the head of the CID Division of Scotland Yard and as the head of the short-lived Intelligence Directorate that was housed within Scotland Yard. He gained renown for his success in capturing and convicting spies, including the interrogation of Mata Hari, whom he sent on to the French, who shot her. His reputation has been tarnished by his blatant anti-Semitism and other attitudes that are now considered unforgivable bigotry.

I have no idea if in 1919 *Simpson's on the Strand* rolled trollies to your table bearing massive cuts of roast beef or ham. However, they do today, and we were lucky to enjoy such a lunch in January of 2020. Highly recommended.

The Curse of the Roaring Tiger
by Nick Cardillo

I had traveled to the Sussex Coast for an extended weekend in the company of my friend, Mr. Sherlock Holmes, when we became entangled in one of the oddest and certainly most tragic investigations in the detective's long history. It is curious, as I look over my notes anew, that despite Holmes's retirement from public life, he did not retire his brain. Even as he tended to his bees on the Downs, he was ever the master reasoner, a thinking engine that could conjure up the solution to any problem that was presented to him. In my heart, I do believe that he relished this – Sherlock Holmes was never content to go the way of idleness. In his earlier days, a dearth of cases invariably led to black moods and his reliance upon artificial stimulants to rouse him from his doldrums and, though my friend's constitution had changed since then, at his core, Holmes still needed the cases just as much as his clients needed him to solve them.

It was a summer morning in the year 1919. The Great War had come to an end and England was healing itself. It was on days like that one that one could almost be forgiven for thinking the great conflict had never happened at all. The sun shone brightly and gulls called noisily over the seas as the waves crashed against the rocks. I could not think of a more perfect tableau. I was seated, enjoying a cup of coffee on the terrace of Holmes's cottage overlooking the Downs, while my companion bustled about in his study within. He emerged from the house a moment later clutching a stack of papers in his hands, tossing a manuscript down upon the table.

"I haven't been entirely indolent between my *other engagements*," he said with customary tact, referring to several missions that he'd recently undertaken at the best of his brother Mycroft and, by extension, the King himself. "That, my dear Watson," said Holmes pridefully, "is the sequel to my *magnum opus*. Another volume that shall be indispensable to apiarists everywhere."

I flipped through the pages – neatly handwritten and accompanied by more than one detailed diagram of the beehive and the honeycomb.

"Most interesting," I said. The topic was much above my head, but the excitement that was manifested upon my friend's countenance was infectious. Holmes looked ever the same, only a touch of grey in the hair and a few lines of age about the face betraying his advancing years.

"I do hope," Holmes said, slipping into a chair across the table from me and reaching for his pipe, "that you would do me the service of reading the thing over. I am, alas, no wordsmith like you. My humble attempts to follow in your footsteps and recount some of my own little exploits have met with less-than-favorable early notices from those who have read them."

"I had no idea that you'd taken to writing," I said. "This is news to me indeed!"

Holmes lit his pipe, his head encircled in pipe smoke as he shooed away my words, with a flick of the wrist. "They were trivialities," he replied. "Few would rank the exploit of the Blanched Soldier among my loftiest success. Have no fear, my dear Watson, I leave the care of my adventures in your capable hands."

"I do wish that you had shared these tales with me," I said. "Who has had the pleasure of reading them?"

"Curiously enough, here comes one of those distinguished few now."

My gaze followed Holmes's as he observed a short, stout figure ambling his way along the back path. He too was advancing in years, a short crop of grey hair peeking out from beneath the brim of a battered hat. As he neared, I observed his clerical collar and the look of anxiety that was etched into his aging skin.

"Thank goodness you are here, Mr. Holmes," the cleric said. My friend rose in greeting.

"Your arrival is felicitous in the extreme," he replied. "Watson, allow me to introduce you to the Reverend Julius Salt, in whose company I've had the pleasure of spending many an afternoon. I do hope, Reverend, that you don't mind my company, and you aren't simply after jars of my honey."

The reverend mustered a grin with what seemed Herculean effort. "It is a pleasure to meet you, Dr. Watson," he said to me. "I've followed your accounts of Mr. Holmes's work for many years. I do wish that our meeting could come under better circumstances."

"And what tragedy it is that brings you to my door?" asked Holmes, gesturing for the man to take the vacant chair. He did so, sitting hunched forward on the chair, the fingers of his hands interlocked in anxiety.

91

"It is no less than work of the Devil," said Reverend Salt.

We were surrounded with silence for an instant – as though time itself stopped and the gulls wheeling above us ceased to call. Sherlock Holmes pulled on his pipe and leaned forward in his chair, a familiar look springing up in his eyes.

"Perhaps you ought to explain."

Reverend Salt drew in a deep breath. "To do that, sir, I shall have to go back a great many years. I haven't bothered you with much local folklore, Mr. Holmes, as I realize well enough that shall things are mere trivialities to you. Fairy stories are of little interest, and though I too regard such with dubious aspect, I know that many of the villagers have taken these stories to heart. There are tales aplenty in these parts of the unexplained – ghosts and ghouls and pirates whose ships crashed on these rocks many moons ago, and whose spirits wander in search of their lost treasure. I know for a fact that Mrs. Higgins in the village believes to have seen one of these specters on the shore, and her superstition is emblematic of so many of the people in these parts.

"One such story that has gained some modicum of infamy in this area," the reverend continued, "concerns a man – a very real man, the town records from two centuries ago attest to that – called Jacob Cicero. He was something of a despot who lived here, lusting after some of the local young women, and was reputed to have practiced witchcraft. One night, after the gruesome death of a local girl, suspicion naturally fell upon him. The town flocked to his door, breaking it down and hauling the man out of his house and into the street. They found the nearest tree and, taking up a length of rope, one man climbed a ladder and hanged Cicero from the highest branch."

"Horrific," I said.

"It is true, Doctor," Reverend Salt agreed. "However, before he was killed, Cicero put a curse on those who killed him. He said that all those who had taken part in the lynching would go uneasy to their graves and, it seems, that Cicero's words have come to fruition. In the days, weeks, months, and years that followed, a great number of the town fell ill, many dying. Mysterious accidents befell several others. At the center of many of these inexplicable happenings was an item of great curiosity – the ladder that was used to hang Jacob Cicero. It seemed that whoever climbed that ladder met with a horrific fate shortly after ascending it. The ladder changed hands over the centuries, and each owner fell victim to its strange curse.

"This all brings us to yesterday afternoon. As it happens, the ladder is now the property of the landlord of the Tiger Inn, Mr. Stokes. As you are doubtlessly aware, Mr. Holmes, Stokes has been an upstanding member of the community for a number of years and, according to him, four years ago he came across a ladder in the possession a neighbor who had passed away. Having a feeling about the ladder, Stokes recognized it for what it was, and had it installed over the bar in the inn – as a curiosity. There, he said, no one would be able to climb it, and at last the curse of Jacob Cicero would be brought to an end. However, tragedy occurred yesterday. Stokes and the rest of his household – his two daughters, Eve and Melody – were welcoming home his son, George, who had served in France during the war. George had been wounded just before the Armistice and has been recovering in hospital for many months. It was the opinion of his doctors that George was shell-shocked like so many unfortunate young men who came back from the front.

"George returned yesterday afternoon and was warmly received by the family. Stokes even closed the pub early so that the family might properly welcome him. It was the first time that the whole family had been together under one roof since before the war. George, of course, had been serving in France and, for much of the war, Stokes's eldest daughter, Eve, had been in America. She only returned last Christmas and was equally and warmly-received by the village. It should have been a day of great celebration, but it turned black very quickly. Stokes was called away from the inn while the two women and George made preparations for that evening's festivities. Melody says that she heard George say something about the state of the inn's sign – one that depicts the image of a roaring tiger – and a few moments later, she, upstairs in the family's living quarters, heard George leave the inn. Almost immediately, they heard a terrible sound and, rushing downstairs, she discovered that George had taken the ladder down from over the bar. Running outside, they discovered their brother dead – having fallen from the ladder while trying to clean the sign. Stokes had been doing some gardening earlier in the day and, at the foot of the ladder, he had left a wheelbarrow, a rake laid across it. Poor George Stokes had fallen to his death, impaled on the points of the rake.

"The curse of Jacob Cicero had claimed another victim."

"A tragedy," I murmured. "A true tragedy."

"Reverend Salt," said Holmes after several moments of silent consideration, "am I to understand that you are won over by this supernatural solution? That the curse of this warlock Jacob Cicero is

93

real and has claimed the lives of God-only-knows how many villagers over the past two centuries?"

"I do not know, Mr. Holmes," the cleric replied. "I fear that something unexplainable is responsible for poor George Stokes's death. Inspector Mackenzie of the local constabulary has begun an investigation. Of course, he believes that the matter is simply an unhappy accident, and I'm inclined to agree with his presentment, but I knew that if there's a man alive who can shed some light on this terrible business, it's you."

"I'm flattered by your assessment of my powers," Holmes said. "Nonetheless, if the Devil himself is somehow involved in this matter, then I should imagine that you are more suited to combating the evil than I. However," he considered, "if a more cogent agent is involved, then I shall do all in my power to find out what is at its source. I am no stranger to Inspector Mackenzie," he continued. "Perhaps I ought to invite the young detective around for a few words?"

Holmes disappeared inside and made a telephone call. Within the hour, our party was joined by the youngish inspector whose acquaintance I had made during the strange case of the Weeping Stone, the particulars I have drawn up elsewhere. I knew the animosity that still persisted between Holmes and the young man – Holmes thinking him to be an arrogant and cocksure representative of the law, the other thinking my friend to be an aging meddler whose days of interfering in police matters ought to have been long behind him. Both were at their cordial best that afternoon, however, Holmes proffering the inspector a glass of cognac which was gratefully accepted. The reverend and the inspector spoke of village matters for some little time while Holmes repacked his pipe in relative silence.

"I expect that you'll be wanting to know about the tragedy at the Tiger Inn," said Mackenzie with more than a touch of vehemence in his tone, "though I must assure you, Mr. Holmes, this is one case where it simply cannot be murder. Unfortunate as the circumstances may be, George Stokes simply slipped from that ladder while trying to clean the inn's sign. The placement of that wheelbarrow and rake at the foot of the ladder was an unhappy accident. It is a tragedy, sir, but I do not think that you'll be able to make a case that anything untoward is afoot."

"So you give no credence to the tales of Jacob Cicero's death and the curse he put on this village?"

94

"Of course not, Mr. Holmes," Inspector Mackenzie replied. "If I had a shilling for every ghostly apparition that someone claims to have seen here, I should be a very wealthy man and I could retire in peace tomorrow afternoon. I cannot – and will not – cloud my judgment with tales of bogeys, you understand, and I do admit that I find it rather odd that you should elect to do, sir."

"You misunderstand," Holmes said waving his pipe. "I wish to merely appraise the landscape in which I move. It's simplicity itself to chalk up George Stokes's death, and the many that no doubt preceded his, upon that ladder as accidents. And even without possession of all the facts, I can pass judgment that that is exactly the case." Holmes pulled on his pipe. "However," he added darkly, "do you not wish to lay this ghost to rest? If you, Inspector, can divine the precise circumstances of Stokes's death, then perhaps the supposed curse of Jacob Cicero shall be lifted forever. To that end, perhaps you can share with me what you gathered from your investigation thus far?"

Inspector Mackenzie reached for a little notebook. "There are few facts by which you can begin your theorizing," he said, "but I shall tell you what little I know. Mr. Stokes was away from the Tiger Inn altogether. He had been working in the garden outside that morning and had decamped to the home of another villager to gather up a few supplies for that evening's celebration. He admits to having left the wheelbarrow and the rake outside, and says that he had intentions of restoring them to his toolshed upon his return. Inside the building itself, Stokes's youngest daughter, Melody, says that she was in the storage room in the inn's basement gathering up supplies. The floorboards, aged and creaking as they are, gave her some idea of what her brother was doing upstairs and, what is more, she says that she had the door to the storeroom open. She heard her brother announce that he was tired of looking at the dirty sign and that he was going to do something about it. Melody had no idea that anything was the matter until she heard her sister running down the stairs and shouting to her. She met Eve in the pub, and from there they rushed outside and discovered the grisly scene.

"This is all corroborated by Eve Stokes's testimony. By her own admission, she was upstairs at the time of the accident. The family's living quarters are above the pub, occupying the largest room at the inn. She had a window open, and was standing at the stove popping some corn for that evening's celebration. It is an American custom, which she brought back with her to England.

Nonetheless, she heard her brother fall and then rushed outside with her sister."

Holmes pulled on his pipe intently. "You have aroused my suspicions, Inspector."

The policeman drained his teacup. "And what has provoked you so, Mr. Holmes?"

"Eve Stokes does not say that she heard her brother cry out. That is singular. A man who slipped and lost his footing on that ladder would surely have cried as he fell."

"As peculiar as that may be," the representative of the law said, "I fail to see how that proves that George Stokes's death was anything other than an accident."

Holmes held an index aloft. "I never suggested that it was anything more than an accident, Inspector," he said bluntly. "I was merely indicating a point of interest in this case. I rather think that there is more here than meets the eye."

Inspector Mackenzie said little in response to my friend's claim. He thanked us courteously for the refreshment that Holmes had provided and then bustled away. Shortly thereafter, the reverend too took his leave, but only after Holmes had assured him that he would do all he could to look into the matter. The cleric seemed much relieved as he departed, leaving Holmes and I seated in silence, both lost in thought. It was just gone noon when Holmes laid aside his pipe and stood.

"Sitting about," he announced, "shall do us no good, Watson. No good at all. We must, like days of old, apply our methods to the scene itself. What say you – would a short walk tax you unduly?"

I replied in the negative and, after collecting our hats and sticks, we set out along the main road into nearby East Dean, the location of the Tiger Inn. As we walked, Holmes remained oddly quiet, his face drawn of emotion. He looked quite unlike the determined investigator at whose side I had shared so many adventures. I pressed him for information but he remained reticent. Finally he turned to me and asked what I thought of the case. I told him that my professional opinion aligned with that of the official representative: The death of George Stokes, tragic as it was, possessed all the hallmarks of an unfortunate accident, and I found it odd that Holmes seemed intent on making something more of it than it was. In response, he clicked his tongue derisively.

"Tut, tut, Watson, I am doing no such thing. I'm inclined to agree. George Stokes did meet his end in a particularly nasty turn of fate. However, I suspect there is something deeper here than a man simply slipping from that ladder. The circumstances suggest a scene that is altogether darker and infinitely more tragic."

"You aren't suggesting," I said, "that there is some credibility to the reverend's tale of the curse of Jacob Cicero? Surely you haven't taken leave of your senses? That a ladder could deal death to all those that ascend it is surely impossible. Posterity hasn't recorded the tens – possibly hundreds – of men who have climbed that same ladder and lived to tell the tale."

"You are right in every particular," said Holmes. "I don't credit Cicero's curse in this matter. Nonetheless, something did happen to George Stokes on that ladder, and what it was is what I intend to find out. Ah, here we are."

The Tiger Inn is a humble dwelling, unremarkable in almost every way. However, I looked on it now with the knowledge that a terrible fate had befallen one of its occupants, and I read only sorrow and death in its bricks and mortar. What should have been a cheerful, seaside inn – a haven for tourists and residents – was now a veritable monument to tragedy. I strained to overcome the negative connotations – a feat of which Sherlock Holmes seemed quite capable. He was standing back admiring the building, his eyes traveling up the wall to an open window, and back across to the front door over which hung its sign hanging on two rusted spokes. It was faded with age, but still clearly depicted the form of a great tiger's head, its mouth open as its massive, pointed teeth seemed to scream out at the world. Above the portrait of the roaring tiger were the words *The Tiger Inn* written in bold, black capitols.

My study of the sign was interrupted a second later by the voice of a young woman calling to us. I looked up and saw the form of a pretty young lady in the open window. From meeting her many times before, I recognized her as Eve Stokes, the daughter who had traveled to the United States. She was plainly dressed, but that seemed to accentuate her youthful features which were clouded with tragedy.

"Miss Stokes," Holmes called up. The young woman nodded her head. "Doctor Watson and I are here to offer our condolences."

She informed us that the door was open and we stepped through. We were greeted within and followed the woman up a cramped staircase to the first floor, where we were shown into the Stokes family living quarters. Although Spartanly furnished, the family seemed to have a quite comfortable arrangement. A table was tucked in the corner of the room and beside it a stove. On the opposite side of the room, overtop a basin, was the open window from which the young woman had just spoken to us.

"I regret that we aren't here under better circumstances," Holmes said. "And I am sorry that you and your brother each haven't had a better homecoming."

Eve Stokes nodded. "I've only been back in England for a few months now. I was overjoyed, however, when I learned that I would be joined so soon by George. He saw even less of England than I did. He was only back for a day before . . . before . . . ." Her voice trailed off. "I do apologize, gentlemen."

"No need, Miss Stokes," I said. "What part of America did you visit? I had a number of acquaintances there, you know."

I distracted the girl with talk of America for some few minutes, during which time Holmes stood and made a turn around the little room. "Miss Stokes," he said at length, "if you think you can manage it, I should like to put to you a question or two regarding your brother's death."

"If I can be of help, Mr. Holmes." Her eyes grew wide. "You're suggesting that George was murdered?"

"On the contrary," Holmes said raising his hands in protestation. "I'm certain that your brother met with an unhappy accident."

"Yes," she said. "He was the victim of that horrible curse. The curse of Jacob Cicero. I take it you gentlemen have heard the tale told?"

"We have, Miss Stokes, and we don't put much credence in it. However, I should like to clarify a point: You claim that you heard your brother fall from the ladder. However, from the position of the stove relative to the window and the sign outside, which we are to understand that he was cleaning at the time of his death, then I fail to see how you couldn't have *seen* your brother too. Did you perhaps see something, Miss Stokes, that you didn't tell Inspector Mackenzie?"

The young woman wrung her hands. "Yes," she said at length. "I did see something. I couldn't tell a soul, though, for fear that I should be thought mad. You see, Mr. Holmes, I have proof that my brother was the victim of the curse."

Throughout the many years that Sherlock Holmes and I spent together, moments of great revelation were no strange occurrence. There always seemed to be an instance when, in the midst of an investigation, someone would reveal something that flipped the case

98

on its head, invariably sending us away on a new course. However, in all of those scenarios, I think few had such a profound impact upon me as that moment sitting in the Stokes's room in the Tiger Inn. I'll wager that the same effect was felt upon Holmes for, though he had been standing, staring out of the open window, he turned now to face Miss Eve Stokes with the inevitable portentousness of a condemned man going to his death. The detective's face was drawn, utterly inscrutable. The young woman's was also long. She suddenly appeared aged, as though the revelation had snatched from her youth itself. Great sorrow welled up within my breast. Tears manifested in her eyes and I proffered my handkerchief.

"Thank you, Doctor," she said, dabbing away the tears. She composed herself after a moment. "I'm sure you think me mad, Mr. Holmes, but if I live to be a hundred, I shall never ever forget what I saw yesterday. For fear that Inspector Mackenzie would put me down as a raving lunatic, I said nothing to him, but I saw it, Mr. Holmes. I saw my brother die."

Elation, or something masquerading as its exact twin, danced in Holmes's grey eyes. He subdued himself and moved across the room swiftly, spryly kneeling and taking the young woman's hand as though he were a man half his own age.

"Please, Miss Stokes," he said, "will you tell us what it is you saw? I can assure you that I shall not judge you for anything that you share with me, and what you say shall be held in the strictest confidence until such time that it may be of use."

Eve Stokes cleared my throat. "It's simple enough, Mr. Holmes," she began, "but the simplicity of it all makes it ten times more terrifying. I was in this very room, preparing for the evening celebration. George was with me. I was trying to persuade him to indulge in the making of some paper hats for the occasion. I thought that he would like that. He was seated on the windowsill and we both sat joking and teasing one another. With his back to the window, he suddenly leaned back and cast a glance at the pub sign hanging just a few feet away. 'Ugh, Evie,' he said, 'when will Dad clean that damned sign?' He stood and started off down the stairs. I called after him, telling him I was just going to pop some corn for the occasion, and he told me that no, he was off to clean the sign. 'If you want a thing done right,' he said, 'then I suppose you have got to do it yourself.'

"Well, I grabbed a pot and filled it with kernels. I lit the flame in the stove and set the pot there to pop. A moment later, I saw George climb into view on the ladder, take a rag out of his back pocket, and begin to clean the sign. The corn began to pop as I bustled about, and I was just turning to tend to it when I caught sight of George. His face was blank, his eyes wide and staring at some point beyond me. I turned to look and see what he was fixed upon so intently, but I saw only the back wall. It was as if he was possessed, Mr. Holmes. And then, a moment later, he seemed to lull backwards, as if pushed by an invisible hand, and he fell from the ladder without a sound. That was the very last that I saw of my brother. I screamed and rushed down the stairs. Melody, in the cellar, heard me and we rushed out into the yard . . . where we found him."

A new onslaught of tears welled up in her eyes and strangled her words. Sherlock Holmes stood and turned to stare at the back wall. I followed his gaze and was met with only a bare white expanse. What could George Stokes have seen? Or, I considered as my reasoning wandered further from the realm of possibility, what had overcome him? Could the cursed ladder indeed have claimed another victim? The very possibility sent a chill down my back.

"Miss Stokes," said Holmes in his most hushed, compassionate tone. "I cannot thank you enough for this intelligence. Beyond that, I wish you my most sincere condolences."

"I wish that he had waited," she cried. "If only he had waited, perhaps I could have stopped him. Father hung that horrible ladder over the bar four years ago while George was away. I was lucky enough to be told the legend as soon as I returned. With the preparations for the happy day, we never thought that we should ruin it with talk of witchcraft, curses, and death. Oh, if only we had!"

"In all my experience," Holmes murmured as we descended the stairs to the inn's ground floor again, "I have never encountered a tragedy the likes of this one. There are forces at work here, Watson, that are beyond the comprehension of man."

"You really have been won over by this supernatural talk," I sputtered incredulously.

"No," my companion rebuked darkly. "I talk of Fate. It was Fate that manipulated the pieces on the board so that they should intersect with truly horrific results. Ah, unless I am much mistaken, we're about to encounter the bereaved father, and I shall make everything plain."

The door to the inn opened and a large, broad-shouldered man stepped through, a petite woman at his arm. I had known him for several years, and knew that he had once been a hale and hearty fellow, but he looked tired and drawn, with purple rings beneath his bloodshot eyes, their present condition brought about by tiredness or tears – I couldn't tell. His hair was white and he looked every year of his advanced age, though ordinarily he looked anything but. The young woman resembled her pater as well as her elder sister. Upon their entrance, the old man's eyes went wide.

"Well, if it isn't Mr. Holmes," he said. "And Doctor Watson."

"You have our sincerest condolences, Mr. Stokes," I replied.

The man hung his head and wordlessly crossed the room, the air of a deflated balloon hanging about him. He sat down at a stool before the bar, cupping and uncapping his hands.

"I suppose," he said, his voice cold, "that you're here, Mr. Holmes, because you suspect some deviltry in my son's death? Have you come to see that he died as the result of the terrible curse that has hung over his village for centuries?" The poor man huffed. "It's almost funny," he said. "George lived through four years of being shot at in the war. He lived through an ordeal in hospital. He lived through all of that, only to die here at his home in the simplest accident imaginable."

Stokes stared hard at the face of his younger daughter, Melody. "I really do blame myself, you know. I should have taken that wheelbarrow back to the tool shed when I was finished with it. Maybe – just maybe – if I had done that, and George had still fallen, he would have lived. But, that damned curse . . . it's truly hopeless."

"I can assure you, Mr. Stokes," said Holmes, "that your son didn't die because of a curse. He was merely the victim of the perfect set of circumstances that could only have ended in his death."

"What do you mean?" asked the publican coldly.

"I shall make everything plain to you," replied my companion, "but I must first insist on inviting Reverend Salt and Inspector Mackenzie. They deserve to hear the thing through to the end, and then perhaps we shall lay the ghost of Jacob Cicero at last."

A quarter-of-an-hour later, we were all assembled within the comforting confines of the inn. Usually I have found the place homey and inviting, but the atmosphere of the pub was cold and clinical. Mr. Stokes had remained unmoving in his seat since his return. His two daughters bustled about, tending to duties as both the reverend and the inspector arrived after just a few moments. Once we were all seated, Sherlock Holmes stood and began to speak.

"I shall make it plain to all," he began, "that there is and never has been any curse. Dr. Watson could not have spoken more aptly when he said that history has failed to record every instance when a man climbed the supposedly cursed ladder used to kill Jacob Cicero and lived to tell about it. It would be nigh impossible to keep such a record. We can, therefore, dispel any notion of the supernatural from our subsequent investigation.

"As I've intimated from the beginning, the circumstances of yesterday afternoon led to the inevitability that George Stokes would die. It was fated that he should fall from that ladder and land on the rake that his father left out in the garden. What no one has questioned is *what precipitated George Stokes's fall from that ladder*? The simplest explanation was that he merely slipped and fell. However, according to Miss Eve Stokes, only a few minutes earlier, her brother had been seated on the windowsill of their living room upstairs, perched on the sill like a bird on a branch. A man with such a keen sense of balance one moment seems unlikely to slip from the ladder only a few moments later. We return then to the question I raised: Why did George Stokes fall from the ladder?"

Silence fell over the room. Holmes leveled his gaze at Eve Stokes. "You, Miss Stokes," he said, "ought to know."

"What do you mean?" she cried. "Are you implying something, Mr. Holmes?"

"Not in the least," said Holmes. "I merely suggest that you hold the answer to my question and you answered it yourself earlier today. What were you doing while your brother stood outside on the ladder? You were popping corn for that evening's celebration. You just so happened to be doing it at the exact moment your brother was up on the ladder and, according to your own testimony, his eyes went wide, his face blank, as he stared at some point in the distance."

The detective was met with the same frosty silence. "It is no secret," he continued, "that George Stokes was wounded in the war and had to recuperate for several months in hospital. Reverend Salt informed me this morning that George was suffering from shell-shock. No doubt, to a man with a fragile, recovering constitution, the sound of corn popping so near his ears – a sound that he's probably never heard before, as the tradition of popping corn is enjoyed rather more in America than here in England – reminded him of the sound of gunfire.

"Though my complete grasp of the specifics is beyond my reach, I do believe that in that moment, your brother imagined himself back in the trenches. He was under assault and, in a panic, his mind and body simply shut down. You witnessed it, Miss Stokes, without even noticing it. You said that he appeared to fall backwards, which hardly accords with the actions of a man who has lost his footing on the rungs of a ladder. As Mr. Stokes suggested, perhaps if the garden tools hadn't been below the ladder, his son's life would have been saved. But as I've outlined, Fate had other ideas."

The chilly atmosphere of the room only grew colder. George Stokes's father stared at a spot on the floor while his two daughters grasped hands in solidarity, fresh wells of tears springing up in their eyes. The Reverend Salt stared with a gloomy expression on his face, which was mirrored in the countenance of the young inspector. He suddenly looked not so habitually boyish and young. He was the first to rise after a spell of what seemed like eternity.

"I shall," he said, "fill out the requisite paperwork concerning this matter and it shall be dealt with speedily. This tragedy shall not have to haunt you on my end, Mr. Stokes."

Mr. Stokes, a man I'm sure seldom shed a tear in his life, breathed heavily through his large nose. "But it will still haunt me," he said.

"Come, Watson," said Holmes touching my arm. "Let us leave this family in peace."

And so we departed from the Tiger Inn, vainly trying to leave behind the memories of the tragedy that now hung over it. I stopped only for a moment on my way out, turning back to cast a glance once more up at the sign of the roaring tiger. Half of the image, I noticed now, though faded in the sun, was dark and coated with dirt and grim.

The other half was spotlessly clean.

The Search for
Mycroft's Successor
by Chris Chan

As much as it pains me to admit it, none of us are immortal. Sooner or later we all must leave this world and face whatever comes next. In the months following the Armistice at the conclusion of the Great War, I found that I was not the only one reflecting on the fact that all of our times must come to an end. While every life has value, some admittedly have a deeper impact than others on the fates of nations. This was the case with Mycroft, Sherlock Holmes's elder brother.

When a monarch dies, the heir to the throne is always in waiting. As much as Britons may revere their best kings and queens, deep in all of our minds is the unspoken realization that all crowned heads are replaceable, and the line of succession is well-known. But there are other individuals who are genuinely and unquestionably indispensable. One such man is Mycroft Holmes.

He had invited us to his rooms a few months after the signing of the Treaty of Versailles. It was a time when most were relieved, even jubilant, in the knowledge that the long years of war were over, and peace was restored. From the expression on Mycroft's face, he was nowhere near relaxed. His eyes had the fog of a man who hadn't slept as much as he ought to have, and his clothes appeared rather tight, as if the already corpulent man had turned to his favorite foods in order to assuage the stress that was evident in his demeanor.

Holmes sized up his brother's mental state with a swift up-and-down glance. "I can see that you've been worrying lately, my dear brother."

"Can you blame me, Sherlock?"

"I most certainly cannot. The last four years have been a terrible strain for most people. It must have been exponentially horrible for the man who at times, to all intents and purposes, *is* the British Government."

"The world could have been spared a great many needless deaths and sleepless nights if the Prime Minister had not sidelined me at the worst possible time in 1914," Mycroft groaned. "Those fools informed me that they had no further need of my services, gave me a miniscule pension and a gold watch that loses two minutes every hour, and then, not two weeks after the start of hostilities, called me back to work without so much as a "Please". I have spent the last years trying to clean up their messes and prevent the nation from crumbling, and now that the wretched war has finally ended, those silly diplomats have put together a so-called "peace" treaty that will lead to yet another massive war within a generation. Possibly I may be able to assuage the situation, or maybe delay the horrors for several more years, but I doubt it very much." Mycroft sagged back in his chair, and he looked far older, more exhausted, and weaker than I had ever seen him.

"Cheer up," I informed him. "I'm sure that all will turn out for the best."

I had never seen so much pure contempt in Mycroft's face. "No, Doctor, it will not! I am not a particularly vain man, but I know for a fact that without me, England will not be able to withstand another terrible war. I'm not flattering myself when I assert that my presence is necessary to the nation's survival. And I will not live forever. I have never fussed much over my health, and it is too late to start now. I may have another year or two in me, perhaps another couple of decades if I'm extraordinarily lucky, but eventually, I will meet my Maker and there will be no one to take my place. We cannot trust our statesmen to handle the increasingly volatile situation. I need a replacement for myself. I cannot rest until I know that when I finally pass on, the nation will be in sound hands.

"I'm too busy with my work to launch a search of my own. That is why I have summoned you today. Find my successor. Search England for the best and the brightest, and when you believe that you have found a man – a young man, mind you, one who will be able to handle this job for decades to come – convince him to come work for me. We need someone with a mind sufficiently clever and dexterous to handle all of the complexities connected to managing the intricacies of the British government. This is a full-time job, so we need someone willing to devote his entire life to this project, preferably one who is content to forgo the distractions of a wife and children as well so he can focus on his work."

Mycroft shifted his weight in his chair and took a long sip from a glass of water on the table beside him. "I have never regretted not marrying – at least, not until now. Perhaps I might have had a son who could have taken over this position. Then again, I might have been too overwhelmed by the duties of fatherhood to have saved England from hundreds of near disasters. In any case, dear Brother, you know as well as I do that intelligence of the kind that the two of us possess does not necessarily pass from father to son. We have many clever fellows in our family, and one or two might make fine detectives like yourself, but none of them have the brain stamina and calculating abilities to take over my role in the government. In any event, it's likely that I might have sired an utter dunderhead, fit for nothing more cranially strenuous that the easy life of a country squire. And that would have done us no good whatsoever in this situation."

"Have you come across anyone in your work who might be able to take on the duties of your protégé, Mycroft?" Holmes asked.

"None. The British Civil Service is filled with a handful of smart men and a great many workaday pudding-heads. Many are called out of a sincere desire to serve their country, but men of the kind of inspired genius that we need are nonexistent." Mycroft drank more water. "I trust that you will not think me arrogant by using that word to describe the brainpower that is essential for this position, but it is a simple fact that one needs a certain kind of mind to handle the facts, figures, and intricacies of my job. When I created this position for myself, I observed a need and chose to fill it. At the time, I didn't realize how essential I would become to the well-being of England, nor did I ever suspect the seeming impossibility of teaching someone else how to perform this job. But it must be done, and you, Brother, are the only one who has the wherewithal to find a worthy man."

"Or woman," I suggested.

"Don't be ridiculous," Mycroft snapped at me.

"What about Bancroft?" I asked, referring to one of the brilliant Pons brothers. "He's already employed by the government – doing much of your work already. Or so I understood."

Mycroft shook his head. "He has already made himself too invaluable in his own areas of expertise. To disengage him from those and have him take my place would cause as many problems as it solves."

"Do you have any suggestions on how to proceed?" Holmes asked.

"Nothing that will significantly improve success. I know of only three young men who might have the brains to take on the position. One is from southern China, another lives in northern India, and the third calls the American Midwest home. But they are all loyal to their current nations, and two of them already have large families. None of them will be persuaded to come to England and

106

serve our interests. That means that you can limit your search to our country. I have initiated a study of the students and recent graduates of our nation's universities and best schools, and though we have lots of able men – "

"None of them are what we are looking for," Holmes finished.

"Precisely. And you, dear Brother, would not find my intellectually stimulating yet physically sedentary job to your tastes. Is there no one of your acquaintance that springs to mind?"

"No specific living person. There was one man who might have managed this epic task, but he chose to devote his incredible abilities to more destructive habits. However – "

"Of course!" A glint flashed in Mycroft's eyes. "I wondered if you would consider that possibility, Sherlock. It is possible that a member of his extended family might be up to the task, if genetics are any guide – which, as I mentioned earlier, is not always the case."

"But we must be careful. While some of them may have the ability, I doubt that most of them have the character necessary for the job. Indeed, that is the curse of that family. The decent, moral members of that family uniformly have pedestrian, mediocre minds. In contrast, the most brilliant individuals with the name in question are dangerous. Upon reflection, I can think of one man from that family, who at thirty-nine probably isn't too old for our purposes, and who could very likely learn how to take over your job . . . but he would use it to take over the nation as well. Within ten years, Parliament would be his puppets, and he would be the dictator of England, and possibly of most of Western Europe as well."

"You have maintained your files on that family?"

"Of course. I'm forever on the lookout for the possibility that one will follow in their patriarch's infamous footsteps."

Holmes went into another room and spent ten minutes making telephone calls. Soon afterwards, the two of us were in a car heading to the West End. "Holmes," I asked, "are you seriously considering turning over England's security and stability to a Moriarty?"

"I can assure, Watson, that I am *not* exploring this possibility lightly. No one is more aware than I am of how dangerous a Moriarty can be. I'm also aware that while intelligence may be passed on from one generation to the next, there is no scientific proof that criminality is inherited as well. In any case, most of the Moriarty family is composed of harmless blockheads. Colonel James Moriarty was a man of no great ability, but he rose in the ranks thanks to the well-hidden intervention of his brother, the Professor. The Colonel's main claim to fame is an insistence that his brother was completely innocent, and that I am a malicious fool who slandered an innocent man. Their other brother, the stationmaster James – "

"I can't understand why the Moriarty family named all three brothers James."

"It is a family tradition. Most male members of the family go by their middle names. In any case, Stationmaster James is a decent enough man, who has no particular aptitude for anything in particular save for crossword puzzles. Meanwhile, the children of Colonel and Stationmaster have reached adulthood, and their mental abilities are a mixed bag. Both brothers have three children. The Colonel has two daughters, one of whom is an amiable featherbrain, and the other is woman of rare intelligence who is unhappily married to a philanderer. I might consider this woman for the position, were it not for the fact that she has devised no less than four brilliant schemes to murder her husband and put the blame on his latest mistress, and it is only thorough my own fortunate intervention that her plans have never succeeded. The couple has separated many times, yet for reasons I cannot understand, a reconciliation inevitably follows a couple of weeks later."

"And the Colonel's third child is a son?"

"Yes. James Albert Moriarty is an actor, and he is currently taking on a part that is made for him – the role of his uncle, Professor Moriarty – in one of those endless revivals of that play by William Gillette very loosely based on my career."

"An actor? Do you really think that he has the ability to replace Mycroft?"

"I grant you that his talents lie in the creative arts, but he is surprisingly talented. His Iago was a minor sensation, and he has risen to fame as a skilled portrayer of villains. I have attended a couple of his performances before the war, and he has a certain amount of charisma, but more important, he has imagination. I believe that he is consistently able to bring a fresh and innovative approach to a well-known character, which shows a certain level of innovation and an ability to take the familiar and make it fresh."

"Could that ability be applied to handling the affairs of government?"

"It has been my experience, Watson, that creativity is a great asset when it is combined with logic and extensive knowledge. Albert – I shall refer to him by his middle name for the sake of clarity – has never been to university, and he is primarily an autodidact. I know that he studied the history of ancient Rome extensively for his preparation of the role of Brutus in Julius Caesar. He served in the military before being wounded and sent home after four months, and he has no known attachments, either romantic or those of ordinary friendship. His fellow actors consider him talented but distant. He is respected as a thespian but not particularly well-liked as a person."

"But can an actor perform Mycroft's duties?"

"From what I've heard, he has taken an active role in the management duties of one performing company, where he managed to clean up their financial situation and eliminated their debt. A stunning achievement, especially for those working in the dramatic arts. Again, I need to view this with some skepticism. There may be something less-than-honest behind the company's sudden solvency. We shall see."

Moments later, we arrived at a small, shabby-looking theater and walked inside. When we asked to see Albert Moriarty (it should be noted that he performed under a stage name, but for reasons of clarity I have chosen to refer to him by his real moniker), we were told he had not yet arrived, but would within the hour. Holmes asked to wait in the manager's office and, after slipping the stage manager two one-pound notes, we were allowed inside.

"What are you looking for?" I asked as Holmes started rifling through the papers on a desk.

As he withdrew a ledger from under a stack of assorted playbills and posters, Holmes explained, "Financial records. If this is what I hope to find . . . ." His voice trailed off as he flipped through the pages, running his finger along columns. I could see the calculations flashing in his eyes as he totaled the numbers in his mind.

I said nothing for nearly thirty minutes, until a knock on the door snapped Holmes out of his reflections, and he shoved the ledger back under a pile of paper just as the door opened. The stage manager informed us that the man for whom we were looking had arrived, and we were led to a dimly lit dressing room.

Albert Moriarty was sprawled out in a chair, with a silver-headed cane across his knees. "Ah! Sherlock Holmes! Have you come to play yourself on the stage? That certainly would be a boon to ticket sales. I wish I'd thought of it earlier."

"That isn't why I am here," Holmes said as he lowered himself onto a rickety-looking bench. I didn't think that it would support my weight as well, so I leaned against the corner walls.

"A pity. I should have liked to have been paired against you on the stage. And you as well, Dr. Watson," he told me with an expression that I thought was a combination of a leer and a sneer.

109

"Wouldn't it be wonderful to have the three of us on stage together? You as yourselves, and me as my illustrious relative?"

"Illustrious?" I snorted.

Albert shrugged. "I chose my words without much thought. He was a magnificent man, even if he was a criminal. Most of our politicians are like that. Power-hungry, unscrupulous, and caring nothing for other people. Yet because they have managed to persuade people to cast ballots for them, they are respected, while my relative is now one of history's greatest villains. He could have been Prime Minister if he'd set his mind that way. But he wouldn't have been happy pandering to constituents or his party. He'd have much preferred to have been king, but monarchs don't have any real power these days anyway. So maybe it was best that he made his mark on the world in the way he did."

"As a criminal and murderer?" I asked before I could regain control of the tone of my voice.

Luckily, Albert didn't seem offended. "Well, if you're going to be judgmental about it . . . ." He leaned back in his chair and kicked up his legs, resting his feet on the ends of the table.

Holmes stood up with a little groan. "Thank you for seeing us. We'll be leaving now."

"Will you be coming to see the show tonight?"

"No."

"Aren't you going to tell me to break a leg?"

"I think you've had quite enough damage to your legs, haven't you? Good day." Holmes strode out of the dressing-room with impressive speed, and I followed him back to the car.

Holmes was clearly in a sour humor, and I said nothing for several minutes, until the awkwardness overwhelmed my desire to allow him the quiet time he so deeply appreciates. "Well? What was wrong with him?"

"Where to start?"

"How about the ledger? There was clearly something wrong with that."

"Indeed. The totals make it look like the dramatic company's in sound financial health, which is suspicious in itself. In any case, I performed some simple arithmetic, and it seems as if their debts have been paid off with nonexistent funds."

"I don't understand. How is that possible?"

"Simply put, Alfred has created a financial house of cards. It allows for seeming prosperity for a limited period of time, but everything will fall apart eventually, and at that point, the company

110

will be totally bankrupt, and even though Alfred is responsible for the financial malfeasance, he won't be on the hook for the debts himself."

"Are you sure he's behind the . . . creative accounting?"

"The handwriting on the ledger matches the scribbles on a script in his dressing-room."

"What was that comment you made about his leg?"

"You remember I mentioned he was injured and invalided out of the war?"

"Yes."

"And he carries the cane as an affectation. He doesn't really need it. But when he raised his leg, I saw his trouser leg slide back enough to see the wound caused by the bullet that sent him home from the front."

"I didn't get a close enough look at it to examine it properly."

"That is understandable. Had you been able to apply your trained medical eyes to it, you would have discovered that from the angle of the scarring, his wound was almost certainly self-inflicted. He shot himself with a handgun, just badly enough to be released from his duties."

"What a coward."

"Well, enough young men saw such terrible horrors on the front lines that I cannot judge them too harshly for wanting to escape with their lives. Still, combined with his accounting, it shows a distinct lack of character. Possibly with sufficient guidance and influence he could be molded into what we are looking for, but he's over thirty now and far too old for his character to be reshaped. Had he received proper training at a younger age, he could have replaced Mycroft eventually. As it is now, his moral compass is too shaky for us to trust him with anything. I suppose I should tell the owners of the theater to hire a proper accountant to examine the books to find out just how deep a hole they're currently in, and we'll see what happens. I doubt that Alfred will learn a lesson, though. I saw no signs of conscience or contrition in his face. He is clearly off the list."

"So where are we off to now, Holmes?"

"The Old Bailey, Watson, to speak to James Walter Moriarty. He is the elder son of Stationmaster James. Walter is a barrister of moderate reputation who specializes in criminal cases."

"Are any of his clients connected to his uncle?"

"A few low-level miscreants. Petty thieves and brutal lads who fell into the Professor's webs as youths and grew up to be inept professional criminals who spend their wasted lives drifting in and out of prison. No one of particular interest to me. Walter does, however, defend the occasional client of means, and is able to make a simple living off of these fees."

"Is a mediocre barrister our best hope of finding a successor for Mycroft?"

"I doubt it. Yet Walter intrigues me. According to my records, he was a brilliant student and on track to become one of the most celebrated attorneys of his generation. And now he languishes in relative obscurity. I wonder why this is the case."

"Perhaps his excellent grades were the result of cheating, and he was unable to find a similar path to success in the workforce."

"That is suspicious-minded of you, Watson, but what you say is not impossible. The only way to find out for certain what is behind his undistinguished to career is to meet with him."

Soon afterwards, we arrived at the Old Bailey, and were informed that Walter was still in court, but he would be finished for the day soon. Not wishing to wait any longer than necessary, Holmes and I quietly entered the courtroom where the case Walter was defending was being heard, and found seats in the gallery.

We arrived in the middle of Walter's summation to the jury. " – it is clear that the prosecution has failed to prove beyond a reasonable doubt that my client was responsible for the thefts. Their sole witness is an elderly man with a degenerative eye condition. There is no proof that the pound notes in his pockets were not his own, won earlier that evening in a card game. Furthermore – "

At this point, Holmes nudged me, and we both exited the courtroom. "I've seen enough," Holmes told me as soon as the door had closed behind us.

"We were there less than thirty seconds."

"More than enough time for me to determine the reason for Walter's middling career. I could see it in his eyes. He has contracted pupils and a skin pallor . . . He's a drug addict."

I nodded. "I observed what you did. He clearly isn't a well man. I would say that he has been abusing drugs for years."

"While I'm in no position to criticize someone who is addicted to drugs, I can state definitively that such a man should not be considered for a position as important as Mycroft's."

I chose my next words very carefully. "Holmes, are you completely . . . certain that Mycroft's role is absolutely necessary? After all, England survived for centuries without him. Other countries appear to be functioning fine without men like Mycroft behind the scenes." A thought struck me. "At least . . . I think that other countries don't have men like Mycroft performing vital roles out of the sight of the average citizen. I could be wrong."

"I'm afraid you are, Watson. Most of the world's great powers have their own versions of Mycroft, though to the best of my knowledge, most of them are not nearly as skilled as my brother. And it is not an exaggeration to say that Mycroft's temporary sidelining was directly responsible for the Great War. The Boer War only occurred because Mycroft was laid up for three weeks with influenza. If Mycroft dies, and we have no one to replace him, it will lead to disaster on a global scale."

"After all we've endured with the Great War, no one will want another conflict on that magnitude," I assured Holmes.

"That may be at the heart of the problem, Watson. If one side is determined to avoid another war, a belligerent nation may be able to extract concessions up to the point where either the other country will fall, or will be forced to fight. Either possibility is unacceptable."

"Then do all of our hopes rely on Stationmaster James's younger son?"

"Unless you can think of an alternative, you are correct. He is known as 'J.J.'"

"J.J." I mulled over this for a moment. "No, his parents couldn't possibly have named him – "

"They did. James James."

"Why?"

"The Moriarty family is an odd one, full of eccentricities and inside jokes, as well as copious amounts of brilliance and twisted psyches. It's quite possible that J.J.'s father considered this a great joke. It's also within the bounds of probability that it was some sort of sadistic plan to make sure the boy would be mocked by his schoolfellows. I cannot tell at present. I can say that J.J. has taken it upon himself to follow in the footsteps of his uncle, the Colonel, and become the protector of his family name."

"How so?"

"You are not the only one to take an interest in writing about my cases, Watson. Shortly before the war, J.J. wrote a lengthy book in defense of his uncle, arguing that dear old Uncle James was nothing more than a misunderstood, slandered academic who was framed by a cocaine-addled, overrated, incompetent consulting detective."

113

"But surely he must have realized that you weren't trying to slander the Professor."

"Oh, J.J.'s book posited that I was sincere enough in my convictions. His thesis is that Colonel Sebastian Moran was the real mastermind of the criminal gang, and the Professor was nothing more than a sacrificial lamb – an innocent man plucked from obscurity to serve as a dupe. J.J. reached out to several publishers, but none would touch it. One of them informed me of the manuscript, and after reading it, I realized that J.J. had a brilliant and creative mind, even if his conclusions were utter tommyrot. I confronted him shortly before the War began and tried to persuade him that he was mistaken, but he did not take kindly to my arguments, and became quite enraged by what I had to say. He has a terrible temper, which is why I put him at the bottom of the list. Still, it's possible that the years have mellowed him."

"Where is he now?"

"He was a medic during the war. According to my informant that I telephoned earlier, he is currently at the Dunstable Hospital. Perhaps he has become a doctor, or at least an orderly. We shall see."

We soon arrived at the hospital, a grim and unsettling place on the outskirts of London, surrounded by massive walls. After some cajoling, Holmes was allowed to speak to the head nurse.

"Why do you want to see Mr. Moriarty?" she asked.

"I wish to interview him about a job," Holmes replied.

"He will not be able to accept any position you offer."

"Is he under contract at this hospital?"

"You misunderstand me. He is a patient here."

A sudden flash of realization passed over my face. "This hospital . . . it is an asylum."

"Yes. Mr. Moriarty had a breakdown three years into the war. The doctors have done their best, but they believe that he is incurable . . . ."

This news left Holmes looking desolate. He said nothing as we rode back to my home in Queen Anne Street, and he refused to join me for dinner. He locked himself in his room, and I heard no more from him until after breakfast the following morning, when he emerged looking disheveled and unslept, but triumphant.

"I may have a solution to our problem, Watson," he said as he buttered a piece of cold toast that had been brought to his room hours earlier. "It is unwieldy, but it could serve our purposes adequately."

"What is it?"

114

"I need a few more minutes to refine my ideas. In just a few minutes we have a meeting with Mycroft and a representative from the government, a Mr. Chumbley. Apparently he is well-connected and has the ear of the Prime Minister. You will learn all when we meet with them."

Thirty minutes later, we were gathered in Mycroft's rooms, as the young, lean, dour-looking Mr. Chumbley glared at us. "Why did you wish to speak to me?"

"You are aware of how indispensable my brother is to the workings of the British government. In matters of foreign policy, spycraft, economics, domestic affairs, and other issues, he is absolutely vital. When he dies, which will hopefully not be for many more years, England will be crippled. If a replacement for my brother exists, I do not know of him. Then I realized, if no one man can replace Mycroft, perhaps several can. Consider this: A specialist or team of experts, maybe two or three, each handling one aspect of what Mycroft does. I have broken Mycroft's duties down into seven fields. I have adjusted the wording for reasons that will become evident once you read the first letter of each topic." Holmes withdrew a piece of paper from his pocket and set it on the table in front of Mr. Chumbley. It read:

Military Strategy
Yeomanry
Commerce and Currency
Royal Issues
Ombudsman
Foreign Affairs
Tradecraft

"Think of it," Holmes explained. "The brightest minds in their fields, all contributing to do the work that Mycroft does now. A secret team of the cleverest men in the country, all working in their respective topics for the good of the nation. It would . . . ." Holmes's voice trailed off as he caught Mycroft's eye.

"Not a bad idea, Brother," Mycroft sighed. "But I came up with something very similar months ago. Only without the silly acrostic."

"And I rejected it then and will again," Mr. Chumbley replied. "We already have quite enough supposed geniuses on the government payroll. There is no need to hire more."

"But who will replace – ?"

115

"People higher up than me put a great deal of faith in your brother. I do not share this high opinion. When he retires or dies, or once his patrons in the upper echelons of the British government are no longer there to protect him, the work he does will cease."

"But Mycroft is – "

"He's a relic! A superannuated fat fossil who has no place in the modern world. He should have died of a heart attack years ago. We don't need him!"

"Mr. Chumbley and I have a complicated history," Mycroft growled. "I proved a few years ago that his wife was leaking secrets to a paramour in the German government."

"It's a lie!"

"It's the truth. Your wife is a traitor and an adulteress and you are a fool for shielding her. But as you see, dear Brother, Mr. Chumbley resents me, and due to his parentage, he is extremely well-connected and has been placed in a position of power he has not earned and does not deserve."

Chumbley rose. "Insult me all you want. My friends in the government agree with me. You are no longer necessary. The world is too complex for the British government to rely upon the caprices of an old-fashioned man like yourself. Our current crop of politicians, diplomats, and civil service employees can handle the workings of the country perfectly well without one enormous crank telling us what we can and cannot do. We forced you into retirement once, Mycroft. I will do what I can to make sure you are put out to pasture again and stay there. Good day to you all." With that, Chumbley flounced out and left the room.

After a few moments I spoke. "Well. What do we do now?"

"Sit back and watch the world burn," Mycroft seethed. "I've made too many enemies, especially amongst the younger generation. They don't like me, and they don't want me in a position of power."

"But does that mean that they'd be willing to harm the nation to spite you?"

"They genuinely believe that I'm no longer necessary," Mycroft sighed. "In any event, they're jealous of the power I hold and they want it for themselves."

"What will this mean for the future of the nation?" I wondered.

Holmes pressed his hand against his forehead. "I'm very much afraid that it means that the future of Europe is not as bright as we may have hoped. Without someone performing Mycroft's duties at his level of competence, I believe that another Great War is inevitable . . . ."

116

I felt utterly despondent. "So there's nothing we can do?"

Mycroft shrugged. "Sherlock and I will continue to look for a solution, but if the fools in the government continue to resist, they may cause the annihilation of another generation."

Holmes nodded. "For now, unfortunately, you must view this case as one of my failures."

As I write these words, Mycroft remains in his position, and continues to fend off those who would cause irreparable damage to this country by removing him. I hope that someday I will be able to pen a conclusion to this case that proves that Holmes's statement was wrong. I have never before wished so desperately that one of our investigations will have a sequel.

The Case of the
Purloined Parcel
by Naching T. Kassa

It had been one year since the end of the Great War and Sherlock Holmes's return to England. My companion had been busy in the intervening months and hardly a month went by without my seeing him. His work had increased ten-fold, and when he decided to take a two- week holiday in Sussex with his bees, I could not fault him.

One can imagine my surprise when, a week later, I found him in my sitting room. He greeted me with a hale and hearty handshake.

"What brings you back to London?" I asked as he resumed his seat on the settee. "Have you taken on another task from the King? Will Altamont make yet another appearance?"

"You act as though only an event of extreme importance could call me up from Sussex," Holmes said with a smile. "I'm not here on matters of state."

"Then what else could've called you from your holiday? Surely you've come here on an investigation."

"You think so?"

"I know so. You've thrust your cloth cap into the pocket of your overcoat. You only wear that cap when on a case, as any other hat will slip from your head when you conduct your investigation. There are fresh chemical stains on your right thumb and forefinger – stains I've observed on several occasions when you are testing ink on various forms of correspondence. And you've that keen, eager look in your eyes when your mind has turned to a problem which challenges your formidable intellect."

"Bravo, Watson. You have applied my methods well. I am indeed on a case."

He pulled a small parcel from the inside of his coat and handed it to me.

"What do you make of this?"

"There is no return address," I said examining the wrapping. "And the box is made of cardboard. I trust there's no salt inside. For if there is, I'm afraid I'd rather not open it."

Holmes laughed. "You've grown squeamish in your advancing years."

"If I have, it's because Miss Susan Cushing and her sisters made me so."

"That case took place over thirty-one years ago."

"And it seems things have grown worse instead of better. Or have you forgotten the monstrosities we witnessed during the Great War?"

"I haven't forgotten," Holmes replied. "Fear not. There are no severed ears in this package. Open it and study the contents."

I opened the box and took a photo, a note, and a ring from within. I dealt with the note first.

"This is written in a woman's hand," I said. "The paper is expensive."

"Pray, read it aloud."

"'*Mr. Holmes, I am in great need of your aid. Come to Carswood Hall, outside the village of Rye, on the morning of February 16th. I need to discuss a problem with you.*'" I looked up into his grey eyes. "It is unsigned."

"Our client wished to remain anonymous, but gave away a vital clue. Do you know who resides in Carswood Hall?"

"I'm sure I don't know. I've never heard of the place."

"You have, no doubt, heard of the young woman who vanished from her room at The Savoy last Tuesday evening?"

"Lady Ellen Carswood? The papers carried the news of her disappearance far and wide. Her mother has offered a substantial reward for her safe return."

"Lady Elizabeth Carswood is her mother. I spoke to her over the phone when I received the parcel in the post. She was rather unnerved by how quickly I deduced her identity. No, Watson, not the photograph. Study the ring next."

I picked up the band of gold and turned it back and forth between my thumb and index finger.

"It's a wedding ring. It must belong to a man. It's far too large for a woman's finger.

"You have read the inscription?"

I squinted at the engraving inside. "The words are too small to make out."

"Perhaps you should put your spectacles on."

"I'm afraid I cannot. They have been missing for over a day now and I – Great Scott!"

Like a magician of old, Sherlock Holmes had produced my wire-rimmed spectacles from the inner pocket of his coat. He placed them on my palm.

119

"I don't know why you find them needless and ugly. You need them for reading."

"Wherever did you find them?"

"I found them where you placed them – near the boot dryer by the front door."

"How on earth did you know I dislike them?"

"A man will treat the thing he loves with utmost care. If he dislikes or even hates it, he will not care where he sets it. The fact that you've hidden your use of them, and the lack of telltale markings on your face, led me to deduce that their wear isn't usual. You don't wear them all day long, only when the need suits you."

"I am astounded."

He smiled. "And I'm glad you're still surprised by my methods. But come, we are far afield now. What does the inscription say?"

I placed my horrid spectacles on the tip of my nose and read, "'*To my darling A.T. With much love, E.B.*' It is a wedding ring."

"And now, we come to the strangest thing of all, Watson. Examine the photograph."

A chill crawled over my skin as I took the picture in hand.

"It looks to be a soldier, Holmes. But . . . his face is missing. Everything but the eyes have been scratched away."

"As have all signs and emblems of military insignia," Holmes said.

I turned the photograph over. A date had been scrawled on the back. It read "*September 9, 1880*".

"Who is he?" I asked. "And why would anyone wish to deface him?"

"That is what we must discover. These items are undoubtedly connected to the Lady's disappearance."

He rose from the settee. "My appointment with Lady Carswood is three hours hence. Can your wife spare you the rest of the day?"

"She can. She is visiting a friend and will not return until this evening."

The eager light burned bright in Holmes's eyes.

"You still have your service revolver?"

"I do. You think we have need of it?"

"I believe the photograph is all the indication we need. A sane mind wouldn't prove so vicious."

We arrived at the village of Rye in Surrey on the afternoon train. Lady Carswood had sent a motor car to retrieve us and within minutes, we arrived at Carswood Hall.

120

"I have often given you my opinion of the country," Holmes said, as we stood before the stone building's large and imposing doors. "And this is a prime example of it. In a place like this, one could commit a crime with impunity."

The door opened a moment later and a tall woman clad in black appeared on the threshold. She looked upon us with red eyes and a small, white handkerchief protruded from her left sleeve.

"Mr. Holmes?" she asked.

"Yes."

"I am Mrs. Manderly, the housekeeper. Her Ladyship has been expecting you."

The woman led us to a sumptuous and opulent sitting room. Paintings in gilded frames adorned the walls and thick rugs covered the floors. Firelight gleamed in the polish of the cherrywood furnishings.

Lady Elizabeth sat in a chair near the fire with two armchairs opposite. She seemed a matron of the old guard. Her white hair had been styled in an austere bun, and her aquiline nose resembled that of a bird of prey. She stared at us with a steel-grey gaze, her mouth in a perpetual frown.

"Mr. Holmes?" her eyes focusing on my face, and then on his.

"I am Sherlock Holmes."

"And this . . . person – Who is he?"

"My friend and colleague, Dr. John Watson."

"This is an extremely delicate matter, Mr. Holmes. I don't wish to share it with interlopers or members of the press."

"I assure you, my Lady. Watson is the soul of discretion."

"Hmmph. He writes for *The Strand*. I've read his narratives regarding your many adventures. He has no gift for keeping secrets."

"If you remember," Holmes said with a smile, "Watson has never written of anyone unless they have passed from this world. History is an odd thing, my Lady. When you have shuffled off this mortal coil, would it not be better for the world to know your side of the story?"

"I suppose you are right there," the matron said. "Very well. You may stay, Dr. Winston."

"Watson," I muttered.

"That is what I said." She motioned to two armchairs. "You may be seated."

We took our seats. Holmes leaned back, his long legs stretched out before him.

"I suppose I should begin at the beginning," Lady Elizabeth

121

said.

"That would be wise," Holmes replied.

"My daughter, Ellen, has always been a shy and retiring young woman. Her father, a Captain in the 66th Berkshire Regiment of Foot – "

"Why, that is my old regiment!" I exclaimed.

"Was it? Well, I don't think you would have known him. He was wounded at the Battle of Maiwand and died on the return trip home."

"How extraordinary! I too was wounded in that battle. Was the Captain a passenger on the *HMS Orontes*?"

"I – I am unaware of his ship. It was sunk when he left the harbor. All hands were lost. As it stands, his death is unrelated to the abduction of my daughter."

"You are quite certain?" Holmes asked. "Did the Captain possess family other than yourself and your daughter?"

"He had none. He was the last of an illustrious line." The Lady's gaze grew fierce and red spots appeared on her cheeks. Her knuckles grew white as she gripped the arm of her chair. "Gentlemen, may we return to the matter at hand?"

"My apologies, my Lady," said Holmes. "Please, continue."

Lady Elizabeth composed herself and returned to her story.

"My daughter grew up rather sheltered from the world. In these forty-one years, she hasn't left my side. It is unusual for her to leave the house without me – though there have been times. She is a devout woman, and often attends church services in Rye on Sundays. She has never gone as far as London, however, and I was as surprised as anyone when I learned she had traveled there."

"There was no message? No telephone call which might lure her there?"

"My daughter is my fondest confidante, and I hers. She would have told me."

"What of the parcel? Was it sent to her?"

Lady Elizabeth blinked. "Parcel?"

"The one you sent with your note."

"I know of no parcel."

Holmes's face grew red. He lowered his eyes and, for the first time in my life, I recognized an element of shame in the face of my friend.

"Ah. I must apologize once more. I suppose, my mind is playing tricks on me in my old age. It seems I have confused your case with another."

Lady Elizabeth smiled for the first time and I railed inwardly at the smugness she conveyed.

"Tell me," Holmes resumed, "was your daughter abducted from her hotel room?"

"That is what the police tell me."

"There were signs of a struggle?"

"They didn't say. I know it must be an abduction. She wouldn't leave of her own accord and fail to return."

"The police have a suspect?"

"A young man was seen in her company. I believe there was an argument, and when he tried to follow her up to her room at the hotel, he was rebuffed. The police are looking for him as we speak."

"May I see her room here?"

The lady paused and gazed at Holmes, stone-faced.

"I don't see how it will help."

"She may have left us a clue to her abductor. It is obvious she has kept something from you."

Lady Elizabeth sighed and waved a hand toward the door. "You will find her room up the stairs. Mrs. Manderly can show you the way."

"Once we have looked the room over, it will conclude our visit," Holmes said, rising to his feet. "I will keep you appraised of my investigation as it develops."

"I suppose we should discuss the matter of your fee?"

"We may do so when the job is done."

The lady rose and pulled a bell pull near the fireplace. A few moments later, Mrs. Manderly appeared at the door.

"Show these gentlemen to Ellen's room," Lady Elizabeth said.

Mrs. Manderly nodded and led us from the room and up the stairs. We found Lady Ellen's room on the right.

It stood in stark contrast to the rest of the house. A simple table, wardrobe, and bed were the only furnishings. No paintings decorated the stone walls and the wooden floor lay bare beneath our feet. The place seemed more akin to a monk's cell than the bedroom of a Lord's daughter.

"Will you be needing anything else, sir?" the housekeeper asked.

"I will, Mrs. Manderly. Would you mind closing the door? Ah, thank you. The place is decidedly drafty, and my poor old bones are quite unused to it. I have one or two questions for you."

"Yes, sir?"

"You are quite fond of Lady Ellen, are you not?"

123

The housekeeper nodded. "I've known her since she was a baby, sir. I've always felt kindly toward her."

"Is that why you sent me the photograph and the ring?"

The woman's eyes widened and her face blanched. "I – I don't know what you mean."

"Come now, Mrs. Manderly. Your employer has lied enough for the both of you. Surely, you can tell me the truth. You sent those items, along with the note Lady Elizabeth charged you with. I want to know why."

The woman shook her head. For a moment, she swayed, and I thought she might fall to the floor. I put out an arm to steady her and she gently pushed it away.

"I didn't send the items, sir. You are mistaken."

"Then I'm mistaken as well. You do not care for the woman."

The housekeeper's shoulders slumped. She stood with her eyes on the floor, her body trembling.

"I care for that girl – that woman – more than you could ever know," she said at last. "And if you find her, Mr. Holmes, you mustn't allow her to return here. You must let her stay lost."

She turned and hurried from the room.

"The parcel wasn't evidence in a different case?" I said after the housekeeper had gone.

Holmes's eyes twinkled. "You think I have lost my faculties with age, Watson?"

"I am somewhat relieved," I admitted.

"Overconfidence is often the downfall of a criminal mind," he said, as he paced, his eyes on the floor. "I wish our opponent to believe me a semi-senile old man, capable of solving this case, but incapable of uncovering other secrets."

"You think Lady Elizabeth possesses such a mind?"

"I do. She is a clever one. I knew it when I first spoke with her on the telephone. As I said, her surprise at my discerning her identity was quite unwarranted."

"Why did Mrs. Manderly send you the ring and the photograph?"

Holmes didn't answer. He knelt beside the bed and brushed the floor with one hand. Then he rose to his feet and pulled the bed away from the wall.

"Reasonably light," he muttered to himself. He pushed the bed to the center of the room and returned to the wall.

"Ah! Here it is."

"What is it?"

"A secret crevice in the floor. Have you a penknife, Watson?"

I delved into my pocket and withdrew the needed item.

"Lady Ellen would've used a piece of cutlery to open this. Something she could easily pocket and return to the scullery later."

He pried a small section of flooring up and set it to one side. A pocketbook lay inside. Holmes took it out and, as he lifted it, a small scrap of paper fluttered to the floor. I picked it up.

"It's a name," I said, as I read the neat and masculine script. "'*Richard Singh*'."

Holmes took the scrap from my hand. "This paper . . . it's the type used in hymnals. See here, you can just make out the bottom of the stave."

He turned his attention to the pocketbook. It was empty, apart from a calling card.

"Our friend, Richard Singh again. It appears he is a reporter and for *The Times* no less."

Holmes replaced the pocketbook and continued his investigation of the room. His face grew grim as he approached the wardrobe.

"There is dried blood here on the floor," said he. "And this wardrobe . . . it has a padlock. A strong one."

With his lock-pick, he opened the wardrobe doors. Two modest and old-fashioned dresses hung from the hangers within.

"I must admit I'm perplexed," I said. "The girl is surrounded by luxury, and yet, she dresses as a housemaid. And this room – a cloister would be more welcoming. I suppose she takes her devotion to the Lord quite seriously."

"Perhaps, though I would lean toward another answer."

"Such as?"

"I believe she lives this way against her will."

"You think that her mother has forced her?"

Holmes didn't answer. His gaze had fallen on the interior of the doors. Several long scratches had been cut into the wood and he traced them with the fingertips of his right hand. A chill prickled my skin.

"My God, Holmes."

"I think we shall take Mrs. Manderly's advice," he said. "And ensure Lady Ellen never returns to this house."

Lady Carswood's car returned us to Rye, where we stopped at a local inn. Holmes took this opportunity to use the telephone, and two of his conversations took several minutes. When he'd finished, he retired to the dining room.

"The Chief Inspector sends his regards," Holmes said.

"Is that who you called? How is Hopkins these days?"

"Doing considerably well. He does miss his days as an inspector."

"As well he should. He was a fine investigator. One of your best protégés. Did he have any information regarding the Carswood matter?"

"Funny enough, he did. And it appears, I'm not the only one Lady Elizabeth engaged for this case."

"She consulted other detectives?"

"Hopkins said the consultations were on a strictly informal basis. It appears she is acquainted with our dear friend, Solar Pons. She engaged him for a week and then discharged him. Coincidentally, the discharge came in conjunction with his investigation into the life of Lord Carswood. She came to me on Hopkins' recommendation."

"She is rather sensitive on the subject of her husband. I feared she might experience an apoplectic fit when we discussed him earlier. I still don't remember such a man in my regiment."

"He wasn't Lord Carswood then. I called Pons after speaking with Hopkins and he informed me of the man's name. He was known as Arthur Templeton, the second son of Hugo Carswood."

"Templeton? I did know a fellow by that name. He was a good fellow, kept to himself. I don't think he was married though. There was talk of a woman, but she was from one of the high born castes in India. Why was he called Templeton?"

"He had a falling out with his father over a love affair and decided to go by his mother's maiden name. Both his father and brother were killed in the Battle of Kandahar and he inherited the title."

I shook my head. "Holmes, that is impossible. According to Lady Elizabeth, he died following the Battle of Maiwand."

"I think we can discount anything the Lady has told us," Holmes said. "The parcel Mrs. Manderly sent me is proof of that."

"How so?"

"Think, Watson. You must know by now to whom the ring belongs."

"*A.T.* . . . . Arthur Templeton. But . . . how can that be? If his ship were sunk, how could she recover the ring?"

"Precisely. Now, what of the photograph?"

The defaced picture returned to mind. I thought of the date

written on the back and the lack of insignia on the soldier's uniform.

"It is also Arthur Templeton. Taken after the Battle of Maiwand and when his ship supposedly sank."

"Very good. Pons has corroborated this information. He assures me that Templeton did not die in a shipwreck."

"Why would the Lady lie about such a thing?"

"Shame. Arthur Templeton was married to Lady Carswood before the Battle of Maiwand. It was a marriage his father forced on him, and one he intended to end when his father passed away."

"What happened to Templeton?"

"Pons says he vanished soon after he reached England. No one has seen him since."

"I'm surprised Pons didn't remain on the case."

"He has many to occupy him. He doesn't mind if I pick up the crumbs."

Holmes reached for his cigarette case and lit a cigarette. The smoke curled above his head.

"What has this to do with the disappearance of Lady Ellen?" I asked.

"Everything."

"I must confess, I don't see the connection."

"That is because you have allowed Lady Elizabeth to prejudice your thinking. As I said before, you must discount all that she has said."

"Then . . . there was no abduction?"

"According to Hopkins, no such thing took place. By all accounts, the lady left her room at The Savoy of her own accord."

"No struggle? No argument with a young man?"

"None."

"But what of the article in *The Times*?"

"As you recall, it never said she had been abducted, only that she disappeared. Again, Lady Elizabeth has clouded your mind. Can you deduce who the author of the article was?"

"Richard Singh?"

Holmes nodded.

"Do you believe he is her lover?"

"Perhaps."

"Where on earth would she have met such a fellow?"

"You have forgotten the hymnal, Watson? She met him in church, of course."

I happened to peer out the window then, just as a familiar person passed. Mrs. Manderly hurried down the street.

"I knew she couldn't stay away long," Holmes said, rising from his seat. "Come, Watson! The game is afoot!"

We hurried out of the inn and into the street. Mrs. Manderly seemed unaware of our presence as we followed her to the parish churchyard. When she disappeared within the church, Holmes and I slipped in after her. Voices echoed as we entered the nave.

"You cannot stay here," Mrs. Manderly said. "Return to London if you must. But don't remain in Surrey another moment!"

"I cannot leave," a woman replied. "Not until I have discovered the whereabouts of my father."

Holmes crept passed the pews and I followed at his heels. We hid in a shadowy corner and observed the drama before us.

Mrs. Manderly stood opposite a woman of perhaps forty-five. Gray streaked the lady's hair which had been cut in a stylish bob. She was clad in a blue dress and matching fur-lined coat.

The woman's companion, a well-dressed man of about forty, stood beside her. Tall and olive-skinned, he stared at the woman with piercing blue eyes. Something about him seemed quite familiar, though I couldn't say what.

"Your father is gone," Mrs. Manderly said. "Gone these forty years. There's nothing you can do for him. But there is something you can do for yourself. You must live now, my poppet."

"He is truly dead then?" Lady Ellen said. "Mother has told me so many lies, I don't know quite what to believe anymore."

"He is dead, though I wish I could say he wasn't. It was a quick one, and he did not suffer much. I think that's what angered her most. She couldn't torture him, and so she tortured you, the one person who reminded her most of him."

"She was there then?" the man said.

"We both were," Mrs. Manderly replied. "And I have had to stay ever since. We are like the snake which eats itself. You can't tell where one of us begins and the other ends. Our guilt is – "

"Look out!" Holmes cried.

Too late. No one save he had noticed the entry of a sixth to our little group. Lady Elizabeth raised her arm and the pistol in her grip gleamed. A shot rang out.

Holmes dashed forward. I couldn't keep up with him and so I drew my revolver, aiming at the Lady in question. Holmes reached her before I could call out and wrested the weapon from her.

The old woman screamed and thrashed like a banshee in Holmes's grasp. It took the sight of my revolver to quiet her.

"No!" Lady Ellen cried.

I turned and found the housekeeper lying on the stone floor. Scarlet seeped from between her fingers.

"Shh, Poppet," Mrs. Manderly said. "I knew this day would come."

"Watson, your revolver," Holmes said. "See to Mrs. Manderly."

I did as he bade me and hurried to the woman's aid. She gazed at me with feverish eyes.

"There is no hope for me," she said. "I wish to tell my story with what time remains."

"Hush, you – you Judas!" Lady Elizabeth screeched. Her hair had tumbled from the bun at the back of her head and she raised clawed fingers in Mrs. Manderly's direction.

"Quiet," Holmes said. The single word, expressed in so masterful a tone, drove the woman into sullen silence.

"I pitied her when first she came to Carswood Hall," Mrs. Manderly said. Her voice had dropped near a whisper and I could barely make out the words. "I pitied Miss Elizabeth Braiden. I knew Lord Arthur would never love her. Course, as time wore on, I realized she didn't care if he loved her or not. What she wanted was wealth, and all the power that goes with it. She wanted control, and she would never control him.

"You see, Sir Arthur loved another woman. His father, however, didn't approve of the match. He forced Arthur into marrying Elizabeth. Said it might settle him down, make him more responsible. I think it had more to do with Arthur's choice. Lord Hugo Carswood didn't want an Indian woman in his house, even if she was high born.

"Lord Arthur still loved his lady, though. And when he was sent overseas to fight in the war, he sent for her. There was nothing Lord Hugo could do. Arthur enlisted in another regiment to escape both him and his brother. He lived with the lady as his wife, even though they couldn't be married. When Lord Hugo died, and Arthur was free of him, he decided to divorce Lady Elizabeth. She didn't take the news too well. I remember, she went through the house once, collecting all his photographs and scratching out the faces with a pair of scissors.

"She'd had Ellen by that time and never was a sweeter baby born to Carswood Hall. Elizabeth hated her. Saw her as a burden ever since she came into the world. She ignored her most times. It wasn't until after . . . after he died that the horror really began.

"Arthur was wounded at Maiwand and shipped home soon

after. But he didn't come here. Instead, he took lodgings at the family home in the city. One night he arranged to meet with Elizabeth and have it out, as it were. There was an awful row. She threatened to take Ellen away because she knew he loved the girl, but he wouldn't have it. He was going to have her driven from the premises. He made the mistake of turning his back on her and, in a fit of rage, she hit him with a candlestick. He dropped down dead, right there at her feet.

"Well, I still felt sorry for her then, and I believed he'd done her a great wrong. When she came to me and begged me for help, God help me, I did it. I helped her bury the body and I helped her clean up. What I didn't know was how conniving she was. She tricked me into grabbing the candlestick and said she'd tell everyone I'd killed Lord Arthur if I ever told on her. I was trapped with her and she with me.

"Things grew worse for Ellen after Arthur died. Elizabeth used to burn the poor babe with candle wax and lock her in the wardrobe of her room. I used to fear for Ellen's sanity – but she was strong, and she wouldn't break. And when she cried 'cause her mother didn't love her, I showed her I did. I did my best to protect her – you. I'm so sorry, Poppet."

Tears flowed down Lady Ellen's cheeks. She clutched the housekeeper's hand.

"She lies!" Lady Elizabeth cried, her face twisted in a malignant sneer. "*She* killed Arthur! I had nothing to do with it! You'll never convince a jury to believe her over me!"

"I think you're wrong there," the young man spoke up. "I think they will find her story quite convincing once it appears in the papers."

"And just who do you think you are?"

"I am Richard Singh," the young man replied. "A reporter with *The Times*."

"I'll have your job for this, you insufferable pup! And I'll have them send you back to India where you belong!"

Lady Ellen rose to her feet. "You will not speak to him in that manner."

"Why? Have I hurt your lover's feelings? You little whore – Conspiring behind my back!"

"He isn't a lover," Holmes said. "He is her brother."

I recognized the man's eyes then. They were the same as those in the damaged photograph – the only feature of Lord Arthur Carswood which could still be seen. Lady Elizabeth's eyes bulged.

"He is my last living relative on my father's side," Lady Ellen continued. "He met me in church five months ago, looking for father, and we have been friends ever since. Because of him, because of his kindness, I have finally found the strength to escape you, Mother. I no longer fear you. Nor do I hate you. I feel nothing for you now. You will never hurt me again."

Lady Ellen turned her back toward her mother, and as we continued to administer to Mrs. Manderly, Holmes led the dreadful woman away.

Mrs. Manderly did not survive the injuries Lady Elizabeth had inflicted. She passed away that night, leaving two crimes on the matron's head.

Holmes and I returned to London on the morning train, and as he perused the morning papers a wreath of smoke about his head, I couldn't help but think of something he'd said the day before.

"You are correct, Holmes."

"Hmm?"

"If a man or a woman loves something, they will treat it with the utmost care. I should've known the moment I walked into Lady Ellen's room exactly what kind of person her mother was."

"Do not berate yourself, old fellow. Believing your fellow man is basically good is an admirable quality – one in which I'm quite deficient. I suppose that is why we work so well with one another. We make up for one another's deficiencies."

"I had never thought of it that way."

"It is something I've considered many times. I don't think I would be Sherlock Holmes without my Watson."

It was one of the kindest things he'd ever said to me.

I thought of it many times in the years to come.

The Game at Chequers
by Roger Riccard

Chapter I

It was the spring of 1920 when I happened to be visiting my friend, the retired detective, Sherlock Holmes, at his bee farm in Sussex. We had been lunching when a telegram arrived:

Sherlock, your presence required. See me soonest.

M

The housekeeper had laid it upon the table by his plate. A quick perusal by him resulted in a grunt and a toss of the paper over to me. Cryptic as it seemed, I had known Holmes long enough that I recognized the significance immediately.

"It appears your brother has something beyond his ability to solve from his desk in Whitehall, or his chair at the Diogenes."

Sir Mycroft Holmes [1], according to my companion, was the smarter of the two brothers and held an unusual government post of key importance, no matter which party was in power. His one flaw was his lack of ambition at proving solutions he had deduced. His physical bulk made him notoriously inactive. When proof was required through on-the-spot investigation, he often called upon his younger sibling to "do all the traipsing about to uncover the physical evidence necessary". This would usually occur when there were legal or political ramifications necessitating absolute proof, as opposed to Mycroft's stated theories.

"An astute deduction," Holmes replied, though I could not tell if there was sarcasm behind that remark or not. "Would you care to accompany me up to London this afternoon to see if we can put Mycroft's mind at ease?"

"I wouldn't mind a dinner at the Diogenes," I replied, nonchalantly, giving him back a little of his own. Not being a member of the Diogenes myself, I was only able to sample the exquisite cuisine on those rare occasions when I was an invited guest.

"I shall see to it, Doctor, though it may have to be after the case is solved, since Mycroft appears to be in a hurry."

Having agreed to terms, we finished our lunch, packed our bags, and were at Eastbourne Station in time for the three o'clock train. We had a third companion with us. Holmes seemed to feel he might be helpful on whatever task Mycroft would lay before us. Upon reaching St. Pancras, we took a cab to my Queen Anne Street residence, where we dropped our friend off. We then proceeded on to the Diogenes, assuming that Mycroft would practice his normal custom and go straight there after his office hours.

The Diogenes Club was founded by Mycroft Holmes, among others, for the purpose of having the benefits of a club where they could have privacy away from work or home in absolute peace and quiet. These were the "unclubable" gentlemen of London, those who were social introverts. There was no talking allowed, save in the Stranger's Room where Holmes and I always met with his brother. Even the dining room was silent. One was given a card with the choices of the day, filled it out, and was served accordingly. There were also refreshments available in the Stranger's Room, such as tea and biscuits, wine or brandy.

As so happened, our arrival coincided with that of the elder Holmes. We greeted him as we disembarked from our cab, while he was just beginning to move toward the door. He was in his seventies now, being seven years his brother's senior. He had lost some of his bulk with age, though he was still overweight. His hair had receded halfway back upon his scalp and, along with his mutton chop whiskers, had gone completely white. His cane now was a necessity rather than an affectation, thus he held it tightly as we made our way to the door.

We walked inside to the Stranger's Room where Mycroft ordered brandies all around as we sat in a triangle of overstuffed chairs. The room itself was paneled in walnut with several tapestries of historical moments in British history. In addition to decoration, these tapestries also provided a measure of sound deadening. Therefore any conversations would not filter through the walls into the silent areas of the building. There were heavy green drapes drawn across the windows now that dusk was falling. The chairs, sofas, and settees were a combination of solid and patterned upholstery in green, tan, mauve, and burgundy.

Mycroft began the conversation with a statement. "You are aware that the Chequers estate has been turned over to the government for the private, exclusive use of the Prime Minister."

Surprised by this opening remark, I recalled that in October 1917, it became public knowledge that the historical estate had been bequeathed as a gift to the government of Great Britain. It was to be used as a country home for the Prime Minister, in perpetuity, whenever the pressures of 10 Downing Street required a respite from London and Parliament.

Chequers was an ancient edifice dating back to the twelfth century. It gained its name from the office of Exchequer, or Treasurer, held by many of its inhabitants. The final private owners, Arthur Lee, Minister of Agriculture and First Lord of the Admiralty, under Prime Minister David Lloyd George, and his wife, referred to as Lady Ruth Lee, had undertaken major renovations to the manor in 1909-1910, while they were still leasing the property. In 1912 they bought it outright. Chequers had also served as a military hospital during the war.

Mycroft continued. "Its use as a hospital has concluded and the few remaining patients have been transferred to other facilities. Now that preparations are under way for the Prime Minister's occupancy, we must be certain that the manor is secure. Lord and Lady Lee are not in residence at the moment. They're taking a holiday in Rome. While they're gone, you are to go up to Chequers and examine the estate for any security weaknesses. Your government is requesting your observational skills in this matter, Sherlock. Report your findings to me and suitable corrections will be made."

"Then it is well that I brought Lestrade along," said Sherlock Holmes. "He should be quite adept at sniffing out irregularities on a country estate."

I stifled a chuckle at this statement as Mycroft nodded at his brother's foresight. The *Lestrade* we were discussing was the Basset hound which Holmes had been given as a gift from a grateful client. [2] Holmes named him after our friend, Inspector Lestrade. He was an excellent scent hound and just as determined as the old Scotland Yard official.

Chapter II

The next morning we left Marylebone Station for the forty mile journey northwest to Wendover Station near Chequers. Once beyond London's city limits, we passed through some of the greenest meadows and forests in all England. While I enjoyed the view of spring's arrival, my companion was focused deeply into papers provided by Mycroft regarding the history and layout of the estate.

Lestrade was curled up sleeping quietly on the seat beside me, having received special dispensation to ride with us, instead of in the baggage car. About two minutes before pulling into the station, Holmes suddenly folded up the documents and put them into his bag.

"Finished already?" I asked.

"Hardly," he replied. "The history of Chequers dates back to the twelfth century. However, we are about to reach our stop."

I looked out the window. My seat faced forward while Holmes view was to the rear. All I could see were green fields. "How could you know that?" I asked, just as the locomotive sounded its whistle. "You've never checked your watch and the station is not yet in sight."

"I knew how long the journey was scheduled to take, dear fellow. I also know how fast I read, depending on the type of material I'm perusing. It was a simple calculation to know how many pages I could review in the time allowed."

I shook my head as the train slowed to a stop. Even after four decades, there were still depths of Holmes character I had yet to learn.

Mycroft had arranged rooms for us at The Crowe's Nest Inn. A moderate cab ride deposited us at the establishment, which was less than a mile from the manor house. It was located in the hamlet of Butlers Cross, directly across the street from The Russell Arms, an attractive pub steeped in history. Originally The Russell was an eighteenth-century coach house. Its name dates back to the family that once owned Chequers, and the pub itself was where many of the Chequers staff lived.

The manager of Crowe's Nest Inn, Harvey Boyle, was a tall, lean fellow with receding brown hair and a prominent nose. He wore a white shirt with black braces and bow tie. He greeted us with enthusiasm. "Welcome gentlemen! I've arranged a ground floor room per your request, Mr. Holmes. It's near the back door for the convenience of your dog."

"I made no such request, Mr. Boyle," stated my companion.

The fellow handed Holmes a telegram from his pocket, "I received this two days ago."

Holmes glanced at it and handed me the form, saying one word, "Mycroft".

I read it aloud, including the signature, "*M. Holmes, Foreign Office*".

Addressing Boyle I asked, "How did you get '*Sherlock*' from the letter '*M*'?"

He replied, "I thought it just meant *Minister* or some title. Frankly, I thought you were retired, Mr. Holmes."

"My brother seems to have anticipated me," Holmes mumbled. "Again."

To Boyle he replied, "One never retires from his duties as a British citizen, Mr. Boyle. This is Lestrade."

"Yes, sir," replied manager as he knelt and gently petted Lestrade, who welcomed the attention as he sniffed the man's hand. "Ah, he smells my Galahad. We should introduce them, just to get acquainted and avoid any unpleasantness later on."

Holmes agreed and a quick whistle from Boyle brought forth a heavy Clumber Spaniel. With his thick white coat and brown ears, he approached us cautiously. Being a short-legged breed, he went easily nose to nose with Holmes's Basset. They sniffed each other as dogs do and seemed satisfied with each other's company.

Boyle showed us to our room. As promised, it was in the back, away from the noise of the lobby. It had two bedrooms and a common room. I noted there was a padded basket for Lestrade. Holmes thanked Boyle and we set about to unpack.

The manager handed Holmes two keys for the room and a third oddly shaped key. "Your automobile is in the carriage house out back and filled with petrol. Dinner is served at six-thirty. Let me know if you need anything else, gentlemen."

In our younger days, the journey to Chequers would have been a pleasant walk on a spring day. Now, however, we were given the use of a 1915 Ford Model T to drive back and forth.

Completing our unpacking, Holmes and I went out to the carriage house. The automobile was parked in an area convenient to the door. Other carriages and wagons were in place around it, and a small stable of horses was adjacent. There was also an area fenced off for numerous crates and barrels of supplies for The Russell Arms, as well as The Crowe's Nest. I thought it a convenient arrangement for the two establishments to share a common storage space. Kegs of beer, foodstuffs, extra bedding, tablecloths, and various and sundry equipment were stockpiled in an orderly fashion.

As to the Ford: Holmes, being in better physical shape than I, operated the crank while I inserted the key and adjusted the timing and throttle stalks. I admit I was somewhat perturbed at Mycroft for his choice of vehicles. There were certainly easier ones to start and operate, and this had no side windows to protect against weather. However, I accepted the situation and followed Lestrade's example.

The dog sat patiently in the back seat and gave a sharp bark when the engine started.

Holmes insisted that I drive slowly, as he wished to examine the roadway leading to the manor. It was a pleasant day with scattered clouds and a bright sun. We headed due south on Missenden Road. It was a narrow, two-lane affair and much of the way was through heavy forest, thick with fresh spring growth, and often with embankments on either side. Lestrade sat up straight and woofed on several occasions at movement in the brush. Rabbits and squirrels seemed to abound, and I once thought I spotted a deer. We passed only one structure, about halfway along our journey. It was a good-sized building made of multi-colored brick with a scalloped roofline of descending arches. A pair of black Labrador retrievers roamed the front yard, confined by a wrought-iron fence.

As I was occupied with driving, Holmes was forced to make his own notes. His frequent scribbling and grumbling told me he already was unhappy with the security of the roadway into what would become the Prime Minister's country home.

The trees on our right thinned out about three-hundred yards before the turnoff to Chequers, giving us a view of the high roof and chimney stacks of the structure itself. We turned down a long drive, bordered by thick hedges. There was no gate, merely a small sign posted stating *Private – No Admittance.*

"Well," I said, sarcastically, "that should certainly keep intruders out!"

Holmes merely grunted and replied, "Our task appears daunting, old friend. Let us hope the house itself affords better protection."

At least there was a wrought iron gate at the entrance to the east circular drive which was open wide, and there were no guards posted. Arriving at the main house, we found a magnificent manor with manicured grounds. The multi-storey structure of red-and-tan brick almost seemed out of place in its bucolic surroundings. Its many large, multi-paned windows spoke to the appreciation of its builders for the surrounding view of the lush countryside.

A well-dressed gentleman was waiting for us in front of the high-arched eastern entrance. I took him to be about forty, with dark brown hair cut short and clean-shaven. He raised his hand and pointed to a spot where I should park the vehicle. He walked smartly over to us and reached for the door, but Holmes beat him to it, stuffing his pad and pencil into his inner breast pocket before extending his hand.

137

"Good afternoon, Major," said the detective as he took the gentleman's hand. "I trust your lookouts telephoned our approach. I hope that our speed didn't leave you standing here too long, but I insisted the Doctor drive slowly so I could make my initial observations."

As good a soldier as he was, the officer couldn't hide his surprise at Holmes's statement. By this time, I had also exited the auto and come around to join the two of them. He shook my hand almost absent-mindedly as he pondered a response. Finally, he spoke.

"A pleasure, Dr. Watson. My name is Nathan Hunter, gentlemen. I'd prefer that you not use my rank, as my true purpose here is unknown to the staff and refurbishers. They believe me to be the majordomo, acting on Lloyd George's behalf. Did your brother tell you about me, Mr. Holmes?"

"Only your name, Mr. Hunter," answered my companion. "Your rank was a mere deduction. As to your scouts, I observed them and their binoculars trained upon our vehicle and the singular phone line which ran straight from there to this property, in addition to the regular telephone service."

"I'm aware of your reputation, sir," replied the Major. "I confess I didn't believe such things were possible until I was assigned to Sir Mycroft and observed him do the same thing. How did you deduce my rank?"

Holmes conceded to answer, "My brother has a penchant for using brave and bright military personnel for certain assignments. A military presence for security could certainly be assumed for the estate of the Prime Minister. Such responsibility would be entrusted to no less than a captain, but not likely to be thrust upon a colonel. Your military bearing gives you away as a soldier. As we drove up you were, out of habit, standing at parade rest. Your attire is crisp and clean, with trouser creases sharp as a sword and shoes shined to a mirror finish. You have shaved off your moustache, so common to military men, but there is a slight difference in the skin tone, indicating it has been done recently and not had a chance to obtain the same tanning as the rest of your face. When you raised your hand upon our arrival, it moved toward your forehead, as if in salute, until you caught yourself and waved us to this parking spot. Finally, your age indicates you are likely to have risen above captain to the rank of major. Someone who is still a captain at your stage of life has not likely distinguished himself in a manner which would gain him such an important assignment as this."

138

Major Hunter nodded. "Very good, Mr. Holmes. You noted our outpost and the extra telephone line. You should also be aware that we have a wireless radio set up there with a receiver in a special attic room here."

Holmes nodded, "Excellent, Mr. Hunter. Might I suggest that the telephone line from the outpost to here be run through an underground conduit? That would make it less likely to be spotted and pulled down by an attacking force."

"I'll make a note of that," replied our host. "Do you wish to step inside or walk the grounds first, gentlemen? I have an office set aside on the ground floor for your work."

He nodded toward me and my walking stick, as if he had made this concession to our ages and my game leg. I returned his nod with one of my own as Holmes replied, "I think we could use a turn about the grounds, Mr. Hunter. Between the train and the car it would be pleasant to stretch our legs while we have a warm spring day to do so. What say you, Watson?"

"It's a nice day for a walk," I replied, "and I'm sure Lestrade could use the exercise."

"Lestrade?" queried Hunter.

"Our companion," I answered as I opened the car door and coaxed the hound out of the back seat to join us.

Chapter III

With most people, Lestrade has a natural tendency to draw one down to a kneeling position to pet him, for he has a winsome appearance and friendly countenance. Major Hunter, being a disciplined soldier, did not deign to do so.

"You've brought your dog with you?" he asked, curiously.

Holmes, in an uncharacteristically doting fashion, crouched and stroked the animal's back, "Lestrade is an invaluable assistant to my work. Like the Scotland Yard Inspector for whom he was named, he is brave and determined. If I put him on a scent, he will run it to ground. He is also adept at warning of danger and is a fair judge of character."

Standing again and taking the dog's leash from me, he asked Hunter a question. "Before we begin, I should like to know if there will be a military force assigned to these grounds, and whether or not they are to be on display or clandestine?"

The Major, still looking askance at Lestrade, answered, "There will be a military presence here, Mr. Holmes. As to how many and in what capacity, that is still under debate. I only know that it will be increased whenever the Prime Minister is in residence.

"Personally, I prefer a strong show of force – discourage anyone who has any thought of attacking this property or doing the P.M. harm. However, I have heard the argument made that this estate should present a peaceful image to the British people and, except for ceremonial guards, any troops attached would be assigned to barracks which are either underground or surrounded by high hedges."

"Very well," said the detective. "We'll table that discussion for now. If you'll lead the way, Mr. Hunter, I should like to observe the exterior of the house and any approaches from the surrounding woods."

We started off toward the south side where there lay several hedge squares surrounding multiple rose gardens, with each square designated for a particular type or color of rose. The spring blossoms created a heady odor as we strolled through. To my mind they provided a thorny barrier to advancing foot soldiers, and the hedges were too low for effective concealment. South of that area the land was flat and green for a goodly distance, with only a single line of trees running perpendicular to the manor house some one-hundred-fifty yards away.

Swinging around to the west, we found multiple tennis courts surrounded by a grove of trees some fifty feet thick. Beyond the western border of that grove, the land was again flat for well over two-hundred yards before the border of Box Tree Wood, a small rolling forest of about a quarter-acre. Coming around to the northwest corner, there was a scattering of trees some two-hundred feet from the north side of the manor. About two-hundred-fifty yards due north, there were the woods which had been on our right as we had driven down Missenden Road. After a hundred yards of trees, it flattened again to a wide level field, directly across from the house we had passed.

Other than the occasional woodland creature drawing his attention, Lestrade seemed quite content with his walk and showed no sign of alarm. Holmes had me make a few notes regarding the aforementioned measurements and the types of trees. He then requested Hunter to conduct us on a quick tour of the house so we could see what we were up against from a security perspective.

Room after room of magnificence and splendor greeted us. Marvelous works of art and historical memorabilia were everywhere. I shall not attempt to list them all here. Holmes

140

questioned Hunter on the provenance of several pieces and how long they had been in the house. He was particularly concerned with anything which may have been added after the plans were announced to turn Chequers into the Prime Minister's country home.

One such piece was a bust of General Oliver Cromwell, which sat on a shelf immediately behind the desk in what would be the P.M.'s working office. Lestrade had sniffed at it rather anxiously, even sitting up on his haunches and waving his paws like some circus animal. A rare feat I hadn't seen in him before, and was not aware he was capable of.

This caused Holmes to examine the bust carefully, then he lifted it off the shelf and held it down for the Bassett to get a good whiff. Lestrade immediately barked and Holmes told us all to clear the room as he set the piece on the desk where he could scrutinize it more closely.

Hunter started to question this command, but I took his elbow, along with the dog's leash, and hurried them both out into the hallway. We waited there for an anxious two minutes before Holmes called out to the Major.

"Mr. Hunter, I need you to clear the north side of the building. I'm taking this bust out through the window and getting it away from the house."

"Mr. Holmes?" cried the man. "That was a gift from the Duke of Holdernesse. Certainly it cannot be dangerous."

"I've no time to explain, sir. Please do as I say," ordered the detective in his most commanding tone.

"Watson, go outside and tie Lestrade up somewhere safe. Then meet me by the window. I need your assistance to hold this while I climb out."

I did as instructed and, once at the window, was able to feel the heft of the bust. Somehow the weight did not seem appropriate to the size. After Holmes stepped out, he took up the work of art and carried it to the edge of the trees where he carefully set it down.

Returning to the house, Holmes found that Major Hunter had joined me near the northeast corner where we could duck back to safety. Lestrade was tied up by the east door and the staff had been evacuated to the southern patio.

"Are you telling me that the Duke of Holdernesse sent a bomb to David Lloyd George, Mr. Holmes? That's preposterous!"

"I quite agree, but we'll get into that later. Do you have any ordinance experts nearby who can disarm a bomb?"

"Not at this time, Mr. Holmes. What do you propose we do?"

Holmes thought for a moment, then clapped my shoulder as he spoke to the Major. "Bring us one of the hunting rifles from the gun room."

To me he said, "Watson, it's time to put your weapons proficiency to use. I'm quite certain you can make this shot. We'll have to examine the pieces later."

I had long ago proven my shooting skills to Holmes, although the first time I did so was on an indoor range using a Colt .45 pistol nearly forty years ago. [3] I had discovered this trait early in my army training, though I never cared much for hunting. Hunter returned with an M1917 .30-06 bolt action rifle and handed it to me per Holmes's instruction. It had been some time since I'd used a weapon of this size and its nine pound weight nearly threw me off balance. I knelt quickly before embarrassing myself and set my cane on the ground. Shooting from the corner of the building gave me the advantage of being able to brace myself against the sturdy bricks. I wrapped my forearm around the sling and steadied my shoulder against the wall with my elbow on my knee. Taking my time, I checked the wind and adjusted the sight. Taking a deep breath, I gently squeezed the trigger.

The bust shattered into dozens of pieces, but the expected explosion did not occur. Hunter's voice grew tense, "Holmes, what have you done?" he demanded through gritted teeth.

Holmes declined to answer, instead striding quickly toward the now ruined work of art. We followed a few paces behind, the Major taking the rifle from me so I could walk more steadily with my cane and bring Lestrade along. Reaching the scene, we found Holmes kneeling and scooping up scatterings of black powder from the ground and off the inner surfaces of the plaster bust. The dog immediately began sniffing studiously at the varying pieces scattered about, giving little *woofs* as he did so.

"It was a black powder device," remarked Holmes before Hunter could complain any more. "Certainly safer for them to send it that way, as smokeless powder is more likely to detonate should the item have been dropped. See here – this fuse was at the back of the base of the neck, nearly impossible to detect when covered with wax. They must have assumed that someday they would be able to infiltrate the staff and some servant could enter the room with refreshments or what not for the P.M., then scrape away the wax with his thumbnail, pull out the fuse, and light it, giving him several seconds to leave the room.

"Look at what is embedded in the plaster forming the back of Cromwell's face."

We bent and looked closely where Holmes pointed. There were dozens of nails which would have shot out at whomever was in the line of fire, likely killing or severely wounding such a person.

Hunter's demeanour changed immediately, "Surely Holdernesse could not be involved in this!"

"Very likely not," replied Holmes. "Do you still have the card which came with it?"

"Yes, it's in my files awaiting an opportunity for the Prime Minister to send out thank you notes."

"Do you know who put the bust in that position?" asked the detective.

"We've had multiple decoraters of varying specialties working on this project," replied the chagrined officer. "I'll have to check the files and see if we can reconstruct who did what."

"Very well. Advise the servants that they may return to their duties, but no word of what we discovered. We'll meet you in your office to discuss this further."

In a matter of minutes Holmes, Lestrade, and I were in Hunter's office as the Major began scouring various ledgers for information. It was a dark-paneled space, unadorned by the artwork and décor which permeated the rest of the mansion. There was no window due to its location. Thus, it was dependent on ceiling lights and a banker's lamp on the desk for illumination. Shelves of ledgers and several dark wooden file cabinets took up the majority of the room – altogether a utilitarian space meant for work, not comfort. Holmes and I were seated in hard wooden chairs in front of the desk with the dog lying at the detective's feet.

At last, Hunter seemed to find the information we sought. First, he handed Holmes the card which had come with the Cromwell bust. "You can see for yourself, Mr. Holmes – the Duke of Holdernesse signed the letter."

I looked over at the document in Holmes's hand. It appeared to be quality stationery, worthy of a peer's station. It was a single typed paragraph with Holdernesse's bold signature affixed underneath. An envelope was attached by a paper clip and my companion gave it a cursory glance before handing it back to Hunter.

"This is a forgery," declared Holmes. "We once provided services for Lord Holdernesse and were rewarded with a sizable cheque. [4] One does not forget the signature on such a significant document. It is similar, but even accounting for his Lordship's

143

advancing years, there are certain characteristics inconsistent with his penmanship.

"Also, the stationery does not bear Holdernesse's custom watermark, nor does the envelope include his seal. It was a clever ruse to get the bomb inside the manor. Have you found who is responsible for placing it in the Prime Minister's office?"

The majordomo consulted a ledger he had opened on his desk. Running his index finger across an entry he shook his head as he read, "That particular office was the responsibility of Mrs. Katherine Casey. She is a noted historian and was recommended by the Cashman Museum in Oxford, where she is an assistant curator."

"Where is she now?" asked Holmes.

"She completed her work three weeks ago. Just in time, I should say," recalled Hunter. "She was heavy with child and has probably given birth by now."

Holmes tilted his head, "I presume she was vetted by your people?"

"We verified her identity, of course," replied Hunter. "We were assured by the museum that she came to them upon her graduation with honors from Somerville College at Oxford as Katherine Doyle in 1914. She married Sean Casey, a prominent solicitor in Cowley with a good reputation, in 1917. He was exempted from war service due to an injury he suffered during his army training which severed his left foot."

As I sat listening to this, it seemed that such detail was rather thorough, and I wondered how the young woman could be involved in this apparent plot. Holmes steepled his fingers at his lips momentarily, then asked, "If she was that far along in her pregnancy, I presume she had someone assist her with the placement of the heavier articles in that room. Do you have any idea who that might be?"

Hunter shook his head, "It could have been any of the servants or workmen. All such items are received into the cellar where they are cataloged for assignment. There are still many items down there. They will be stored and rotated for display on various occasions or to fit the tastes of the particular prime minister in residence at the time."

"We'll need to examine that area, of course," declared Holmes. "Is the telephone in the Prime Minister's office a private line? I need to call London."

Chapter IV
144

Hunter unlocked the door to the office, for Holmes had locked it before he passed the bust out the window to me. We gave him his privacy on the telephone and I enquired of the Major if there were somewhere convenient where I might obtain water for the dog panting at my feet. He took me out to the kennel by which we had walked on our earlier exterior excursion. "There are no dogs in residence at present," he remarked. "Your Basset is free to wander this area. There is a water pump over there and containers of dog food in that shed."

I took Lestrade off his leash and let him wander about as I filled a metal bowl with water from the pump. I found more bowls and food in the shed and set out a fair-sized meal for the hungry hound. I knelt and spoke gently to the animal as I scratched behind his ears, assuring him that I would be back. He seemed to accept that, going immediately to his food bowl.

The Major and I returned to the house and met Holmes coming from the office, having finished his telephone call. Hunter spoke first, "What next, Mr. Holmes?"

My friend glanced at the floor and replied, "I presume Lestrade is enjoying a meal out in the kennel. We will require him later. For now let us continue the tour of the house."

The rest of the afternoon was spent going floor by floor and room by room, Holmes having me take so many notes that I nearly filled my notebook. This was only a cursory tour and a more detailed examination would take place over the next several days. We found many other items regarding General Cromwell. Hunter informed us that John Russell, a grandson of Cromwell, Lord Protector of England during the English Civil War, had married Joanna Thurbarne, who had inherited Chequers in 1707.

Once we finished with a quick look of the attic, we descended to the ground floor again where we examined the kitchen and pantry. Holmes paid particular attention to the dumbwaiter which brought supplies up from the cellar. He even took some measurements.

Finally, he turned to Hunter and said, "I believe we should retrieve Lestrade and examine the cellar."

Our canine companion was napping in a shady spot when we returned to the kennel, but perked up immediately at the sound of the opening gate. He trotted over to Holmes in that swaying fashion unique to stout, short-legged dogs, sat down, and stared up at his master. Holmes gave him a biscuit from his pocket and attached the leash.

"I should like to take a closer look at the outside entrance to the cellar, Major. Please lead the way."

Hunter did so and, upon arrival, took keys from his pocket to unlock the doors, prompting Holmes to question, "Who else has keys to this area?"

"Only the kitchen steward, the groundskeeper, and I can enter through here. From the inside the door for the kitchen has a lock, but it is left over from years ago when servants were less trusted. Nowadays it is never locked."

Once inside, Hunter turned on the electric lights and I noted a quiet hum. When I questioned the noise, the majordomo replied, "That is a dehumidifier, Dr. Watson. You'll notice that this room does not exhibit the damp feel or smell typical of most cellars. It prevents the growth of mildew and the spoilage of food."

Holmes knelt by the Basset and pulled the envelope of black powder from his pocket to give the dog a scent. He then ordered, "Seek," and walked the room with Lestrade sniffing all around. Everything seemed to pass muster, until they reached the coal bin. The bin itself was full. However, there were several crates of charcoal next to it and Lestrade crouched and barked until Holmes put him at ease. Using a crowbar that hung there for the purpose of opening such crates, Holmes pried the top off of one and dumped the contents onto to floor. One would expect coal dust to have settled to the bottom of the crate so it was no surprise when the charcoal tumbled out amidst piles of black powder. What was concerning was the amount. The crate was probably two thirds full of black powder with just two or three layers of actual charcoal on top.

Holmes called the Major and me over, pointed at the pile on the floor, and said, "More gunpowder. We are in deep waters, gentlemen. Major, you must keep the Prime Minister's office locked so no one knows we have discovered the bust. Explain to the staff that we merely shot a prowling scavenger earlier. Do you have men who can come and haul away these crates tonight under cover of darkness?"

"Yes, Mr. Holmes, I can arrange that," replied Hunter.

"Good. You will also need to replace the crates. No staff member can know we've discovered this deadly cache."

Holmes looked about the cellar once more, "Are all the supplies and artifacts delivered to this room directly from the supplier, or is there another warehouse from which you draw items that have been bought in bulk?"

"There are two storehouses with whom we contract for overstock," replied the army officer. "I can get the names and addresses for you from my office if you like."

"That would be prudent," answered Holmes. "I presume they're nearby?"

Hunter's answer sent an alarm off in Holmes's mind and he demanded, "I must use the telephone again. Quickly, Major!"

Late that afternoon, we left in time to be back to The Crowe's Nest before dark. This time, Holmes drove and I sat with Lestrade on my lap, poking his nose out the side. When we reached Wendover Road and were almost there, Holmes turned right instead. When I enquired where we were going, he stated, "I'm expecting a telegram at Wendover Station."

"Surely they would have delivered it to The Crowe's Nest." I said.

"I prefer to pick this one up as discreetly as possible," was his only reply.

After forty years of friendship, I knew better than to question Holmes's reasons and merely sat back and enjoyed the ride. The temperature was beginning to drop, but our overcoats were sufficient for now. I waited in the car with the dog while Holmes went into the station telegraph office. He was out in about five minutes, stuffing a message into his inner breast pocket.

"Forgive my tardiness, Watson," he apologized. "This required another inquiry on my part."

"Were you writing to Mycroft?" I asked.

"Among others," he said.

"Could you possibly request another vehicle? This old bucket is deucedly cold, uncomfortable, and nearly impossible to crank up. I should hate to have an emergency come along and need to start it without your assistance."

He smiled, "Already done, my friend."

Upon return to our lodgings, Holmes backed the Ford into the carriage house and parked it where it had been. When we got out, though, instead of immediately going into the inn, Holmes chose to poke around a bit at the supplies in storage. This went on for nearly ten minutes before he was satisfied. He wouldn't answer my query as to what he was looking for, merely stating, "Something that is not here."

We took to our rooms and cleaned up for dinner. The menu at The Crowe's Nest was in keeping with its seafaring name and offered a variety seafood in addition to the more common dishes of the English countryside. The dun-colored walls were decorated with fishing nets, harpoons, and mounted fish. A large painting of *H.M.S. Vanguard* hung on one wall, and an anchor leaned on top of the fireplace mantel.

Such an atmosphere inspired me to have a halibut steak with assorted vegetables. Holmes chose to eat lightly as he so often does on a case, when he eats at all. His plate arrived with various cheeses, a platter of bread, and a glass of wine. Our table was off in a corner, as Holmes preferred not to be overheard.

"You have suffered your usual patience with this investigation, old friend. As always, I appreciate your silence so that I may concentrate my thoughts. Now, however, I would require you to speak your mind upon any conclusions you may have drawn."

I took a sip of the white house wine, a combination of Chardonnay and Chenin Blanc, which the innkeeper referred to as *Blarney's Blend*, to wash down my last bite of fish. I dabbed my lips with my napkin and sat back. Looking at my companion, I sniffed. "I could hardly have seen any more than you, Holmes. I daresay likely not a tenth as much."

Holmes shook his head. "I need an intelligent layman's perspective. Your education and military background is ideal, for you are the type these assassins are attempting to bypass."

"Very well then," I paused, hooked my thumbs into my lapels, and looked to the ceiling to gather my thoughts. Finally, I leaned forward, arms folded upon the table to keep my voice low, and spoke.

"There could be any number of enemies who would want to do harm to the Prime Minister. This could be the work of German agents in retribution against the treaty terms they were forced to sign. It could be radicals of the opposition party. At some future point, there may be a ransom note forthcoming from some criminal element, and failure to pay would have required a demonstration of their power."

"You are convinced, then, that it is a group plot and not an individual?"

I shook my head, "Too many elements for one person, or even two. Had it just been the bust in the office, we might be able to lay the blame at the feet of this Katherine Casey person. But even then, she would require an accomplice on the serving staff to set off the bomb at some future date. The stockpile of black powder in the cellar indicates a much larger group."

148

Holmes hummed in apparent agreement, then asked, "Why an explosive? A member of the serving staff could just as easily slip poison into the Prime Minister's food or drink."

"Poison is too quiet," I responded. "Whoever is behind this wants a public demonstration. Death by poisoning could be covered up as merely a heart condition or other such ailment. The public might never know the truth, and these people want to make a statement."

Holmes pulled his pipe from his pocket and sat back to light it, "You are a reflection of luminescence my friend, as always. Thank you."

Chapter V

The next morning there was a knock upon our door at seven-thirty. Lestrade sat up in his basket as I went to answer. Holmes emerged from his room just as I opened the door to reveal Lt. Harry Wiggins. He was not in uniform, as he was during our adventure just the previous Christmas [5], so I merely said, "Wiggins, a pleasure to see you again."

The young man shook my hand, "Doctor, always a pleasure, sir."

Turning to my companion, he held up a key as he said, "Ah, Mr. Holmes, I believe you requested a new car? I've been sent to take that relic off your hands."

Holmes traded over the key to the Model T and thanked the young man. I could never get over the resemblance of the Lieutenant to his father, Joe Wiggins, former head of the Baker Street Irregulars and now owner of Jabez Wilson's old pawn shop. He then held out a briefcase to Holmes, saying, "From Sir Mycroft."

Holmes took the case, removed a folder, and began a quick perusal of the papers within. "As I thought," he said, without expounding. Looking back to the young man he asked, "Will you be joining us, Wiggins?"

"I'm afraid not, sir, although I will be gathering information you may find useful while I'm on assignment to Oxford. I'll send any findings to the Wendover Station, per your request. A telegram to the Oxford Constabulary will reach me if you need anything."

"One question, if I may," I said. "Why on earth did Mycroft inflict that old rattletrap on us to begin with?"

Wiggins shrugged his shoulders, but Holmes answered, "It was merely an identifier, Watson. The lookouts were told to watch out for such a vehicle on the day we arrived. It merely established our bona fides."

I shook my head, looked at Wiggins, and said, "Tell Mycroft he should try something out himself before inflicting it upon others. Thank you for bringing us something better." I paused. "It is better, isn't it?"

The young man smiled, "Yes, Dr. Watson. It's an Army surplus, 1919 Lanchester Forty, but it's been painted a royal blue and rides very well."

"Thank goodness," I replied. "You be careful on your assignment, young man."

"Yes, sir," he said, starting to salute, but he caught himself and shook my hand instead.

After Wiggins left us, Holmes sat at our common room table, beginning a more thorough examination of the papers, and saying to me, "You go have breakfast, Watson. I need to digest this information rather than food. Meet me at the car in forty-five minutes."

I took his advice to heart and ate a hearty breakfast, not knowing whether Holmes would take time for lunch. I returned to the room and found him and Lestrade both gone, so I continued out the back door and was greeted by the sight of a beautiful Lanchester automobile. It was a four-door model with a royal blue body, black roof, engine compartment, running boards, and fenders. It also featured actual windows to enclose the passenger compartment from the elements.

I was greeted with a bark from the Basset who was seated in the back, with the window partially open and the car already running. I slid into the passenger seat and Holmes drove us smoothly out onto Missenden Road and at a moderate pace to arrive at Chequers in less than five minutes. We pulled into the same spot as the day before, and Hunter greeted us.

"All is as you requested, Mr. Holmes. The crates with the black powder were replaced last night and taken away by horse-drawn wagons, so as not to draw attention. My men and I are the only ones currently spending the night here. The nearest neighbor is only a half-mile away, and I felt motor vehicles in the middle of the night may arouse suspicion. My men down the road have been examining the crates and found that the ones containing the explosives had a unique mark of identification. We also found one packed with dynamite and a concealed fuse, much like the one on the bust. We

150

have left the fuse intact, but replaced the dynamite with empty tubes, in case someone checks."

"Excellent work, Mr. Hunter. Has everyone shown up for work today?" asked the detective.

"All accounted for, Mr. Holmes."

Holmes held up the briefcase, "Mycroft's agents have been digging deeper into certain backgrounds. We may uncover this conspiracy very soon. In the meantime, I should like to lock this up somewhere and then go about a more thorough inspection of the premises."

We went on to the known secret passages and rooms to ensure that they were either locked or sealed and that nothing harmful was stored in any of them. There were more than I expected, but then, this estate had been through many a war and persecution. Priest holes and even a "prison room" were a part of its history.

Holmes also made an inspection of the gas pipes and electrical circuits, making note of vulnerable areas where more precautions should be taken. Every ground floor entrance, whether by door or window, was checked for locks or bolts. These proceedings took up most of the morning, and even Lestrade was exhibiting signs of wanting to get off his feet.

At last, Holmes stated, "I believe that is sufficient for this morning. Mr. Hunter, if you could prevail upon the chef to provide us with a light lunch, it would be most appreciated. Watson, would you see to Lestrade? I'll be in the office."

After provisioning our four-legged friend with food and water, I stopped by the kitchen where a cart with trays of food and beverages had been prepared. I offered to take the cart myself, but the kitchen steward insisted upon serving us. Thus, he followed me to the office where Holmes was going over Mycroft's papers in greater detail.

Holmes glanced up briefly at our entrance and nodded to the gentleman, "Thank you. Walsh, isn't it?"

"Yes, Mr. Holmes," the steward replied. "Will there be anything else, sir?"

Holmes took a quick look at the cart and answered, "This should be quite sufficient."

Walsh turned on his heel and left us. I set a plate with a sandwich and fruit next to Holmes and took one for myself. I also picked up a bottle of brandy, but before opening it, Holmes asked to inspect it. I handed it over and he carefully examined the foil and

151

cork and even checked the bottom of the bottle. Handing it back to me, he merely said, "Thank you, Watson. You may pour."

"Really, Holmes," I said as I poured us each a measure of the amber liquid. "Do you think someone would dare to poison us while we are here?"

"It would be foolish to poison both of us, Doctor," he replied. "It would bring down suspicion rather hard and make their further plans even more difficult to move forth. However, we have dealt with fools before."

I looked at the bottom of the bottle after I had poured our drinks and enquired, "I assume you were looking for needle marks in the foil or through the cork. But why the bottom of the bottle?"

Holmes took a sip of his brandy and replied, "A diamond drill could be used to make a hole for inserting poison. Someone, with glass blowing skills could then re-seal the hole. However, the heat required to do that would distort the glass around the hole and leave a discernible mark."

I sighed, "Sometimes I pity the way your mind must work, Holmes. Always having to be on guard like that. It must be a terrible strain."

"On the contrary, Watson," he replied. "It has become second nature to me, and I rarely notice the extra precautions I take, unless they prove to be life-saving."

Major Hunter stuck his head in the door just then and enquired if we needed anything else before he went to eat lunch with his men in the radio room. Holmes handed him a slip of paper with two names written upon it, and asked for the employment records and references of each of them. "After you've eaten will be sufficient, Mr. Hunter. At that point, I may need to use the private telephone in the P.M.'s office again."

The information that Hunter brought back an hour later did, indeed, prompt a phone call by Holmes. Afterward, he informed Hunter that we would be leaving for the day and returning later that evening. We asked to leave Lestrade to the Major's care and he agreed.

When we got into the Lanchester, I asked Holmes where we were going. He replied, "The sparks that have been going off in my mind are starting to burn more brightly. I just spoke with Wiggins. He gave me a piece of kindling and is now investigating another possible match. We are headed to Oxford, but first we must make a quick stop at Crowe's Nest."

Arriving at the inn, Holmes pulled straight into the carriage house. Like the previous evening, he strode among the supply area for the two establishments. This time, however, I saw him making notes as I stayed out of his way, standing by the entrance. I was smoking a cigarette and also serving as lookout. I let out a loud "Halloa!" when I saw Boyle coming from the inn. Holmes quickly opened up the engine compartment of the automobile before the manager came into his line of sight. Boyle asked if anything were wrong.

"I saw you pull in a few minutes ago, Mr. Holmes. When you didn't come in straight away, I thought I'd see if I could help you with something."

"Thank you, Mr. Boyle. The engine seemed to be running a bit warm," answered the detective. "I was just letting it cool off so I could check the water level. It appears adequate. I should like to borrow a canteen if I may, in case it acts up on our next drive."

"You're going out again today?"

"Just a quick trip over to Oxford. One of my old professors has asked us to tea with him this afternoon."

"I'll fetch something for you right away."

"We do appreciate your assistance, sir. Doctor Watson and I will just step into the pub for a bit of ale, then be on our way." Holmes closed and latched the engine cowling and the three of us walked back to the pub where Doyle poured Holmes and me some Smithwick's Red Ale.

As we drank, Boyle disappeared for a minute, then returned with a full two-quart-sized canteen. We thanked the man and then returned to our car for the trip westward to Oxford.

As we turned right on Ellesborough Road, I turned to my friend, "I assume that was a ruse about tea with an old professor?"

Holmes's kept his eyes on the road and replied, "Certainly. All of my professors at any of the schools I attended are long retired to warmer climes or have passed on. We're meeting Wiggins to pick up more information, and then calling upon a young lady."

He would say no more but, after retrieving a report from the Lieutenant at the Oxford Constabulary office, our next stop was Trinity Hospital, whereupon Holmes asked for a piece of equipment from my ever-present medical bag. We made our way toward the maternity ward, and he asked me to keep lookout outside the room of Mrs. Katherine Casey.

As it was mid-afternoon, Mr. Casey was likely at work. This allowed for my friend to be alone with the new mother, who was still

153

recovering from giving birth to a son – whose name, Wiggins had learned, was Patrick.

"Good afternoon, Mrs. Casey," Holmes smooth mellifluous voice filtered out into the hallway where I stood. "I'm Dr. Scott. How are you feeling today?"

"I'm much stronger, Doctor. Frankly, I feel I could do better if I could take Patrick home and start eating decent food again."

In spite of the words, the complaint was couched in a humorous tone which I found to be a pleasant sound. Holmes replied in like manner. "I understand. Hospital food is not exactly *haute cuisine*. Well, let's see what your heart tells us."

Holmes, using my stethoscope quite expertly, listened to her heart and lungs. I should have known that, after all the years of observing me, he would be able to mimic a cursory examination.

"Your heart and lungs are fine," he stated. "Any pelvic pain?"

"It has quite subsided, Doctor. Only hunger pains now," she joked.

"Very good," replied Holmes with a chuckle as he took her wrist to check her pulse. "I see on your chart that you are married to Sean Casey. Would that be the solicitor of Casey, Stengel, and York?"

"Yes, that's his firm," she replied with no little pride. "You know of it?"

"I'd written an opinion for them on a medical case years ago, but was never called to testify. I understand they're quite successful."

"Yes, my husband has many prominent clients. Just recently he was entrusted to deliver a gift for the Duke of Holdernesse to the Prime Minister for his new estate at Chequers. I was doing some work there as an historian and was able to assist in the delivery. It was a bust of Lord Cromwell, and the Duke was quite insistent that it be placed overlooking the Prime Minister's desk as a source of inspiration."

"How interesting," replied Holmes. "You were most fortunate to obtain such a prestigious post. Were you solicited, or did you apply for it?"

"My husband heard of the position and used his connections to make a recommendation. I was thrilled to obtain it. I only wish I could have finished, but Patrick had other plans."

Out in the hall, I was finding this lady quite charming, even though I couldn't see her.

154

"Did you get to meet the Duke yourself when he gave over the bust to your husband?" asked Holmes.

"No, Sean was given it while meeting at the Duke's estate. His Lordship preferred to have him deliver it rather than entrust it to some delivery service, for it was rather fragile."

"I presume Mr. Casey drove you there? He didn't let you carry anything too heavy?" said Holmes, feigning concern.

"Oh, no, Doctor. He insisted on driving me and setting the bust up in the office himself because of the weight."

"Very good," replied the detective. Then added, "Your blood pressure is slightly elevated, but not alarmingly so. Have you done your walking exercises today?"

"Yes, Doctor. I'm feeling quite well. No pain, no dizziness."

"You seem fine to me, and I shall add my voice to a recommendation for your release. Congratulations on your new son. Good day!"

As Holmes and I were walking away from the room a nurse came by with a tea cart. Holmes, the stethoscope still around his neck, asked the young lady if it was for Mrs. Casey. "Yes, Doctor, it's her afternoon tea."

Holmes looked over the tray, finding a thin porridge and crackers. He looked at me and said, "I believe she can have something more substantial than this at this stage."

I nodded and he turned back to the nurse. "Please bring her a proper sandwich and some ginger ale. She needs to be weaned back onto solid food."

"Very good, Doctor," said the nurse who turned to go back to the kitchen. We continued out the door to the Lanchester and I questioned my companion.

"She seemed quite sincere. It appears she had no knowledge of the explosive device."

"Her charm can be quite disarming," he replied. "She is also attractive. A two-edged sword in the weaponry of deceit. However, I believe you are correct."

"What tipped the scales toward her innocence in your eyes?" I enquired.

"I was taking her pulse the whole time I questioned her. There was no significant change, as there would be if she were lying or hiding something. Just a slight elevation due to her pride in her husband and her son. No, she is innocent in all this. More's the pity, for her words have all but condemned her husband."

Chapter VI

"Will you have Sean Casey arrested then?" I asked as we stepped into the car.

"Not yet. We need more proof, and this admission does not explain the dynamite in the cellar. There is more data to gather, and more players in this little game at Chequers."

We drove back to the Oxford constabulary office and met with Wiggins and a police sergeant. Holmes instructed them on actions they needed to take regarding the solicitor and left them to their own devices for doing so. The return to Chequers went smoothly. Walsh answered our knock and informed us Hunter was awaiting us in his office. The Major greeted us enthusiastically when we appeared and bid us to close the door and sit down.

"I've found a discrepancy, Mr. Holmes. We get regular coal deliveries by way of a service which brings in a vehicle once a month to fill the bin through the outdoor chute. However, the charcoal that was in the crates is used for outdoor cooking, and is only ordered in the spring and summer when the weather permits such activities. The crates we found were ordered in February, far ahead of schedule, and sent to the storehouse of The Russell Arms to await the first spring delivery."

"Ordered by Walsh, no doubt," declared Holmes.

Major Hunter's countenance fell as his thunder was knocked out from under him. Recovering, he asked, "Why, yes, Mr. Holmes. How did you guess that?"

Holmes shook his head impatiently, "I never guess, sir. As head kitchen steward, Walsh is the only one in authority to make such an order, save for Lord Lee himself, until you arrived. It also fits the pattern I've detected."

"We should take him into custody!" demanded Hunter.

Holmes shook his head, "There are more players in this game than he. We need absolute proof before we make our move to round them all up."

"You mean Brockmeyer, the desk manager at The Russell Arms? Likely a German agent if you ask me."

Holmes shook his head and responded, "People are being used in this plot, Major. I'm awaiting one more piece of evidence before we close in on the true culprits. In the meantime, we remain diligent and don't let any potential target visit this facility until we've sprung our trap.

156

It took two more days, and Holmes continued a vigilant inspection of the grounds and buildings. At last, we brought in an army stenographer to transcribe all the notes that he and I had taken into some semblance of a report of recommendations for Mycroft to act upon. When a telegram arrived from Wiggins at Wendover Station, Holmes emerged waving the flimsy in the air as he returned to the car. Handing it to me he cried, "We have them, Watson! Now we can act."

The following Saturday afternoon, a party was planned for the staff and other special guests who were so instrumental in the preparations of Chequers for the Prime Minister's occupancy. A contingent of Royal Horse Guards were brought in for ceremonial purposes, and the servants were relieved of their normal duties so they could be waited upon by an outside agency that was hired.

All the decorators and refurbishers were invited, including Mrs. Casey and her husband. Brockmeyer, Boyle, and other suppliers were brought in as well. All were gathered in the ballroom until Hunter, in his role as majordomo, stood before them.

"I welcome you all to this special occasion where the Lord and Lady Lee wished to express their gratitude for your diligent work in preparations for this grand estate to be turned over to the government for the use of all future Prime Ministers. They have returned from Italy, but are currently stuck in London. Hopefully, they will arrive in time for dinner. In the meantime, you are all to proceed to the south patio where tables have been arranged for your comfort and refreshments will be served.

Holmes had stayed out of sight, not wishing to be recognized by Mrs. Casey, but I knew that he was in disguise as one of the cooks. Hunter stayed close to Walsh and Casey as we emerged onto the patio. There were several round tables covered in tablecloths and place settings. Beyond them were serving tables and a row of large grills. A line of Royal Guardsmen with rifles and bayonets, resplendent in their red coats and tall beaver hats, took their place along the doorways leading back into the house.

When Walsh saw the grills and the crates of charcoal being place in them, he froze. When Holmes, as a bearded cook, threw a match onto the kindling underneath one such box, Walsh grabbed Casey's arm and whispered, "We must get away from here, now!"

Hunter and three of the guardsmen grabbed the two men when they turned to flee, while Mrs. Casey cried out in confusion at being left behind. Several feet away, Boyle had also tried to run for it and was detained by two more guardsmen. Walsh looked back at the grill

157

in horror as the flames began to grow. In panic at last he screamed, "It's going to explode! We must get away now!"

He struggled against his captors to no avail as Holmes called out to the crowd, while removing his false beard, "No need to panic, ladies and gentlemen! The explosives he refers to have been removed and everything is quite safe. I am Sherlock Holmes, and we do have some arrests to make, but the rest of you feel free to relax, have some wine, and enjoy yourselves."

The guests returned to their conversations, much more animated than before. Casey, Walsh, and Boyle were handcuffed and taken inside. Mrs. Casey went up to Holmes and demanded, "How dare you pass yourself off as a doctor! What is the meaning of all this? Why have you arrested my husband?"

Holmes bowed his head to the lady. "I am sorry for your situation, Mrs. Casey. I have no doubt you are an innocent pawn in your husband's game."

She started to protest, but Holmes held up his hand and indicated me, as I was standing close by. "This is Dr. Watson. He will introduce you to the Duke of Holdernesse, who is a guest here tonight. He will confirm that he never gave your husband the Cromwell bust. It was a bomb meant to be set off by your husband's uncle, Mr. Walsh, to kill the Prime Minister. I'm afraid they are both members of an Irish underground rebel group, as is Mr. Boyle of The Crowe's Nest."

"No!" she cried, on the verge of tears. "It cannot be!" Her voice faltered and she began to swoon. I caught her and eased her into a chair. Holmes caught Holdernesse's attention and he came over to speak with the unfortunate lady.

Later, after the military guards had removed their prisoners, Holmes and I met with Hunter in his office, away from curious guests.

Hunter began the discussion. "How did you make the Irish connection, Holmes? I thought surely Germans would be behind this."

Holmes nodded as he lit a cigarette, "With the late war so fresh in our minds, gentlemen, it was natural to lean toward German agents perpetrating this scheme. But a different spark was struck in my mind at the mention of Katherine Casey's name. When I heard her maiden name as '*Doyle*', then her husband '*Sean Casey*', I left that ember to smolder in the background. Then, when you showed me the list of storehouses and I saw '*Russell Arms*'. I knew that

158

Boyle, another Irishman, as evidenced not only by his name, but the drinks he serves and the painting of the Vanguard on his wall, was involved. His establishment was used for their storage. That ember began to burn like kindling. Finally, there was *Walsh*, the steward. Certainly you realize that we had the makings of an Irish bonfire here?"

"My agent's name is *Doyle*, and he's Scottish," I interjected.

"One of the many names developed from the Gaelic language roots they share. Just as is *Walsh*, which is also a Welsh name," answered my friend patiently. "When I had Mycroft and Wiggins dig deeper into the family backgrounds of these people, my suspicions were confirmed. Walsh and Boyle were both involved in the Easter Uprising last year, though under different identities. Casey blames the British government for the loss of his foot, and was a natural recruit for his uncle, especially with his connections."

Hunter nodded, "You are sure the wife is not involved?"

"Mrs. Casey, in spite of her Irish roots on her grandfather's side, loves Great Britain and is passionate about our history. It is what makes her a successful curator for the museum. It was shameful of her husband to use her so. I only hope this bitter experience will not dampen that enthusiasm and turn her against England."

I spoke up at that. "If she recognizes the lack of trust her husband had in her, and that his love for her was was not as deep as hers for him, I'm sure that will go a long, though painful, way toward her resolve to go on and provide a good life for her son."

"I leave the thoughts of women to your expertise, Doctor," he replied, waving the cigarette in my direction. "All the same, I do believe a recommendation to Mycroft to keep an eye on her, and her son as he grows up, would not be out of order. The Irish independence question is not likely to go away for at least a generation to come."

NOTES

1. Mycroft Holmes was knighted after the Great War, ostensibly for his decades of loyal service. Sherlock Holmes suspected it was rather to placate him for the government ignoring his advice regarding post-war treatment of Germany. Mycroft had predicted that the harsh terms imposed by the Allies would build nothing but resentment and determination for the German nation to rise again. – See "The Five Gold Rings" in *Sherlock Holmes Further Adventures for the Twelve Days of Christmas* by Roger Riccard.
2. See "The Five Gold Rings" in *Sherlock Holmes Further Adventures for the Twelve Days of Christmas* by Roger Riccard
3. See "The Eighth Milkmaid" in *Sherlock Holmes Adventures for the Twelve Days of Christmas* by Roger Ricccard
4. See "The Priory School".
5. "The Five Gold Rings" from *Sherlock Holmes Further Adventures for the Twelve Days of Christmas* by Roger Riccard.

The Adventure of the
Swiss Banker
by Frank Schildiner

"Watson," my friend Sherlock Holmes said to me, "Could I interest you in a brief visit to the London Underground?"

I looked up from my newspaper, quite taken aback by the suggestion. Holmes never asked such questions unless he was on the scent of an investigation. As I've written in the past, by that time London's first consulting detective and my closest friend was retired, having chosen a life of beekeeping in Sussex over his previous existence. I was married and acted as a consultant for various medical matters about the city – far more sedentary lives than our days residing in Baker Street.

"I have no appointments," I said. "What is this about, if I may ask?"

Holmes, who was visiting my home while Mrs. Watson was assisting her niece's wedding preparations, turned over my newspaper and pointed towards the headline on the bottom of the first page. There was a simple article, mentioning the disappearance of one Dritan Muller, a former Swiss banking clerk.

"'*Last sighted near Victoria Station*'," I read aloud. "Why does this inspire your interest in visiting the Underground? It appears a common enough missing persons case."

The corner of Holmes's lips lifted briefly in the ghost of a smile, one I remembered quite well from our more adventurous days.

"Normally such an event wouldn't receive my attention. The event does raise a unique coincidence that occurred when I visited Mycroft yesterday. He remarked upon several persons I've encountered in the past appearing at the same time in London. I don't fancy that they traveled here for me, most having arrived four days ago. However, I do believe their presence and this apparent disappearance are connected in some way."

"Which is?" I asked, rising slowly from my seat.

Holmes turned his back, heading for the guest room down the hall.

"Each were followed to Victoria Station and were observed walking randomly about the vicinity. I shall meet you in the front hall in twenty minutes," he said. "Oh, and Watson?"

"Yes?" I asked.

"Do bring your revolver," he called over his shoulder. "The individuals we may encounter are a less-than-savory lot."

Victoria Station on a spring afternoon is a sight to behold, one that writers of fantastical tales of the future would struggle in explaining. Dozens of people bustled about, moving in every conceivable direction – their expressions ranging from determined to the quite confused. I spotted well-dressed gentlemen and ladies striding purposefully while liveried men lugged mountains of luggage in their wake. There were smartly dressed young blades with waxed mustaches, filth-stained workers, children of all ages, and elderly couples moving with deliberate slowness.

And none behaved as if their fellow travelers were somehow of a lesser breed. Having visited other lands, both before and after my association with Sherlock Holmes, I knew this was a far from common phenomena. Britain, or more specifically London, is truly a land of dreams, and I felt a glow of pride in my chest as Holmes and I joined the throng.

"Mr. Holmes," a familiar voice said to our right, "and Dr. Watson. Now this is a propitious turn of events."

I smiled as I turned, extending my hand towards a voice I recognized instantly.

"Harry Dickson!" I said, shaking the man's hand after Holmes. "You do look well!"

Young Harry Dickson, for I still thought of him as Holmes's young pupil in the arts of crime detection, had aged since that distant time. His sandy hair appeared lighter, and I spotted the faint traces of a scar or two on the back of his right hand and at the edge of his collar.

"Thank you, Doctor," he said, favoring me with a warm, almost boyish, grin. "How is the lovely Mrs. Watson?"

"Quite well, I thank you," I said, stepping back slightly as Holmes edged closer.

"Given your earlier statement," my friend said, "I presume you're in search of a certain Swiss gentleman's whereabouts."

Harry Dickson nodded, his demeanor shifting to one of grave concern, I observed.

"Just so," he said, his unusual accent an odd co-mingling of English and American tones. "As are representatives of at least two governments, based on those present."

"If you refer to the French gentleman pretending to be reading the train schedule," Holmes said, "I think you will find he is following the short plump woman with the poorly hidden pearl necklace within her sleeve."

"No, Mr. Holmes," Dickson said, "I believe he is an inquiry agent from Marseille, based upon his luggage and brand of tobacco. No, I meant the Prussian man who keeps checking his watch while gazing towards the south exit."

I noticed the man immediately, a tallish, slender figure in a dark suit and a Homburg hat. He had short dark hair and a neat Van Dyke beard that appeared slightly lighter in color than his hair.

"How did you know he was Prussian?" I asked, not glancing toward the possible agent's direction.

"His boots," Holmes said. "A particular brand favored by members of the Prussian cavalry."

"Also," Dickson said, "his pocket watch is one made exclusively by a Königsberg firm whose dials are distinct."

"There are several other factors," my friend added, "which need not be stated since the point is clear. Are there others?"

"I believe I observed a squat figure dressed in a coat I recognized as Siberian," Harry Dickson said, his eyes shifting left and right. "However, I lost sight of him, thanks to a blast of steam from a departing train."

Holmes turned away, purchased a newspaper from a passing boy, and said, "Then we had best begin our search in the Underground. If Herr Muller is in fear for his life, I doubt he would remain above ground for any length of time."

Both detectives turned and I joined them, heading for the staircase that lead to one of the Underground lines. I didn't ask why they chose this particular tunnel, but I expected each could recite a long list of observations on the subject.

"This tunnel," Holmes said, airing my unspoken question, "leads to the most exits in the station. Banker Muller would feel that was the best choice, since it provided him with the most directions in which he could flee."

I shook my head and said, "And the most in which someone could assault him from behind."

Dickson laughed, stating, "True, Doctor. Herr Muller is a banker, not a former officer in the military. He would choose the direction that offered him the best chances of escape."

"Escape from what?" I asked, though my question was ignored by both detectives.

We halted at the bottom of the stairs, which opened to a tunnel that ran left and right before turning and sloping downward. Both Holmes and Dickson halted, their heads moving in both directions. Their swiveling skulls ceased simultaneously, focusing upon one location upon the wall.

"What is it?" I asked, not spotting anything untoward.

Both men ignored me as Dickson walked over and held a magnifying glass above a tiny stain along the tiled wall. Then he and Holmes stared through the lens for a moment and exchanged a look.

"Blood, Watson," Holmes said. "A single drop."

I knew better than to question at any find by my friend and his former pupil, but this did seem slightly ridiculous.

"Surely that could have been there for weeks," I responded.

"The stain is less than twenty-four hours old," Holmes said. "The cleaning staff haven't arrived in this location, though their work from past work is clear. You will observe a thin line of soap along the left bottom edge. It hasn't been covered by the dust of multiple travelers yet."

"Anyone could have tossed that there," I said in protest.

"Not based on the angle and shape of the stain," Dickson said. "The elongated teardrop shape, as well as the direction of the thinner edge points indicates a person quickly swinging his or her arms from a location above. Any additional drops probably fell on the pavement and were destroyed by the pedestrians."

"South then," my friend said, turning and leading us that direction. "A-ha! Another two of them, five feet forward on the right. A hand injury."

Dickson pointed to several more spatters further along. "Quite a bad one, based on that series."

Holmes shook his head and sighed. "I fear we may be too late for Herr Muller."

Neither Harry Dickson nor I said anything in reply. We merely trailed in Holmes's wake until we were back in the station. The young and old consulting detectives stepped to the left and right of the doorway, with Dickson squatting low and duck-walking several feet.

"Here," he said. "I believe he ran in this direction. The stain is dried, but not older than one hour!"

I started as young Dickson ran forward and laughed triumphantly. "Yes! A clear handprint, my friends!"

Holmes's former pupil stood next to a ladder that led downward next to the tracks. A clear concrete walkway lay below, trailing into the dark rail tunnel. There were several bloodstains heading down the ladder, and some that I observed splashed across the crumbling brick wall near the metal rungs.

"Capital!" Holmes said, following Dickson down the ladder. "Come along, Watson. The game's afoot!"

Both Holmes and Dickson produced electric torches, lighting the way as we stepped into the stygian, dank murk beneath the city of London. The air felt fetid and my nose wrinkled from the odors of mildew, rotting wood, and other foul scents I couldn't identify. I fancy that I heard the sounds of skittering, tiny feet on each side and above where I slowly strode.

Shivering in disgust, I placed a hand on my old service revolver. I also gripped my stick tight as we moved further from the lit station and deeper into the hidden tunnels. I disliked tunnels since our experience with the Great Rat of Sumatra, a tale I shall never tell for fear of being labeled mad by my readers.

"Blood," Holmes said. "A few feet ahead, I believe."

Harry Dickson sighed, his shoulders slumping. "Yes, sir. There is the corpse of a man just ahead of our position. I see his hand wound from here."

I moved closer and peered between both of them, spotting the silhouette of a figure lying on his back about ten feet ahead. The details were indistinct to me, but growing clearer as we approached.

The body was that of a young man, garbed in a dark suit that glistened with dried blood. A thin cut lay across his right hand and neck, the weapon having dug deep into the flesh.

"Dritan Muller," said Dickson softly.

The man was of average height with light brown hair, blue eyes, and mottled skin indicating he survived smallpox or some other terrible disease. His face was black, and his eyes and dried tongue protruded from his gaping mouth. All his pockets were turned out, with a cloth wallet, a silver watch and chain, and a slim gold ring lying next to the body.

I squatted down beside Holmes, who studied the cuts across the hand. Harry Dickson examined the neck wound, as well as the rest of the walkway near the corpse.

165

"A thin blade," I said. "A razor perhaps?"

Dickson and Holmes shook their heads, neither looking my direction.

"Piano wire," Dickson said. "A favorite form of garroting used by various criminal gangs and assassins. The wire cuts deeply into the flesh and can sever the jugular vein as well as strangle the victim. No doubt we'll discover a small bruise in the center of Herr Muller's back in the autopsy, where the killer braced his knee."

"This is the *modus operandi* of Strelnikov," Holmes said, "the former Nihilist who was an early fanatic of the Communist government that arose recently in Russia."

"Reports are that Strelnikov is dead," Harry Dickson said. "Shot by White Army troops two years ago."

"Until I see a body . . . ." my friend said, waving the suggestion aside. "The downward angle is the same that assassin used in past encounters. Either Strelnikov, or someone very like that terrible killer, is responsible for this murder."

"Took some time searching through the body . . . ." I said, observing the items near the corpse.

Holmes straightened, his eyes twinkling as the investigation suddenly grew more interesting to his facile mind. "And failed to discover that they sought," he said. "You will notice the tears near the vest. The murderer was desperate at that moment, hastily realizing that the one person who had access to the prize was executed."

"The police had best be summoned," Dickson said, sliding past me towards the station. "I'll return to the platform and call Inspector Caldwell of Scotland Yard,"

"Good, good," Holmes said, absently frowning as he shuffled through the cards contained in the dead man's wallet. "Ah, now this does present some unique possibilities."

"What does?" I asked as my friend showed me a common business card in the light of his torch.

I read that Herr Dritan Muller was a clerk in the venerable Wegelin and Company Bank, located in St. Gallen, Switzerland. I handed the card back, still not seeing the oddness Holmes suggested.

"All shall reveal itself in time, old friend," Holmes said as Harry Dickson's torch flashed in the distance. "Simply put, the presence of foreign players on London soil is now more apparent."

Inspector Caldwell proved an efficient, small, bustling man who displayed open respect to both my friend and Harry Dickson upon arrival. Presently, after establishing the facts, we left the scene. Dickson led us to a long black-and-silver roadster parked by the curb near the west exit. Soon we were motoring down the road, a gentleman named Parker driving.

"You needn't worry about Parker," Dickson said. "Completely deaf from a shell explosion near Verdun. He volunteered as my driver while my vehicle is receiving a bit of maintenance."

Holmes waved that away. "I assumed as much when I detected the scent of cigarette smoke from the rear compartment. Not at all what you would choose, even when you lack funds."

"Correct," Dickson said, "and you observed my ensuring eye contact when I instructed him as to where we should go."

Surprisingly for me, we didn't proceed to the infamous Diogenes Club. I'd assumed that would be Dickson's choice, since Mycroft Holmes used the location as his secondary office.

My readers know of Sherlock Holmes's older brother, though for the few that do not, I shall briefly elucidate. Mycroft Holmes possesses an even greater genius than my friend, but lacks the energy and interest in pursuing the art of detection. He occupies a high, though completely inexplicable, office in the government which the loftiest members respect and, I believe, obey.

Therefore, when our conveyance halted before a small building near Cannon Street, I followed Harry Dickson and Holmes into an odd organization known as the Gresham Club. Unlike Mycroft's Diogenes, which was a bastion of silence run by misanthropes, I heard the buzz of conversation and laughter the moment we stepped through the doors.

"The Gresham Club," Dickson said while handing his coat to a waiting footman, "is one devoted to bankers and personages who inhabit the City. It is quite possibly the best location for gossip that one can find in the whole of London."

"Gossip?" I asked. "Would it not be better to learn why the Swiss gentleman met his demise?"

"If you're referring to my brother Mycroft as a possible source of information," Holmes said. "I'm afraid that would be a waste of time. He mentioned the presence of foreign agents to me in hopes I might have some knowledge upon the subject. When I expressed no knowledge, he scribbled off a quick note to an underling – no doubt one of his Foreign Office wags is charging about, seeking answers."

"Gossip," I said, shaking my head. "It feels quite sordid."

Dickson laughed and led us off to a large chamber filled with well-dressed, chattering gentlemen and three clicking tickertape

167

machines. The men sat in club chairs or stood leaning against the columns in the room, many gesticulating with lively animation.

"I think this shall prove quite useful," Holmes said, nodding across the room towards a slender man with ebony hair that flowed and bounced across his shoulders. "I recognize another player in our game."

"Count Iosef Romanov," Dickson said, accepting a drink from a waiter but never lifting it to his lips. "Claimant to the Russian throne, and agent of the White Russian cause in Europe. I hadn't known he was back in London."

"Nor did I," Holmes replied. "Last I heard, the Germans chased him out of their country. Beggar, liar, thief, swindler, and, I believe, murderer. One of the worst criminals in the whole of Europe."

I followed my friend and his former pupil across the room, joining the throng of bankers seated near the Russian nobleman. Count Romanov glanced our direction and I fancied I caught a spark of recognition in his eyes. He was a handsome sort if one admires the hairy, bestial type. His beard and mustache barely hid large square teeth and thin, almost invisible crimson lips. An odd scent hung over him, emanating from his shining, curling hair in a way I found unpleasant. I couldn't say why, but I felt a shiver of cold fear spread up my spine . . . feeling almost as if his pale-eyed gaze was that of a wolf rather than a man.

The Count returned to the others and bowed while backing away. "I look forward to your presence tonight," he said.

There was a rumble of conversation that followed, with Holmes and Dickson stepping after the Count. The rapier-thin nobleman whirled in place, his feral face momentarily registering what I took as unconcealed fury towards Holmes and me for several seconds. Then he straightened and smiled, bowing deeply once again.

"Mr. Dickson," he said. "As always a pleasure. Whom do I have the honor of meeting today?"

"Mr. Sherlock Holmes, Dr. John Watson," Harry Dickson said, "may I introduce you to Count Iosef Romanov, formerly of St. Petersburg, Russia."

A scarlet flush spread across the Russian nobleman's long, swanlike, neck. "Gentleman," he said, "I must depart. So good to see you again, Dickson."

Count Romanov stalked away, his fury evident across his monstrous, taut frame. I waited until the man vanished from view before guffawing openly.

I shook my head and adopted a falsely chiding tone. "Now that was very naughty, Mr. Dickson. It seems that you insulted the Count by simply introducing him to us."

Dickson chuckled and shrugged. "I'm an American. We make such mistakes."

Holmes joined me in laughing, knowing Dickson was fully aware of his intended insult. Though born in the United States, our young friend spent most of his life on these shores.

"I do believe we have found the first step in discovering the truth of this investigation," Holmes said, glancing my direction. "Watson, do you still have a good set of evening dress?"

"Yes," I said, "a fine new outfit bought for a wedding next month."

"Capital!" Holmes said. "I'll obtain some from my tailor and tonight we shall discover the reason the late Herr Muller died in that terrible manner."

I blinked several times, confused by this inexplicable jump in the situation.

"Did I miss something?" I asked. "Where are we going tonight?"

Holmes clapped me on the back and said, "To an event being held by Count Romanov. Think man – would a thief hold a gathering of important bakers if he didn't have a reason? The coincidence of his presence, the death of Dritan Muller, and appearance of enemy agents in London – I surmise we'll soon find the next clue in this mystery."

I frowned, thought for a moment, and raised a finger, halting any possible conversation from the detectives.

"Ah, but he didn't say where the gathering shall occur!"

Harry Dickson performed a cutting gesture in the air. "Leave that to me, Doctor. I shall mingle among the monied men and discover the answer within the hour. I'll send word as to the time and place of our next meeting."

"Good Lord!" I said as I stepped from the oversized automobile. "This is quite the spectacle, is it not?"

Holmes barked a quick laugh and said in a murmur, "Some wealthy men believe the only means of proving their worth is through conspicuous consumption. Gird yourself, Watson. The display this evening shall rival the dreams of Lucullus."

The home was that of Cyrus Manning, a beer manufacturer who invested in his father-in-law's silver mine. By happenstance, they discovered a new and very rich vein of the precious ore and sold their interests out to a massive American firm. Manning was now vastly, fabulously wealthy, and determined to prove he was an important figure worthy of note.

The dwelling itself was three-stories high and built in a fashion that seemed a bizarre combination of Regency and French Baroque in style. Detailed scrollwork covered the outer facing, and the sheer number of carven images were overwhelming. Three fountains were in evidence, each possessing cavorting children and nymphs dancing across crystalline, bubbling waters. The final image I viewed was a distant statue of what I took to be our host atop a horse, dressed in a semi-knightly costume.

I smothered a laugh as a pair of liveried men in red jackets with powdered white wigs opened a pair of monstrous wooden doors and admitted us within. An elderly man in a long, curly white wig and carrying a black wooden pole awaiting us several feet away. He possessed a curved nose that resembled a vulture's beak, and tiny, dark eyes surrounded by deep crevasse and creases across his frowning face.

"Your names, sirs," he said, his voice softly sneering as he examined our trio with what I took as open distain.

"Sherlock Holmes, Dr. John Watson, and Harry Dickson," Dickson said as our hats, gloves, and capes were received by a host of children dressed as pages from the Georgian era. "You will find us on the guest list."

The haughty servant lifted a small page before his eyes, squinted for several seconds, and sniffed with what I took as dismissive acceptance. I considered kicking his posterior as a lesson in manners but dismissed the notion as futile. Nobody can match the overbearing cheek of a servant who secretly believes himself the true master of a domicile.

"Proceed, sirs," he said in a drawling voice, followed by a second sniff.

Holmes steered me away from the offensive fool, pressing a champagne glass between my fingers.

"Ignore the man," Holmes said. "He provided us an excellent clue by his demeanor."

"He did?" I asked, sipping the sparkling, amber liquid.

"Just so," my friend said. "His behavior is one of true self-satisfaction and gratification. He believes, based on his no doubt unsavory act of listening in proverbial keyholes, that a momentous event shall occur tonight. This gathering is no mere ball in which the

170

wealthy seeking to cozen connections with the titled members of society. Our vulture-beaked friend believes he shall receive secondary elevation through his master's success."

"You received that from a simple sniff and the haughty behavior of a servant who acts above himself?" I asked, amazed.

Holmes laughed and shook his head. "No, Watson, simply confirmation – a solution derived from our host's willingness to indulge the disreputable Count Romanov, as well as said person's presence in the Gresham Club."

I slipped a bit more of the wine, finding the flavor too sweet for my tastes.

"Who is this Count Romanov?" I asked.

"He represents himself as a cadet member of the deceased royal family of Russia," Dickson said. "He resided in Austria most of his life and escaped to Switzerland when the war commenced. He is actually a professional criminal who pretends to represent the interests of the White Russian cause against the Bolsheviks."

Holmes nodded once and said, "A professional seducer of women and thief. Based on the callouses along the inside of his right hand and thumb, I would suggest he practices fencing for both self-defense and exercise."

I indicated that I hadn't noticed those details, as my attention had been upon his thick, foul, black beard. "Reminded me of a bear's hide," I said in closing.

"Scars," Dickson said. "The brief examinations I've had of the man in the past have revealed little. Our total encounters lasted not above fifty seconds in total. Despite that, I observed several tiny indentations across his brow that resembled burns of some sort."

We mingled among those gathered and I spotted several important persons from the political and mercantile classes. There were at least three sitting ministers present, several wealthy bankers, and a host of others that I recognized as rising members of the important political parties.

The talk proved dull, as would be expected among such persons. The politicians debated politics heatedly, the bankers spoke of stock prices and markets, and the hangers-on pretended enthrallment at their every statement. Holmes and Dickson seemed to move in and out of various knots, murmuring a word or two before drifting to another clique.

As for me, I found myself involved in an enjoyable chat about the upcoming test match in which our side now held a fast bowler. Two men, whose names I didn't know, appeared as disinterested in the proceedings around us as I did, having attended out of some unspoken obligations to their wives.

"Much rather be watching a bit of sport or spending time at the club. Are you a member of the Reform Club, Doctor?" the heavier of the asked said while clapping me on the shoulder. "You must consider joining! Be nice to have another member who enjoys the best sport on Earth!"

I was prevented from answering when a loud series of horns shook the gaudy home and hushed the guests into a confused silence. The horns blew again and the lights dimmed slowly as the echoes died away.

"Sounds like the opening of Ascot," one of my companions said and we three laughed quietly.

Holmes appeared at my elbow, silently stepping spectrally from the gloom, and steering me away from my new-found friends.

"We will now discover the reason for the death of Herr Muller," Holmes said, his voice a near whisper, "and the reason the Count finds himself among a class of men who otherwise wouldn't entertain him in a woodshed."

"Ladies and gentlemen!" Count Romanov said, stepping into view on a raised platform at the far end of the ballroom. "I thank you for agreeing to my humble invitation. My host, the most excellent gentleman Cyrus Manning, has granted me permission to speak to you. Please indulge me briefly."

A light ripple of applause followed, though the reception was tepid at best. I heard voices whispering in the darkness and doubted the bestial Count would hold their attention for many minutes.

"As you know," he continued, "my poor country was overrun by the lowest of the low, the most horrific creatures known as 'Communists'. They murdered my dear uncle, the Czar, as well as many of my people."

"Oh, do get on with it!" a voice said from somewhere, causing several hoots of laughter and coughs hiding the derisive sounds.

Surprisingly for me, the Count laughed too and bowed deeply. "Forgive me, I feel quite emotional when speaking of my dear Fatherland, Russia. The reason the good Cyrus Manning gathered you here tonight is because there is a new hope for Russian freedom! Through the actions of my agents in Russia and Europe, I hold the means of returning Russia to the land of peace of beauty! Allow me to present, Her Royal Highness, Grand Duchess Anastasia Nikolaevna Románova, last surviving member of the Royal family, and my wife!"

A girl stepped to his side, and I use the word "girl" correctly. To my eyes, she could be no older than twenty years, with thick, curling dark hair, a long, somewhat pretty face, and a smile that appeared quite forced. Her clothes were obviously new, though she wore them with open discomfort as she gently waved towards those present.

A loud round of applause followed, and the remainder of the Count's remarks were incomprehensible. The house lights rose again, and the musicians began a merry waltz. The count, who I believed was old enough to be her father, led the child to the dance-floor and soon the party began anew.

"A quite unexpected turn of events," Holmes said, his eyes fixed upon the dancing Count and his youthful bride.

"More than you realize," Dickson said. "The implications are very interesting."

I sighed audibly. "I would appreciate if you gentlemen would cease speaking in riddles."

Dickson laughed and said, "Same old Watson. You never enjoyed couched speech. For my part, I apologize. There are many possibilities regarding Count Romanov and this so-called 'Grand Duchess Anastasia' – or whomever this imposter really is. Basically, all the information that we possess states that the entire royal family died in mid-1918 at the hands of the new Communist rulers of Russia."

I nodded, recalling the terrible tragedy, and Holmes added, "It is as close to certain as anyone connected to intelligence could determine. I learned some of the details from Mycroft some months back. Our royal family held little love for the Russian cousins, but they did wish some knowledge of the truth."

"Outrageous!" I said, a fresh wave of disgust filling me as the song ended.

Holmes led us towards the exit. "Common enough, my friend. Throughout history, false kings, queens, and other royal persons have attempted using their facial similarities as a means of garnering wealth and power. Perkin Warbeck, Constantine Diogenes, Terentius Maximus . . . the list is long and sordid."

"Then how does the death of the Swiss banker connect to this event?" I asked.

"That is the difficulty, Doctor," Harry Dickson said as we, and I noticed several others, left the party quite early. "The coincidence is too great for there not to be a connection."

173

"It begins to appear that Herr Dritan Muller died by the hands of a Russian assassin," Holmes said. "But the new rulers of that country wouldn't dispatch one of their lethal assets unless there was an important reason."

Moments later, we sat in silence in Harry Dickson's automobile, both detectives silent and, I believe, meditating upon this problem. Neither man said anything save a simple good night upon dropping us at my home.

Inside, Holmes changed into his dressing gown and then returned to stand in the sitting room, his eyes upon the fire. Unconsciously he pulled from his left pocket his oily briarwood pipe and filled the bowl with the foul shag he always favored.

"I believe I face a three-pipe problem," he said, more to himself than me.

Retiring to my bed, I reflected that I would request the maid air the room out and sweep the rugs with greater efficiency before Mrs. Watson returned. She was not as indulgent as our former landlady, Mrs. Hudson, over the tobacco ash that often followed in Holmes's wake.

The next morning, I found Holmes where I left him, his eyes possessing a fierce determination that I recognized from our younger days. I left him to his thoughts, accepting a full breakfast from our cook and reading *The Times*. Count Iosef Romanov and Grand Duchess Anastasia managed a small column on page three. I supposed this to be *The Times*'s method of reporting the incident without stating their disbelief of the young girl's supposed identity.

"Watson," Holmes said, "there are far too many questions that must still be answered for a full picture of the infamous Count's motive. Therefore, I've determined a new course of action."

"Which is?" I asked while pouring him a cup of tea.

"To learn more of Muller's murder. I believe that, regardless of the identity of the killer, the reason for unfortunate man's death shall reveal the complete picture."

I wiped my face with a napkin and rose. "Then what do you propose we do now?"

Holmes swilled his tea down in a single gulp and said, "The killer searched the body of Dritan Muller after his garroting. Based on the state of the corpse's pockets, I doubt that Strelnikov discovered what he sought. This only means one thing."

I knew the answer this time. "Muller hid the item somewhere before his murder."

174

"Correct!" Holmes said. "Come, Watson. Let us change our clothes and repair to Victoria Station and hope we discover the truth before it is too late!"

Harry Dickson met us in the same spot as before, his face shining with the delighted joy I remembered from his youth. There was an almost electric energy emerging from him which reminded me of Sherlock Holmes when he was on the scent of a criminal.

"Gentlemen," he said, greeting us as if we recently emerged from a train, "the Prussian agent we observed yesterday is present. I arranged a small diversion for him in the next thirty seconds. I haven't seen the false Count or a squat figure who may be Strelnikov. Oh good, my assistance has arrived."

An elderly woman with snow white hair, a ramrod stiff back, and clothing I recognized as being the latest fashion in the 1890's, marched past our position. She didn't glance our direction but strode with angry steps until she reached the German man Holmes and Dickson had recently recognized. She bumped into him, stumbled, and shrieked in a high-pitched, wailing tone.

"Thief!" she cried. "Masher! Help! Help me!"

"I did not touch you, lady," the German agent said, straightening and stepping back several inches.

"Stop him!" she cried while clutching her heart and moaning. "He stole my change purse!"

A crowd quickly surrounded the pair, with the man protesting louder as accusations and threats emerged from different directions. I suppressed a burst of laughter as Holmes steered me towards the Underground, Dickson trailing at a small distance.

"Hattie Craig," Holmes said. "I thought she retired some years ago."

"She did," Dickson said, "but she considers herself in my debt. I assisted her grand-niece from a spot of difficulty. Since then, she sends me the occasional dollop of gossip or extricates me from situations."

I shook my head while saying, "She looks like an old granny who runs a tea shop."

Holmes barked out a quick laugh. "Carefully cultivated, Watson. Mrs. Craig is one of London's most accomplished pickpockets. She moves among society with the skill of a chameleon and the dexterity of Hermes. No doubt our Germanic competitor will discover himself unknowingly in possession of her change purse once a policeman has arrived."

"Which will keep him detained for the remainder of the day," Dickson said as well strode down the stairs that the dead banker Muller had used before his terrible murder.

"Back to the tunnels?" I asked with a shudder.

"Probably," Holmes said. "Muller possessed the item in question as he fled before suffering a murderous assault. The item in question would have been hidden once out-of-sight of his pursuers."

"He could have hidden it before that time," I said. "Also, what are we looking for?"

"I have no notion," Holmes said as we stepped onto the underground platform. "But I believe I shall discover the hiding place, and the answer shall present itself to us."

He and Harry paused for a moment at the division between the left and right passages, exchanged a glance, and moved away. Neither looked behind them, but I did notice that Harry held a small one-shot revolver in the palm of his left hand.

The Underground station appeared deserted at first glance, though I corrected myself a moment later. An elderly woman with a cloth shopping bag sat upon a bench near the end of the platform, her body hunched and still. She didn't look up as we walked in her direction, though one rheumy eye lifted as we approached.

The echo of distant footsteps appeared and from the entrance to a nearby passage stepped Count Romanov himself. He held a thick cane in one hand and tipped his top hat with the other. Unhurriedly, he came in our direction, stopping eight feet from our position.

"You didn't know that I awaited you around the corner," he said. "Not particularly observant, Holmes. You and your toadying doctor are growing less efficient in your elder years."

Holmes paused, pulled a pair of leather gloves tightly across his hands, and gripped his stick tighter. For my part, I held my gun in hand, raised and ready should the nobleman or an unseen henchman attempt to attack us with a firearm.

"Possibly so," he said. "However the distinct odor of the hair oil you wear did linger. Mr. Dickson and I recognized the scent, but we were unsure whether that was you or another Austrian with a taste for expensive scents."

"You are growing childish, Holmes," Romanov said, drawing a sword from his cane. "I am not Austrian, but Russian."

"You are no more Russian than I am," Dickson said. "I suspected that in the past, but your mistake last night proved my supposition."

Count Romanov paused, stared his direction, shook his head and raised his weapon. "I do not have time for such nonsense. I shall cut you to ribbons, Mr. Dickson."

Holmes chuckled, raised his cane in a matching pose and said, "I think not. Shall we begin? You have no doubt dreamed of this moment for many years."

The Count spat out a series of guttural sounds that I recognized as oaths of the lowest variety. I raised my handgun, sighting on the Count in case he attempted some clever trick. I vowed I would shoot the man in the head should he kill my greatest of friends.

Holmes and the Count exchanged a few passes, neither achieving a touch. They danced back and forth for a moment, sword and cane slicing the air and sending odd, echoing, tapping sounds through the air.

According to Holmes, the Count was a devoted fencer and, based on my observations, I believed this to be true. The man moved with uncanny lightness and his weapon flashed across my vision with uncanny speed. Holmes, for his part, appeared to be the man's match. I knew my friend practiced singlestick fighting, and I felt some relief that he didn't appear to have ceased training in that form of martial attack.

"Watson, duck!" Dickson said and I felt a rush of air behind my position.

I quickly dropped to my knees as a thin cord whistled through the air where my head had been. My bowler hat fell from my head, dropping to the concrete floor in two pieces. A single shot shook the air and I heard a cry of agony, followed by the meaty, wet, sound of a falling body.

Slowly straightening, I beheld the elderly woman with the rheumy eyes prone upon the floor. A widening pool of blood lay around her head, resembling a crimson halo. Her body was rotund, and I noticed she possessed arms that were as thickly corded as a sailor. Her nose appeared to be broken from past days, and her right eye and ear were naught but a mass of scar tissue

"Galina Strelnikov," Harry Dickson said, shaking his head. "The only picture I ever viewed of her was from 1882. She was quite pretty in those days. From what I gather, a bomb she built went off prematurely and injured her badly."

"We must help Holmes!" I said, turning back to my friend as his duel continued.

I observed that his shirt was cut in two places, and a thin line of blood was across his right arm. I raised my revolver and sighted.

177

However, I couldn't in good conscience shoot the evil Count as he honorably battled Holmes.

Several minutes passed as the pair dueled away, their weapons rarely touching, their bodies perpetually in motion. Holmes appeared to be damp with sweat and his breath became labored as the battle continued. The Count scored a second thin slice across my friend's leg, his thin lips smiling and flashing his ivory incisors.

Then Sherlock Holmes stumbled, losing his footing as he stepped to the side while avoiding another slash. Count Iosef Romanov cried out in triumph and lunged, the point of his thin blade poised and positioned for a perfect pierce of Holmes's heart. I felt my heart sink as the attack moved with deceptive slowness for the kill.

Holmes neatly parried the lunge, batting the blade aside. His cane fell heavily across the Count's wrist and I heard a sickening crunch as the bones snapped. As he cried out in pain, the sword fell from his grasp, clattering and rolling across the floor. With a single strike to the head, Holmes dropped the villain, who fell with a moan upon his back.

"So ends the career of the infamous Baron Adelbert Gruner," Holmes said, "alias Count Iosef Romanov."

"Gruner?" I said, lowering my firearm. "He looks nothing like that infamous rogue!"

Holmes chuckled, reached down, and pulled free a portion of the overwhelming beard that covered his face. The burns beneath the false whiskers were gray with age, the deep pockmarks marring the previously perfect flesh.

"You will recall, Watson," Holmes said as dropped the beard on the man's chest, "the Baron's true downfall, in addition to his diary of perversions, came from a vitriol attach by one Miss Kitty Winter. When our friend Dickson here remarked upon the Count's burn scars, I realized several details. First, he demonstrated open recognition and rage in our presence. Second, Baron Gruner was never a fool and possessed a keen intelligence. Then he made his fatal mistake in his joy and effusiveness last night."

"What mistake?" I asked.

It was Dickson who chimed in. "He referred to Russia as his 'Fatherland'. That is a Germanic construct of words. The 'Motherland' is the Russian version of that term."

"When a man becomes enthusiastic and is in the height of his triumph," Holmes said, "his tongue often loosens and reveals information that he would best wish unspoken."

"Uncanny!" I said.

"Elementary," Holmes and Dickson said at the same moment.

Holmes sighed and leaned upon his cane for a moment. "I am far from the sprightly figure I was in my youth. I'm quite fatigued. Dickson, would you do me the honor of guarding the prisoner? I must retrieve the object in question from its hiding spot before we contact Inspector Caldwell."

Dickson agreed and reloaded his gun as Holmes led me to the ladder. He halted me at the top and then climbed down a single rung, examining the left and right of the yellow metal. He repeated this action twice more before feeling along the wall for several seconds.

"A-ha!" he cried, removing a tiny wax-covered packet from the crumbling bricks. "In the words of the great Archimedes, 'Eureka!'"

"Congratulations, sir," Dickson said as we returned with the item in question.

Holmes accepted the words with a nod. "Say nothing to the police. We shall discuss the contents later in greater privacy."

I puzzled by those words but remained silent as the stolid Caldwell and his men arrived. They removed the corpse of Strelnikov with little ceremony and handcuffed Baron Gruner, taking his still barely conscious form away.

"I think you shall find," Holmes said to Caldwell, "that his host, Mr. Cyrus Manning, will proffer a charge of fraud once the Count's identity is revealed."

Caldwell accepted those words, leaving with little ceremony. He reminded me of Inspector Gregson, with whom we shared so many adventures over the years.

Dickson's dwelling had papers strewn on every surface, and a pleasant scent of pipe smoke hung in the air. He had chosen a curving calabash that was a gift from me many years ago. After a small cloud covered the room, Holmes retrieved the wax cylinder from his inside pocket.

Breaking the seal, he removed a curl of paper that he read for a moment. His eyes twinkled as he handed the item to Dickson. The younger detective grinned openly before passing said paper into my hands.

The paper read:

9918272737217171723727828902201375 9038

I looked up with obvious bewilderment.

179

"Swiss banks are notorious for their protectiveness and secrecy of their clients," Holmes said. "As a means of ensuring the safety of their most important assets, they assign lengthy numbers."

"The Romanovs, sensing danger, moved many of their greatest assets into the oldest Swiss banks in case they needed to flee their country," Dickson continued. "It's rumored that Czar Nicholas learned the number by rote as a security measure."

"Oh dear," I said, realizing the fullness of the tale. "Then Gruner, posing as a Romanov, realized that Muller had the number —"

"And he planned on using it to claim the untold wealth that rests within the Swiss vaults," Holmes said, completing my thought.

"What of the Grand Duchess?" I asked. "Is she real?"

"Doubtful," Dickson said, relighting his pipe. "The Germans are also said to be holding a different woman who also claims that *she* is Anastasia. There will doubtless be other women who make the same claim in the coming years."

I nodded, hoping the poor, frightened girl found a means of escaping the terrible rogue. Then my thoughts turned back to the man who had used her.

"Sadly, Gruner will merely spend a year or two in prison on fraud charges," I said, "but he escapes true justice yet again!"

Holmes laughed and shook his head. "Doubtful, my friend. His ruse as Count Romanov will have earned him a great many enemies among the Russians throughout Europe. His life will be a constant struggle each day, hoping he will stay alive. No, Watson, killing Baron Gruner this day would be have been a mercy . . . which I do not believe that he deserves . . . ."

NOTES:

Harry Dickson, also known as *"The American Sherlock Holmes"*, was a creation from several sources. They were originally written as a German series of Holmes stories under the name of *Detektiv Sherlock Holmes und seine weltberühmten Abenteuer* (*Sherlock Holmes's Most Famous Cases*). With issue No. Eleven, the series changed names to *Aus den Geheimakten des Weltdetektivs* (*The Secret Files of the King of Detectives*), with the hero becoming one "Harry Taxon".

Dutch-Flemish publisher Roman-Boek-en-Kunsthandel launched a reprint of the series, renaming the stories, *Harry Dickson de Amerikaansche Sherlock Holmes* (*Harry Dickson, the American Sherlock Holmes*). Belgian writer Jean Ray translated the German tales and later began writing his own, subtly changing Harry Dickson into a character that lasted one-hundred-seventy-eight issues.

The Harry Dickson stories under Jean Ray took on a horror and science fiction element, with the detective and his assistant, Tom Willis, battling vampires, ancient mummies, evil gods, and terrible criminals. Most of these stories take place in the 1920's and 1930's. A few were translated into English. Recently, the character has had something of a resurgence, with interest in the wild tales being newly translated and republished.

181

The Adventure of the
Confederate Treasure
by Tracy J. Revels

It was a lovely morning in the spring of 1920 when I received a note from my good friend, Sherlock Holmes, bidding me to come to our old Baker Street abode that afternoon. Though retired, and more generally engaged with his bees than the pursuit of criminals, Holmes had retained his famous lodgings to facilitate his occasional trips into the city, whether to visit his brother Mycroft – these days a sometime-invalid, though with a mind as sharp as ever – or to simply enjoy the company of his former Irregulars and his erstwhile rivals at Scotland Yard. I knew it gave him great pleasure to receive a summons to the police headquarters, to deliver a lecture, or provide practical demonstrations to the young inspectors.

This communication, however, set all my nerves to quivering. It was delivered in two parts by a fresh-faced messenger who had been duly instructed on how to handle the components. I first read the note, written in Holmes's firm hand:

> *Watson – I have need of you. A young lady proposes to call upon me at four today. As you know, I refuse most cases, but in the second envelope you will find the reason I find myself inclined to hear her story. I will see that your favorite chair is cleared of debris for your arrival.*

I nodded for the youngster to give me the yellow envelope. I split it open over my desk. Five orange pips dropped out.

My knees complained as I slowly climbed the well-worn seventeen steps, but my friend's cheerful call for me to enter quickly made me forget my aches. Holmes's manner, as always, was kind if not effusive. Though he was in his mid-sixties and his hair was gray, his spine was straight, and his eyes were bright.

"Really, Watson, still fond of games of chance? At your age?"

I would not give him the satisfaction of knowing how straight his little deductive dart had flown. I had just lost half-a-month's pension on an ill-advised wager.

"Tell me of your client," I said. "I was startled by the contents of the missive."

"As was I," Holmes said. "But since her note arrived yesterday morning, I have been doing some reading at the British Library. It seems our assumption – that the last remnants of an invisible empire of terror perished in the Atlantic aboard the *Lone Star* – was premature. The Ku Klux Klan has returned."

"How?"

"Do you recall a motion picture called *Birth of a Nation*? It played in our cinemas five years ago."

I shrugged. "It was a melodrama about the American Southland, was it not?"

Holmes settled into his chair. "Of a sort. Directed by the notable auteur D. W. Griffith, it is based upon a novel called *The Clansman*, which celebrates the activities of the scoundrels who sent my client, Mr. John Openshaw, to his doom."

"But what possible relation could a book or a cinema feature have to these pips?" I asked, removing the envelope from my pocket. Holmes took the packet from me.

"They have inspired a re-awakening of the strange society," Holmes said. "New chapters of the infamous Ku Klux Klan have been organized, and have become quite powerful across the American nation. It is a disgrace that citizens of a country which so recently joined in our Great War – to 'make the world safe for democracy', as their president declared – are now eager to embrace villainy. From what I have read, the Hun couldn't have been more abusive to his victims than these 'respectable' men in robes and hoods are to Negroes, immigrants, and Catholics – all those they deem 'un-American'." Holmes sighed and placed the withered pips on the little table at his elbow. "But as to my potential client – I know only that she has received these pips, along with a threatening note, which she sent along to me. Here it is."

I took the small, folded paper. I will not offend my readers by recording the vile language it employed. Only one line was direct and not tinged with vulgarity:

> *Leave the spectacles and the map at the feet of Apollo*
> *at the stroke of midnight on Saturday, or you shall meet*
> *your brother's fate.*

"To what does this refer?"

Holmes spread his hands. "I have no data. But I think that shall soon change, for I hear the lady's footsteps upon the stair."

A few moments later, a lovely young woman of African blood, Miss Celia Howard, was seated on our sofa. She was smartly but discreetly dressed and carried a fashionable alligator bag.

"Thank you for agreeing to see me, Mr. Holmes," she said, with some shyness. "I know you are a very famous man, one who is surely not accustomed to being called upon by a distressed person of my race."

"Problems and predicaments do not discriminate, and neither do I. Besides," he said with a chuckle, "Lady Morley would no doubt be displeased if I were to refuse her private secretary."

The client gave a little start. "How could you know? I did not mention her in my communication to you."

"There is no great mystery," Holmes said. "Your employer wrote to me on her own, and her letter arrived in the post just after yours. She is incensed that you should be so persecuted, and virtually orders me to bring your torment to an end. As she is a third cousin by marriage to the King, I have no choice but to obey."

Miss Howard smiled. "Lady Morley is kindness personified, sir. I begged her not to worry herself about me, but she was greatly offended by the letter. She has taken this bizarre business to heart."

"As well she should." Holmes gestured toward the pips. "We have seen this warning before, but in another context. Please, tell us your story, from the beginning."

The lady nodded. "To do so, Mr. Holmes, I must begin with what will seem like a fable, but I promise you that every word is true.

"My people were enslaved in the state of Georgia for many generations, until freedom came to us at the end of the Confederate rebellion. My grandfather, Jim Howard, lived on the Greenbriar Plantation, near the little town of Washington – he was a widower with only one child, Eddie, who grew up to become my father. When the master went off to war, and many of the other slaves ran away, my grandfather remained – not because he felt his enslavement was deserved, but because he was a devout, godly man who pitied the mistress, a weak and foolish woman who would have starved had not some of the people stayed behind and tended to the crops.

"As you know, the war ended in April 1865, but news of the surrender only trickled into the countryside. My father was just a boy

184

at the time. One night in early May, an event occurred that my father would remember very clearly for the rest of his life.

"It was after midnight when my father was awakened by a cry of pain. He tumbled from his cot to find his father half-carrying a wounded white man into their cabin. The man was clad in a blue uniform, but it was ragged and dirty. My grandfather gave the injured stranger what little whisky he had and offered to run to fetch a doctor, but the man grabbed his shirt.

"'No – if you call someone, the Rebs will come, and I must not let them get it. Ha! I have fixed the rascals, even if I die! Stay, do not leave me.'

"My grandfather did all he could to help the sufferer, but the soldier grew weaker, and it soon became clear he would perish. As he began to struggle for breath, he pulled my grandfather to his side.

"'My name is Hiram Johannsen, and I have lived a wicked life,' he said. 'I deserted the Union army; I betrayed my country for pillage and plunder. But I will make amends now, and perhaps God will forgive me. Listen – draw close – I will tell you my secret!'

"My father could not understand what was being said between the two men, but he saw his father shake and pull away as the soldier's soul departed. Warning his son to stay quiet in his bed, my grandfather picked up the dead man and bore him from the cabin. My father heard the hoofbeats as his elder galloped away. It was almost daybreak before my grandfather returned to the cabin, and he would say nothing of what he had done with the dead man or his horse. Instead, he instructed my father to forget what he had witnessed – an impossible task for a curious boy. A few days later, word came to the plantation that the war had ended, and that Jefferson Davis, the rebels' president, had been captured.

"Hard times followed. Though free, the former slaves possessed no money, no land, and no knowledge. They had little choice but to continue to labor at Greenbriar, receiving nothing but the right to remain in their cabins and a small division of the annual crop. My grandfather worked without complaint, but he insisted that my father attend a nearby school established by some missionary ladies from the North. At night, by candlelight, using sticks and the dirt of their floor, my father would teach his father. My grandfather struggled with numbers and it took him great effort to learn his letters, but he was gifted with a prodigious memory. He loved the stories of history, and soon he could recite the names of all the presidents.

"One of the teachers at the school, Mrs. Julia Mather, was a free woman of color from New York City, a young widow with no children. She took a special interest in my family's welfare and often visited the cabin. My father hoped my grandfather would marry her, but my grandfather laughed at the very suggestion.

"Then, three years after the war, the terrible Ku Klux Klan began its reign of terror, threatening the Negroes, the Republicans, and even the gentle ladies who wanted nothing more than to educate the freedmen's children. After a noose was left in the schoolroom, Mrs. Mather told her students that she was leaving for New York on the next day's train. My father came home in tears.

"That night, my grandfather vanished for more than an hour. When he returned, he packed a meager satchel of clothing for my father, as well as a pair of warped spectacles that had belonged to his late wife, and a map he had drawn. Then he taught my father a strange poem, which he made him promise to share with no one, except any children he might have. The poem ran:

> *It rests where only the trumpet shall make it rise*
> *Beneath the stony angel's eyes.*
> *Place the right glass above our father's name*
> *And due west, the left glass, place the same*
> *There you shall find the ladies' baubles*
> *To make an end to all our troubles.*

Miss Howard said these last words with a sad smile. "I fear my grandfather was no Shakespeare. Once he was certain my father would never forget the verses, he hitched his old mule to his little wagon. They hurried to the train station, arriving only moments before the teacher's departure. My grandfather took Mrs. Mather aside, talking with her seriously, away from all the others. My father saw him press something into her hands. Then, to the boy's astonishment, his father put him into the teacher's care, instructing him to always be a good son to her. My grandfather embraced his child and told him he must not return to Georgia. With a kiss goodbye, he sent his son away, knowing he would never see him again."

The lady sniffled. With gentle dignity, she opened her purse and brought a small lace handkerchief to her eyes.

"Once aboard the train, Mrs. Mather showed my father what she had been given. It was a diamond pendant, set round with rubies and sapphires.

186

"I can condense many years into a few sentences. Mrs. Mather was a good and loving adoptive mother to my father. They lived in a neighborhood called Harlem, and my father continued his education, finally becoming a teacher himself. He would write letters to Georgia, and from time to time, small packages would arrive from home. Inside these packages, Mrs. Mather would find bits of broken jewelry or a clutch of precious stones. These she quietly sold, investing the money to great profit, even as she and my father continued to live comfortably but modestly. She raised my father to believe that this unexpected wealth was not a thing to be flaunted, but a tool for raising the fortunes of their race, and that is what they did, enabling many other children of former slaves to be brought North, to receive an education or train for careers.

"The one thing Mrs. Mather would never reveal to my father was why he had been sent away, though my father often suspected it had something to do with the jewels which arrived in the mail. In 1890, Mrs. Mather developed a fatal cancer. On her deathbed, she summoned my father, by then a married man with a home of his own. She said it was time to tell him all that she knew, the things my grandfather had asked her to keep hidden in her heart.

"The man who had been carried into grandfather's cabin that night was a Yankee 'bummer', one of Sherman's troops who had deserted the general's march to the sea and had since been a fugitive, living off the land. He had come upon the caravan that was bearing Jefferson Davis through Georgia. Suspecting that Davis might be travelling with Confederate riches, the bummer slipped into the camp at night and stole a chest, which he found brimming with jewelry. The next day, the bummer was spotted by Union men who recognized him as a deserter. They fired on him, mortally wounding him, but he rode as far as my grandfather's cabin before toppling from his horse. As a dying penance, he had given the treasure to my grandfather, who carefully concealed it that very night. My grandfather had been returning to this spot whenever he felt safe to do so, and removing the jewels bit by bit, sending them to Mrs. Mather to aid both his son and her good works. But in 1888, Mrs. Mather had learned, from another missionary, that Jim Howard had died. She assumed the secret of the treasure was lost with him.

"My father knew otherwise – faithful to his promise, he had told no one about the poem, and had always claimed that the spectacles and the map were merely relics of his childhood. His life was a busy one, and he had no wish to travel to Georgia; not even the thought of still-buried riches could tempt him to the place where our people

187

had been oppressed for generations. My brother William was born in 1893, and I followed in 1895. Our mother died when I was eight, but otherwise we were a very happy, close and loving family.

"During the war, my brother served with 369th Infantry Regiment, which won fame as the Harlem Hellfighters. William hadn't yet returned home when our dear father fell ill with the Spanish Influenza. In his last hours, Father shared his most remarkable story with me. I think I might have dismissed it as the deluded ramblings of a fevered mind, had he not directed me to a small safe on his wall, which contained the spectacles and the map. I have them here."

She removed the two objects from her purse, placing them in Holmes's hands. I rose and examined them over his shoulder. The spectacles were antique, with one lens broken, and the yellowed map was a hand-drawn thing, showing a region of the southern state of Georgia, with crude marks indicating roads, streams, and houses, along with swamps, cemeteries, and half-a-dozen little towns.

"Remarkable," Holmes said. "Your grandfather was quite the cartographer."

"I cannot imagine the labor he must have given to it, he who could barely form his letters. But my father said no one knew the country better."

"And did you try to find the treasure upon your father's passing?" Holmes asked.

"After William returned home, I told him the story and showed him these items. I thought chasing after the treasure would be a very irresponsible thing to do – Georgia is not safe for those of our race, and Father hadn't explained to me what the mysterious poem implied. But I could tell the idea of looking for a buried treasure appealed to William's adventurous spirit. He spent hours toying with the map and spectacles, scribbling down thoughts and theories. As I packed for London, where I was to join Lady Morley's staff, William insisted that I take the spectacles and the map for safekeeping, that he had all the information he needed inside his head. He said he would write to me if he ever went to Georgia. I told him not to be a fool.

"A month ago, much to my surprise, I received a letter, postmarked from Savannah, with William's name on the back of the envelope. For just an instant I imagined that he had found the treasure and was now a rich man. But this is what fell out."

She passed us another piece of paper, a clipping from a newspaper. The headline read "*Negro Neck Stretched*" and the story

188

claimed that a black man named William Howard had "*acted too saucy by far, while visiting in the country*" and was reprimanded by "*the swift justice of Judge Lynch, as administered by our noblest Klansmen*".

"My God, what a horror!" I said.

Holmes's brow was furrowed, his palms flattened together.

"Miss Howard, what do you believe happened?" Holmes asked.

"I believe my brother went in search of the treasure and was apprehended by those who, after two generations, are still seeking it. He must have dug in the wrong place. They captured him, and my address and information about the articles I possessed was tortured out of him before he died. It is possible they know about the poem as well."

"I agree," Holmes stated. "It is the only explanation that makes sense. The lynching was merely a cover for the Klansmen's crimes. This clipping was sent to strike fear into your heart. But the next note, the one with the instruction for giving up the clues, was postmarked from London, as I recall."

"That is correct. You can imagine my horror when that awful letter arrived. The instructions made it clear the author had been watching my movements. Lady Morley's London home, in Bloomsbury, has a large garden, with a replica of the Apollo Belvedere – this is the '*feet of Apollo*' to which it refers. I have no wish to bring trouble upon myself or my gracious employer, but I refuse to betray my brother's memory. Tell me, Mr. Holmes, what should I do?"

My friend frowned, and then asked his client to reprise her grandfather's poem, signaling for me to write it down.

"It is a curious wording," Holmes said. "Though the first part of it is rather simple."

"Simple!" both the lady and I exclaimed.

"Yes. '*It rests where only the trumpet shall make it rise.*' What does that suggest?"

"A battlefield," I said. "The American war had just occurred."

Holmes shook his head, gently tapping the map. "Is there a battlefield indicated here? Try again, Watson. And consider the second line as well."

"'*Beneath the stony angel's eyes*'," Miss Howard quoted. "Wait – a trumpet and rise, an angel . . . surely this refers to a cemetery."

"Much better," Holmes said. "Taking the Biblical reference to heart, and the fact that I count at least eight cemeteries or burial grounds on this map, the deduction seems rather obvious."

189

"But why would he put it there?" I asked. "Wouldn't it have made more sense to have hidden the treasure in or near his home?"

The lady shook her head. "From what I have learned, none of my people would have felt safe keeping something valuable in a cabin, no matter how well concealed. Father told me that the Nightriders, as they called the Klan in those times, would invade and take whatever they pleased, even down to the last morsel of food. No, he would have needed to secure it at a safe distance from himself."

Holmes hummed softly. "Let us imagine ourselves the gentleman's place. On the night he buried his treasure, he needed somewhere to which he could easily return, but also a place where overturned earth might not draw attention. What better place than a cemetery – which is also a location that most individuals would avoid, especially at night."

Miss Howard had taken up the map. "But there are so many cemeteries – and surely several of them have angel statues as landmarks. How can we know which one he meant?"

"Ah, now we come to the crux of the problem. We are clearly supposed to place the eyeglasses on the map, with the right lens over a location and the left lens 'due west' of it. But which location? How does the next line run – *'Place the right glass above our father's name'*? Your grandfather's name was Jim Howard, correct?"

Our client nodded, then abruptly shook her head. "No – I mean, not always. His master called him Pompey, which was a name he despised. His mother had named him Juba, for the day he was born. Just after the war, he was recorded as Jim Wilson by the Freedman's Bureau, but grandfather didn't wish to bear the surname of the people who had enslaved him. A nearby farmer, Mr. Howard, had been kind to my grandfather, loaned him some tools and a mule to work with. When that man died in 1866 with no family, my grandfather took on 'Howard' in his honor."

"This does present a complication," Holmes said. We took the map and placed it on Holmes's desk, so that we could all three study it. Look as we might, nothing on the paper was labelled with any of the names that the lady's grandfather had borne in his lifetime. No Pompeys, Jubas, Jims, Wilsons, or Howards appeared anywhere.

"Wait," the lady said. "Perhaps we misunderstand the wording. If my grandfather said, '*our* father's name', could he be referring to *his* father?"

"What was that gentleman's name?" Holmes asked. The lady looked woeful.

"I do not know I ever heard it spoken."

A dazzling thought suddenly came to me. I slapped my hand to my head. "What are we thinking? '*Our father*' – it is clearly a reference to *God*!"

Holmes snorted. "Watson, I have already considered and dismissed it."

"Have you?" I asked, perhaps a bit more irked in my tone than I intended. Holmes merely smiled and tapped his finger to the map.

"Indeed, it was the first thing that occurred to me, especially as Miss Howard told us that her grandfather was an exceedingly devout man. But it is the map that makes such an interpretation of the poem problematic. See here, there are over a dozen churches indicated – which one does the poem refer to? The entire point of the poem is to allow us to place the spectacles in the precise spot. Having over a dozen spots to choose from defeats that purpose."

I feared we had reached the end of our rope. Holmes folded his arms, staring down at the map as if it had offended him. Just then, there was a knock at the door.

"Ah, I see Miss Howard's bodyguard has arrived."

"Bodyguard?"

"Yes, dear lady," Holmes said. "I have previously crossed foils with the fiends who send out orange pips. As ridiculous as the threat might appear, I have learned, to my everlasting sorrow, that it must be taken seriously. Ah – young Billy – do come in. Watson, perhaps you recall our former page?"

How long it seemed, that the youth had been nothing but a boy-in-buttons, bringing up tea and carrying messages. Now he was grown into a rather handsome and sturdy man, taller than Holmes, with broad shoulders and a military carriage.

"It is good to see you again, Doctor," he said. "Mr. Holmes has been giving me instruction in his line of work. I hope to hang out my own shingle as a consulting detective before much longer."

"And Billy is an apt pupil," Holmes said, making introductions between him and the lady. "My adventuring days are behind me, but – "

He froze. We all turned, wondering what was amiss.

"My God," Holmes whispered. "I am such a *fool*! Why did I not see it instantly?"

The color had so suddenly drained from his face that I feared for his health. I was about to reach out to take his pulse when he threw out his arms.

"Out! All three of you! No – I don't mean to throw you into the streets – only to the kitchen. Perhaps the cook – wretched girl, burns everything – can fix a few sandwiches. Yes, sandwiches, that's what is needed. You appear famished. Give me but an hour, and I will set it all to rights!"

I confess that Holmes's sudden agitation startled and alarmed me, but Billy only smiled and gently herded us down the stairs.

"I think Mr. Holmes misses the old days, the drama of the game," he said. "And Agatha's cooking is not nearly as terrible as he implies. I'm sure she can manage some refreshment for us."

And so, for the next hour, we found ourselves in a companionable knot in the kitchen, sharing some fine roast beef and beer as we waited for Holmes's revelation. Billy had been in the Great War and regaled us with stories. Miss Howard again mentioned that her brother had also served.

"In the Hellfighters? I saw them in action – they were some of the most courageous men who ever carried the American flag. I never saw chaps I admired more."

I leaned back in my chair. It became clear to me, in only a short time, that Billy and Holmes's client were immediately comfortable with each other. He asked her what I had been curious to know – how she came to be employed by Lady Morley.

"She is a collector of what is called 'folk art' – I was working at a gallery in Harlem and I helped her locate and negotiate a number of pieces while she was visiting New York. She is planning more trips to America soon. I had hoped to accompany her, but after these threats – "

"Do not worry," Billy stated. "Mr. Holmes will put it right. And if he will give me the names of these felons, I'll thrash them all for you."

A bell rang, signaling Holmes's readiness for our return. He was himself again, his long legs stretched toward the fireplace. He gestured languidly toward the map on the table.

"It is indeed elementary!" Holmes proclaimed. "Miss Howard gave us the key to the key, if you will." He smiled at the lady's obvious confusion. "You said that your grandfather was a lover of history, that he memorized the history of your nation, including all its presidents. Tell me, who would Americans refer to as their father?"

"Father – the father of our country? Why – George Washington, of course!"

Holmes motioned for us to look. He had settled the spectacles over the small town of Washington. Due west, in the middle of the other lens, was "*Freedom Hill Baptist Cemetery*".

"While you three leisurely dined, I sent inquiries to a bookseller friend of mine, who specializes in travel volumes. Fortunately, among his collection was this little book, *Rustic Georgia*. See here!" Holmes opened the tome to a sketch of a country scene. It showed a small chapel, large oak trees, and a strange monument, a grim-faced angel. "The angel is dedicated to Ebenezer Wilson, a plantation owner who perished in the war."

"Mr. Holmes, this is wonderful," the lady said, "but if these evil men are seeking it as well, how would I ever feel safe in trying to retrieve it?"

"You will be safe because we will set a snare for them. Tonight, you will give them what they want – spectacles and a map at the feet of Apollo." Holmes smiled at our shared looks of surprise. "But not this map, nor these spectacles. Instead – you will place this facsimile out as an offering."

He opened a wooden box. Inside was a crinkled, aged paper and a rusty pair of eyeglasses. I removed the paper, marveling at the crude map.

"How on earth did you find a paper so old and worn?"

"I did not have to find it – I created it. I haven't enjoyed working with my philosophical instruments in some time. It is simplicity itself to make paper seem old and decayed." Holmes pointed at Billy. "You will return to Lady Morley's with Miss Howard. I have already sent word of our plans to friends at Scotland Yard, so that they will be prepared. Billy, see that Miss Howard is able to place these items on the statue unmolested, and assist the regular forces in any way that you can. I note you smacking your fist into your palm, but do not let your emotions overtake your reason. Once these villains are arrested, the field will be clear."

"For what?" I asked.

"For Billy to escort Miss Howard to retrieve her patrimony," Holmes said. "I suspect he may have to take Lady Morley along as well – she is a feisty dame, as I have reason to recall. Hit me with a parasol once, but I bear her no ill will! You must go, so that there is plenty of time to prepare."

The lady gathered her things. "Mr. Holmes, how I can repay you?"

"My work is its own reward – now more than ever. A successful conclusion to this case will be all the recompense that I require."

After our guests departed, I was about to take my own leave, but Holmes caught my sleeve.

"Is the game still afoot, Watson?"

I knew exactly what he meant. "Where you like and when you like," I answered.

"Well, we are both too old to be scaling fences and burgling houses, and I would not trust myself with my pistol, though I would very much enjoy cracking a Klansman's head with my cane. Ah, but action is for the young. Still, we might watch the show from a discreet distance. I know a most obliging cabman who specializes in skulking."

And so, just before the stroke of midnight, we found ourselves lurking in a motorcar in the deep shadows of an alleyway near Lady Morley's stately home. Even in the darkness, Holmes's eyes glittered, and his hands worked compulsively, as if filled with the desire to grab hold of a miscreant's collar.

"I hope we aren't disappointed," I said. "I've seen nothing but ladies and gentlemen returning from the theater."

Holmes chuckled. "I doubt that our prey is stupid enough to wander the streets of London in their Klan regalia, Watson! But I have recognized several of these late night ramblers as men of the Yard – and at least one female detective as well! I do not think – "

At just that moment, a whistle blew and three men – two in evening attire and one dressed all in black, with a knitted cap pulled low – came running down the street. Immediately, a half-dozen other well-clad gents bolted from where they had waited, in doorways and behind lampposts. The two rascals in finery were easily captured, one seized by the flaps of the red-lined cloak that he wore. Much to our chagrin, the third ruffian escaped. He appeared to be clutching a bag as he fled.

"Should we give chase?"

Holmes leaned back in the seat. "No, I think not." He told our driver to deposit us at Lady Morley's door. There, we found the house alight, and were quickly ushered into a front parlor, where Miss Howard was binding a cloth around Billy's bloodied right hand, while the ever-eccentric Lady Morley puffed nervously on a cigarette.

"It's nothing," Billy said, "I barked my knuckles on one fellow's teeth. He was hiding behind a bench when Miss Howard went out to place the bait. He jumped for her. I gave him the business, but his companions rushed me. I fear they got away with the glasses and the map."

"Indeed, we saw the bearer of those items elude the police."

Billy shook his head. "Should we track him to the docks? Post men at the train stations? I wouldn't think he would stay in London."

"No – we will let him go back to America."

"But the treasure! What if he's worked out the clues?"

"Billy," Holmes said, in a voice of supreme disappointment, "do you really think I duplicated Miss Howard's map, or the dimensions of the spectacles? If he believes he knows the way to work the key – "

"He will dig in the wrong place!" Miss Howard said. "Oh, what a wonderful comeuppance."

Holmes smirked. "Especially if he digs where I planted."

Spring had turned to highest summer before I found myself in Baker Street again. Holmes's invitation for a small jollification was welcome, as I had been curious as to the outcome of Miss Howard's case. I was delighted to be escorted inside by Billy, who looked like a man brimming with adventures.

Holmes indicated that Billy should tell his tale.

"Well, Doctor, the two Klansmen we arrested kept their silence. They refused to give anything to the Yard, and the Americans at the consulate put up such a fuss that they were released a few days later, and made contact with their accomplice, who had laid low. They boarded one of the White Star liners, never knowing that their watcher was in the salon just a few paces down from them. I adopted the persona of an American – my cap is off to Mr. Holmes, who played the part of Altamont so well before the war. That accent is brutal on an Englishman's jaw!

"I made my opponents' acquaintance. One was a sot, and while in his cups, he revealed their entire plan to me, bragging that they had a map to a lost Confederate treasure. It seems that rumors of a vanished chest filled with jewels had long circulated among the men of the Ku Klux Klan. Now I understand why Jim Howard never tried to use his own windfall: Everyone was suspicious, and a Negro man with sudden wealth would not have enjoyed it for long. My new 'friend' also told me that they had tortured the secret poem out of young William Howard, and that they had broken its code. He showed me on the map where they planned to dig. I had little to do after that, Mr. Holmes, except to alert the appropriate military authorities."

"Why the military?" I asked.

195

Holmes gave a satisfied puff on his pipe. "Because when I redrew the map, the only 'Washington' on it was in the District of Columbia – and the spectacles landed the erstwhile treasure seekers in the middle of Arlington Cemetery."

Billy laughed. "The servicemen were not amused by a trio of Georgia crackers attempting to dig up one of their war heroes! Those yokels are all behind bars and will be for some time."

"And the real treasure?" I asked.

"Miss Howard and Lady Morley arrived in Savannah two weeks later. We went out together, late at night. We found the treasure in less than a foot of red Georgia soil. Jim Howard had placed it in an old iron box."

"And?" I asked.

Billy's lips twitched. "Doctor Watson, do you recall the Great Agra Treasure?"

I gasped. "It was gone!"

"I believe that Celia's grandfather had exhausted it," Billy said.

"You recall the poem," Holmes echoed. "The loot was referred to as *'ladies' baubles'*. I believe that the women of Richmond donated what remained of their jewelry to their fleeing president, to finance his escape. By that point in the war, there could have been very few ornaments remaining to be contributed to such a hopelessly lost cause. Over the years, Howard senior had been breaking the pieces apart and sending the treasure away bit by bit." He pointed to Billy. "And did I just hear . . . *Celia*?"

The young man abruptly blushed. "Yes, Mr. Holmes, you did. You should know that there was one item left in the container. A single, rather remarkable stone. I have it here."

He pulled a small box from his pocket and opened it, revealing an exquisite yellow diamond set delicately on a band of gold.

"I love her, sirs, and she has done me the honor of agreeing to be my wife."

The Adventure of the Resurrected Brother
by Arthur Hall

In my declining years I feel a certain anxiety as I record a recent meeting with my friend Mr. Sherlock Holmes, who has proved himself able to function much as he always did when a problem or unexplained incident attracts his interest.

My concern springs from the fact that, because of my advanced age, my memory has begun to fail me. It is still relatively easy to recall the many past mysteries, the solving of which gained Holmes a well-deserved reputation, but of late it has become imperative to commit his exploits to paper while my recollections remain clear.

Much has changed since our days in Baker Street. Holmes and myself have survived a war the likes of which the world has never before seen, a conflict in which flying machines and engines of destruction took a heavy toll of life. Poisonous gases and guns of hitherto unseen size brought about devastation greater than we could have imagined, and we came to realise that life could never again be the way it once was.

The year is now 1920, and almost two decades have passed since Holmes retired from his practice as the foremost consulting detective in the land. Yet I've been careful to maintain correspondence with Holmes, and he has on numerous occasions been kind enough to invite me to his Sussex cottage for short visits. Moreover, he has, sometimes reluctantly, related to me certain incidents in which he has chosen to involve himself since taking up residence in this most pleasant part of the country.

After sharing a rather basic but satisfying meal we have often sat, one at each side of the stone fireplace, enjoying our pipes as he enlightened me as to his activities, while daylight gave way to dusk and we felt an easy peace come upon us.

It was during one of these visits, however, that I found myself again assisting him, and some of the feeling of comradeship and the thrill of adventure of former years returned, I like to think, to both our lives.

Since the cessation of hostilities, the hansom and other familiar conveyances had all but vanished, replaced by machines most often referred to as "horseless carriages". Holmes viewed these without interest, saying only that their advent would be the cause of considerable trouble in the years to come, and that he regretted the demise of the horse-drawn cab. As for myself, I had long known how to drive a car, and the steam train remained the favoured vehicle for long journeys and short excursions, but I resolved to learn to drive one of the newer and faster automobiles. This was accomplished with the purchase of a hardly-used Morris Cowley and a great deal of patience.

Spring had hardly given way to summer when I received a letter from Holmes inviting me to join him for the coming weekend. Having mastered, as far as I could tell, my mechanical transportation, I set off for Sussex early one calm and sunny morning. At that hour, I met only sparse traffic on the London streets and the capital was soon left behind. I had studied my map carefully but still, I confess, took several wrong turnings. The route I had chosen was one largely avoiding the main roads, for I was still unsure and had therefore resolved to confine myself to the leafy lanes and village streets as much as possible. Towards the end of my journey, I came upon a fellow cranking the starting handle of what appeared to be a brand new Ford motor car near a roadside cottage, and from him I learned that I was within a few miles of Holmes's residence.

Finally I found my way to and entered the narrow track that led to Holmes's secluded villa. The tall bushes to either side blotted out the sun and gave the impression of travelling through a tunnel as one does on a railway journey, but these suddenly fell away and I brought my vehicle to a halt in a quiet glade within sight of the cliffs and a calm sea. The engine came to rest, leaving only the cries of seagulls to disturb the silence. I approached the front door of the modest little building, which opened before I reached it, and to my delight beheld Holmes standing there puffing at his old briar.

"Good Morning, Watson!" he said after removing his pipe. "I trust you had a pleasant journey with no mishaps?"

We shook hands, and I admitted, "I occasionally went off course."

"I would have been surprised had you said otherwise. We were accustomed to depending on the knowledge of the driver of whatever conveyance we once used. It's very different now. But I'm forgetting my manners. Come in, old fellow. It's too late for breakfast, but I assume you would not object to a mid-morning cup of coffee?"

"I would welcome it," I assured him.

We sat in the small sitting room. As Holmes prepared our beverage I could see through a window the gulls circling above the cliffs and the sun sparkling on the sea beyond. It was easy to understand why he had chosen such a place in which to spend his retirement, for the peace and tranquillity hereabouts were medicine to the nerves.

"Are you hungry?" he asked as he reappeared from the kitchen with a tray.

"Not especially. I find my appetite greatly reduced of late."

"As do I. Not that mine ever matched yours, but the passing years bring many small changes."

"Indeed." We drank the strong brew and replaced our cups, and I asked him whether he passed his days here pleasurably, after the terror and excitement of the war.

"I cannot deny that it was strange at first," he replied. "I've mentioned before how my adjustment from life in the capital to a more sedate existence before the war was not as easy as I had expected. It was more of an adjustment now. Still, my bees take up much of my time – I have fifteen hives now, all flourishing – and there are still the odd times when fellows from the village and surrounding properties have approached me with their little problems. I'm glad to have been of some trifling assistance to them, and such instances serve as reassurance that age has not robbed me completely of my faculties."

"You don't miss the old days then, and Baker Street?"

He smiled, briefly. "This is not the first time that you have asked me that question. Until now I have answered that I do not, with little reservation." He paused thoughtfully, for an instant. "Now, however, I think that my feelings may be changing. I find that I am dwelling on our past adventures a great deal, of late."

"I recall that you often declared your intention to write monographs on various subjects, as a result of our encounters."

He sat back in his chair. "And doubtlessly I will, possibly during the coming winter. I have, however, been contemplating a return, probably of short duration, to London for some time."

"Something, I believe, has brought this to a head."

"You are as perceptive as ever. If your surmise is correct, then perhaps I can identify the cause."

He reached out and took an envelope from the sideboard and for me, a strange thing happened. As he turned back to face me I saw him for an instant as he had been the height of our many adventures together. Then the image faded and I noted that his hair was streaked grey at the temples and his features appeared more hawk-like than ever. As he slid the envelope across the small table that stood between us, I saw in his eyes the same glitter, the same eagerness for the chase that I recalled vividly from of old.

"See what you can make of this."

I peered at the envelope, not yet touching its surface. "It appears to be of good quality paper, and to be postmarked four days ago. It was apparently posted at a City of Westminster Post Office, suggesting that the sender may work in that district since it is not residential. I conclude also that the sender is not familiar with your career or movements."

"Your observations are correct, if a little obvious. The last, however, is not quite so. On what did you base it?"

"The envelope bears a Post Office rubber stamp, indicating that the letter was redirected after being delivered to a former address. It is seventeen years since you left Baker Street."

Holmes clapped his hands. "Excellent, Watson! The years haven't dulled your senses. Now kindly oblige me by extracting the letter from the envelope and reading it."

I obeyed, noting that the paper matched the envelope in colour and quality. The writing was clear but I discerned that the hand trembled slightly. I read it slowly, and then again.

My Dear Mr. Sherlock Holmes,

I have heard much of you in previous years, but I am afraid that your present whereabouts are lost to me. I pray that this appeal reaches you, for if it does not I will surely go mad. This letter I have sent to an address that I know was formerly yours, and I am depending on the efficiency of our excellent Post Office to convey it to wherever you live now.

I beg you to communicate with me so that, if you will permit it, we can meet. I am in great need of an explanation of some recent experiences and, almost certainly, of your advice. I look forward greatly to hearing from you, if indeed you still live.

Yours, in hope and desperation,

Cordon Reeder

"The fellow sounds in a state of excitement," I observed, "and he writes from the House of Commons."

"But the request is a personal one, not to be considered as from an official source."

"Quite." I studied his face intently. "Will you respond to it?"

He hesitated for but a moment. "As I mentioned, I have been aware of a growing restlessness. Perhaps a short return to the capital will relieve it, so that I can give my bees my full attention."

"A capital notion. You must stay with me, of course."

"Pray do not take offence, but I think it better if I do not. I cannot predict the nature of Mr. Reeder's problem, and therefore am unable to exclude the possibility of attendant danger. We aren't the young men we once were, old friend, and I will not risk any harmful exposure to you."

"Nonsense!" I exclaimed eagerly. "We will assume the task together. Holmes, it will be like reliving the old days. If you wish to stay elsewhere, then so be it."

He rose abruptly and walked to the end of the room. I could not help but notice his slowness, compared to our former days. He turned then, and fixed me with a critical glare.

"Very well, but I must have your word of honour that, if I tell you at any time to desist, you will do so at once."

"You have it."

He nodded. "Then it remains, after you have spent a few days here, for me to arrange a room at the Langham Hotel. I'll notify our client and conduct my investigation from there."

"Capital!" I said with some excitement. "But why must we wait? Your prospective client may be in a desperate state, as his letter suggests. I'm perfectly willing to postpone our planned excursions here, in favour of spending one night under your roof before we drive together to London to begin this unexpected, but very welcome, adventure."

A slow, somewhat ironic smile crept across my friend's face. He gazed for a moment at the intricate pattern of the Persian carpet, then out of the window at the distant sea before he answered.

"It shall be as you say, old fellow."

Holmes appeared rather uneasy at first as we sped through the lanes early the following morning. A low, overhanging branch brushed the roof of my vehicle and he looked up sharply, but after that he lit his pipe and became more settled. Unlike many times past when we travelled by train or hansom together, conversation was plentiful. He asked many questions about my new mode of transportation, enquiring both about its mechanical nature and my increasing mastery of its control. After a while he seemed satisfied and we reverted to re-living some of his exploits which I had been privileged to share in our younger days. I was fortunate to find an establishment where I could purchase fuel, as it was running low by the time our journey was half-completed and, on espying an inn nearby, we indulged ourselves by consuming an excellent lunch of roast pork.

Presently we reached the outskirts of the capital, and from there I drove to the Langham Hotel where Holmes had telegraphed the previous evening during our walk through the local village. As he left me, carrying his scant luggage, I recalled that this place had featured in some of our earlier adventures and was gripped, for an instant, by a deep nostalgia.

Holmes had assured me that he would wire a reply to Mr. Cordon Reeder during the morning, arranging an appointment for the following day or sooner. I was to meet Holmes in the hotel lobby at four o'clock in any case, unless I received notification to the contrary.

I received no such message, and so presented myself punctually at four. Holmes, who like myself had effected a change of clothes, was waiting for me. After advising the receptionist to direct Mr. Reeder to a table near the lobby, he led me there.

"Our appointment is for four-thirty. We have time for a brandy before our client arrives."

We sat near a pillar which held a gilt-framed mirror, before which Holmes positioned himself carefully. Several tall leafy plants in enormous vases surrounded us, and there was a muted buzz of conversation from further off. A waiter appeared quickly and took our order. As we drank, I noticed that Holmes fixed his gaze above me, no doubt to make deductions from the reflection of Mr. Reeder before meeting him.

"He is late," I said after consulting my timepiece.

"Not so. Unless I'm mistaken, he stands near the entrance that you yourself used. He is quite young, about twenty-four or -five I would say, with a rather uncertain disposition and hair that is very light in colour. He leans heavily on a cane and is dressed severely in black, as one would expect of a man in his position."

The man who approached our table had a pronounced limp and was indeed as Holmes had described. He appeared rather cautious as he looked at Holmes and then myself with uncertainty.

"Mr. Sherlock Holmes?"

Holmes half-rose from his chair, indicating that Mr. Reeder should sit with us. "I am he, and this is my associate, Doctor John Watson, before whom you may speak as freely as to myself. But I perceive that you are somewhat overwrought, sir. Allow me to order you a brandy to calm your nerves."

"Thank you, no," our client replied. "It's true that I am perturbed by my predicament, but I cannot be away from the ministry a moment longer than is necessary."

"Very well, then. I should explain that I've been retired from my profession of consulting detective for some years, but have recently decided to return to it briefly. Pray tell us of your difficulties, so that we can see if it's possible to assist you."

"I am able to reward you generously, Mr. Holmes."

"That will not be necessary. My fees were always calculated on a fixed scale, regardless of the means of the client."

"Then let me say how grateful I am to you for your response to my letter, and for your attention."

"It will be of no consequence unless you furnish me with the facts."

Mr. Reeder hesitated, as if doubtful that he would be believed.

"In the war, I fought in France with the Fourth Army of the British Expeditionary Force," he began. "In some of the most bloody battles of the war."

"The Somme," I said. "Survivors to whom I've spoken described it as a visit to Hell."

Holmes gave me an irritated glance, but our client nodded. "That is indeed an accurate description. The memories will trouble me until the day I die."

"Undoubtedly," Holmes agreed. "Watson and myself saw action also, but not there. Is it from that experience that your problem arises?"

"It is true to say, I suppose, that it began on the battlefield. Half of our regiment was in the trenches, awaiting the order to charge. When at last it came, my brother Jonathan and I proceeded together with fixed bayonets, but on leaving the trench he stumbled. I reached out with my free hand to prevent him from falling, but not before he had toppled before me and suffered a hit that killed him instantly. Somehow, I and a few of our company survived, but I've been haunted for the past four years by the knowledge that it should be me, and not Jonathan, who lies forever in that French field."

"You aren't my first client to suffer from unnecessary guilt," Holmes recalled. "It would be quite a different matter had you used him as a shield deliberately. But tell us, how does this most tragic event relate to your current troubles?"

Our client hesitated, and I saw from his expression that his conscience troubled him greatly.

"Two weeks ago, gentlemen, I was in my study at my home in Mayfair, near midnight. I'm unmarried and often work on routine ministry papers well into the early hours because I don't sleep well. My maid and valet do not live in the house, and so I was quite alone when I received a telephone call at that ungodly hour. Imagine my horror and disbelief when the caller identified himself as my deceased brother."

I felt some astonishment at this extraordinary statement, but Holmes seemed unperturbed.

"Was the voice that of your brother?" he asked.

"As far as I could tell, it was. It was a voice full of pain and distress."

"What did it say to you?"

"Only that he hadn't died on the battlefield, and wished to meet me."

"Did you arrange to do that?"

Our client fidgeted in his chair. "Jonathan, if indeed it was he, requested that I visit The Tailor's Arms, a public house in the Kings Road, at precisely five o'clock the following afternoon. He was most specific about the time."

"Doubtless that is significant."

"You kept the appointment, of course?" I ventured.

"Until the time of the meeting, I could think of nothing else. I arrived to find the road busy with traffic, which is usual for that time of day. The cab deposited me opposite The Tailor's Arms and I waited for a gap in the procession of vehicles to enable me to cross the road. After a few minutes, I realised that Jonathan watched me from where he stood near the front of the building. When he saw that I had noticed him, he turned away, and I frantically tried to force my way through the approaching cabs and omnibuses. When I finally crossed the road, there was no sign of him. A group of loafers who had been drinking noisily nearby had noticed nothing unusual, only a rather dilapidated soldier in a uniform that was the worse for wear

– hardly an uncommon sight to which you would pay much attention."

"Quite," Holmes said. "How did this man appear to you? Was he indeed your brother?"

"From the distance I was able to observe him, it seemed so. Part of his face was obscured by the collar of his greatcoat, and his stance was lop-sided, as if he were wounded."

"He didn't shout anything that could have been a message or instruction to you?"

"Nothing. Afterwards, I began to wonder if he existed only in my imagination, or if I had seen a ghost."

"I would suggest that you immediately dismiss that notion. I'm sure that ghosts – and I have always doubted the existence of such – do not need to use telephones or arrange meetings."

Mr. Reeder nodded. "Of course, I didn't seriously consider such an explanation. There is more to this, however. A week ago, at exactly the same time as before, I received a further telephone call. The voice was the same, and I immediately began to ask why this person had left the scene of the meeting after observing my arrival. Everything I said was ignored, so that I felt I was speaking to someone who could not hear. The voice then took on a tone that was almost commanding, directing me to present myself at a hotel in Limehouse at ten o'clock that coming evening."

"That is an area best avoided after dark," I commented.

"Indeed it is, Doctor, but I felt compelled to pursue this. I had begun to doubt that my brother still lived, for I couldn't see how this was possible, but I had developed a strong curiosity which drove me. Also, I had confided in a gentleman I know slightly from my work who suggested that I consult you. I regret now that I didn't do so immediately."

"As I suspected from the moment I saw your occupation listed on your letter," Holmes said. "Brother Mycroft's hand is in this."

"He requested that I not mention him by name, but I see that that it was unnecessary to do so."

"This isn't the first time that he has furnished me with a puzzle. Pray continue."

"The venue in Limehouse was by no means a hotel. It was a half-derelict place where rooms were rented individually. Judging by the arrivals and departures that I witnessed as I approached the building, it was frequented by the lowest classes. On nearing the entrance a great brute of a man, reeling drunkenly, pushed his way past me. He then stopped and looked up, as if following the flight of

205

a bird. I did likewise and was astounded to see my brother, or whoever it is who pretends to be him, gazing down at me from a tall unlit window. He shouted to me, and I was astounded because the voice was certainly that of Jonathan, and I confess to trembling as I listened."

"Did he make threats?" Holmes asked.

"No, he just shouted: '*You killed me to save yourself. How can you live after that?*'"

"Did you then seek to enter the building, to confront him?"

"A minute or two passed before the shock left me. Then I rushed to the entrance with that intention. Before I could speak to the *concierge*, two well-built men, extraordinarily so for Orientals, stepped from the shadows and manhandled me back into the street. I'm ashamed to say that I found myself sitting in the gutter near that filthy establishment in complete confusion."

Holmes sat in a contemplative silence for a moment. "On both occasions," he pointed out, "your tormentor – for that is what he is – has ensured that you remain some distance from him. That immediately suggests that he fears that a closer encounter would reveal something to you that he would much rather keep hidden. Was that the last you heard of him?"

Our client shook his head. "No, but it was then that I decided to write to you. Last night as I prepared to retire, and at the exact time of the previous calls, I received yet another. This time the instruction was to meet tomorrow on Platform 2, Victoria Station, at mid-day exactly. May I prevail upon you gentlemen to accompany me?"

"In the clear light of day?" Holmes retorted. "You may depend upon it." He turned to me. "Watson?"

"As ever," I replied with enthusiasm.

"Then it is settled. Before you leave, Mr. Reeder, there is one thing more that I must ask you. During your time in the trenches, was there anyone with whom you or your brother struck up a friendship, or even conducted regular conversations with?"

"There was Corporal Wendell Bright," our client remembered. "In fact, I can recall only him and Nurse Edith Merrow, who attended to me during my stay in hospital, from that terrible ordeal. I was invalided out, you see. Half my left leg had been shot away."

"My military career had the same end," I told him, "although my injuries were less severe."

Mr. Reeder nodded absently, his expression vague. I could see that, for an instant, his mind had slipped back to the awful conflict in which he had participated, as mine sometimes still did to Maiwand.

"Have you, Mr. Reeder, consulted the official force on this matter?" Holmes asked then.

Our client's embarrassment was evident. "I confess that I have not. Apart from the tale being an unlikely one, it would almost certainly damage my standing in the Ministry if a police investigation of such events were connected to me."

"I understand your reluctance," Holmes said then. "I would be much in your debt if you would write down the addresses of Mr. Wendell Bright and Nurse Merrow, and leave us your card, if you will. If you are in agreement we will join you outside Victoria Station, near the newspaper-seller's kiosk, at ten minutes before mid-day tomorrow."

"I cannot begin to express my gratitude, sirs."

"That is quite unnecessary," Holmes said. "We look forward to seeing you then, and perhaps to throwing some light upon these extraordinary circumstances."

The approach of mid-day found us among the crowd that filled the station. Mr. Reeder met us as arranged and we proceeded at once to Platform 2. Military uniforms were much in evidence, queueing among the waiting civilian passengers and in small groups that awaited later trains. Holmes's eyes were everywhere, scrutinizing the entire platform and often returning to the entrance. The babble of various conversations was constant, but temporarily blotted out as mighty engines appeared and came to rest before us. Several came and departed as we waited. It was as an express flashed through, exposing the opposite platform to our view, that our client suddenly stiffened and pointed suddenly. "Look there!"

Holmes and I followed his direction. Separated from us by the tracks, the passengers opposite were equally numerous. Among the uniformed men and others hurrying to and fro, a strange figure stood near a stack of cages of racing pigeons. I glanced at Mr. Reeder's ashen face and put out an arm to steady him.

"He is pointing in our direction, and shouting," Holmes observed.

"Yes, but I cannot hear."

"I read his lips. He said, 'You took my life. You are a coward and a murderer.'"

We watched as the figure turned away to leave the platform. He appeared to be a man of above-average height, in the uniform of

207

a private soldier. He stood and moved in a lop-sided manner and I could see, even from this distance, that his face was unnaturally pale.

I turned to speak to Holmes, but he was no longer there. Less than a minute later he appeared on the opposite platform, looking across at us, breathing hard and shrugging his shoulders hopelessly.

"Now that you have seen him more closely, can you be certain that this man is your brother?" I asked Mr. Reeder.

Our client had been silent and still since his first sight of the figure, but now he struggled to regain himself. Both his appearance and his voice confirmed my opinion that he had suffered from the condition that had become known as "shell-shock".

"His face was full of pain, and his movements appeared to cause him some discomfort but yes, Doctor, I believe it was him."

Holmes returned soon after. "He was nowhere to be seen," he said. "I observed everyone near the other entrance and on the steps."

"How can he have disappeared?"

"That wouldn't have been difficult, among a crowd and with so many men in uniform. I suspect that his awkwardness of movement was part of the deception, and that he fled quite quickly."

"Is there anything more than can be done, Mr. Holmes?" Reeder asked as we left the station.

Holmes appeared to be deep in thought. As we reached the bottom of the steps, he hesitated before replying. "I'm entertaining a theory, Mr. Reeder, based on what we know and what we've seen, but of course it's far from complete at this stage. What I am certain of is that your life is in danger, and that you must take all precautions from now until the hour when you can expect the next telephone call. Accordingly, Watson and I will now accompany you to your place of work, if it is your intention to go there. Have you any friends among your colleagues who would be willing to safeguard your return home later?"

"Two of my fellow-workers will, I am sure, come to my aid. They are sturdily-built men, rugby players who are used to much physical activity."

"Excellent. We will arrange at a later date to meet at whatever venue your tormentor chooses. Never fear, we will put things to right."

Mr. Reeder nodded. "My thanks to both you gentlemen. I have every confidence that you will succeed. Are there other precautions of which I should avail myself?"

"I would recommend that you keep a revolver close by you, even at home. Possibly you have such a weapon retained from your army service. Above all, do not venture from your home except when absolutely necessary, and never alone. Admit no strangers at any time."

"It shall be as you say."

"As for Watson and myself, we will continue our investigation. Several lines of enquiry suggest themselves, and these we must explore."

At Holmes's bidding I hailed a cab, and we presently arrived at Whitehall. His last words to our client, whose pallor had returned significantly, was to the effect that he should not relax his vigilance for any waking moment.

"What now?" I enquired as the cab pulled away.

"Lunch, I think, old fellow. After which we will call upon Mr. Wendell Bright."

Mr. Bright, we saw from the information furnished by our client, lived in Hampstead. We arrived in a quiet tree-lined street in late afternoon. As the cab left us and disappeared around a corner, I saw that Holmes was scrutinizing the tiny front garden.

"I fear that Mr. Bright, like our client, did not emerge from the war unscathed."

"How can you possibly know that? Have you met the man previously?"

"I have never set eyes on him," he assured me. "But between the gate and the entrance there are several patches of mud, and all but one bear footprints accompanied by the imprint of a stick or cane. Be so kind as to make use of that ornate door-knocker, and we will see if time has blunted my observation skills."

I did as he requested, and knew that his deduction was correct from the moment the door was opened. Mr. Bright, although probably not much older than our client, had been aged considerably by his experiences. His hair was almost white and his face bore marks of prolonged strain. I noted that his movements were uncertain, and an instant later realised that the reason was obvious. The blank stare he gave us could only mean that the poor fellow was totally blind.

Holmes showed no surprise at this. "Corporal Wendell Bright?" he enquired.

The man's severe expression was at once relieved by a sad smile. "No one has addressed me as such for a good while, sir. Are you from the military?"

"Not at all, but my friend and I are here on what is essentially a military matter. I am Sherlock Holmes, a consulting detective, and I am accompanied by, Doctor John Watson."

"I have been told of you, but what can you want with me?"

"If you will permit it, I would like to discuss a war-time incident involving your comrade, Mr. Cordon Reeder."

"Lieutenant Reeder!" Mr. Bright exclaimed. "Yes, I remember him well. Won't you come in, gentlemen?"

We entered his home and I saw the cleanliness and tidiness with some surprise. I supposed that he had someone who cared for his needs, but the ease with which he led us to his sitting room caused me to realise that this wasn't necessarily so.

"I can sense that you gentlemen are surprised that I do not walk into obstacles," he said as if he had read my thoughts. "I've lived here since childhood, long before my parents passed away, and so I was familiar with everything before the war took my sight. I get few visitors of late, apart from my niece who helps me greatly. Please be seated and tell me more fully about Lieutenant Reeder's problem. I understand that he has done well for himself, since the war."

We sank into thickly cushioned armchairs and our host offered us tea, which we both declined.

"As we understand things," Holmes began, "Mr. Reeder and his brother served together at the Battle of the Somme."

"That is correct. I spent many days next to them, freezing and starving in the trenches. Waiting to be ordered into action."

"Quite so. Can you recall the day that Mr. Reeder was wounded, and his brother killed?"

Mr. Bright fixed us with his sightless stare. "I will never forget it. The order came to leave the trench, to charge. Jonathan Reeder climbed out slightly before his brother and was immediately cut down. Cordon took his weight and lowered him gently to the ground hoping, I thought, that his brother still lived. I ran past them but I heard Cordon cry out and realised that he, too, was either wounded or dead."

"It couldn't have been, then, that Jonathan Reeder shielded his brother?"

"I cannot see how. He had hardly regained his balance from the climb before he was struck."

Holmes nodded. "It has been suggested that Cordon Reeder deliberately took shelter behind his brother's body."

"That is preposterous!" A tinge of angry red appeared on Mr. Bright's cheeks. "As I have already said, Jonathan climbed out

210

before his brother and hadn't yet stood up fully when he was hit. Cordon was still struggling for a foothold in the loose earth. To imply that there was cowardice involved is a disgrace, a slur on the man's name, and I will not have it!"

"Pray calm yourself, Mr. Bright," Holmes said in his gentlest tone. "There is no danger of Mr. Cordon Reeder being defamed. The suggestion was made by someone with a grudge against him, who most likely did not witness the event as you did."

"I would stand by my recollection in any court in the land."

"Was the charge successful?" I asked Mr. Bright.

"Not at all," he said after a moment. "I could never see the sense in the order, for we were rushing into a fusillade of enemy fire without a chance. To my surprise, I found myself very near the enemy lines, although how I got there unscathed I could not have explained, when I heard an explosion quite close and saw a brilliant flash. When I awoke in hospital I could no longer see, and they told me I never would again."

Holmes and I voiced our commiserations and Mr. Bright related to us some of his earlier war experiences. After a while he seemed in better spirits, and we thanked him and left.

I had dinner with Holmes at the Langham Hotel, and we spent the evening together, inevitably re-living old times. By ten o'clock we were both showing signs of weariness, and I rose from my chair to leave.

"Take care, Watson, as you drive back to your residence. It is perhaps a rather remote possibility, but be watchful that you aren't observed or followed. More than ever in this new age, we must take care to anticipate risk. Good night. I'll see you here at nine sharp in the morning, when we will see what can be learned from a visit to Nurse Edith Merrow."

I was glad to find that Holmes's caution was unnecessary. I drove through the streets of London unhindered, and was lost in sleep shortly after returning home.

At the appointed time next morning Holmes was waiting for me, resplendent in his grey tweed suit, near the hotel entrance. We were bound for Hammersmith, he told me, but on arrival directed me to proceed all the way along the High Street and beyond.

"How are you so certain? You appear to have no map."

I drove more slowly as a boy leading a cow crossed the road ahead. Out of the corner of my eye, I saw Holmes smile.

211

"There is no mystery about that. I simply telephoned the lady earlier to ensure that she would be at home and prepared to receive us."

The road now became a wide track with farms and cottages on either side. Holmes peered before us and gave me directions.

"There! Turn by that great oak at the crossroads."

Shortly afterwards we found ourselves outside a charming stone cottage, with rhododendrons, geraniums, and ivy evident in the small front garden and on the walls. As we alighted the front door opened, and a woman of about thirty welcomed us.

We entered a sitting room that was much as I expected. Dark beams ran the length of the ceiling, while copper warming pans from a distant age glinted upon the hearth. The lady, I have to say, would certainly have been handsome in her youth, but the rigours of her profession had hardened her stare and set her mouth in a straight line. I reflected that I had seen this effect upon the female countenance many times before.

Nurse Merrow proved to be a pleasant and cheerful hostess, offering us comfortable chairs around the fireplace and cups of Assam tea. Holmes surprised me by uncharacteristically confining himself to unrelated subjects and pleasantries until the tea things were placed to one side.

"Now, you wanted to ask me about my service after the Battle of the Somme," she began before either Holmes or I spoke further. "Was there anyone in particular that you wished to enquire of?"

Holmes nodded. "Do you recall, among your patients, Lieutenant Cordon Reeder?"

Nurse Merrow smoothed her grey skirt as she tried to remember. "As I said when you telephoned, I tended many patients. I could not hope to remember the number, but of course there are always some who remain in the mind for one reason or another. If I'm thinking of the man you refer to, then he was a patient with a leg injury. Poor man, it was quite severe, and I knew he wouldn't walk again without the aid of a cane. He struck me as a brave man, both against his pain and, according to his comrades, on the battlefield. I believe he tried to save his brother while under fire."

"So we understand. I take it that you have never heard anything to contradict that?"

She shook her head, brushing a stray lock of auburn hair back from her face. "I can recall no such thing. As far as I'm aware, Lieutenant Reeder was a popular figure." She paused, with the air of someone to whom a sudden thought has just surfaced. "In fact, there

212

was but one other patient, whom I had almost forgotten, who was critical of him."

At once, Holmes leaned forward in his chair. "Pray, elaborate."

"A private, I think, also with a leg wound, but not so serious as that of the Lieutenant. He used to relate humorous stories to the other patients, making them laugh despite their injuries. His impersonations of famous people were, as I recall, quite convincing, but it was he alone who berated Lieutenant Reeder. His comments were wounding, I would have said, on occasion."

"Do you remember the name of this man?" I asked.

She shook her head. "It was a few years ago, and there have been so many patients since."

"Was there anything of significance about him?" Holmes enquired.

"I believe he was of average height and rather pale, I think. But wait! I have it now – His name was Rufus Tiller."

Holmes got to his feet at once and I reflected that, as in the old days, he had lost interest in the lady from the instant that she had furnished the required information.

"My grateful thanks to you, Nurse Merrow. Your assistance has been most valuable."

The lady showed us out. She was a little bemused, I thought, by our abrupt departure.

We had returned as far as Hammersmith High Street when Holmes instructed me to slow down.

"Ah," he said, peering out at the shops and houses. "Stop here, there's a good fellow."

I complied at once, and he scrambled from his seat to walk quickly away in the direction of the Post Office.

"Is everything all right?" I asked when he reappeared.

He slid onto the leather seat and slammed the door. "That we shall know shortly. Bradstreet is still at the Yard, and I've requested that he conduct a search of their files for Rufus Tiller."

"You believe him to be posing as Mr. Reeder's resurrected brother?"

"Possibly. At this stage that appears likely. Consider: According to Nurse Merrow he is pale and has sustained a leg injury, was skilled at impersonation, and for some reason held our client in contempt. Did not the apparition we witnessed yesterday exhibit these features? Mark my words, Watson, the mystery here is not *who* is the villain but *why* he acts as he does."

Inspector Bradstreet had acted quickly. On our return to the Langham Hotel a telegram awaited Holmes.

"I asked Bradstreet to send a telegram rather than use the telephone," he remarked as he tore open the envelope, "since we couldn't be certain to be here at a given time." His eyes quickly scanned the sheet within. "Tiller is unknown at Scotland Yard, they have no record of him. We will now have lunch, I think, before considering another source of information."

We repaired then to the dining room, where an excellent luncheon of roast lamb was served. Holmes ate his with little enthusiasm, as was his way when in the midst of a case, and leapt from his chair the moment his meal was finished.

"Enjoy your dessert, old fellow. I will forego mine and return in time for coffee."

He was as good as his word, reseating himself rather breathlessly as I finished my plums and custard. Moments later, the coffee arrived and we drank our first cups before he would be drawn.

"Are you about to tell me where you've been?" I enquired.

"Just, once again, to the nearest Post Office," he replied. "Since Tiller served with our client, the obvious place to discover facts about him is the Army Records Office. I dare say it is highly irregular, but during the war I assisted Major Simmonds on several occasions, and I am certain that he will wish to be of help to us now."

Holmes seemed to be in no hurry to finish his coffee. When he had done so, he ordered more. We left the dining room shortly after and, at his suggestion, were about to repair to one of the sitting rooms when a young man in the livery of the hotel approached us and handed him an envelope.

"Major Simmonds has been prompt," he murmured as he extracted the form. "This is excellent. He has been thorough."

"What does he tell us?"

"Suffice it to say that I now know considerably more about Tiller than previously. Before his army days, he performed in half the music halls in the capital." He laughed, shortly. "Do you know, he called himself 'The Man of Many Faces'?"

"A master of disguise? Sounds like our man, I would say."

"Indeed, but I'm still curious as to the reason for his persecution of our client. We will, I think, pay a visit to Mr. Cordon Reeder this evening, when he's most likely to have returned from his work."

We sat talking in the comfortable surroundings of one of the quiet rooms near the main entrance. Apart from an aged ex-military man who slept deeply throughout, we were quite alone. After an hour or so I felt the need of the afternoon rest that I now take frequently, and so we parted until dinner.

Although I lived in Queen Anne Street, but a few hundred feet from the Langham, I didn't want depart in case anything happened. Holmes was good enough to allow me to use his room upstairs, where I slept for almost three hours, while he remained where he sat in deep contemplation. I confess to feeling awkward at dinner, having no evening clothes with me. He, in the same predicament, seemed unaffected. I enjoyed the roast chicken and what followed, but Holmes barely touched his and was obviously anxious for us to be on our way.

Mr. Reeder, I remembered, lived in Mayfair. I drove slowly as we entered the area, conscious of the homes of the very rich that surrounded us. I reflected that little seemed to have changed since we were here years ago, as younger men.

"The next turn to the left will bring us to Regal Mews, I think. Our client's residence is Number Eighteen."

I brought my vehicle to a halt in front of an imposing structure. Tall chimneys reached towards the darkening sky, and the house appeared to be of sturdy construction with a sprawling lawn before it. We approached by means of a paved path and Holmes rapped upon the door with his cane. After several minutes the silence within remained. He raised his cane again to knock again but stopped suddenly, as if somehow warned that something was amiss. We exchanged cautious glances before he gripped the ornate door-handle and turned it slowly. The door opened easily.

"All is not well here," he whispered as we stepped into a darkened room.

I noticed that the heavy curtains were fully drawn, and we hesitated to allow our eyes to adjust to the shadows. The door to the corridor leading to the next room was open and Holmes gestured to indicate that we should be silent and still. I strained to hear, but there was no sound and no movement anywhere. After a short while I sensed that Holmes was running his hand over the wall to our left, at about shoulder height. I heard a loud *Click!* and light flooded through the room.

"As I thought," he said. "Electric light. I noticed the cables fitted to the wall outside. The house appears to be empty, and I am curious to discover why it was left unlocked."

"Considering Mr. Reeder's current problem, and his fears, it is hard to imagine such an oversight."

"Precisely. This parlour holds nothing out of the ordinary, but let us see what the sitting room has to offer."

He led the way along the short corridor, again pressing a switch to illuminate the next room. As the electric chandelier came to life we both came to an immediate halt, for the bodies of two men lay sprawled before us. One of them was that of our client.

We approached carefully, disturbing nothing. I observed their condition carefully.

"Both men have sustained gunshot wounds to the head. I would say that death occurred about twelve hours ago," I concluded.

Holmes said nothing, so that I turned to him to ensure that he had heard. He wore an expression which utterly surprised me, one than I can recall seeing rarely in all the years of our association. His eyes held a hint of sadness and when he spoke it was with deep regret.

"I should have foreseen this. In my younger days I would never have committed such an error. I am indeed older, but it is uncertain if I have become wiser."

"You cannot blame yourself, Holmes. You advised Mr. Reeder to avail himself of protection, and judging by this other fellow's physique I would say that he was one of the rugby players that he spoke of. Also, his right hand was in the act of withdrawing a revolver from his pocket, so the attack must have been sudden."

"I have said before now that it is you who are the detective rather than me," he said grimly. "That appears not to have changed."

With that he opened a door at the other side of the room which led into a small study. His gait appeared weary as he entered, and moments later I heard him speak into a telephone.

"Are you all right?" I asked as he returned.

"I've telephoned Scotland Yard, and Bradstreet will be arriving soon," he replied, ignoring my question. "Before then, we have the opportunity to conduct our own examination. I would be obliged if you would look out from the front window and alert me at the first sight of him."

I obeyed, and Inspector Bradstreet, accompanied by two burly constables, arrived in less than half-an-hour. During this time, only the sound of Holmes's movements had disturbed the silence of the house. I admitted the men from the official force and showed them to the sitting room where Holmes stood near the bodies.

"Good evening, Inspector," Holmes said solemnly. "As I explained during our telephone conversation, these men are Mr. Cordon Reeder, about whom I had spoken to you before, and a

216

companion who is as yet unknown. The rear door of the building has been forced, and I believe the murderer awaited them as they entered the house and left the same way." He pointed to an armchair in a corner. "From beneath that chair I retrieved – without touching it, never fear – a six-shot revolver of recent manufacture. With the aid of my lens I discovered a clear thumbprint on the handle. Doubtless you will be able to make something of it. This was a crime of passion, not profit, for what criminal in his senses would leave his weapon for examination if he wished to remain free? "

The inspector, who hadn't said a word other than to return Holmes's greeting, wore a bemused look. Holmes was not usually so forthcoming so quickly, and I attributed this changed behaviour to the shock and regret he had suffered at the discovery of our dead client.

"Thank you, Mr. Holmes," the Scotland Yard man said after a moment. "We will begin our own investigation. Much has changed since the war, you know, and our capabilities have increased somewhat. Nevertheless, I would be grateful for the benefit of any other observations you may have made."

Holmes nodded and proceeded to list his impressions. As of old, Bradstreet listened eagerly and took notes. The constables were silent but paid close attention until they were ordered to search the upper floor. When the conversation was over, we left to return to the hotel.

"I won't detain you, Watson," Holmes said as we arrived at the entrance. "When I learn anything further, I'll communicate with you."

At that he alighted and I, feeling rather snubbed, again drove my vehicle home. It was apparent to me that his failure to prevent Mr. Reeder's death had affected him deeply, and I recalled that this had happened before the war when we were younger men. I resolved to remind him of this with the object of dismissing his fears about his powers diminishing with age.

That night I slept fitfully, hoping that Holmes wouldn't let his disappointment cause him to return to Sussex prematurely. Also, I wondered whether Inspector Bradstreet would further consult Holmes, or keep him informed as to the progress of the case. The early sun shone through my bedroom window and I decided not to delay rising. I had washed, shaved, and dressed, and was at the point of finishing my last piece of breakfast toast, when a telegram arrived.

The message was short:

Come at once.
Holmes

It was still early when I alighted outside the nearby Langham Hotel. Holmes and Bradstreet were near the reception area in deep conversation, and Holmes saw me at once.

"Watson," he began when greetings had been exchanged, "Bradstreet here has been busy since last night. According to the records at the Yard, the owner of the thumbprint on the weapon at Mr. Reeder's house was one Paul Durwin, who resides in Clapham."

"He is known to us from several convictions for petty theft," the inspector volunteered. "A visit to him should establish whether he owns the revolver and is therefore our killer, or if he has some other explanation. I thought you gentlemen might care to accompany me, for old time's sake."

"We would indeed." Holmes sounded much improved from the previous evening. I concurred also.

"I have a police vehicle waiting around the corner."

Presently, we found ourselves in a narrow street of old and rather decrepit houses. Bradstreet identified the number of the one we sought and, after instructing the police driver to wait, climbed out ahead of us.

"Are you armed?" Holmes enquired as we caught up with the inspector and crossed the street.

"I have my hand on my service weapon at this moment."

"Excellent. I doubt if you'll need it, but it is as well to be prepared."

The inspector approached a door that was in dire need of a coat of paint and rapped upon it.

We inclined our heads to listen, but there was only silence within. He raised his fist again, but lowered it as we heard movement. Then the door opened to reveal a dishevelled man whose pale face grew more so as he beheld us.

At once his eyes fell to the floor and I saw utter resignation in his face when he lifted his head.

"Come in, gentlemen," he said in a voice we could barely hear. Without any other word spoken we entered, and I felt that our visit had been anticipated.

We filed into a parlour that was clean but sparsely furnished. Our host let himself fall into the only armchair and we stood around him.

"Are you Paul Durwin?" Bradstreet asked him.

He shook his head.

"Or, more often, Rufus Tiller?" Holmes enquired.

"I cannot deny it."

Bradstreet studied the man carefully for a moment. "We have identified you as the owner of a gun that killed two men in Mayfair yesterday. How do you explain this?"

"I killed them. There is no other explanation."

Holmes and Bradstreet exchanged glances.

"Then I must arrest you for the murder of Mr. Cordon Reeder and Mr. Robert Arlen." Bradstreet produced a pair of police handcuffs, and snapped them on Tiller's wrist. The prisoner remained still and indifferent.

"Must we go immediately?" he asked then.

Bradstreet looked at him curiously. "What do you mean?"

"I would like the full circumstances known, so that whatever accounts and memories of me remain shall not depict me as a criminal. My actions were fired, not from greed or a desire for unlawful possession, but from revenge. A revenge that sprang from love."

Bradstreet looked perplexed, and I saw Holmes raise his eyebrows. I remembered that he had said that the mystery here was the reason behind all that had occurred.

"Surely, Bradstreet, we can afford a few minutes," Holmes ventured.

"It's irregular, but seeing as it's you, Mr. Holmes. I suppose there's no harm in it."

"Very well," Holmes said to Tiller. "You have a chance to tell your story. Pray be concise, and speak the truth."

Tiller, with Bradstreet standing beside him, sat back in his chair. There was a moment of complete silence, and then he seemed to collect his thoughts.

"It began, if there was a beginning, in the trenches at the Battle of the Somme. For days we waited for orders, for the call to action, but none came. We stood in a pool of mud for days and nights. We all ate and slept where we were. In those long lines of men, I found myself next to Cordon Reeder and his brother, Jonathan. There were no exchanges between us but I heard much of their conversation, and it was in this way that I learned of the brothers' devotion to each other. When Jonathan died, I was no more than a few yards away and, like Lieutenant Reeder I suffered a leg wound during the assault."

"You witnessed the elder Reeder's death?" Holmes interrupted.

219

"It happened before my eyes."

"Is there then, any truth in your accusation that Cordon Reeder positioned his brother to shield himself?"

A crafty smile crept across Tiller's face. "No, that was an invention of mine, intended to drive him to the point of madness, as I will explain. I spent my recovery in the same field hospital ward as Cordon Reeder, and it was there that I first saw Nurse Lily Crowther." His eyes flitted across our faces, and I had the impression that he was feeling some embarrassment.

Seeing no sympathy, he continued. "Until the moment when I first saw her, I had little interest in women, always having lived with my widowed mother, but to be confronted with such an angel changed my life in an instant. She was the sweetest girl I could ever have imagined, and I looked forward with all my heart to the occasions when she dressed my wounds or enquired as to my condition. I began to think of her as mine, and turned my head away when she treated the other soldiers."

Here he paused, and I could see that the memory was painful to him. "Can you imagine then my disappointment when I realised that she had eyes only for Cordon Reeder? As the weeks passed, it became obvious to us all. Some of the others laughed and congratulated him on his 'conquest', but to me every smile she gave him was a dagger in my heart."

The reason for his animosity towards our client, as described by Nurse Edith Merrow, now became clear. Holmes's expression suggested that his thoughts were similar.

"Do you mean to tell us," Inspector Bradstreet asked with some incredulity, "that your actions and crimes in all this were because of *a woman?*"

Tiller looked at him in a strange way. "That would not be an inaccurate assessment, but there is more. You see, to me she was becoming my whole life. I imagined us together, and this eclipsed everything that had gone before. The time came for my discharge from the hospital and, unfit to render further service to my country, I resumed my former life. My mother passed away but I hardly noticed her absence, because Nurse Crowther still filled my mind.

"Unable to keep myself informed about her life, I read the newspapers avidly to keep track of Cordon Reeder. The news that I dreaded, that they had married, never appeared, but I saw that he was progressing in government circles. Then came the Spanish Flu epidemic of 1918. At that time he led a committee that was set up to combat the disease, and made the final decision to despatch a contingent of specially-trained nurses to a badly infected hospital in Manchester. This was strongly opposed by most of his colleagues for many reasons, but he would have his way.

"Quite recently I discovered that most of those poor nurses died, and that among them was my beloved Lily. This news caused me such melancholia that I wanted nothing else but to die too. Several times I found myself on the brink of taking my own life as the only way of seeing her again. Then one day it came into my mind that the cause of her death was Cordon Reeder, because he had had the final say in placing her in peril."

"Did it not occur to you," Holmes asked him, "that Mr. Reeder was probably unaware that Miss Crowther was in the group? After all, unless I have misunderstood you, he had no further contact with her after leaving the hospital."

Tiller shrugged his shoulders. "That didn't seem to matter. All that I could see was that he was responsible for her death, and that I couldn't leave this life without making him pay. It struck me as fitting that, using my skills at disguise learned long ago, I should use the guilt he carried about, causing the death of a brother that he loved, to avenge the death he had caused of someone that I, myself, adored."

"Enough of this," Bradstreet said impatiently. "If you are confessing, then get on with it."

Tiller glanced at him, but continued as if hadn't heard. "I had a plan. I intended to appear as Jonathan Reeder unexpectedly and with increasing frequency. I hoped to place doubts in Cordon Reeder's mind about his brother's death, and then to intensify them. Had I not been prevented, a week or two would have seen him fit for the mad-house."

He scowled, looking directly at Holmes. "But after Victoria Station, my task became more difficult. I recognised you, Mr. Holmes, and remembered your reputation of old. I couldn't risk failure, and leaving my Lily unavenged was now more likely, so I decided to abandon my plan and act at once. I forced my way into Cordon Reeder's home, only to find it empty. I therefore resolved to await his return and then to shoot him, which I did a short time later. I didn't expect him to have a companion, but when this other man appeared and attempted to retaliate, I had no choice but to also kill him.

"I cannot remember now, but I believe I dropped my weapon to the floor as I left. That was of no importance, and neither was my fate." He rose to his feet. "You see then, gentlemen, why your arrival, although sooner than expected, came as no surprise."

"I have seldom heard such a story of a man deceiving himself so much, and certainly not to the point of murder," Bradstreet commented. "The best you can hope for, my lad, is to spend the rest of your days in an asylum. Apart from that, it's the hangman I'm sure."

"Yet there is something pitiful about this account," I said.

"Don't waste your sympathy, Doctor. The streets of London will be safer without the likes of him. Who knows who he might have taken a fancy to next?"

Holmes nodded. "This is far from the first time that I've seen a man ruined by his obsession with a woman, even when she is unaware of it. I think, Bradstreet, that you should take him now, as he appears to have come to the end of his tale."

The inspector began to move towards the door with Tiller, held to him by the handcuffs, at his side.

"Thank you for your assistance, gentlemen. It was quite like in our younger days."

The words were hardly out of Bradstreet's mouth when Tiller, passing the sideboard, quickly wrenched open a drawer with his free hand. Something flashed and at first I thought that Bradstreet, now spattered with blood, was injured, but then Tiller sank to his knees pulling the inspector down with him.

"*Watson!*" Holmes cried, and I responded at once. I knelt beside Tiller and loosened his collar but it was quickly apparent that he was beyond my help.

I stood up and shook my head. "I can do nothing for him. He plunged a fork from the cutlery drawer deep into his neck. The rapid loss of so much blood suggests that he has severed the jugular."

With disgust, Bradstreet removed the handcuff from Tiller's lifeless hand. "He has saved the hangman a job, I expect. This is not the way I would have chosen for this affair to end, though."

"It wasn't our decision, Inspector," Holmes replied impassively. "I take it that you would like Watson and me to visit you at the Yard tomorrow to add to your report."

"I would be obliged."

With that, the inspector went to arrange for the removal of the body. Holmes and I left the premises in poor spirits, for tragedy was abundant in this case. My surprise was therefore considerable when he, rather than descending into a dark mood as of old, suddenly smiled and placed his hand upon my shoulder.

"I think, old fellow, that we are in dire need of something to cheer us up. What do you say to a drink in that tavern that I see on the corner, followed by luncheon at Simpson's?"

"At this moment, I can think of nothing better," I replied with enthusiasm.

It was as I replaced my empty glass upon the worn table that I asked Holmes the question to which I dreaded the answer.

"Has it crossed your mind, Holmes, that you could easily re-establish yourself as a consulting detective, perhaps with even more success than before?"

For a moment – it seemed like an age – he appeared to consider. Then a slow smile spread across his face.

"Dear old Watson, it is clear to me that you would like nothing better than for us to resume our activities, and I will confess that a part of me is in accordance. But consider, old fellow, that we are now in a new age. The London we knew has gone forever. Now we see around us machines instead of horse-drawn hansoms. Scotland Yard appears more efficient to the point where my assistance will soon be unnecessary, and you and I no longer have the energy of youth.

"Then there is the certainty that nothing will ever be the same since that terrible war. Witness the increasing strangeness of everyday behaviour and even little things, such as the abominable noise that is now recognised as music, and this becomes clear: We're out of our element. London today is better served by those other consultants who have followed in our footsteps – Solar Pons. Hercule Poirot. Lord Peter, and Campion. You may recall that I have said, on more than one occasion in Baker Street, that you are a fixed point in a changing world. I should have realised then, I now see, that I am also. No, my conclusion – and I gave the matter some thought before you mentioned it – is exactly the opposite."

I knew of course that Holmes was correct, as usual. Nevertheless, my heart sank. Then he looked me in the eye and smiled warmly, and his words restored me instantly.

"But – and make no mistake here, old friend – what I have said by no means precludes our opportunities to meet more often, and re-live our adventures many times before your fireside or mine. And who knows what strange events will present themselves, even in our twilight years, to cause us once more to set off together in pursuit of explanation?"

The Adventure of the
Grave Correspondent
by Robert Perret

It was 1920, and though peace had been declared at Versailles, my beloved England was still very much reeling. The home economy had collapsed even as we tried to rebuild, and our valiant lads still struggled to return to a regular way of life. Holmes, of course, carried on as if he were unaffected, puttering about his Sussex plot in the guise of a simple apiarist. For myself, I had adopted my friend's sliding scale in ministering to the soldiers who had met with disaster in the war. I often went days without seeing a penny, and those were the days that I felt the most like a true man of medicine. In pursuit of my merciful aspirations, I found myself on a train to Worthing and decided a visit to Holmes's villa near Birling Gap was in order. Despite the punishment that my friend had endured in recent years, I did not doubt that no other physician ever had a chance to pass an eye over him. Indeed, I was likely one of the few people who ever spoke to the old hermit. Those who only know of the Great Detective from my stories may be surprised to learn that I found my friend sat upon a rock with a pellet gun across his knee, a plume of blue smoke rising languidly from his clay pipe.

"Haven't found anything for the pot, yet?" I cajoled as I approached.

"For myself, I had only intended some spare greens," Holmes said. "But of course that is no meal fit for a weary traveler."

"You can't have known I was coming. I hardly knew myself!"

"There have been advertisements in the newspaper announcing the arrival of the hospital ship *Britannia*. A thousand men to be discharged, having reached the limits of His Majesty's care."

"There are dozens of doctors engaged in the endeavor. There was no reason to expect I would be among those in attendance."

"My dear Watson, you have yet to miss an opportunity to visit these southern shores since my retirement."

I could hardly deny it, so I simply laid my valise upon the ground and attempted to work the stiffness of train travel from my muscles.

"Do you fancy pheasant or hare tonight?" Holmes asked.

225

"I'm not particular," I said, thinking more of the mead Holmes fermented in his workshop.

Holmes fired a shot into the grass to the north, causing a pheasant to the east to startle and leap into the air. With a practiced hand, he primed the gun and shot the bird.

"There are easier ways to flush a hen," I said.

"This way we shan't have to choose," Holmes said, moving to the north and plucking a hare from the grass. He had shot them both in a matter of seconds.

"The criminal class of London would have shuddered to know what a dead hand you are."

"Justice is rarely found with a bullet," Holmes averred. He collected the pheasant and set about cleaning the game. With a simple rustic blade, he made short work of it, and soon I was sat by his hearth as the stew simmered. I had just settled in and became properly comfortable when there was a knocking at the door.

"Pray enter," Holmes cried, somewhat to my surprise.

With a delicate hesitancy, a woman peered in through the barely propped door.

"Mr. Holmes?" she asked.

"The same. Please, my good lady." He stood and gestured to his seat. For my part, I fumbled to find my heels. As she entered, my heart sank. I had seen too many young ladies dressed in mourning these last few years.

"My name is Penelope Creighton," she said.

"Mrs. Creighton," I asked, "may I offer you a drink?"

"Ah, no, thank you, sir. I was hoping to have a word with Mr. Holmes."

"And a word you shall have," Holmes said. "This is my esteemed friend, Doctor Watson, and I assure you that you may speak freely before him."

The lady gave me a quizzical look. "Forgive me, I suppose it never occurred to me you might also be found in Sussex. You seem as much as part of Mr. Holmes's London as your flat in Baker Street."

"Yes, well, I do get around a bit now and then."

"Of course, how silly of me. Oh, I shouldn't have come, it's just . . . ."

"Take your time, Mrs. Creighton," Holmes said.

"It is these." She held forth a bundle of letters.

226

Holmes's took it but briefly and hardly seemed to regard it before placing it upon the end table. "You have attracted a suitor, even though you still wear mourning."

"The audacity!" I bellowed.

"And yet not completely unwelcome," Holmes replied.

"Holmes!"

"She kept the letters, Watson." He had paused to dramatically regard the mantle.

"Yes, that is true," she said. "I did keep the letters, but there is a good reason."

"Pray tell," Holmes replied.

"These letters – they come from my husband."

"Your late husband?" I stammered.

"Yes."

"Are you certain?"

"Quite. It is his handwriting, and in his voice, as they say. Here, I brought you an example of a letter he wrote to me before he was conscripted. I apologize that it is a bit . . . sentimental."

"That is nothing to apologize about in the least," I assured her.

This letter Holmes did read, and he plucked a letter from the bundle and compared the two momentarily. He then returned the lot to Mrs. Creighton.

"You see it is so," she said. "Don't you?"

"By what means do you receive these more recent missives? I note that the envelopes don't bear an address."

"I have a habit of visiting his grave on Tuesdays. I began to discover these notes left there."

"Perhaps these letters were written before his death?" I offered. "A fellow soldier may have taken up the charge of delivering them to you."

"That was my thought as well," Penelope said. "But as the letters have continued to arrive, they begin to make reference to events after the date my husband supposedly died."

"And, as a practicality, there are too many letters, Holmes said. "A final missive would be one thing, but no soldier writes dozens of letters, just in case tragedy should befall him. Is there a letter every week?"

"Recently that has been so," she said.

"The letters were more sporadic in the past?"

"Yes. The first did not appear for several months, and then weeks would normally pass between them."

"Has the nature of the letters changed as well?"

227

"They have become more . . . ardent over time. I don't understand, Mr. Holmes. If my husband is alive, why does he not simply come home?"

"I dare not yet speculate," Holmes said. "You have received these letters for almost a year. What prompts you to seek assistance now?"

"To be honest, Mr. Holmes, I think I had been trying to ignore the whole business. I saw my husband in his coffin, saw him laid to rest. I know that he is dead, and that these letters have to be some odd business it would be best to ignore. And yet, I saw William – my husband – yesterday."

"Did you speak to him?" Holmes asked.

"No, it was only at a distance. I arrived at the cemetery a bit early on account of another appointment I needed to keep later in the morning. As I neared my husband's plot, I startled a figure knelt by the grave. He looked at me but for a second before fleeing. I called out to him, but a lady in a dress has little hope of catching a man on the run."

"You are certain it was your husband?" I asked.

"It was but a momentary glimpse of his cheek, but the whole figure and the way he moved – I felt it in my heart."

"Was a letter left behind?"

"Yes, I believe he had already placed it. It was the very one you have examined."

"It seems a simple enough matter to wait for the man to appear again next Tuesday," I said.

"Oh, that is an eternity!" Penelope cried.

"In the meantime, I shall attempt to verify the official fate of your gallant husband," Holmes said. "Return to the cemetery per your normal routine. You will not see us, but rest assured we shall be there, standing ready to assist you."

"Thank you, Mr. Holmes!"

"Not a bit," he replied.

"What do you think?" I asked when the woman had departed after providing us with information as to her residence and the cemetery's location.

"The dead do not rise," Holmes replied. "As much as we may want them to." He opened a cabinet to reveal a telephone receiver inside. I recalled many years earlier, when his brother Mycroft had insisted upon it as a condition of Holmes's retirement. He lifted the receiver and depressed the hook switch several times in sequence.

"Colton, please," he said, before providing a string of letters and numbers.

There was a pause of a few minutes.

"Good day, Lieutenant. I am calling to confirm the disposition of an Able Rate William Creighton of the Fifth Sussex. Very good, I shall await your reply."

We sat down to a hearty supper then. Holmes's housekeeper was away, and for all his simple tastes, Holmes was quite accomplished as a cook.

"You aren't absolutely correct," I said as we sipped at our mead and looked out upon clover under the setting sun.

My friend's brow arched precipitously as he turned to me. "Is that so?"

"On occasion, the dead have risen – perhaps even in response to fervent desire."

"You speak of myth and legend," Holmes said.

"No, I speak of you."

Holmes's responded with silence.

"You had no grave, you know. Mycroft wouldn't allow it. I understand why, in retrospect of course. But at the time my grief had no locus. There was Baker Street, but that remained Mrs. Hudson's home, and so I could hardly go there without commiserating with her. It wasn't a place I could go to visit my memories of you in solitude."

"The ruse was an unfortunate necessity, my dear Watson."

"Instead I imagined you at the bottom of that horrible waterfall, the sound of rushing water plaguing my nightmares. We looked for you, you know. For weeks we searched. Sherlock Holmes had just disappeared. The thought that you lay down there undiscovered was agony."

"It was necessary," Holmes replied again, weakly. "When next we part, you shall find me there." He gestured at his apiary. "I intend to nurture the creatures who have nurtured me in my dotage."

What of the creatures who nurtured you in your prime? I wondered. But instead, I said, "You have found a gravedigger who will work among the hives?"

"Old Tom Carriage is a beekeeper himself."

"Seems unwise to consign one's final affairs to a man who has old in his name."

"He is of that hardy stock who will outlive men half his age," Holmes replied. "Honest labor and plenty of fresh air."

At that, the telephone rang. My friend excused himself to answer it. He returned and sparked his clay pipe again.

"As far as His Majesty's Navy is concerned, Able Rate Creighton honorably laid down his life in service to the Crown."

"And you are sure you got an honest answer?" I asked.

"There is no such thing as an honest answer in government, but I find Colton to be trustworthy, and he would have understood that it was not a casual inquiry."

"An impostor then? To what end?"

"I have paid no special attention to Mrs. Creighton. I don't rely upon my famous parlor trick as much as I once did. I don't get the practice I need to stay sharp. Yet, I would hazard that she holds some sort of clerical position and that she lives in a modest flat. She is obviously accustomed to conducting her own affairs, and she had the wherewithal to discover me and my whereabouts. She was polite, but not exceptionally deferential to men who are both strangers and nominally her social betters. If she worked with the public, she would have been compelled to leave her mourning dress behind. Yet her clothes do not suggest particularly manual labor. I'll wager she works in the back office of a moderately large business concern, likely shipping. Someone may believe that she may be privy to useful information, or else that being in her favor might convey some advantage in negotiation."

"It seems all they have managed to do is drive the poor woman to distraction."

"Yes, well, that is a matter for next week."

"You don't intend to investigate further?"

"Mrs. Creighton doesn't appear to be in any mortal danger, so we may afford to wait until we know the villain will present himself. I would hate to tip our hand when we have the unusual advantage of foreknowledge. Who knows what eyes may be upon her? Already her visit to me may have set her bashful correspondent upon his toes."

I found that reasoning rather unsatisfactory, but I was kept quite busy over the next week as I tended to the sorry exodus of newly discharged soldiers. I had once been in their place, cast out upon my own pluck before being yet whole again. Some hurts I could fix with the meager contents of my Gladstone, while I could only prescribe for others, and nearly all needed a friendly ear. That, at least, I could do without reservation. So many sad stories, and yet the same few themes which resurfaced again and again. I was truly wrung out by the time my appointment with Holmes came around. I found him sitting in the lobby of my hotel that morning, the paper draped across his lap as he took languorous draws upon his cigarette.

"Ah, Watson," he said as I approached. "Leave your trunk at the desk. "I've arranged for it to be delivered to my cottage. Unless you prefer it go directly back to London?"

"I can hardly imagine making the journey in my present condition," I sighed. I liked to think of myself as hale and vigorous, but I had to concede that six days of labor had perhaps taken a toll upon me.

"Today shall be nothing more than a stroll in the park," Holmes said. "A cab awaits us out front, and I have taken the liberty of laying in a healthy spread."

"That doesn't much match my memory of our past vigils."

"This one is by necessity in the open and the daylight. Even I no longer relish the thought of wedging myself in some obscure nook and laying in wait these days. No, we shall have a luncheon in memory of Reginald VanDunne."

"Who is that?" I wondered as we made our way outside.

"Some fellow or another who had the good fortune of being buried at the top of the far ridge opposite Able Rate Creighton. We shall enjoy an unobstructed view while remaining inconspicuous by sheer distance."

"I see."

"There is a cold roast to accompany a rather fine brandy," Holmes said.

"I see!"

Holmes's opened the door of a beautiful burgundy Albert with kid interior. The driver gave us no more acknowledgment than to touch his cap before we sped away. Every bump in the road sent great shocks through me, but I had to admit it was great fun to go so quickly. The car threaded expertly through the traffic before us. Just a few years ago there would have been an endless stream of people and animals milling about, but with these new motorcars, the major roadways now stood clear for the most part. Soon enough we were standing at VanDunne's grave, Holmes spreading a tartan blanket upon the bushy grass.

"How do you know that we haven't missed the man already?" I asked.

"I took a surreptitious glance at the grave as we passed," Holmes replied. "Besides which, we know he was here only shortly before Mrs. Creighton was due to arrive. I have no doubt he observes her receiving the note, and he can't be seen loitering about the

231

cemetery for prolonged periods week after week. Indeed, I suspect the delay in the letters being left after the Private's death is down to the widow not having yet settled into a predictable routine."

It was a melancholy thing to watch the mourners shuffle in and out as the day progressed. At the same time, birds flitted between headstones and rabbits and squirrels scampered about, oblivious to the gravity of the place. We had just begun to make a light lunch of cheese sandwiches when Holmes perked up. "Don't look, but our man just arrived."

Had he simply not said anything it would have been no bother, but now I ached to see the scene behind me. Holmes continued to eat his sandwich as if by rote while watching over my shoulder.

"He has left his letter and settled in now," Holmes said. "He kneels near a headstone, not five yards distant, but behind where Mrs. Creighton will stand."

"Do you see her yet?"

"She is not due for another half-hour."

"We could set upon the rascal now," I said. "Before the lady faces danger again."

"I suspect we will get few answers that way, and the man is breaking no law at the moment."

The sandwich was bitter in my mouth, but there was little else to do while we continued to wait. At last Mrs. Creighton came walking through the cemetery gate. I hazarded a glance at the fellow lurking in wait for her. As I suspected, he had seen her already and his attention was completely fixated upon her. For her part, the widow looked a bit hesitant, and I could see from the set of her chin that she was casting her eyes about while trying to appear that she was not. I hoped it wasn't obvious to anyone who wasn't looking for it.

"Steady on," Holmes said as she approached the grave. With trembling hands, she took the letter and, after a moment's hesitation, opened it. Something in the letter seemed to shock her, and she ran back towards the gate. The man jumped up from behind his headstone and I stepped forward to intercept him. I hadn't made two steps before Holmes's sure hand was at my collar, arresting my charge. "Give it a moment," Holmes said. "I don't believe he knows anyone is on to him yet. Let us see where he retreats to."

By now, Mrs. Creighton was out of sight, and her voyeur had done nothing more than make a few false starts at chasing after her. He now hung his head and began to plod across the cemetery.

232

Carefully, we followed him, watching him leave through what appeared to be a service gate for the groundskeeper.

"What of Mrs. Creighton?" I asked just before we stepped through.

"If you hurry now, you just might catch her," Holmes said. "Ask her to meet us at the Mermaid's Garden at six. It is a place she will know of. I'll have a table at the back."

Before I could object, Holmes was gone. I turned on my heel and made my way back to the main gate, leaving the picnic supplies behind me. Holmes had mentioned that he'd made arrangements with the cemetery staff to retrieve them, should be make a sudden departure. I couldn't see Mrs. Creighton in any direction, but I played to Holmes's assumption and made my way towards the center of town where a clerk would most likely be employed. As I made my way forward with rather more grit than I preferred to employ, I heard a woman sobbing over a hedgerow. It took a moment to find my way around it, but there was Mrs. Creighton, having collapsed onto a small bench inside this private garden. She startled when I stepped inside and then turned away when she saw it was I.

"You must think I am dreadfully silly, Doctor Watson."

"Not a bit of it," I said. "It is a most unusual situation. What did the letter say?"

"The writer was making love to me."

"But you are certain now that the writer was not your husband?"

"You have been married, Doctor Watson. I have read of it, and I see even now that you wear a wedding band. You must know how a unique intimacy develops between a husband and wife. Little turns of phrase, sweet nothings – a secret language of sorts."

"Yes, I know precisely what you mean."

"There was none of that which I would recognize," she said. "Worse, there is a brute passion to the prose that would never have come from William. And yet, the writer knows things which he should not."

"May I see the letter?" I asked.

"Not this time, I'm afraid," she said, clutching it close as if I would snatch it away. "Even before a man of discretion, even before a physician, some things are too personal."

"I understand, my dear, and you have my word of honor that I will not pry further." I offered her my handkerchief and helped her regain her feet. "Mr. Holmes is pursuing the man, and I have every confidence he will have some answers for you tonight. He has asked to meet with you at the Mermaid's Garden tonight at six for supper."

Surprise crossed her face for just a moment.

"Do you know about the place?" I asked.

"Yes," she said. "But I wonder at what Mr. Holmes knows."

"May I escort you back to work?" I asked.

"I appreciate the offer but I must decline. I endeavor to be seen as my own person now. Any sign of female frailty shall be leapt upon by my colleagues."

"Might I at least offer this small bit of courage?" I proffered my flask.

After a moment of hesitation, Mrs. Creighton took a long draught of my favored brandy, dabbed her eyes dry, and gave me a brusque nod before making her way back out to the street. I shan't be surprised if we find women to be more than our equal someday.

It seemed like it would be rather a bother to make my way back to Holmes's cottage just to have to come straight back, and so it was that I found myself at loose ends in Worthing. I was exhaustively familiar with the makeshift hospital at the docks, but I had seen little else of the city. I eventually found a satisfactory spot overlooking the Worthing Golf Club and the channel.

At one point I had fancied taking up the great game in my retirement, but my old wounds yet nagged me, seeming to have reasserted themselves in my mature years. Yet it was pleasant to watch the balls soar and the ships catch the wind. My life had been spent in strife across three continents, so I could well appreciate this brief respite. When the changing timbre of the town behind me told me that the workday had ended, I made my way back, eager to hear what Holmes had discovered.

Returning to paved streets I hailed a cab and asked for the Mermaid's Garden. The driver turned and gave me a momentary glance of appraisal, but then pulled away from the curb without comment. I began to wonder, then, what sort of place Holmes had picked out. We left the commercial streets and began to navigate the narrow residential roads beyond. The cabman seemed to be keeping his left eye on the coastline. Brick buildings gave way to wood gave way to stone. At last, he pulled to the side of the street and indicated that the Mermaid's Garden was up the winding path ahead.

"For two pounds I'll wait for ten minutes," he said as I paid him his fare.

"I don't think I shall be back so quickly."

He cocked his head in a way that suggested he disagreed, but then he pulled his car around and sped away. I made the lonely ascent up to the precipice above. It was an ancient stone building, likely some kind of lookout at one point. I heard a pleasant chattering inside so I ambled up to the door at ease, only to find it locked. Curious, I knocked.

"What do you want?" came an unwelcoming voice from inside.

"I have an appointment here," I said. "With Mr. Sherlock Holmes." I could hear the muffled tones of a conversation within.

Finally, the voice said, "Go around back."

I did so, trying not to glance inside the windows as I passed. Even so, I gathered that I was being observed closely by the occupants. At the rear, I knocked again, this time to be greeted by my friend.

"An unusual venue," I said as I stepped into the bare room.

"I suppose I am accustomed to it," Holmes said.

"You come here often?" I asked. "The hospitality leaves something to be desired."

"Come now, Watson, there is no need to be sour."

"Mrs. Creighton has not arrived?" I asked.

"She shall appear presently."

"And your investigation of the grave correspondent?"

"Let us wait a few moments more for the lady."

Presently, Mrs. Creighton did arrive, coming through the inner door rather than the exterior door I had come through.

"I am a bit surprised to find you here," she said.

"I have had the honor of providing some small assistance in the past," Holmes said. "And, of course, we should not have to worry about your admirer here."

"As much as I respect the work done here, I do not reply upon it personally," Mrs. Creighton said.

"What sort of work is done here?" I asked.

"It is a relief society, of a sort, for war widows," Mrs. Creighton said. "But it could just as well be a nunnery. These women have retreated from the world. I shall think of William every day, but I do not intend to drown in my grief."

"To that end, may I assume that you carry a photograph of your late husband?"

She unclasped the locket around her neck and gently opened it.

Holmes's regarded it momentarily. "You cannot think of any other man who might have regarded you dearly?"

"I have encouraged no affections besides my husband's!"

"I did not mean to suggest otherwise – and yet, as dear Watson might attest, women possess a natural charm. You met your husband here in Worthing?"

235

"Yes, he came here as an apprentice to the harbormaster and he would occasionally have business with the trading company at which I work. He would contrive it so that I was the clerk he spoke to, and then he began to come around when he had no official business at all. He would bring me little treasures from all around the world. The ship captains would give little gifts to the harbormaster, you know. And, well, I suppose you gentlemen have been courting a time or two in your lives."

"William Creighton hadn't come to Worthing alone?" Holmes asked. "He had a brother?"

"Yes, that's right. Poor Walter. Unlike William, Walter had hopes of becoming a sailor on a merchantman. The allure of exotic ports and all that. Spent his time bothering all the ships that came in, hoping to be taken aboard as a crewman."

"I am surprised he had difficulty," I said. "Many a merchantman is not particular about which men they take aboard."

"That is true, but he was known to be the dockmaster's apprentice. No one would cross the dockmaster by taking Walter aboard. It is like a little kingdom down there, and the dockmaster can make life very difficult for an unwary captain."

"But such a man holds no sway over His Majesty's Navy," Holmes observed.

"Yes. Walter leapt at the opportunity to enlist when war broke out. William was quite bereft, up until he was drafted."

"You never had any sense that Walter had any affection for you?" Holmes asked.

"No, I was quite firm with him. He had been flirtatious when I first met him, but when William pledged himself to me, I rebuked Walter in no uncertain terms."

"I am afraid the heart does not readily obey," I replied.

"You believe it is Walter who has been leaving the letters?"

"I followed him back to the boarding house where he's staying. It is exclusive to sailors. I managed a look at the registration book. While there was no Creighton on the books, there was an entry in a hand of passing resemblance to the letters. Most tellingly, I had a good look at his face through a window. There are seven points of conclusive physiology, despite the scarring."

"The scarring?"

"Marine Walter Creighton was medically discharged after injuries sustained from a shell blast."

236

"I had no idea. We hadn't heard from him since he enlisted. There were some hard feelings all around over that. Why wouldn't he come to see me? I am yet his sister-in-law."

"And why the subterfuge of being his own brother?" I asked.

"I'm not certain that the subterfuge was intentional," Holmes replied. "The two boys would have learned to write elbow to elbow, and particularly were simultaneously trained in the clerical hand used by the dockmaster. Likewise, even if their temperaments differed, their manners would have been much the same. Each approached Mrs. Creighton in a similar fashion, before what Walter perceived as a developing intimacy allowed for his personality to begin to show in the letters. Of course, they share the same initials."

"I would have seen the difference!" Mrs. Creighton said.

"The hand of the two brothers are strikingly similar," Holmes said. "And I suspect an element of hope crept into your perception as well."

Mrs. Creighton seemed to collapse in her seat. "It sounds ridiculous, but I suppose in my heart I did hope that William was somehow alive." Tears welled up in her eyes, and she buried her face in her hands.

"There is nothing ridiculous about it," I said. "I still have moments when I turn to say something to my departed first wife. Our loved ones stay with us in spirit."

"I know that you don't wish to throw yourself into a life devoid of anything but mourning," Holmes said, gesturing back to the inner door, "but Mrs. Damascus is a good woman who has been a friend to many women who find themselves with unexpected lives after the war. She is available to you in the salon with a most remarkable blend of tea, if I may say. Watson and I can go and have a word with Walter."

"No, I want to do it," she said. "Give me a moment to pay my regards to Mrs. Damascus and we can go."

Holmes and I were savoring the end of our second cigarettes by the time she emerged, flush of cheek and red around the eyes, but seeming to carry much less weight. "Mrs. Damascus is a remarkable woman," is all she said.

"I have found her to be so," Holmes replied.

We picked our way back down the cliffside and Holmes led us on a merry stroll to the less picturesque streets of Worthing. The lady and I waited outside while Holmes knocked upon the door of a rather weary workhouse. He stepped inside and emerged a few moments later with a man wearing his naval dress coat over threadbare trousers. He was wiping his face with a rag even as he stepped out.

Mrs. Creighton stifled a gasp with her gloved hand. "Walter!"

"Penelope," he said sheepishly, still holding the rag to his face.

"I didn't know you had come home!" she said.

"I didn't feel it was my home after William passed."

She stepped forward and pulled his hand down. "We are family, Walter."

He turned the scarred side of his face away.

"You don't have to hide from me. I care for you, even if I do not love you." She emphasized the last by placing kind hands upon his arm. "Not like I loved William."

"I know," he said with a catch in his throat.

"I hope I can still be a sister to you, and you a brother to me. We are all the other has."

I nodded to Holmes and we stepped away, keeping a benevolent watch from a distance. I don't know what further passed between them precisely but in the end, Mrs. Creighton embraced the wounded sailor and slipped a piece of paper into his hand. For his part, he seemed to shrink in his coat before stumbling back into the workhouse.

"Thank you, gentlemen," was all she said when she rejoined us.

When we lived at Baker Street, news of our old clients would often find us, directly or indirectly. No longer residing at a world-famous address, I was often left to wonder whatever became of all those we had assisted through the years. Holmes, it seems, kept a watchful eye upon Mrs. Creighton and her brother-in-law, and so I did at least learn that Walter found work on a Canadian fishing vessel, spending long months at sea with men who likely did not flinch at his disfigurement. Mrs. Creighton, for her part, yet visited her husband's grave weekly. The pair would meet occasionally when Walter was ashore, but that was all the detail Holmes cared to provide. Thinking of those windswept shores reminds me that the Great War left so many vacancies between us all.

The Austrian Certificates
by David Marcum

A coldness had grown in recent months with my literary agent, Sir Arthur Conan Doyle, all on his part, and for the most surprising of reasons. Whereas he had become weary in earlier years of his association with my writings, feeling that it took readers' minds from better things – that is to say, his own historical romances – of late he had been pestering me to revive our long-dormant partnership and provide him with more accounts of Sherlock Holmes's investigations to be published under his own bolder by-line.

Thus, it was with some surprise that I entered the Stranger's Room of the Diogenes Club on that afternoon in early July 1920 to find him sipping the club's notable whisky and swapping stories with Mycroft Holmes. That fact nearly overshadowed that there was a third man in the room, sitting nervously to one side.

I knew that Mycroft and Sir Arthur – or Doyle as I shall always call him – were well-known to one another, although I couldn't say when they had first became acquainted. It was certainly sometime after Doyle first learned of Mycroft's existence when he'd arranged for the publication of "The Greek Interpreter" in *The Strand*. I don't know if Doyle then met Mycroft by happenstance, or if he sought him out. In any case, Doyle became one of Mycroft's occasional cronies, and years later, in 1912 to be precise, I learned that Doyle had been recruited to help spin out the Government's contingency plans for possible schemes that might be useful in the coming war with the Germans, using his writer's ability to plot out various distractions that might be put to good use. *

But the war was behind us now, and while there was certainly no reason that Mycroft and Doyle wouldn't have remained friends, I was puzzled to find them congenially conversing when I had expected a more serious discussion, based on my cryptic summons to the Club earlier that morning.

Before I had time to offer a greeting, let alone raise the question, the door opened behind me, and in stepped Sherlock Holmes.

If he felt surprise upon seeing the unexpected guests, he withheld it, as would be typical. With a nod to me, he stepped forward and offered his hand to Doyle, who shook it warmly. I did

239

the same. We repeated the action with the other man. Neither of us made the gesture toward Mycroft, who didn't expect it.

The club steward who had shown Holmes in now made himself busy providing refreshments to all of us, and then he slipped out. Mycroft took a sip of brandy and then set it aside.

"Thank you both for coming. I was aware that you were in town, Sherlock. Did you settle that little matter for Braithewaite to his satisfaction?"

Holmes smiled, leaned back in his chair, and crossed his legs. "I won't ask how you knew about it. Braithertonn would be mortified to learn that it's being bandied about in a Pall Mall club. But yes, we returned the stolen items to him last night."

"And Adrian Wiley? Did you let him catch the ferry to Dieppe?"

Holmes glanced at the other two men in the room.

"No worries, Sherlock," said Mycroft. "Both Sir Arthur and Armathwaite are discreet. I assume that you let Wiley go. It's what I would have suggested, had you consulted me. Much better for all concerned."

"We did," replied Holmes, glancing my way. "As you say, it's better to have him away from England for a year or two. He's a little worse for wear after tangling with Watson, but he's cowed – at least for the present."

At the mention of a confrontation, Doyle sat up. "Taught him a lesson, then, Watson? Good show! Send the bounder scrambling!" Then he laughed and fit his whisky glass under his massive mustache, taking a sizeable swallow. His right shoulder twitched once – as if he were imagining delivering a resounding blow himself – and then he gave a slight chuckle and looked toward our host.

"This," said Mycroft, with the slightest nod toward the unknown man, "is Cedric Armathwaite – he's the Number Two at the Exchequer, under Chamberlain. He came to me with a problem about the Austrian gold certificates."

Holmes nodded, but as was usual, my face betrayed my ignorance of the matter. Doyle's expression indicated that he was in the same boat, although trying to look more confident about it.

"If you would?" Mycroft gestured to the fifth man. Armathwaite nodded, wrung his hands, and began.

"As you know, after many months of negotiations, preparations are in place to finalize the Peace with Austria in just a week or so, officially declaring that portion of the war to be complete. As part of that, there are a number of behind-the-scenes pieces of the puzzle that have had to be negotiated and put into place. These include the delivery to Austria of a sizeable amount of gold certificates obtained during the conflict and held by us for their eventual return.

"While some here in England are quite vested in heaping crushing punishments upon our defeated enemies, there are others who realize that it's best for all concerned to help them rebuild – we are better off to encourage friendly relations and help develop trading partners than to simply create a broken wasteland where Germany and her allies stood."

"If we don't help them rebuild," added Mycroft somberly, "we'll be at war again within a couple of decades."

After several months of coming to terms that we were once again at peace, that knowledge rocked me back considerably. Holmes and I, along with Mycroft, and occasionally Doyle, had worked for decades to avert the seemingly inevitable war with Germany – and if not prevent it, at least to delay it so that England would be on a firmer footing when it finally arrived. Now, after the terrible years that had dragged in nation after nation, even the United States from the other side of the world, and had resulted in over twenty millions deaths, it was brutally crushing to hear that it might have been for naught.

Armathwaite apparently read my expression. "Yes, Doctor, it's a very real possibility that a defeated Germany, if not offered the true hand of peace, will withdraw into poverty and bitterness, festering with resentment until a wave of nationalism stirs them to lash out with even worse deeds."

"And consider the advances in warfare," added Mycroft, "and the new ways for man to rain death upon his enemies that were developed in the last conflict. Is there any doubt how much worse the next one will be?"

"So a way to ease some of this pressure," said Holmes, "and to attempt to get things off on the right foot, is to return these gold certificates – which I assume have now been stolen. Or worse."

"Stolen," said Mycroft. "That's bad enough."

"The shares were printed by the Bank of England," explained Armathwaite, "for transfer to Austria – nothing unusual about it. Such transactions occur all the time, far beneath the awareness of the general public. Squabbles may come and go – even something as terrible as the Great War – like storms passing across the surface of the sea, but underneath, deep below where such things can cause any disturbance, the steady currents remain unaffected. So it is with international finance. Throughout the war, men on both sides

241

remained in contact with one another, understanding that the war would eventually end and that normal relations would need to remain and resume. This plan to transfer – that is to return – the ownership of the Austrian gold was in place as early as 1916. But now that's been upended – by treachery within our own ranks."

"I take it," said Holmes, "that these are bearer documents, and that whomever holds them effectively owns them, no questions asked."

"That is correct. And if the man who has taken them can find a way to get them to Switzerland, he will exchange them for equivalent and more usable amounts of currency, while the documents themselves will slip away like water running through a sieve, never to be recovered *en masse*."

"So prevent him from getting to Switzerland," I said. "Arrest him for crossing the street illegally until a better reason can be found. Stop him from making arrangements with an agent who can slip away in his place and make the exchange for him."

"I agree," said Mycroft. "We plan to recover the documents while they are still in London."

"You know where they are?" asked Doyle. "Who has them?"

"We believe that they may have been taken by – " began Armathwaite, but Mycroft interrupted.

"They were lifted three days ago from the Armathwaite's desk by Sir Rodham Molesworth."

I raised an eyebrow in surprise. Sir Rodham was a not-so-distant relative of the King, and one of his close cronies. I understood now the difficulty of the situation. It was this relationship and that alone which had protected him from more criticism and scrutiny than he would have otherwise received for his often irresponsible escapades – particularly during the war. His particularly virulent comments advocating harsh treatment of the enemy following the conflict had achieved a certain popularity with the more violent populists to be found throughout the country, but those of us with more sense had viewed his leanings with a certain amount of disgust. The King's association with one such as him was often an embarrassment.

"He was part of a committee that has been meeting with the Exchequer," explained Mycroft. "I would have preferred that he have nothing to do with our affairs, but we had to bow to the Sovereign's request. It was mentioned in passing that the documents in question were in my office. At one point during the meeting, Sir Rodham excused himself. Soon after his return, the meeting ended,

242

and the participants departed. I returned to my office to find the certificates gone. An aid in our department confirmed that Sir Rodham had been seen in the vicinity of my door."

"Is there any other evidence?" asked Holmes. "Were any attempts made to see if the man left fingermarks? Were there any other witnesses confirming his actual entry into the room?"

"Not at all," replied Mycroft. "And he didn't drop the ash from a unique Trichinopoly cigar either. But an interview with the aid confirms that he was the only one there."

"And what's been done since then to get the certificates back?" asked Doyle, a canny and interested look on his face.

"Nothing," replied Mycroft. Then, seeing the surprise on my face, he added, "One simply can't accuse a man of Sir Rodham's standing of such a crime without proof. I can't just ring up Inspector Parker at the Yard and have him obtain a warrant."

"That's why I – we – need your help, Mr. Holmes," added Armathwaite, rather breathlessly. "You're the only one who can get the documents back."

Only those who knew Holmes well could recognize that the statement had pleased him – there was a slight upturn of one corner of his mouth in something like a secret smile. I have no doubt that Mycroft observed it too.

Holmes started to speak, but Armathwaite continued.

"Mr. Pons is away from London right now, and M. Poirot has just left for Egypt. You are my last hope."

Mycroft's unexpected laugh was something of a snort, and Holmes's small smile turned to a tight-lipped frown. "So this must be carried out quietly," he said, without acknowledging Armathwaite's *faux pas*. "You can't simply have the King summon him and demand their return."

"We would prefer not to," countered Mycroft, still smiling.

Holmes abruptly uncrossed his legs and stood. "I'll let you know something in a day or so." Then, nodding to each of us, he departed.

Doyle shifted forward on his chair. "That's the Holmes I expect to see – the definitive man of action." He glanced toward Armathwaite. "I think you lit a fire under him by mentioning Pons and Poirot."

Armathwaite looked confused. "I . . . I didn't mean to offend him. It's simply that he's retired now, you know, and I had first thought of approaching some of the active consulting detectives here in London. I already know Mr. Pons from his work with the

243

Cryptographic branch during the war – we had need of creating secure informational channels – and of course everyone is aware of M. Poirot's rescue of the Prime Minister near the end of the war, and then his recovery of the Victory Bonds a few months later."

Mycroft flipped a hand. "It is of no matter. My brother would like to claim that he is an emotionless and logical being, but it isn't true, and he knows it, and we know it. If his pride is a bit wounded, it will simply spur him to try harder." He glanced my way. "You will certainly hear from him before I do. I may know nothing further until he delivers the recovered bonds. If you need my assistance, feel free to let me know."

I nodded and stood. Doyle and the man from the Exchequer rose as well. "Stay for a bit, Armathwaite," added Mycroft. "We have other matters to discuss besides this distraction." The man resumed his seat.

Having been dismissed, Doyle and I made our way to the street. Outside, he suggested that we adjourn to a pub and catch up. As I had no appointments for the rest of the day, I agreed. Ten minutes later, after a short cab drive down Pall Mall, across Trafalgar Square, and into Northumberland Street, we were to be found seated in the quiet pub on the ground floor of the Northumberland Hotel, aptly named for its location on Northumberland Street close to the intersection of Northumberland Avenue. (Sometimes I despaired at the quaint uniqueness and lack of imagination of London street names.)

With pints of the pub's excellent beer before us, we did indeed begin to catch up, and the coldness that I previously referenced seemed to melt away. I hadn't seen my old friend for quite a while – too long, I realized. I'd had numerous letters from him for a long stretch, asking about the use of my writings in future projects, before my repeated negative responses caused him to stop writing. I supposed that the last time I'd seen him in person had been at the funeral of his poor son in late 1918, just a month or so before the end of the war. His brother Innes had died only a few months later, a victim of the influenza pandemic. Both events seemed to have renewed his long interest in spiritualism.

To be fair, he'd initially approached the topic with a certain healthy skepticism, looking to disprove charlatans and weed out those who would take advantage of the grieving and the gullible. But as time passed, and as various tragedies caught up with him, he seemed willing to suspend his disbelief and give many homegrown false fakirs the benefit of the doubt.

244

He sighed and I realized that I'd let my mind wander as he explained his latest spiritual interest. As I attempted to regain the thread of the conversation, he took a deep swallow before wiping the foam from his mustache. "You'll have heard that I'm preparing to go to Australia for a lecture tour, so I haven't been able to get up to Cottingley as I'd like, but Edward Gardner of the Theosophical Society went in my place. His investigations aren't complete, but the evidence for fairies is looking most encouraging." He glanced at the much-diminished beer as if considering another swallow, but then he lowered his voice, as if conveying a confidence. "There are photos of them, you see . . . ."

It was all I could do not to roll my eyes. As much as I'd looked forward to reacquainting myself with Doyle, I now wondered how I could disengage and return home to Queen Anne Street. My wife had been ill recently, and I hated to be gone too long. When I mentioned her, as a preface to raising the subject of my departure, Doyle pivoted to the subject of his own bride. "Jean is showing great promise, you know. We're not ready to announce it yet – there are still tests and verifications to perform – but apparently she has the gift of spirit writing. Some of her messages, from The Ma'am – " (His mother.) " – and Innes are too accurate to be from some other spirit taking their place for its own malicious reasons."

I was tempted to mention one of Holmes's past investigations involving spirit writing, and how such a thing could be used to fool those easily deceived, but I didn't feel like entering into such a discussion, which would undoubtedly grow heated, requiring more effort than I wished to provide, and with the possibility of losing a friend. As I mentioned at the beginning of this account, a coldness had grown between Doyle and myself in recent months as he pressed me for the renewed use of my stories – an idea which I was then resisting, as my wife didn't always care for that aspect of my past. In 1917, I had allowed Doyle to publish an account of one of Holmes's war-time activities, both as a patriotic gesture, and also as something of a coda to the 1914-1915 appearance of *The Valley of Fear* in *The Strand*. Both narratives had featured the adventures of brave detectives going under cover for extended periods in the realms of theirs enemies – Birdy Edwards amongst the killer miners in the coal valleys of Pennsylvania, and Holmes as "Altamont" from 1912 to 1914, working his way from the Irish criminal syndicates of the United States all the way to a nest of entrenched German spies in England.

245

As I considered this, I became aware that Doyle had worked his way back around to the Cottingley fairies.

"If Edward can gather enough initial corroboration," he continued, a gleam in his eyes, "I was hoping that Holmes would look into the matter as well. With his stamp of approval – his validation, if you will – I think that the question of the existence of fairies will be settled once and for all. I only wish that I was going to be here, instead of in Australia, when Holmes goes up to Cottingley."

Clearly in his mind it was already an established appointment. I could only imagine Holmes's reaction when asked to affix his professional reputation to the existence of fairies in Yorkshire. Before I could gently warn Doyle away from asking Holmes about it, he shifted his aim.

"And what about you, Watson?" he asked. "You've been rather discouraging in your replies to my letters. I know that I once tired of being associated with Holmes years ago, but I've rather changed my mind on the subject. The public still wants the stories, you know, and you have to admit that they've made both of us a pretty penny over the years. I don't mind admitting that the additional income more of them would generate will certainly help fund some of the more ambitious spiritualistic activities that I hope to support."

This was only getting worse, and I began to take larger sips of my beer to finish it more quickly. "What about some of the investigations where you and Holmes encountered actual spiritual manifestations?" he asked. "Something along the lines of that one about the Dartmoor hound years ago, but without the human explanation at the end."

I shook my head. "Holmes always disproved any spiritual involvement in the solutions of his cases. And when there was still some doubt at the end – when I saw something that he couldn't explain . . . ." My voice drifted off, remembering a number of occasions when the case was over and I still had questions about something that hadn't been adequately addressed. A mysterious and ghostly figure, or a presence that had generated feelings of unease or fear – there were a number of these occurrences which were beyond the scope of Holmes's rational solutions. But instead of relating any of them, I glanced at Doyle's look of interest, like a terrier sensing the movement of a rat, and I quickly changed the subject.

"My wife," I said. "Well, you see, she would prefer it I didn't publish any more of the stories. It isn't like the old days. While I still join Holmes for the occasional investigation – "

"She'll come around," countered Doyle, rubbing his hands. "My first wife objected to some things too, but when they were a *fait accompli*, she supported me faithfully. When we went to Switzerland for her health in '93, and I wanted to see the Reichenbach Falls where we all thought that Holmes had died, she was terrified, but she went up there with me anyway. It sometimes just takes a firm hand, you see, for a man's wife to understand what's required. You pick the stories – I'll get them sold."

I was skeptical, and I wondered at his enthusiastic change of heart. Back in the mid-1880's, a few years after we met and both realized that we were writers as well as doctors, I'd mentioned my desire to make Holmes's work better known, and to make sure that he received the credit that was being otherwise misplaced. Doyle was keen, and when he read my first effort, the tale of how I met Holmes, and a decades-long blood feud that began in America and ended in our Baker Street rooms, he was quite encouraging, and even asked if he could write a long middle section, fictionalizing the American-set events that had led to the London murders. I agreed, and when he sold the entire combined document under his name, with references to my reminiscences as a sub-heading within the text, I tolerantly went along, as by then I was in practice, and didn't necessarily want the attention that I'd receive as an author detracting from my work as a doctor. (Doyle, still a doctor then, desperately wanted to abandon that career to be a full-time writer.) The decision to allow his name such prominence over my work was one that I would come to regret.

He and I published another of my writings in 1890, concerning the search for a treasure stolen in India and hidden in London for many years. Then, when Holmes was presumed to have died at Reichenbach in May 1891, and I was compelled by my grief to record more and more of his adventures, it was Doyle who managed to get them placed in a newly created magazine, *The Strand*, which had gone into business earlier that year. Since my first two works were already dubiously under Doyle's by-line, he convinced me to continue in that same manner, as people who were interested in the current stories would then seek out the older, and keeping the same name on them would avoid confusion. But it caused confusion in my own home, as my wife as quite unhappy indeed with the misdirected attention, even as we did reap the financial benefit.

247

(Not all we deserved, my wife would correctly point out, stating that it was *my* writing and time and effort that was being published, and by that point I could have adequately served as my own literary agent, or found another who didn't insist that his name be shown with such prominence.)

In any case, by late 1893, Doyle was jealous of the attention that my works were receiving over his own historical novels and essays, and when I was forced to write up the events of Holmes's supposed death at the Reichenbach Falls, and his battles with Professor Moriarty, in response to the scurrilous published comments by the Professor's brother, Colonel Moriarty, Doyle saw it as a way to draw the series of stories to a fitting close. I disagreed. By then, my wife had passed away, and my practice held very little interest for me. I filled my lonely and empty hours writing more and more of the adventures that I'd shared with the best and wisest man I'd ever known, Sherlock Holmes, but Doyle was finished with it. And in my despondent state, I let the series die then, too depressed to go forth and make my own arrangements with *The Strand* to continue publication.

But time passed, and Holmes was not dead. When he returned to London in '94, he was rather appalled to read of his cases in what he regarded as a low-end periodical instead of a scientific journal, and he requested that I write no more of them. Yet I continued to record them for my own records – a writer simply cannot stop writing. And in later years, Holmes relented, leading to further intermittent appearances in *The Strand* – the tale of the Baskerville Hound at the turn of the century, for instance, and a year or so later a full series of stories that were published around the time that Holmes retired.

(This wasn't entirely due to the demands of the reading public. Holmes retired in part because he needed to devote much more of his time and energy to the upcoming war with Germany, and it helped his efforts for people to believe that he was retired and apparently living the life of a reclusive Sussex apiarist, or to be reminded of his days in Baker Street so that they wouldn't think too much of what he was doing afterwards.)

Doyle and I had placed other stories on a very irregular basis in the years leading up to the war, concluding with the narrative of Holmes's capture of the German spy, Von Bork. That story, which appeared in *The Strand* in September 1917, had been appropriately titled "His Last Bow", as I thought it was the last time that I'd relate one of Holmes adventures – I'd even referred to it as "*An Epilogue of Sherlock Holmes*". But now Doyle wanted to share more of them, and in spite of my wife's misgivings, I felt my resistance weakening.

"I have an idea for a play," Doyle was saying. "Something like when we produced *The Stonor Case* back in 1910. What do you think? Do you have anything that might work well on stage? Or we could rework one of the published cases. I think we could make a fortune. I've been talking with someone about leasing a theatre. And if the interest is there, perhaps we could run another series of stories in *The Strand*."

I nodded, feeling as if I were making a concession of some sort. "I'll consider it. And I have an idea for something that might be adapted to the stage – one of Holmes's cases from not long before he retired. That affair of the Crown Diamond, and Count Negretto Sylvius. But – " And I raised a finger, wagging it in his face like a teacher. "Nothing supernatural. You want to fund your studies, but I can tell you that Holmes will want nothing to do with anything like that. And you would be well advised to steer clear of him with this fairy business as well."

He seemed to deflate a bit. As he'd been speaking, his fervor had grown to where he looked like a loaf of bread rising and expanding in the oven, only to collapse. But he saw the sense in my words and nodded.

"You're right, of course. I should have remembered that. Holmes told me that a long time ago: 'No ghosts need apply.'"

I sighed, nodded, and lifted my glass. "As long as you keep that in mind, then here's to our renewed partnership."

We drank, and Doyle – having secured the permission he sought to move forward with his plan – relaxed. Rather than consider how I would explain this to my wife, I asked what I'd been wondering since first seeing him in the Stranger's Room – Why had he been there?

"Oh, I'd dropped in to see Mycroft about a bit of other business," he replied vaguely, and I couldn't blame him. Discretion was a watchword when involved in Mycroft Holmes's affairs. Although he'd remained active throughout the war, Mycroft had relinquished a great many of his duties in the last year or so to others, particularly the brilliant and similarly minded Bancroft Pons. Physically, he'd never been in the best of shape, but even though the war had wearied him and he was showing his age, he had lost weight and in some ways seemed healthier than he had in years. I was glad that he still took an interest in various affairs, a sure sign that his mind was sharp.

"Mycroft told me about Armathwaite's appointment, and that you and Holmes would be along, and suggested I stay. I suspect that he planned to involve me somehow, before Holmes abruptly left to handle it on his own." He took a sip. "It's too bad – I had a bully idea for getting back the certificates . . . ."

I wondered what it might have been – clearly Doyle wanted me to ask, and yet for some reason I was reluctant to delve into it, possibly fearing a spiritualistic stratagem. He'd originally been recruited by Mycroft as an "idea man", and I knew of several of his schemes that had been used to great success during the war. It's certain that whatever he had planned for Sir Rodham would have been most interesting.

We parted soon after, and I chose to walk home, ambling along through Trafalgar Square and Piccadilly Circus, observing with interest how the typical citizens were oppressed by the early July heat which, after my service decades before in India and Afghanistan, bothered me not at all. By that time of afternoon, Regents Street was clearing somewhat, and the entire stroll was much more pleasant than it might have been otherwise. Almost before I knew it, I'd passed the Langham and made my way through the nearby lanes to Queen Anne Street, and my own home at Number 9.

Holmes had been staying with us while in town to settle the outstanding questions related to Adrian Wiley, and I'd thought that he planned to return to Sussex soon after, but now he'd become involved in this new business, and I was uncertain of his plans. I shared the latest news with my wife, without being too specific in deference to the nation's security concerns. She had always liked and admired Holmes, but enjoyed – as had I – the tweak he'd received when Pons and Poirot were referenced as Armathwaite's first choices. As I was concluding with the statement that I didn't know how Holmes intended to proceed, he arrived, being let in by the maid. (He had his own key, but would only use it in emergencies.)

As it was time for dinner, he explained his intentions as we ate. "I've been researching Sir Rodham to find what is known beyond the usual newspaper reports – quite a bit, if one knows whom to ask. During times when my own resources are in Sussex, I have access to Pons's scrapbooks in Praed Street. I believe that I now have enough information to settle this matter quickly." He took a sip of water and asked, "Are you free to join me this evening for a small

250

dramatic performance?" Then he glanced toward my wife. "Purely as a spectator, I assure you."

She smiled and I agreed. Thus, a couple of hours later we found ourselves in Bolton Street. Holmes was disguised to appear twenty years younger, and as part of his new mien, he seemed to be carrying twice that amount in extra pounds across his middle. He'd used padding to fill out his cheeks, and artful makeup changed the shadows that fell across his face. His hair was darkened and combed differently, and in his hands was a small cardboard box containing what he'd described as an "artifact" – a hideous construct of leathery shrunken head decorated with crude and ragged-cut primitive gemstones and slivers of dull-looking jade.

"I borrowed it from the British Museum," he'd explained as we walked. "It's a primitive talisman used for talking with the dead – or so the Pvali Tribe believes. While it's supposedly the preserved human head of a revered ancestor, clearly it's that of a small ape, quite likely a child." He closed the box. "Sir Rodham is an aficionado of the occult – a collector with the funds and means to build his collection. After I sent a message that it is available, he hopes to purchase this rarity tonight. He seemed quite anxious that we should meet as soon as possible to discuss the terms."

"And you plan to use this gruesome little piece of fish bait as a means to gain access to his home," I said as we turned into Bolton Street, which seemed exceptionally crowded for such an address, and at that time of night. I glanced at the various congregants along the street, and then toward Holmes. "The Darlington Gambit?"

"I prefer to call it 'The Arnsworth Castle Distraction'."

I tended to think of it in my own mind as the method he'd used when trying to determine where Irene Adler kept her damning photograph of the King of Bohemia, but kept that to myself.

"It has worked well for me in the past, as you know, on several occasions," Holmes continued.

"And will I be required to throw a plumber's smoke rocket to set things in motion this time?"

"I think not." He nodded his head toward the throng spread up and down the street. "I did tell your good wife that you were simply to attend as a spectator. I've arranged for others to take the lead on this occasion. I'll meet you back in here in half-an-hour or so." And with that, he increased his pace, lightly mounted the steps to Sir Rodham's substantial townhome, and was soon admitted.

Having nothing else to do, I stood under a plane tree, watching as the sky darkened and the drama before me played out to its own

251

script. Soon after Holmes's entrance, several nondescript men came up to Sir Rodham's house, carrying something that I couldn't identify. They dropped silently over the railings into the areaway between house and walkway. Then, I happened to glance up toward a movement along the roofline. Two more men were there, coming along from an adjacent house, carrying some flat boards which they proceeded to lay across the house's chimneys. Even as this occurred, greasy smoke began to billow up from the areaway and along the front windows of the house, opened to catch some of the evening breeze that was carrying away the day's July heat. The entire performance was escalated by the sudden cries up and down the street of "Fire! Fire!"

Five minutes later it was all over. The smoke had mysteriously vanished, as had the loiterers who had filled this normally quiet street. Holmes, still in disguise, exited the building rather quickly, came down the steps two at a time, carrying the cardboard box and walking hurriedly my way. I stepped from the shadows as he reached me, and we kept going, turning into Piccadilly and heading the short distance west until we reached No. 110, where we turned into the hotel there. I wondered if Holmes had plans to visit our friend Lord Peter, who had moved to an apartment upstairs just the year before, but instead he led me into the small bar on the ground floor. Finding a secluded booth at the back, we seated ourselves, gave our order to the quickly attentive waiter, and then, with a look both ways, Holmes pulled a large and thick envelope from underneath his coat.

"So you got it then," I said, "instead of simply finding where he'd hidden it and deciding to go back tomorrow."

"I learned my lesson long ago from The Woman," he explained. I still perfectly recalled that morning over three decades earlier when Irene Adler had beaten him. His scheme – the Darlington Gambit or the Arnsworth Castle Distraction, or whatever he wanted to call it – involved the faking of a fire or some such potential disaster, prodding the person in question to try and save that which is most value to them. "A married woman grabs at her baby," he'd explained at the time, "and an unmarried one reaches for her jewel-box." Presumably in this case, a scoundrel with a penchant for offensive occult detritus would try to save an envelope containing a fortune in gold certificates.

Which was what I expected to see as Holmes carefully opened the envelope. Instead, he pulled out a stack of sheets which held his attention for nearly a minute before he began to laugh – a thoroughly unabashed eruption of joy that turned the heads of several in the quiet bar.

He tossed the packet my way, and without picking it up, I could see that it was a stack of old photographs, all apparently the same, each of the type manufactured by theatres for publicity – in this case portraying Mr. William Gillette wearing a deerstalker and looking suitably intimidating.

"It seems," said Holmes, wiping his eyes after his laughter ceased when the waiter delivered our drinks with a suitably admonishing expression, "that Sir Rodham is an admirer of your works."

"Or at least aware of them. And one other thing is true: He was expecting you."

"Yes, and he was expecting this tired gambit as well – further evidence that the capital is in good hands without me."

I was surprised that he took this set-back so well, but I had known him long enough at that point – nearly forty years – to realize that he wasn't defeated, and that he likely had so many threads in hand that he was still several moves ahead of this player on the other side.

As we sipped our drinks, Holmes explained that he'd been welcomed into the house and shown into Sir Rodham's presence. "He's around our age, and slim and sly-looking – nothing like that up-and-comer Spode, with whom he publicly debates so often. The house is well-decorated, but there's just a whiff of decay – which fits what I learned today. He's outlasted his father's money, which is no doubt why he was tempted to make a play for the Austrian certificates.

"He was fascinated by the little head – and rightly so, as he knows enough to realize that it's real. But then the cry of fire started, and the chimney started to back up into the room. As the smoke thickened, he thrust it back into my hands while he dashed to his desk, anxiously pulling out an envelope – *this* envelope." He tapped his finger on the stack of photographs. "Then, changing his mind, he set it back down and excused himself, quickly leaving the room. I presumed it was to check on the fire. Rather than lose sight of the envelope, I snagged it and made for the front door. No doubt he was watching from the shadows, laughing to himself when I fell for his trick."

He provided a few other irrelevant details about what he'd seen of the man's macabre collection, and soon we finished the drinks and obtained a cab for the ride back to Queen Anne Street, with a

253

single stop along the way to send a telegram to Mycroft from the Wigmore Street Post Office, relating the night's failure. When we arrived, he said good night and went up to the guest room, while I reported to my curious wife. It was still early, but even if it had been late, she would have waited for news of our quest.

The next morning, Holmes and I were sitting at the dining table, having just finished breakfast, when the doorbell rang. I heard a hearty voice that I recognized, but was surprised when Doyle entered the room, his eyes squinted and his broad face garbed in a thick black beard, spilling down over his chest.

"Challenger's the name!" he boomed, his voice muffled behind the tangled black creature dangling beneath his nose. "Glad to be of assistance!"

Even Holmes was surprised.

"Is that the beard you used when portraying Challenger years ago?" I recalled it very well. Nearly a decade before, at the time when his account of Professor Challenger's trip to South America was published, he'd portrayed the man for a publicity photograph using this very beard. He'd invited me to be part of it, standing alongside him with a few of his other friends, but for some reason I'd declined – either due to a previous engagement, or more likely out of some sense of dignity-preserving discretion.

Doyle nodded, pulling out a chair and seating himself. I indicated to the maid, who was peeking into the room, to pour our visitor some coffee.

"It is the same," was the reply as Doyle wisely removed the scrofulous-looking thing before trying to find his mouth with the coffee cup. He drank deeply, ignoring the heat of the beverage, and then looked toward Holmes. "I was visiting your brother this morning in his office – regarding a bit of separate business that we have going on – and heard about what happened last night. I decided to see what I can do."

"How so?" asked Holmes, clearly amused.

"I intend to make Sir Rodham's acquaintance," he said. "I understand that the fellow is interested in the occult. I'll play that up – in character of course – and win his confidence – all while I wait for the opportunity to retrieve the certificates."

Holmes cast his eyes toward the beard, now lying on the table. "Why that? You are noted for your occult researches. Why not simply introduce yourself under your own name?"

"He'll be suspicious now, of course, after your visit last night. Clearly he expected you. What happens when I show up as myself, with our known association? I would never win his confidence that way."

"And you just happened to have that beard from a decade ago with you?" I asked.

That seemed to rattle him. "I . . . umm . . . ."

Before I could press him as to why he carried such an item with him from his home while traveling up to London, Holmes let him off the hook.

"As much as I appreciate the gesture," he said, "and your willingness to pull my burnt chestnuts from the fire, it's really unnecessary. I was about to invite Watson to join me at Scotland Yard for the *denouement* of this affair, but you're certainly welcome to join us, Doyle."

Seemingly grateful for the change of subject, our friend quickly agreed, and it wasn't long before we were outside and walking around the block toward Cavendish Square to find a taxi. I was grateful that Doyle had stuffed the beard in his pocket, rather than try and wear it – or worse, leave it on my dining room table for my wife to discover like a deceased cat when she returned from her morning errands.

After entering the Yard, Holmes requested that we be taken to wherever Inspector Stanislaus Oates was holding a prisoner. The constable nodded, and we were led through the long-familiar halls, deeper and lower into the building. Along the way, I was struck by how many strangers surrounded us, in contrast to those long-ago days when we seemed to know – to one degree or another – every constable, inspector, and superintendent on the premises. Now I recognized just the occasional face, while in turn we seemed likewise to be recognized by only a few as well. Inspectors Japp and Jamison were in conversation in a hallway that we passed, and as they nodded, I could see that they were wondering why we were there. Finally we reached a plain heavy door, opened to reveal Inspector Oates and a young man in his mid-twenties, seated at a plain table and looking wide-eyed and harried.

"We've held him as you asked, Mr. Holmes. He bolted overnight, just as you'd predicted."

Holmes nodded and thanked him. The inspector then walked out of the room. Only then did I notice another man standing in the shadows to one side. He stepped forward.

"Evanston," he explained. "Your brother sent me to keep an eye on things, Mr. Holmes."

255

"Excellent," replied my friend. "I'm happy to pass this over to you. I simply wanted the chance to speak with Mr. Mantooth, here."

He pulled out a chair and sat opposite the young man, looking at him closely. Yet, instead of speaking directly to him, he explained to Doyle and me.

"Knowing that Mycroft was anxious to delegate this matter elsewhere, I suspected that he hadn't done a great deal of research to obtain all the facts – and that's no discredit to him, as he knew that I was to be involved, and that I'd be verifying facts on my own, whether or not they'd already been obtained. It occurred to me that the claim against Sir Rodham was based on the fact that the certificates were in fact stolen while he was in the building, and that he had been specifically implicated by an employee in the Exchequer's office who placed Sir Rodham in the area at the time. I became interested in that employee – Mr. Mantooth here."

The young man's eyes widened as Holmes laid out what his investigation had revealed.

"In this modern age of interconnected and immediate communication, it took very little time to determine that Mr. Mantooth is Sir Rodham's illegitimate son – although never acknowledged publicly, or legally." He addressed Mantooth for the first time. "I understand that you're in Sir Rodham's will."

The man nodded. He swallowed and replied, his voice thin, "So I'm told. He has no other heirs."

"Perhaps, then, you might hope to make the case that you were coerced into helping him with this curious scheme in the hopes of staying in his good graces as his prospective heir."

"So Sir Rodham is still involved?" I said.

"Of course. If Mr. Mantooth had simply stolen the certificates, he might have gotten away with it, although it's unlikely without Sir Rodham being available as a distraction. That was their plan. Working together, Sir Rodham would be implicated by this man's accusation, but very little action could initially be taken against him. Yet he would draw all the attention as the supposed thief. In the meantime, Mantooth himself took the certificates.

"We might have dithered for a while, thinking Sir Rodham too powerful to accuse – assuming that his familial connection with Mr. Mantooth remained undiscovered – if he'd only had the sense to appear puzzled at how he was involved in these events. But he had to be arrogant about it – either knowing that I was likely to be involved, or learning of it somehow by hearing that I'd been summoned to a meeting with Mycroft – and he decided to be clever.

Apparently he's read your narratives, Watson, for he was familiar with my methods. He prepared a decoy packet of documents in advance for me to retrieve, simply having to have his little joke. He couldn't have known for certain about the false fire gambit, but as it played out, he understood who I was and what was happening. He left the envelope for me to take and congratulated himself. Sadly for him, his prior preparations of the packet only showed that he knew more than he should have about all this if he was innocent.

"Of course, I'd already researched enough about him and Mr. Mantooth to see what might be going on, and that Sir Rodham was deliberately drawing attention to himself. Once he was sure that I was focused on him, he felt safe enough to have Mr. Mantooth depart for Switzerland in order to sell the certificates for untraceable cash. He was arrested at the station."

He turned to the young man, now staring between his feet at the floor. "You've been poorly manipulated by your father. You would do well to admit everything and save yourself as much as possible."

Without looking up, the young man nodded. He was still looking down when we left him there.

From Scotland Yard, Evanston joined us as we made the short walk to Mycroft's office (which he still maintained, in spite of his supposed "retirement"), where the details of the story was explained. Doyle alternated between amazement and admiration at seeing Holmes in action, and a certain tenseness when it seemed as if the beard in his pocket might be mentioned in front of Mycroft Holmes. However, he needn't have worried, as the conversation was quickly concluded, and the certificates – held closely by Evanston after their retrieval from Mantooth – were placed into Mycroft's care.

Outside, I invited Doyle home for lunch, where I intended to discuss our renewed partnership with both Holmes and my wife – as I'd avoided the subject with both of them the night before. I doubted that either would express terribly strong objections, but still it was something that I wasn't particularly anticipating. Perhaps, if there was any tension, I could suggest that Doyle don his beard and explain it in the guise of Professor Challenger . . . .

NOTE:

*   See "The Adventure of the Missing Missing Link" by David Marcum in *The Papers of Sherlock Holmes.*

About the Contributors

The following contributors appear in this volume:
After the East Wind Blows
Part II - Aftermath (1919-1920)

Brian Belanger is a publisher, editor, illustrator, author, and graphic designer. In 2015, he co-founded Belanger Books along with his brother, author Derrick Belanger. He designs the covers for every Belanger Books release, and his illustrations have appeared in the MacDougall Twins with Sherlock Holmes series, as well as *Dragonella, Scones and Bones on Baker Street*, and *Sherlock Holmes: A Three-Pipe Problem*. Brian has published a number of Sherlock Holmes anthologies, as well as new editions of August Derleth's classic Solar Pons mysteries. Since 2016, Brian has written and designed letters for the *Dear Holmes* series, and illustrated a comic book for indie band The Moonlight Initiative. In 2019, Brian received his investiture in the PSI as "Sir Ronald Duveen". Find him online at *www.belangerbooks.com*, *www.zhahadun.wixsite.com/221b*, and *www.redbubble.com/people/zhahadun*

Nick Cardillo is the author of *The Feats of Sherlock Holmes*, as well as several short stories that have appeared in collections for both MX Publishing and Belanger Books. A devotee of Sherlock Holmes since the age of six, Nick is also a lifelong fan of the Golden Age of Detective Fiction and Hammer Horror. He is a recent graduate from Susquehanna University and earned his ShD – Doctorate of Sherlockiana – from the Beacon Society in 2019.

Chris Chan is a writer, educator, and historian. He works as a researcher and "International Goodwill Ambassador" for Agatha Christie Ltd. His true crime articles, reviews, and short fiction have appeared (or will soon appear) in *The Strand, The Wisconsin Magazine of History, Mystery Weekly, Gilbert!, Nerd HQ*, Akashic Books' *Mondays are Murder* web series, *The Baker Street Journal*, and *Sherlock Holmes Mystery Magazine*.

Craig Stephen Copland confesses that he discovered Sherlock Holmes when, sometime in the muddled early 1960's, he pinched his older brother's copy of the immortal stories and was forever afterward thoroughly hooked. He is very grateful to his high school English teachers in Toronto who inculcated in him a love of literature and writing, and even inspired him to be an English major at the University of Toronto. There he was blessed to sit at the feet of both Northrup Frye and Marshall McLuhan, and other great literary professors, who led him to believe that he was called to be a high school English teacher. It was his good fortune to come to his pecuniary senses, abandon that goal, and pursue a varied professional career that took him to over one-hundred countries and endless adventures. He considers himself to have been and to continue to be one of the luckiest men on God's good earth. A few years back he took a step in the direction of Sherlockian studies and joined the *Sherlock Holmes Society of Canada* – also known as *The Toronto Bootmakers*. In May of 2014, this esteemed group of scholars announced a contest for the writing of a new Sherlock Holmes mystery. Although he had never tried his hand at fiction before, Craig entered and was pleasantly surprised to be selected as one of the winners. Having enjoyed the experience, he decided to write more of the same, and is now on a mission to write a new Sherlock Holmes mystery that is related to and inspired by each of the sixty stories in the original Canon. He currently lives and writes in Toronto and Dubai, and looks forward to finally settling down when he turns ninety.

Margie Deck (Spanaway, Washington) lives in the Pacific Northwest with the books, the husband, and a dog. She whiles away her time talking about Sherlock Holmes on Twitter (*@pawkypuzzler*) and volunteering for *The Sound of the Baskervilles* and *The John H. Watson Society*.

Sir Alfred Gilbert RA (1854–1934) was an English sculptor and illustrator. He also explored other techniques such as goldsmithing and damascening. Additionally, he painted watercolours and drew book illustrations. He was made a member of the Royal Academy of Arts in 1892, but his efforts declined around that time as he took on too many commissions and entered into debt, whilst at the same time his wife's mental health deteriorated. In 1892, he received a royal commission for the tomb of Prince Albert Victor. However, he was unable to complete it and complaints from other dissatisfied clients began to accumulate. Eventually, Gilbert was forced to declare himself bankrupt and to resign from the Royal Academy. However, in the 1920's his career was rehabilitated, and he returned to England and completed the tomb of Prince Albert Victor, as well as the Queen Alexandra Memorial. In 1932, Gilbert was knighted and reinstated as a member of the Royal Academy.

Arthur Hall was born in Aston, Birmingham, UK, in 1944. He discovered his interest in writing during his schooldays, along with a love of fictional adventure and suspense. His first novel, *Sole Contact*, was an espionage story about an ultra-secret government department known as "Sector Three", and was followed, to date, by three sequels. Other works include six Sherlock Holmes novels, *The Demon of the Dusk*, *The One Hundred Percent Society*, *The Secret Assassin*, *The Phantom Killer*, *In Pursuit of the Dead*, and *The Justice Master*, as well as two collections of Holmes *Further Little-Known Cases of Sherlock Holmes*, and *Tales from the Annals of Sherlock Holmes*. He has also written other short stories and a modern detective novel. He lives in the West Midlands, United Kingdom.

Paul Hiscock is an author of crime, fantasy, and science fiction tales. His short stories have appeared in several anthologies and include a seventeenth century whodunnit, a science fiction western, and a steampunk Sherlock Holmes story. Paul lives with his family in Kent, England, and spends his days chasing a toddler with more energy than the Duracell Bunny. He mainly does his writing in coffee shops with members of the local NaNoWriMo group, or in the middle of the night when his family has gone to sleep. Consequently, his stories tend to be fuelled by large amounts of black coffee. You can find out more about his writing at *www.detectivesanddragons.uk*.

Naching T. Kassa is a wife, mother, and writer. She's created short stories, novellas, poems, and co-created three children. She lives in Eastern Washington State with her husband, Dan Kassa. Naching is a member of the Horror Writers Association, Head of Publishing and Interviewer for *HorrorAddicts.net*, and an assistant and staff writer for *Still Water Bay* at Crystal Lake Publishing. She has been a Sherlockian since the age of 10 and is a member of The Sound of the Baskervilles. You can find her work on Amazon: *https://www.amazon.com/Naching-T-Kassa/e/B005ZGHTI0*

David Marcum plays *The Game* with deadly seriousness. He first discovered Sherlock Holmes in 1975 at the age of ten, and since that time, he has collected, read, and chronologicized literally thousands of traditional Holmes pastiches in the form of novels, short stories, radio and television episodes, movies and scripts, comics, fan-fiction, and unpublished manuscripts. He is the author of over eighty Sherlockian pastiches, some published in anthologies and magazines such as *The Strand*, and others collected in his own books, *The Papers of Sherlock Holmes*, *Sherlock Holmes and A Quantity of Debt*, and *Sherlock Holmes – Tangled Skeins*. He has edited over sixty books, including several dozen traditional Sherlockian anthologies, such as the ongoing series *The MX Book of New Sherlock Holmes Stories*, which he created in 2015. This collection is now up to 27 volumes, with more in preparation. He was responsible for bringing back August Derleth's Solar Pons for a new generation, first with his collection of authorized Pons stories, *The Papers of Solar Pons*, and then by editing the reissued authorized versions of the original Pons books, and then volumes of new Pons adventures. He has done the same for the adventures of Dr. Thorndyke, and has plans for similar projects in the future. He has contributed numerous essays to various publications, and is a member of a number of Sherlockian groups and Scions. His irregular Sherlockian blog, *A Seventeen Step Program*, addresses various topics related to his favorite book friends (as his son used to call them when he was small), and can be found at *http://17stepprogram.blogspot.com/* He is a licensed Civil Engineer, living in Tennessee with his wife and son. Since the age of nineteen, he has worn a deerstalker as his regular-and-only hat. In 2013, he and his deerstalker were finally able make his first trip-of-a-lifetime Holmes Pilgrimage to England, with return Pilgrimages in 2015 and 2016, where you may have spotted him. If you ever run into him and his deerstalker out and about, feel free to say hello!

Robert Perret is a writer, librarian, and devout Sherlockian living on the Palouse. His Sherlockian publications include "The Canaries of Clee Hills Mine" in *An Improbable Truth: The Paranormal Adventures of Sherlock Holmes*, "For King and Country" in *The Science of Deduction*, and "How Hope Learned the Trick" in *NonBinary Review*. He considers himself to be a pan-Sherlockian and a one-man Scion out on the lonely moors of Idaho. Robert has recently authored a yet-unpublished scholarly article tentatively entitled "A Study in Scholarship: The Case of the *Baker Street Journal*". More information is available at: *www.robertperret.com*

Tracy J. Revels, a Sherlockian from the age of eleven, is a professor of history at Wofford College in Spartanburg, South Carolina. She is a member of *The Survivors of the Gloria Scott* and *The Studious Scarlets Society*, and is a past recipient of the Beacon Society Award. Almost every semester, she teaches a class that covers The Canon, either to college students or to senior citizens. She is also the author of three supernatural Sherlockian pastiches with MX (*Shadowfall*, *Shadowblood*, and *Shadowwraith*), and a regular contributor to her scion's newsletter. She also has some notoriety as an author of very silly skits: For proof, see "The Adventure of the Adversarial Adventuress" and "Occupy Baker Street" on YouTube. When not studying Sherlock, she can be found researching the history of her native state, and has written books on Florida in the Civil War and on the development of Florida's tourism industry.

Roger Riccard of Los Angeles, California, U.S.A., is a descendant of the Roses of Kilravock in Highland Scotland. He is the author of two previous Sherlock Holmes novels, *The Case of the Poisoned Lilly* and *The Case of the Twain Papers*, a series of short stories in two volumes, *Sherlock Holmes: Adventures for the Twelve Days of Christmas* and *Further Adventures for the Twelve Days of Christmas*, and the ongoing series *A Sherlock Holmes Alphabet of Cases,* all of which are published by Baker Street Studios. He has another novel and a non-fiction Holmes reference work in various stages of completion. He became a Sherlock Holmes enthusiast as a teenager (many, many years ago), and, like all fans of The Great Detective, yearned for more stories after reading The Canon over and over. It was the Granada Television performances of Jeremy Brett and Edward Hardwicke, and the encouragement of his wife, Rosilyn, that at last inspired him to write his own Holmes adventures, using the Granada actor portrayals as his guide. He has been called "The best pastiche writer since Val Andrews" by the *Sherlockian E-Times.*

Frank Schildiner is a martial arts instructor at Amorosi's Mixed Martial Arts in New Jersey. He is the writer of the novels, *The Quest of Frankenstein, The Triumph of Frankenstein, Napoleon's Vampire Hunters, The Devil Plague of Naples, The Klaus Protocol*, and *Irma Vep and The Great Brain of Mars.* Frank is a regular contributor to the fictional series *Tales of the Shadowmen* and has been published in *From Bayou to Abyss: Examining John Constantine, Hellblazer, The Joy of Joe, The New Adventures of Thunder Jim Wade, Secret Agent X* Volumes 3, 4, 5, and 6, *The Lone Ranger and Tonto: Frontier Justice*, and *The Avenger: The Justice Files.* He resides in New Jersey with his wife Gail, who is his top supporter, and two cats who are indifferent on the subject.

Frederic Dorr Steele (1873-1944) was born in Marquette Michigan, and studied at the National Academy of Design before becoming a free-lance illustrator. In 1903, he received the commission from *Collier's Weekly* magazine to provide the illustrations for *The Return of Sherlock Holmes.* Rather than base his likeness on Holmes's true appearance, as shown in Sidney Paget's drawings, he instead modeled his drawings on William Gillette, whose portrayal of The Great Detective was very popular during that time, particularly in the U.S. This led to the American perception for a generation that Holmes mistakenly resembled Gillette. Steele passed away in New York on July 6, 1944.

Nicholas Utechin BSI joined *The Sherlock Holmes Society of London* in 1966, aged fourteen. Ten years later he became Editor of *The Sherlock Holmes Journal* – a position he held for thirty years. The year 1976 also saw the publication of two Holmes pastiches he co-wrote: *The Earthquake Machine* and *Hellbirds.* This is his first venture in the field since then. He is a *Baker Street Irregular*, an honorary senior member of *The Sons of the the Copper Beeches* scion society, a founding member of *The John H. Watson Society*, and has contributed extensively to Sherlockian scholarship over the decades. The fact that he is related to Basil Rathbone could have something to do with this madness. In another life, he was a senior producer and occasional presenter for BBC Radio in the field of current affairs. Now retired, he lives in Oxford, UK with his wife, Annie, follows the careers of their two sons with interest, and the lives of their two grandchildren with love. He believes he knows quite a lot about fine wine and silent films (meeting and interviewing Lillian Gish was something special,) and is lucky enough to own a Sidney Paget original (sadly not one for a Sherlock Holmes story.)

Richard W. Wallace was an American illustrator who, in 1919, provided images for three Holmes stories in *Lectures Pour Tous*, a French magazine. These included "His Last Bow", "The Dying Detective", and "The Red Circle"

*The following contributors appear
in the companion volumes:*

Part I: The East Wind Blows (1914-1918)
Part III: When the Storm Has Cleared (1921-1928)

Wayne Anderson was born and raised in the beautiful Pacific Northwest, growing up in Alaska and Washington State. He discovered Sherlock Holmes around age ten and promptly devoured The Canon. When it was all gone, he tried to sate the addiction by writing his own Sherlock Holmes stories, which are mercifully lost forever. Sadly, he moved to California in his twenties and has lived there since. He has two grown sons who are both writers as well. He spends his time writing or working on the TV pilots and patents which will someday make him fabulously wealthy. When he's not doing these things, he is either reading to his young daughter from The Canon or trying to find space in his house for more bookshelves.

Derrick Belanger is an educator and also the author of the #1 bestselling book in its category, *Sherlock Holmes: The Adventure of the Peculiar Provenance*, which was in the top 200 bestselling books on Amazon. He also is the author of *The MacDougall Twins with Sherlock Holmes* books, and he edited the Sir Arthur Conan Doyle horror anthology *A Study in Terror: Sir Arthur Conan Doyle's Revolutionary Stories of Fear and the Supernatural*. Mr. Belanger co-owns the publishing company Belanger Books, which has released numerous Sherlock Holmes anthologies including *Beyond Watson, Holmes Away From Home: Adventures from the Great Hiatus, Sherlock Holmes: Before Baker Street, Sherlock Holmes: Adventures in the Realms of H.G. Wells, Sherlock Holmes and the Occult Detectives, Sherlock Holmes and the Great Detectives*, and *Beyond the Adventures of Sherlock Holmes*. Derrick resides in Colorado and continues compiling unpublished works by Dr. John H. Watson.

John William Davis is a retired US Army counterintelligence officer, civil servant, and linguist. He was commissioned from Washington University in St. Louis as an artillery officer in the 101st Air Assault Division. Thereafter, he went into counterintelligence and served some thirty-seven years. A linguist, Mr. Davis learned foreign languages in each country he served. After the Cold War and its bitter aftermath, he wrote *Rainy Street Stories, Reflections on Secret Wars, Terrorism, and Espionage*. He wanted to write about not only true events themselves, but also the moral and ethical aspects of the secret world. With the publication of *Around the Corner*, Davis expanded his reflections on conflicted human nature to our present day traumas of fear, and causes for hope. A dedicated Sherlockian, he's contributed to telling the story of the Great Detective in retirement.

Sir Arthur Conan Doyle (1859-1930) *Holmes Chronicler Emeritus*. If not for him, this anthology would not exist. Author, physician, patriot, sportsman, spiritualist, husband and father, and advocate for the oppressed. He is remembered and honored for the purposes of this collection by being the man who introduced Sherlock Holmes to the world. Through fifty-six Holmes short stories, four novels, and additional Apocryphal entries, Doyle revolutionized mystery stories and also greatly influenced and improved police forensic methods and techniques for the betterment of all. *Steel True Blade Straight.*

Sonia Fetherston BSI is a member of the illustrious *Baker Street Irregulars.* For almost thirty years, she's been a frequent contributor to Sherlockian anthologies, including Calabash Press's acclaimed *Case Files* series, and Wildside Press's *About* series. Sonia's byline often appears in the pages of *The Baker Street Journal, The Journal* of the *Sherlock Holmes Society of London, Canadian Holmes*, and the Sydney Passengers' *Log*. Her work earned her the coveted Morley-Montgomery Award from the *Baker Street Irregulars*, and the Derek Murdoch Memorial Award from *The Bootmakers of Toronto*. Sonia is author of *Prince of the Realm: The Most Irregular James Bliss Austin* (BSI Press, 2014). She's at work on another biography for the BSI, this time about Julian Wolff.

Tim Gambrell lives in Exeter, Devon, with his wife, two young sons, three cats, and now only four chickens. He has previously contributed stories to *The MX Book of New Sherlock Holmes Stories*, and also to *Sherlock Holmes and Dr Watson: The Early Adventures* and *Sherlock Holmes and The Occult Detectives*, also from Belanger Books. Outside of the world of Holmes, Tim has written extensively for Doctor Who spin-off ranges. His books include two linked novels from Candy Jar Books: *Lethbridge-Stewart: The Laughing Gnome – Lucy Wilson & The Bledoe Cadets*, and *The Lucy Wilson Mysteries: The Brigadier and The Bledoe Cadets* (both 2019), and *Lethbridge-Stewart: Bloodlines – An Ordinary Man* (Candy Jar, 2020, written with Andy Frankham-Allen). He's also written a novella, *The Way of The Bry'hunee* (2019) for the Erimem range from Thebes Publishing. Tim's short fiction includes stories in *Lethbridge-Stewart: The HAVOC Files 3* (Candy Jar, 2017, revised edition 2020), *Bernice Summerfield: True Stories* (Big Finish, 2017) and *Relics . . . An Anthology* (Red Ted Books, 2018), plus a number of charity anthologies.

John Linwood Grant is a writer and editor who lives in Yorkshire with a pack of lurchers and a beard. He may also have a family. He focuses particularly on dark Victorian and Edwardian fiction, such as his recent novella *A Study in Grey*, which also features Holmes. Current projects include his *Tales of the Last Edwardian* series, about psychic and psychiatric mysteries, and curating a collection of new stories based on the darker side of the British Empire. He has been published in a number of anthologies and magazines, with stories range from madness in early Virginia to questions about the monsters we ourselves might be. He is also co-editor of *Occult Detective Quarterly*. His website *greydogtales.com* explores weird fiction, especially period ones, weird art, and even weirder lurchers.

Paula Hammond has written over sixty fiction and non-fiction books, as well as short stories, comics, poetry, and scripts for educational DVD's. When not glued to the keyboard, she can usually be found prowling round second-hand books shops or hunkered down in a hide, soaking up the joys of the natural world.

Stephen Herczeg is an IT Geek, writer, actor, and film-maker based in Canberra Australia. He has been writing for over twenty years and has completed a couple of dodgy novels, sixteen feature-length screenplays, and numerous short stories and scripts. Stephen was very successful in 2017's International Horror Hotel screenplay competition, with his scripts *TITAN* winning the Sci-Fi category and *Dark are the Woods* placing second in the horror category. His two-volume short story collection, *The Curious Cases of Sherlock Holmes*, was published in 2021. His work has featured in *Sproutlings – A Compendium of Little Fictions* from Hunter Anthologies, the *Hells Bells* Christmas horror anthology published by the Australasian Horror Writers Association, and the *Below the Stairs, Trickster's Treats, Shades of Santa, Behind the Mask*, and *Beyond the Infinite* anthologies from OzHorror.Con, *The Body Horror Book, Anemone Enemy*, and *Petrified Punks* from Oscillate Wildly Press, and *Sherlock Holmes In the Realms of H.G. Wells* and *Sherlock Holmes: Adventures Beyond the Canon* from Belanger Books.

John Lawrence served for thirty-eight years as a staff member in the U.S. House of Representatives, the last eight as Chief of Staff to Speaker Nancy Pelosi (2005-2013). He has been a Visiting Professor at the University of California's Washington Center since 2013. He is the author of *The Class of '74: Congress After Watergate and the Roots of Partisanship* (2018), and has a Ph.D. in history from the University of California (Berkeley). *John has stories in Parts I and III*

Gordon Linzner is founder and former editor of *Space and Time Magazine*, and author of three published novels and dozens of short stories in *F&SF, Twilight Zone, Sherlock Holmes Mystery Magazine*, and numerous other magazines and anthologies, including *Baker Street Irregulars II, Across the Universe*, and *Strange Lands*. He is a member of *HWA* and a lifetime member of *SFWA*.

David Marcum *also has stories in Parts I and III*

Will Murray has been writing about popular culture since 1973, principally on the subjects of comic books, pulp magazine heroes, and film. As a fiction writer, he's the author of over 70 novels featuring characters as diverse as Nick Fury and Remo Williams. With the late Steve Ditko, he created the Unbeatable Squirrel Girl for Marvel Comics. Murray has written numerous short stories, many on Lovecraftian themes. Currently, he writes The Wild Adventures of Doc Savage for Altus Press. His acclaimed Doc Savage novel, *Skull Island*, pits the pioneer superhero against the legendary King Kong. This was followed by *King Kong vs. Tarzan* and two Doc Savage novels guest-starring The Shadow, and *Tarzan, Conqueror of Mars*, a crossover with John Carter of Mars. He is the author of the short story collection *The Wild Adventures of Sherlock Holmes. www.adventuresinbronze.com* is his website.

Dan Rowley practiced law for over forty years, both in private practice and with a large international corporation. He is now retired and lives in Erie, Pennsylvania, with his wife Judy. He inherited his writing and creative abilities from his children Jim and Katy.

Andrew Salmon has won several awards for his Sherlock Holmes stories and has been nominated for the Ellis, Pulp Ark, Pulp Factory and New Pulp Awards. He

265

lives and writes in Vancouver, BC. His novels include: *Fight Card Sherlock Holmes: Work Capitol, Blood to the Bone* and *A Congression of Pallbearers* (collected in the *Fight Card Sherlock Holmes Omnibus*) *The Dark Land, The Light of Men,* and *Ghost Squad: Rise of the Black Legion* (with Ron Fortier) and his first children's book, *Wandering Webber*. His work has also appeared in numerous anthologies covering multiple genres. His tales from the *Sherlock Holmes Consulting Detective* series were collected in *Sherlock Holmes Investigates*. He is currently at work on the first in a series of Eby Stokes novels, the female pugilist turned Special Branch agent, who debuted in the *Fight Card Sherlock Holmes* trilogy, as well as a myriad of other projects. To learn more about his work check out:

amazon.com/Andrew-Salmon/e/B002NS5KR0

Shane Simmons is the author of the occult detective novels *Necropolis* and *Epitaph,* and the crime collection *Raw and Other Stories.* An award-winning screenwriter and graphic novelist, his work has appeared in international film festivals, museums, and lectures about design and structure. He was born in Lachine, a suburb of Montreal best known for being massacred in 1689 and having a joke name. Visit Shane's homepage at *eyestrainproductions.com* for more.

Robert V. Stapleton was born and brought up in Leeds, Yorkshire, England, and studied at Durham University. After working in various parts of the country as an Anglican parish priest, he is now retired and lives with his wife in North Yorkshire. As a member of his local writing group, he now has time to develop his other life as a writer of adventure stories. He has recently had a number of short stories published, and he is hoping to have a couple of completed novels published at some time in the future.

Kevin P. Thornton is a seven-time Arthur Ellis Award Nominee. He is a former director of the local Heritage Society and Library, and he has been a soldier in Africa, a contractor for the Canadian Military in Afghanistan, a newspaper and magazine columnist, a Director of both the *Crime Writers of Canada* and the *Writers' Guild of Alberta*, a founding member of *Northword Literary Magazine*, and is either a current or former member of *The Mystery Writers of America, The Crime Writers Association, The Calgary Crime Writers, The International Thriller Writers, The International Association of Crime Writers, The Keys* – a Catholic Writers group founded by Monsignor Knox and G.K. Chesterton – as well as, somewhat inexplicably, *The Mesdames of Mayhem* and *Sisters in Crime.* If you ask, he will join. Born in Kenya, Kevin has lived or worked in South Africa, Dubai, England, Afghanistan, New Zealand, Ontario, and now Northern Alberta. He lives on his wits and his wit, and is doing better than expected. He is not one to willingly split infinitives, and while never pedantic, is on occasion known to be ever so slightly punctilious. *Kevin has stories in Parts I and III*

Daniel D. Victor, a Ph.D. in American literature, is a retired high school English teacher who taught in the Los Angeles Unified School District for forty-six years. His doctoral dissertation on little-known American author, David Graham Phillips, led to the creation of Victor's first Sherlock Holmes pastiche, *The Seventh Bullet,* in which Holmes investigates Phillips' actual murder. Victor's second novel, *A Study in Synchronicity,* is a two-stranded murder mystery, which features a Sherlock Holmes-like private eye. He currently writes the ongoing series *Sherlock Holmes* *and the American Literati*. Each novel introduces Holmes to a different American author who actually passed through London at the turn of the century. In *The Final Page of Baker Street*, Holmes meets Raymond Chandler; in *The Baron of Brede Place,* Stephen Crane; in *Seventeen Minutes to Baker Street*, Mark Twain; and in *The Outrage at the Diogenes Club*, Jack London. His most recent novel is *Sherlock Holmes and the Shadows of St. Petersburg* and *Sherlock Holmes and the Pandemic of Death* will be published later in 2021. Victor, who is also writing a novel about his early years as a teacher, lives with his wife in Los Angeles, California. They have two adult sons.

Joseph S. Walker is an active member of the *Mystery Writers of America*. His fiction has appeared in magazines, including *Alfred Hitchcok Mystery Magazine, Mystery Weekly*, and *Dark City*, and in anthologies such as *Seascape, Day of the Dark*, and the MWA collections *Scream and Scream Again* and *Life is Short and Then You Die*. In 2019, his story "Haven" won the Al Blanchard Award, and his story "The Last Man in Lafarge" won the inaugural Bill Crider Prize for Short fiction. He lives in Indiana and teaches college literature courses. Follow him on Twitter (@JSWalkerAuthor) and visit his website at: https://jsw47408.wixsite.com/website

I.A. Watson, great-grand-nephew of Dr. John H. Watson, has been intrigued by the notorious "black sheep" of the family since childhood, and was fascinated to inherit from his grandmother a number of unedited manuscripts removed circa 1956 from a rather larger collection reposing at Lloyds Bank Ltd (which acquired Cox & Co Bank in 1923). Upon discovering the published corpus of accounts regarding the detective Sherlock Holmes from which a censorious upbringing had shielded him, he felt obliged to allow an interested public access to these additional memoranda, and is gradually undertaking the task of transcribing them for admirers of Mr. Holmes and Dr. Watson's works. In the meantime, I.A. Watson continues to pen other books, the latest of which is *The Incunabulum of Sherlock Holmes*. A full list of his seventy or so published works are available at: *http://www.chillwater.org.uk/writing/iawatsonhome.htm*

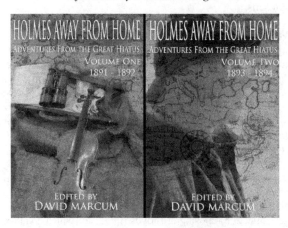

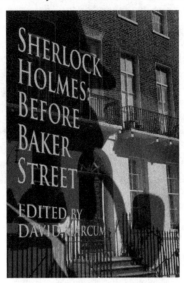

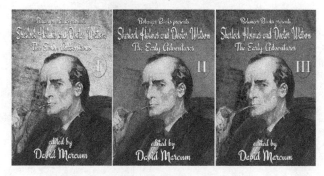
271

Belanger Books